ADRIEL PEREGRINE

ADRIEL PEREGRINE

THE TALE OF A WANDERER WHO BECOMES A PILGRIM

MICHAEL G. TAVELLA

atmosphere press

"And a highway shall be there,
and it shall be called the Way of Holiness;"

(Isaiah 35: 8a ESV)

CHAPTER ONE

ADRIEL PEREGRINE

I would be a pilgrim to the Holy City. My family name, Peregrine, indicates that I am a palmer, a pilgrim to the Holy Land. Yet, I have wandered restlessly through near and distant places with no goal or end. My soul is weary. I have been Adriel Vagus, wandering and inconstant. I wish again to be Adriel Peregrine.

— A Wanderer Who Becomes a Pilgrim, *Adriel Peregrine.*

In a secluded corner of a rural central Pennsylvania church cemetery stands a grave marker close by several willow trees, planted sometime after the interments, with low-hanging boughs that, in a breeze, tap against the top of the simple monument. The trees are symbolic of both grief and eternal life. The weeping willow is called thus because rain runs down its leaves as if it is weeping. In their distress, the people of Israel wept about their captivity under the willows of Babylon. All of us weep because of the suffering and loss we experience in this mortal life. The willow also represents hope, life, and the strength of God. The stone reads, "Adriel Peregrine," and also bears the name of his beloved. A willow tree is carved on the stone.

Stories of extraordinary people linger long after they have died. Tales of Adriel's life were no exception. Though little known by most folk in his life and death, he was a hero in the little world in which he lived. His writings had a limited circulation; but, those who read them did not come away disappointed. The oral tradition and family records have together carried faithfully over several generations the narrative of his life. His words and deeds reflect the conversion of life that turned him from the self-destructive tendencies all of us on some level exhibit. One habit in his youth was laden with the possibility of his total disintegration and ruin, an account of which one will find here.

When young, Adriel would wander through the hills, fields, and forests surrounding his family home. He called himself, "God's Vagrant," or "Wandering Sky" (his middle name was Skylar), laughing to himself about how clever he was. Though he did not shun the company of other boys his age—Caleb Landis was his closest friend—he enjoyed his solitude more.

During his peregrinations, he would imagine himself a wanderer through lands exotic and strange where he encountered beings of the same character. Without evidence except for a vivid imagination, Adriel believed that humans shared the world with a host of outlandish folk who shielded themselves from exposure to human beings. At times, in the rustling of a bush or the soughing of the wind through the trees, he believed he could hear these elusive denizens of the forest and fields fleeing his presence so they would not be exposed to his sight. Exposure was hazardous to them; for, when in danger of being sighted by a human, they would evaporate into the air with no assurance that they would re-materialize, or so Adriel concluded in his fancy.

Adriel was always on the lookout for evidence of their existence. He convinced himself that the objects of the world that he saw and touched were not all that existed. Many things escape detection either because of our inattention, their elusiveness, or both.

The gentle breeze would take his own yearning into itself and, in the local dialect of field and forest, speak for him to all the inhabitants of this fairy land. When alone, he would sometimes say, "I am your friend. Speak to me." He was convinced he heard them respond through the messenger-breeze. Their voices were indistinct; but, he would sometimes hear some-one from that world call his name. At other times, he would hear indistinctly a chorus singing songs of love and joy. He was convinced that he had heard a song more than once that his mother had taught him.

The elfin girl stood under an elfin tree
Stirred by the wind to an elfin glee.
Her true love took her by the hand,
To dance to the tunes of an elfin band.

Such is the imagination of many a child that with adulthood dies.

Agatha, his mother, knew that Adriel was a dreamer; for, he didn't hide his yearning in his questions and comments to her. Sometimes, she would embrace him and place her cheek next to his, rock his head, and answer the best she could without disillusioning him.

His father, a hardworking and practical man, was pre-occupied with his duties on the estate. Many things, not pertaining to his responsibilities, escaped his notice. He felt a strong loyalty to Massey Alden, for whom he worked. Sylvan didn't want to disappoint his employer, who treated his family well.

Sylvan didn't have the imagination of his son, nor did he understand it. Though perplexed by Adriel's dreams and wanderings, Sylvan loved Adriel and gave him time and attention despite his many responsibilities. He wasn't demonstrative in his love, but expressed it. He would make Adriel wooden toys with his skilled hands, join his wife and son in walks in town and fields, read stories to him and join in prayers before bedtime, and teach Adriel skills that would be helpful to him throughout life. Sylvan expected much good to come from his only son and child. He could be demanding.

Adriel dreamed of faraway places, both imaginary and real, but such dreaming didn't make him an inattentive student.

Reading filled his imagination, and so, he read voraciously. Among his favorite authors was the great Washington Irving, who died on the day of Adriel's fourteenth birthday. With the great writer, he traveled to Granada and walked through the Alhambra. He learned of Moorish Spain and Spanish conquest. He traveled the road on which Ichabod Crane fled the headless horseman and came upon Rip Van Winkle as he was sleeping his long sleep. He built in his thoughts Knickerbocker New York.

Adriel wandered with Odysseus, campaigned with Caesar, hid away with David from Saul, slept in the mead hall with Grendel's victims, overheard the "Open, Sesame!" with Ali Baba, traveled from hell to the gates of heaven with Dante, and beheld with the poet the Beatific Vision accompanied by Beatrice Portinari, then Saint Bernard. Someday, he thought he would travel through exotic lands and write about them. Keeping a diary and writing poetry and short stories were pre-occupations with him.

Adriel asked Joshua Schreiber, who became the teacher of the one room school when he was ten, many questions about distant exotic places and people, often remaining after class to speak with him. Joshua was generous with his time on behalf of his students, especially Adriel, whom he regarded as conscientious and imaginative. Before settling down to wed, teach school, and tend a small farm, Schreiber served in the U.S. Navy, his last assignment being on the steam frigate *USS Susquehanna*, with Commodore Matthew C. Perry during his two expeditions to Tokugawa Japan that the United States insisted on opening to the world.

Aware of Adriel's great promise as a scholar and writer, Mr. Alden made it financially possible for the boy to attend a private boarding school from which he graduated. He had spent one year studying to be a teacher at the local Normal School, also financed by Alden.

He had returned home to attend a party thrown by the

father of a young woman in the vicinity. It was during the last Christmas break that he fell in love with Abigail Dunlap, a classmate in the schoolhouse and a good friend from childhood.

Abigail was as beautiful as a morning glory opening at the beginning of the day. Her black hair curled over her forehead and fell half way down her back. Her eyes were a deep green like the green of the ocean. Her face was a perfect symmetry, long but not too long. Her skin was pale, but not so pale as to make her look like a black-haired ghost. She was of medium height. She walked with a certain non-affected elegance, improved and nurtured in the days she attended a private girls' boarding school not far away from her home. She graduated from the school in the spring of 1863.

Abigail's father was a prosperous local farmer, owner of a grist mill and a general store, a stockholder in the very recently completed Columbia-Reading Railroad that began operation a few months before through the nearby town of Manheim and involved in various other commercial enterprises.

He adored his only daughter, as did his wife, her mother, Katherine. The parents were protective of Abigail and noticed when she spoke of boys.

Whenever he had an opportunity during vacations, Adriel stopped by the Dunlap farm to visit Abigail as he was concluding one of his long walks. On the first day of his visit home, he had missed her, for she had gone into town with her mother to do some shopping. Conrad Kraybill, a long-time, trusted servant of the Dunlaps, met him at the door of the stone farm house that looked more like a manor house.

"Is Abigail home?"

In a formal and cold voice, Conrad answered, "Not at the moment. She won't be back for hours." He was lying. Abigail and her mother were expected within the hour.

He didn't invite Adriel in, nor did the servant encourage him to come back some other time. Abigail's father, Hamilton

Dunlap, was not warm to Adriel. He hoped that Abigail would not become interested in a young man who didn't have the social standing and prospects of his own family that he worked so many years to achieve.

Hamilton rued his own childhood poverty. His wealth was a result of his own hard work and the fortunate circumstance of receiving an inheritance from a childless employer who thought of him as a son. In his wishes for his daughter, he forgot his own humble background. Hamilton communicated to the servant his negative attitude toward Adriel Peregrine.

Not to be discouraged, Adriel stopped by the next day and had the good fortune of meeting Abigail on the long lane that extended from the Dunlap house to the road. She was picking flowers and putting them in a basket hanging from her arm. Her wide-brimmed sun hat matched the basket. She didn't notice him until he was but a few yards away.

"Adri, you frightened me!" Abigail and a few other friends called him by this nickname; his parents always called him Adriel.

"Abigail, I'm sorry." He was unnerved that he caused her any grief.

"It's nice to see you. Come with me." Abigail said no more. As Adriel drew near, she took him by the hand and walked slowly with him down the lane toward the road. His hand began to sweat, and his heart was overcome by her gesture. She was unaware of how her touch affected his emotional state of mind. Many times they had held hands as children. Her gesture was not new, nor meant in any romantic way. Adriel, timid in the matter of love, was incapable of expressing his love for her; for, he feared she would reject him. Abigail also was reticent regarding romance. She loved Adriel as a friend, not as a future husband. Adriel didn't tell Abigail he loved her; she didn't tell him she didn't love him.

Abigail was well-acquainted with her father's attitude and wanted to spend time with her good friend without having to deal with her father's hostility. She reminded her father that she was not in love with Adriel; but, he was worried something might develop. At no time did she wish to mislead Adriel about their relationship, but said nothing partly because he said nothing. During the previous Christmas vacation, friendship had blossomed into love for Abigail in Adriel's heart. The two hearts were not beating to the same cadence.

Adriel never spoke of his love to his mother or father. His mother had to guess what was in his heart from the few things he said about Abigail; his father did not speculate, or even think of speculating, about Adriel's longing. Adriel wanted to speak about what was in his heart, but he couldn't. Knowing him so well after many years of friendship, Abigail had some insight into his heart regarding her. She tried to relieve it with her natural warmth and gentleness; but, she couldn't say that she loved him. She continued her reticence as he did.

Abigail dropped Adriel's hand and turned toward him. With great earnestness, she said, "I'm so glad that you have come home to attend my graduation party."

"I don't know if your father would approve. He doesn't like me very much."

"Father doesn't dislike you, Adriel. In any case, he has let me make the guest list. Don't mind him." Abigail was not going to let her father discourage her from inviting Adriel to the big event. She had a strong will that was not easily thwarted.

"I can't say no. That's why I'm home."

"Good."

Abigail again took his hand, accompanied Adriel to the end of the lane, and bade him farewell with a kiss on the cheek. He walked home in a reverie that took him two miles out of the way. By the time he was in the vicinity of home, he had composed a not so good one stanza poem, expressing boyish love.

"My father's joy" explains her name.

I would she knew she's my joy too.
How do I tell her without rue?
Her radiant love I would attain.

He opened the door of his parents' home as the sun reddened in the west.

CHAPTER TWO

ADRIEL'S EXCURSION

Though the view from my door was still more contracted, I did not feel crowded or confined in the least. There was pasture enough for my imagination. The low shrub oak plateau to which the opposite shore arose stretched away toward the prairies of the West and the steppes of Tartary, affording ample room for all the roving families of men. "There are none happy in the world but beings who enjoy freely a vast horizon"—said Damodara, when his herds required new and larger pastures. — Walden, Henry David Thoreau

In the summer of 1863, Adriel was seventeen years old. The Civil War had been raging for a little over two years. Only fifty miles away from where Adriel lived, the little town of Gettysburg would become, in a few short weeks, forever famous. Many local boys were in uniform. Some would come home; others lay or would lie in faraway battlefield graves, many unmarked, casualties of disease or battle wounds. Though he pondered enlistment that summer, Adriel was not yet of age for the army. His mother and father didn't encourage him to enlist when he spoke about it. He felt uneasy about the prospect of staying safely at home while so many were fighting to keep the country united. He didn't want to be known as a coward, and he had a heartfelt commitment to do his part to preserve the Union.

When he came of age, he could avoid service. Conscription did not bear much fruit for the Union army. Enlistment was the usual way of entering it. Some men provided a substitute or paid for commutation. Mr. Alden would have insured that Adriel could continue to attend college and not go to war. Alden supported Adriel's plans to go to a four year college after Normal School. Adriel was interested in joining the army, in becoming a teacher, and in Abigail. He couldn't do all three at the same time. If he had a choice, he'd join the army and return after the war to marry her. Then, he would pursue a career as a teacher after finishing college. The experience of most of us tells us we don't always get our way.

Adriel would think often about reading her the poetry of love, but feared an adverse reaction. He thought, "Had we but world enough and time, This coyness, lady, were no crime." (Andrew Marvell, *To His Coy Mistress*). He feared, though, that Abigail's coyness was actually disinterest in being Adriel's lover and future spouse. His assessment was right. In his timidity he revealed none of his struggle to her. He was *Adriel Agonistes*, an epic made of the matter of love. In his youthful agony he had passed from childhood to early manhood.

Adriel woke early from a long night of little sleep. He had tossed and turned thinking about Abigail and how he would tell her that he loved her. Despite his lack of sleep, he had so much energy on waking that he took a long walk toward the Dunlap farm. From a nearby hill, he looked down on the green fields, thickening with corn and tobacco, across to the stately farm house where Abigail lived. The breeze was blowing softly; the honeysuckle filled him with its sweet scent. He thought he saw Abigail coming down the farm lane toward him. When he came to his senses from his reverie, she disappeared. He stood there for a long time, but not knowing how much time had passed. He pulled out the pocket watch that his father and mother had given him as a graduation present. A half hour had gone by while he stood on the crest of the hill.

Adriel decided to hasten the day with a hike in the woods. He loved to walk except in the heart of winter. He would walk and walk and think about many things. His ever-active mind would burst with manifold thoughts.

The beautiful Pennsylvania countryside was an elixir that stimulated Adriel's imaginative inclination. It was a formula that invigorated his young life. He took the land into himself as a restoring potion. Love of the nearby inspired his thoughts of the far distant. He exulted in the panorama of his home that lent to his appreciation of the faraway and exotic. Both worked together to give ecstatic vision to his young mind.

The Pennsylvania landscape was dotted with groves of trees. Adriel loved most to walk in wooded areas. Though an extensive forest covered the hills, often called mountains in Pennsylvania, north of home, Adriel, not wanting to stray too far, chose a grove close to the Dunlap farm. On that warm summer day, he walked until tired. He found a magnificent tree under whose branches he rested. Soon, he fell asleep and dreamed of pleasant things—of denizens of the forest making merry under the ferns and May apples. He was suddenly awakened by a man who stood before him. Though unsteady from sleep, Adriel stood up quickly to face his visitor without losing his balance.

The man was old with a short grey beard, extending from sideburn to sideburn and without a mustache, and a pipe sticking out of his mouth. His nose was of definitive prominence on his face. His eyes were of a color difficult to ascertain. His hair looked half combed. He was very lean and slightly bent over. He didn't show agitation; but, he did reveal an intensity that bordered on it. In his right hand was a walking stick with the image of a falcon carved into the handle. Adriel thought he looked somewhat like a picture he had seen of Henry David Thoreau, though aged by many years beyond Thoreau's own life span.

"Sorry to disturb you, young man. I wanted to make sure you were all right," said the mysterious senior.

"I'm fine, sir. I'm fine," was Adriel's reply. He felt uneasy, but didn't sense that he was in danger.

"Beautiful day, isn't it?"

"Yes. It would be heartless to stay indoors on a day like this," Adriel replied.

"Ah, you're a poet."

"No, but I'd like to be," Adriel replied modestly, and then changed the topic. "Are you from around here?"

"No, I'm not. I'm a wayfarer."

"Where are you going?" Adriel inquired.

"I'm traveling nowhere in particular. I've no goal. I walk from place to place without itinerary and destination," said the man. "I've been doing it for the last year, ever since my wife died. By the way, my name is Pontiac Rowbottom, Ottawa and Englishman. I apologize for not introducing myself from the outset. What's yours?"

"I'm Adriel Peregrine. Some call me Adri."

"Ah, you too are a traveler."

"Not much of one. I've been few places," responded Adriel.

"But, you like to wander."

"Yes, I've walked all over these hills and fields many times," Adriel said.

"Here and there?"

"Yes, here and there." Adriel was feeling a bit of irritation, perceiving that Pontiac was interrogating him.

"I've not found a place to call home since my loss. I think I never will. I'll die on the road, far from my original home in Ohio."

"How sad! Why don't you return home?" Adriel asked.

"I see my wanderings as a symbol of my life. I have no goal. I have no stability. I'll probably die among strangers and far from home. I'm not a pilgrim. I seek no holy place or place of rest. I do not yearn to go on pilgrimage. I don't have the fervent longing of the palmer for the journey. 'Thanne longen folk to goon on pilgrimages, And palmeres for to seken straunge strondes.' (*The Canterbury Tales*, Geoffrey Chaucer) I have no goal to Canterbury or the Holy Land or Santiago de

Compostela or the Kingdom."

"A little bit of Chaucer," Adriel responded. He realized that Pontiac had some education.

"Ah, you do like poetry."

"Indeed, I do. But, where will you stay?" Though a person unknown to him, Adriel was concerned about Pontiac's physical comfort.

"I'll stay in this grove. A campfire will keep me warm. My bed roll will keep me comfortable. Some food I bought in the nearby town will fend off hunger." Pontiac had made some provision for the road. He took odd jobs along the way and had saved some money during his working days.

"May I share with you some bread I brought along for my walk?" Out of his haversack, Adriel took some bread his mother had made.

"I much appreciate it, young man." Pontiac took the bread without hesitation, took off his backpack, and stored the gift in it.

"I'll pray for you, Mr. Rowbottom."

Adriel was about to continue on his way when Pontiac said to him, "One of these days you may wander like me."

Perplexed, Adriel responded, "How would you know this?"

"I've an intuitive sense. I can't explain it. I've never been misled by it. You'd be a pilgrim; but, by the circumstances of your life, you will be misdirected into wandering."

The young man felt an uneasy sensation, a knot in the stomach. *Was this old man simply a crank, or did he have an extraordinary gift of perception? Was he some sort of prophet?* "Thanks for the insight. I appreciate it." Adriel was not so sure he appreciated it.

"You may wander until you are directed to the road that leads to the Promised Land, where all pilgrims are headed. I hope someday that I will become a pilgrim in heart and mind. Right now, my sadness, grief, and anger prevent me from doing what my heart is urging me to do and not allowing me to do. I often struggle within myself. I often feel as if I am in an ongoing debate with myself, sometimes taking one view and at another time taking the other view. I may die a divided man before I come to join the path of pilgrims. The direction of my life may remain moot. Keep in mind what I have said," Pontiac said with conviction.

"I thank you. Ask God to help me find my way in this world."

"I'll do that," replied Pontiac.

Adriel felt very sad about the old man's circumstances. He was affected by Pontiac's pain at a great loss--his beloved wife called Sarah. May he never bear such a loss. Later, he wondered much about what the old man said to him about his own life.

The two men shook hands and departed from one another, Pontiac to his night in the woods, Adriel to home.

Adriel was confounded by his encounter with Pontiac and disturbed by Pontiac's revelation to him. Adriel loved to wander in the woods, but had no desire to wander purposelessly in the world. He believed in God and attended Church with his parents at St. Jude Thaddaeus, located on land given by the father of Mr. Alden. Adriel loved opportunities to talk about the world, God, the Church, and the meaning of life with Father Derek Ledford. These occasions were brief encounters as the two were each on their way to someplace else, hardly opportunities for profound discussions. The priest's firm opinion was that theology was meant for daily living, and communicated this perspective in his teaching and preaching.

Adriel hurried home to get ready for the party at Abigail's. He was beside himself with both apprehension and excitement. When he arrived home, he ran upstairs without greeting his parents. Fearing he would become a greybeard like Pontiac, he looked in the mirror and saw an old, despairing face before it returned to the freshness and hopefulness of youth

CHAPTER THREE

THE OCEAN VOYAGE

From my early teenage years, I have had a devotion to love poetry. Dante had his Beatrice; Petrarch had his Laura; and, I had my Abigail. Love poetry has been written where love has been unrequited. — Reflections on Romantic Poetry, *Adriel Peregrine*.

Adriel was weary from his long walk, so he decided to rest before getting ready for the evening's festivities. When he entered his second floor room, he flung himself on his bed, accompanied by a deep sigh. Many strong emotions ran through his head and heart as he lay there—anxiety about the coming evening, perplexity about his encounter with Pontiac, desire to be Abigail's beloved, apprehensions about the future as the Civil War claimed the young manhood of the nation, and fear of death and of being called a coward if he did not enlist. He knew that at any time, Principal Wickersham at the Normal School would organize a regiment to defend Lancaster County from a possible Confederate invasion. He would be part of this expedition.

As he lay there, Adriel focused his attention on a print of a clipper ship hanging on the wall. In the quiet and warmth of the afternoon, with a gentle breeze blowing through the opened window, Adriel fell asleep.

The house turned into the deck of the clipper with Adriel standing on it. He looked toward the bow of the ship. A figure whom he recognized as Abigail Dunlap was struggling toward him, holding tightly to the ship's rail. She was calling out to him for help; because, the sea had become rough so that the ship was rolling violently. Suddenly, a large wave swept Abigail off the vessel. Adriel stumbled toward the bow of the rocking ship, almost falling into the sea, in an attempt to rescue her. She was gone. All he could hear were her cries.

Adriel woke up with fear and grief in his heart. He began to weep. When he realized it was a dream, he began easing down from his panic with a sense of great relief.

Adriel sat up in bed for the longest time, attempting to figure out why he had such a dream. He wondered if Abigail was in some sort of danger. What could he do to warn her? Or was he being silly? He put his face in his hands and thought very hard about what he was going to do. He decided that he would say something to Abigail. Should he tell her tonight at the party? No, he couldn't do that. Yes, he must. He finally decided to keep his unfounded fears to himself.

He sprang out of bed, washed up, and put on the clothes he would wear to the festivities. He was on edge about what might happen that night. He was excited; he was anxious; he was happy—a mix of emotions as he awaited the hour. Feelings are below the level of the logical and reasonable; nonetheless, they insist on being heeded, if not obeyed; for, they have important things to say to those who experience them. It is usually best to put them through the test of good judgment. In his callow youth, Adriel had much yet to learn.

After dressing, he went downstairs, where his mother was preparing the evening meal. She greeted him with a question, "Are you ready for the big night, Adriel?"

He responded in a weak voice, "Yes, I am."

Mothers know their children very well. She marked his halting reply. "That wasn't very enthusiastic."

"I'm a little nervous, Mother," he said, somewhat irritated.

As she stirred a pot of beans, she said, "I understand. I hope you have a good time."

"I will." Adriel headed out of the house through the door of the kitchen.

His mother cried after him, "Dinner's at six."

He responded, "I'll wait till the party to eat." His mother said something else that he didn't hear, nor did he return to find out what it was. Adriel would have no appetite before the festivities. He walked into the woods next to the little settlement where his family lived. He was not concerned that his clothes might get dirty, though he did want to make a good impression on Abigail. He would be careful.

A path, lying between the Peregrine house and Saint Jude Thaddeus Church, led to the limestone quarry owned by Mr. Alden. Though his parents warned him about the danger, Adriel had often taken the path to this place of quiet, interrupted during the work day by the distant sounds below where the workers were cutting limestone. His favorite perch he called *frithstow*, two Old English words meaning "place of peace." Another trail, beginning at the large stone on which he often sat, led around a portion of the quarry to the limekilns owned by Mr. Alden.

He sat down on the rock and dreamt. He fantasized about far off places and times—of adventures like those of King Arthur fighting the Anglo-Saxons, of traders traveling the Silk Road, of crusaders embarking for the Holy Land, of worshippers entering the temple of Apollo at Delphi, of pilgrims' following the way to the Temple in Jerusalem and of sailors' suffering shipwreck on a remote island—a wide span of scenes that his broad, well-read imagination could summon. Then, as he thought of clipper ships, he remembered his terrible nightmare of Abigail's being swept overboard by a wave. He was again troubled deeply in his heart. He shook his head as if to cast away the thought. A chill went down his spine.

Maybe he could save Abigail. Adriel struggled to think of ways to win her affection. All that was left to him was a growing dejection. Perhaps tonight would be a turning point that would lead them from friendship to romance.

The dreamer lay back on the rock, unconcerned about the

state of his dress-up clothes. He daydreamed himself to sleep until the sun turned from bright yellow to deep orange as it slipped below the ridge.

CHAPTER FOUR

THE PARTY

My lady carries love within her eyes;
All that she looks on is made pleasanter;
– Dante Alighieri, La Vita Nuova, trans. Dante Gabriel Rossetti

Adriel woke up with a sick feeling in his stomach as the time of the party approached. After a moment, he realized that it was getting late, very late. Shadows were lengthening below in the quarry. After quickly brushing off his clothes, he sprang up and ran down the path to home. When he got there, he headed straight for the barn and saddled his horse, Bunyan.

The horse and man moved at a rapid pace to the Dunlap farm. Their speed stirred up the dust of the road that, from a distance, looked like an advancing dust storm. Adriel arrived at the farm sooner than he expected, not realizing how fast he was going. He hoped no one saw his panic in motion. After a brief respite for Bunyan and him to catch their breath, they jogged to the main entrance of the house. Adriel didn't want Abigail or anyone else to think that he was overly excited about attending the festivities.

A servant took Bunyan as Adriel stood at the end of the walkway that led to the front door. As he concentrated on the door, it seemed to move further away from him. His heart was pounding so hard he imagined it would burst from his breast. He felt a contraction in his throat that made it hard to swallow. His stomach muscles were as hard as a rock. His legs were weak and ready to give out. Would he make it to the front door was his only thought. He was in a daze. Somehow, he summoned the strength to walk the few yards to the entrance where Conrad Kraybill met him.

No sterner face had Adriel ever seen. "Master Adriel, please enter the room to your left. The party has already begun." Adriel sensed reproach in the servant's voice.

"Thanks, Kraybill." Adriel addressed the steward in the way that he wished to be called.

Adriel entered the house. Joyful sounds came from the hall. The guests included Abigail's friends and members of her family, including her two brothers. Abigail chose a formal evening party rather than a summer picnic for the celebration.

Adriel walked into the large hall where a small orchestra was playing, people were dancing the two step, and others were seated around the room enjoying one another's company while eating food from the sumptuous spread that the Dunlap's provided. The room was bright with the light of candelabra, chandeliers, and wall candles. The windows were open to allow a breeze. The growing darkness outside contrasted starkly with the bright light of the hall.

The brightness made it difficult for Adriel to see as he tried to locate Abigail in the crowd. His eyes then fell upon her sitting in a corner of the room where she was talking with Caleb Landis. He thought that she stood out as the moon among the stars, dimming all that was around her. The dancers were an obstruction to the far side of the room; but undeterred, Adriel found his way to where Abigail sat. As he approached, he wondered if he should tell her of his disturbing dream. He decided not to.

Abigail was particularly lovely that evening. Her face was radiant and her eyes sparkled. Her light blue dress contrasted well with her black hair. Her smile revealed a joyful soul that expended most of her thoughts on the beautiful things in life.

"Adri, how good of you to come to my party!" Abigail knew he would. She got up from her seat and embraced her good friend. "Please, come and sit down and join Caleb and me." Adriel greeted Caleb and then sat down. Adriel had been Caleb's friend from the time they started school. They shared many walks, swims in the creek, and skating on the pond. Now a little tension was afoot. Adriel wondered if a relationship between Abigail and Caleb was developing. He had no ground for thinking such except that they were sitting together.

"Adri, it's good to see you. It's been a while since we've gotten together. How's school?" Adriel lived in Old Main at the Normal School; Caleb was employed by his prosperous father in his father's cabinetmaking business.

"It's going well. How about you?" Adriel said coldly.

"It's the daily bustle in the shop, but I've nothing to complain about."

Adriel began thinking of himself as being silly for his suspicions. Abigail was free to befriend whomever she wished. He was afraid he was becoming a tyrant in mind, soon to become a tyrant in his actions. He hoped his condition didn't show. He resolved to clear his mind and tend his heart. It was very difficult for him to do this.

"Adri, it's time for a waltz. Join me." Abigail stood up and took Adriel's hand. She led him to the dance floor. She was a deft dancer; he wasn't so light footed. Every time he danced, which was seldom, Adriel felt as if he was flushed with embarrassment for everyone to see, though he was never able to confirm his feelings.

Adriel wondered if Abigail was playing games with him. Was he imagining that she loved him as more than a friend? He concluded again that night that she was not being coy like Marvell's mistress. That she loved him as a friend, not a suitor, was his reluctant conclusion.

When the two returned to their seats, Abigail took Caleb's hand and drew him onto the dance floor. The orchestra struck up another of Johann Strauss' waltzes. Abigail and Caleb, an excellent dancer like his partner, danced away across the floor with people looking on with admiration at the skill of the handsome couple. Abigail and Caleb both knew they were the center of attention. Adriel was close to miserable.

When the dance ended, the couple came over to Adriel. Abigail invited Adriel to join her and Caleb in partaking of the banquet board of tasty food, inspired by Pennsylvania Dutch cuisine. He followed Abigail and Caleb and picked out his favorites.

They sat together where they were before until Abigail invited Caleb for another dance. As Adriel was glumly sitting alone, a young woman approached him from the other side of the hall.

As with Abigail, Adriel had known her since his first year in school. Jennie Hallewell did not have the looks of Abigail; nonetheless, she was pretty. She was of medium height with short reddish-brown hair. Her eyes, somewhat obscured by wire-rimmed glasses, were a pale blue-grey – sometimes more blue than grey and sometimes more grey than blue. Her face was sprinkled with some freckles, but not excessively. She was not timid, but not bold either. Her shyness was made more of humility than a lack of confidence.

Jennie's parents were farmers, helped in the enterprise by Jennie, her sister, and two brothers. She desired to be a teacher, but had not yet gotten off to the Normal School. In her heart and mind, she hadn't dismissed her hope someday to teach children in one of those one room schoolhouses spread across the central Pennsylvania countryside.

Jennie loved Adriel. She had loved him from the last year they attended school together. She would look in his direction on Sunday mornings at church. Like Adriel with Abigail, she was shy about expressing her interest in him.

"Good evening, Adriel. How have things been?" Adriel had seen her coming toward him and wished he could escape. He was in no mood to talk to her or anybody but Abigail.

"Well, thank you, Jennie. What have you been doing these last months?"

"I've been helping Mom and Dad on the farm. My life has been quiet and uneventful."

Jennie was hoping Adriel would invite her to dance; but, she expected the likelihood was small. When the music stopped, Caleb and Abigail came over to them.

"Jennie, how good of you to come to my party," Abigail said with some surprise. She had not seen Jennie in the crowd of guests.

"I couldn't miss. Congratulations on your graduation. What are you going to do now?"

"I'll help Mom and Dad here on the farm. Dad may need me at some of his other businesses. I have plenty to keep me busy."

Adriel felt awkward; for, he knew he loved Abigail and was sure that Jennie loved him. He made the best of the situation by returning to the buffet. "I'm going to refill my plate," he said as he fled to the serving table. His stomach had gone from tense to hungry since he arrived at the party.

When Adriel returned, Jennie had departed. He scanned the room but couldn't find her. He was relieved. The rest of the evening, Adriel toured the hall to seek out friends. He half-heartedly danced with several other young women he knew, and then he slipped out into the evening air. He called for his mount and rode home. It was dark.

Adriel found his way home after a considerable time; because, he rode Bunyan home at a walk in the dark. He wanted some time to think and sort things out. He was convinced that Abigail didn't love him in any way but as a friend; but, he'd not give up on his yearning for her to be his future wife.

When he arrived home, he settled Bunyan in the barn and went directly to his room. The house was quiet. Nobody greeted him as he entered. He remembered that he forgot to tell Abigail of his disturbing dream. Then, he remembered that he decided not to tell her.

CHAPTER FIVE

RETURN TO SCHOOL

In this summer of 1863, I realized much more so than before the desperate state of my native land.

— A Wanderer Who Becomes a Pilgrim, Adriel Peregrine.

Sunday morning after the party, Adriel's mother knocked on his bedroom door to give him a telegram that came in the early evening of the preceding day. "Adriel, I have something for you I think you should read. It's a telegram."

Between lack of sleep and the rigors of the night before, that is, the party, Adriel was hard to awaken. His mother's persistence paid off. Adriel found his bedroom door and took the telegram from his mother. Accomplishing her task, she did not remain to find out the nature of the message. Adriel stood in the middle of his room and opened it. His roommate promised to send one to him if the Confederates were likely to enter the Commonwealth and threaten Lancaster. He read it through and then cast the paper on his bed. He quickly got dressed and hurried downstairs. He was in an excited, agitated state when he entered the kitchen, where his mother was preparing breakfast for him and his father.

"The Rebels are threatening to come into Pennsylvania. Principal Wickersham is organizing a regiment at the Normal School that will go over to Wrightsville to assist in preventing them from crossing the Susquehanna. I've got to get back to school as soon as possible."

Adriel's father was planning to return Adriel to the school

on this very day. Adriel wanted to leave right away.

"Your father needs to complete some chores for Mr. Alden before he takes you, and we all need to go to church at nine o'clock." Adriel's mother was piling pancakes on a plate as she spoke.

"Where's he right now? I've got to tell him how important this is."

Adriel's mother was not excited about the idea of his going off to war. He wasn't eighteen yet. "He'll get you there soon enough."

Adriel disagreed. "I will miss the action."

"You'll miss getting hurt. After church, he can take you."

Adriel resigned himself to his mother's wishes. She told him to sit down and have some pancakes. And so he did. Pancakes were at the top of the list of his favorite meals. As he ate, his father came through the kitchen door.

"Father, will you take me back to school this morning?"

"After church, Son. Adriel's father sat down to join him in the pancake feast. The stack became an empty plate.

Sylvan, Agatha, and Adriel walked down to the church, only a few steps from their house. They entered the lovely little church and sat in their usual places. The Peregrine and Hayhurst (Agatha's maiden name) families had been Anglicans since the Reformation and Roman Catholics before that.

The congregation sat quietly, anticipating the first hymn as the organ played the prelude. The service began with "Thou, whose almighty word chaos and darkness heard, and took their flight; hear us, we humbly pray, and where the Gospel day sheds not its glorious ray, let there be light." Then, Father Ledford began Morning Prayer from *The Book of Common Prayer.* "The Lord is in his holy temple; let all the earth keep silence before him." *Hab. ii.20.*

While the service continued with the Confession and further on, Adriel thought of God's light scattering darkness at creation and now among people who have not known the

Word of God. He was quite earnest in his thoughts. He took matters of Christian faith quite seriously. He thought of himself as a pilgrim like John Bunyan. He was on a journey to the great City of God.

But, most on his mind was the growing crisis in Pennsylvania. Now and then during the service, the restless young man was thinking about joining his fellow students who would defend the Commonwealth from the southern rebels, helping in the Union cause. He didn't want to miss whatever may happen. How the mind can wander! It is so human.

Father Ledford preached from I Kings, the story of Naboth's vineyard. The king of Israel and his wife Jezebel committed grievous injustice against an innocent man. Adriel thought of how unjust the affairs of the world stood. He would have to speak to Father Ledford about his troubled thoughts on this matter.

After the service ended, the Peregrines greeted their rector at the door and walked home. Adriel could not contain his excitement about returning to school.

"Father, can we go soon?"

Sylvan smiled, looked at his son, and said, "Very soon."

When they arrived home, Sylvan hitched the horses to the buggy while Agatha made them lunch to take with them. Before long, father and son were on their way to the outskirts of Lancaster on the southwest side where the Normal School was located.

CHAPTER SIX

THE NORMAL SCHOOL GUARDS

The enemy is coming close, and I, with my school friends, will come to meet them. During this time my head spins with excitement.
– Diary of Adriel Peregrine, June 22, 1863.

The conversation between father and son moved from one particular to another; but, a topic Sylvan kept coming back to was giving Adriel advice on how to conduct himself during the crisis of the Confederate army's entering Pennsylvania and approaching Lancaster County. Adriel listened attentively, but had some resentment in his heart, as older youth often do when being counseled by parents. *Aren't they aware of the wisdom attained by a person at the age of seventeen?*

"Adriel, you may be going into a dangerous situation. Be careful and prudent. Be brave but keep your head down if there is shooting. Mom and I aren't very happy that you're chasing such danger. You're only seventeen. I hope Wickersham knows what he is doing. The Conscription Act doesn't apply to anyone under twenty. You don't have to walk into this danger. You're not even in the army."

"When I'm twenty the war will be over. Principal Wickersham is a fine man. He won't mislead us. And thanks for letting me join in. I couldn't face my friends if I didn't."

Then Adriel asked, "Father, what will become of our country if we lose?"

After an uncomfortably long silence, Sylvan said, "If we lose, we'll have no end of trouble. The two nations will fight again over one thing or another; slavery will exist for who knows how long; foreign nations will try to take advantage of us, as they already are doing; and other things that I can't begin to think of." Sylvan was an early defender of emancipation when it was not popular, and the abolitionists were reviled. Though he attended school only through sixth grade, Sylvan was a reader who had learned much on his own.

"Sounds awful."

"It'll probably be worse than we can imagine."

They traveled without words for some miles. Sylvan thought of the safety of his only child; Adriel thought of an exciting adventure and face-saving among his friends who had gone, or soon would go, to war; yet, he knew about the slaughter that had already occurred. He had wanted to see Matthew Brady's collection of pictures from Antietam, displayed at his gallery, but never got to New York. The pictures of the battle shocked Americans, who had their first look at the dead on a battlefield.

At the same time, Adriel was conflicted about joining the army because of Abigail. Yet, he realized that the possibility of a romance and marriage was slight. With this in mind, he retained his fervid interest in serving in the army.

After being on the road for two hours with a way to go on the sixteen mile trip, Sylvan stopped. "It's time for lunch. Let's see what tasty things your Mom packed." He hopped out and retrieved the closed basket. The two of them sat under a tree and ate the very adequate meal.

During lunch, Sylvan brought up the possibility of Adriel's enlistment, "Adriel, you already know that Mom and I are worried about your possible enlistment in the army. We wish that you would wait until sometime after you're eighteen."

"I'll return to school, if school is in session. Because of the likelihood of invasion, school may be let out for this term."

"If you attend the October term, I'll not oppose your joining the army afterward." Adriel would be eighteen in November.

"This seems fair enough."

They ate to their hearts' content, almost finishing what Agatha had sent. After they packed the basket and returned it to the buggy, Adriel's father said, "Let's go. I'd like to get home before sunset."

Sylvan and Adriel arrived on the campus in the middle of the afternoon. A crowd of young men and some of the women students had gathered in front of Old Main on lawn and porch. When a friend named Philip Hollinger saw Adriel, he ran toward him and stopped at the side of the buggy. "Hello, Mr. Peregrine." Sylvan nodded. "Adriel, glad you're back. It's reported that the Confederates are about to enter Pennsylvania."

"Bad news."

"It looks like we're going to march over to Columbia to defend the Wrightsville Bridge."

"I'm so glad I'm here. Thanks, Dad."

"You're welcome." Sylvan told Adriel that he must leave and also told him to telegraph him for an update on what was going on if he got a chance. He shook his son's hand. Adriel jumped off the conveyance and retrieved his bag. Philip and Adriel walked together up the steps of the imposing Victorian building to the porch. The students, in a celebrative mood, were gathered together there.

Wickersham was organizing the Normal School Guards. The young men were excited about the chance to participate in the great conflict that had wracked the nation for over two years. The North had recently had setbacks at Fredericksburg and Chancellorsville. Was the war coming to an end in favor of the South?

Adriel spent some time with the crowd, and then went to his room in Old Main. Greeting him there was his roommate,

Jacob Brenneman. "Adri, it's great that you're back."

"Jake, it's good to see you. The last few days must've been pretty exciting. Thanks for the telegram."

"Sit down. Let me give you an update." Adriel threw his travel case on the bed and then sat on it. Jake was sitting on his desk chair. He turned it to face Adriel.

"We're going to Columbia to help prepare for the defense of the bridge. It's estimated that we will leave on Wednesday. It's expected that Confederate troops will try to cross the river to take Lancaster. Can you imagine? We must stop them. The Normal School will respond. Principal Wickersham is organizing us into a fighting unit. Are you with us?"

Adriel responded, "Of course. I wouldn't miss it." His heart beat fast and hard. He was excited and anxious about the prospects ahead of him. After a long talk with Jake, he lay down and fell fast asleep. His dreams were full of the historical events of the day.

The following days would be filled with the drama of Lee's invasion of the North. Adriel and his friends at the school would in some way be part of the great events. The excitement on campus was a sustained hurrah.

On the night before departure to Columbia, Adriel was restless. He got very little sleep. During the night, when he was awake, he noticed that across the room, Jake wasn't doing very well either. Adriel's dreams were of battlefields. A sea of gray stood before him with muskets aimed. His company mates were falling under the intense gunfire. He thought he was hit, too, but not mortally. He lay on the field, calling for help. Then he awoke suddenly.

The sun was peeking through the small opening left by the curtains. Adriel could hear the birds through the open window. One of them was chirping what sounded like, "I hate you. I hate you." It was not exactly a cheerful greeting. He felt quite morose until he remembered the words of Wesley's hymn, "Christ, whose glory fills the skies, Christ, the true and only light." The hymn's lyrics reminded him that without Christ the morning is cheerless and joyless. And then he prayed the last stanza, "Visit then this soul of mine, Pierce the gloom of sin and grief; Fill me radiancy divine, Scatter all my unbelief; More and more thyself display, Shining to the perfect day." He got up, washed his face, and got dressed while Jake was yet asleep, trying to recover the sleep he lost during the night.

"Wake up, Jake. Wickersham won't wait for you." Jake jumped up, tripped over his shoes, and almost fell.

"That won't do, Brenneman. If you get injured, you can't go with us; but, I'll bring back some sort of souvenir."

"Don't be funny, Peregrine. I'll be ready in time."

Adriel and Jake reported for duty with many other young men of the school. They would walk to the Susquehanna River to defend their state and country.

CHAPTER SEVEN

THE WRIGHTSVILLE BRIDGE

So difficult was my decision to return home after my adventure in Wrightsville. Many of my friends joined the army. I languished during that very long summer.

    – A Wanderer Who Becomes a Pilgrim, *Adriel Peregrine.*

At the call of Principal J.P. Wickersham, the young male students were assembled on campus to walk to Columbia, located on the Susquehanna River. They were mostly from the farms and towns of central Pennsylvania, where the conflict of war had not come so close since the French and Indian War, the Revolution, and the Whiskey Rebellion. The War of 1812 brought the British navy to the Chesapeake Bay, Baltimore, and Washington. The students' lives had not known anything but peace. Now, a large hostile army was approaching central Pennsylvania, where the "dogs of war" (*Julius Caesar*, William Shakespeare) would do their damage. There would be no distance at all between the Confederate Army and Lancaster County. Their hearts stirred with the call to defend their homes. The fervency of youth would rouse them on this occasion to do all they could to keep the rebels from home soil, where the Confederates would endanger Philadelphia and Harrisburg.

The eyes of state and nation were drawn to the Wrightsville Bridge, the longest covered bridge in the world, spanning over a mile across the Susquehanna River. Indeed, it was an engineering marvel. Trains, hauled by horses over the bridge to prevent fire; a towpath for canal boats, and a pedestrian path were included in the second bridge at Wrightsville. When Adriel saw it, his eyes stared in wonder.

The young men from Franklin and Marshall College and the Millersville State Normal School, that Adriel attended, bivouacked in Columbia. Food was provided to them. The contingent worked on the Wrightsville side, preparing breastworks to defend the bridge against capture. Adriel's excitement and trepidation competed with one another. He worked off the energy with the other college students. With ears wide open, the work crews listened for the sounding of the alarm.

Rumor was spread that the term ending in September would be canceled. It turned out that this was what happened. Principal Wickersham announced to the student body in the chapel of Old Main that the students could return for the October term.

On June 25, the Twenty-seventh Pennsylvania Volunteer Militia relieved the students. The young men stopped off in Lancaster's Center Square on June 26, where they left their muskets. Some of the men of the Normal School had or would join the army. With respect for his parents, Adriel returned home, as he promised.

Union forces burned the bridge at Columbia-Wrightsville to forfend Confederate forces under General Gordon from achieving the east bank of the Susquehanna River. The Confederates were prevented from taking Lancaster, Philadelphia, and Harrisburg, saving the Commonwealth from havoc and destruction.

Adriel said good-bye to Jake, a year older than Adriel. His good friend joined the Union army. With great misgiving, Adriel sent a telegram to his parents to retrieve him from the school so he could remain home until the October term.

Adriel read in the local papers all about the burning of the Wrightsville Bridge. It irked him that he had not been there during the action. After the October term he would join the army and fight for the preservation of the Union. He would not be frustrated in his desire.

CHAPTER EIGHT

THE INJUSTICE OF IT ALL

The injustices of the world have no simple explanation. Theodicy is a difficult subject that has challenged the human mind for many centuries; but, a world without God is far more unjust than one with God. A world without God does not permit the possibility of redress. A world with God involves ultimate judgment and setting things right.

– A Wanderer Who Becomes a Pilgrim, Adriel Peregrine.

On June 28, Adriel returned home with his parents. He would spend the summer months there until school re-started in October. He wanted to finish the curriculum so that he would be able to teach; but, even more, he wanted to join the army to fight against the secessionists. His thoughts about the war caused him considerable disquiet, motivating him to take a long daily walk in the fields and woods of the district in which he was born, grew up, and lived. The frequency and length of his peregrinations were a measure of his need to think through the events of the day and how they applied to him.

On these excursions, Adriel would find a soft patch of grass, lie down, and gaze at the clouds, attempting to find a message embedded in their forms. They would float by gently, quietly, smoothly, like ships on a calm sea. Their calm was his agitation; for, in them he would find images of the violence of the war instead of the peace that they seemed to represent. On a particular day he saw in the cloudscape, red with light and white with water droplets, the discharge of many field pieces—a display of fire and smoke. At times, the sky would join in Adriel's imaginings. When a storm with its lightning and dark clouds was approaching, he felt the arrival of the apocalypse, as if the War was a sign of the end of the world. He could only imagine the battlefield; for, he had no experience of its reality.

Adriel justified the war as a God-given power of the state to perform its duties of defense and protection of the people. The government was fulfilling its function as stated in the Preamble of the Constitution: "to form a more perfect Union, establish Justice, insure domestic tranquility, provide for common defence, promote the general Welfare, and secure the Blessings of Liberty to ourselves and our Posterity."

Adriel thought of the terrible war as a threat to what he cherished. He saw portents in the clouds of alarm and devastation. He wanted to participate in his own small way to bring the war to a satisfactory end. Projected onto the sky were his concerns and fears. He would then close his eyes, fall asleep, and dream unsettling dreams.

On the Sunday after returning home, July 5, just two days after the Battle of Gettysburg ended, Adriel went to church with his parents. Father Ledford greeted the family at the door where and when Adriel made an appointment to see him. He trusted the priest whose opinion he desired.

Worship that Sunday was the Service of Holy Communion, celebrated once a month, from *The Book of Common Prayer*. Father Ledford preached on a text from I Peter, admonishing the Christian community to avoid evil and do good. The biblical text, according to the 1789 *Book of Common Prayer*, includes this translation of one of the verses: "For the eyes of the Lord are over the righteous, and his ears are open unto their prayers:

but the face of the Lord is against those who do evil."

Adriel asked himself then and often, "*Is there justice in this world? Do the evil suffer punishment? Or do they get away with their evil?*"

The great Battle of Gettysburg that began on July 1 and ended on July 3, just fifty-five miles from Adriel's home, had been fought between Adriel's time at Columbia and Wrightsville and the following Sunday, July 5. The slaughter on the battlefield had caused certain questions about justice and suffering to drum in his head like they never had before.

On the following day, Adriel knocked on the outside door of the vestry, where Father Ledford was at his desk. The priest came to the door, invited Adriel in, and offered him a seat. Adriel was a bit nervous. *After all, he was the priest of the parish. What if I say something clumsy or dumb?* Adriel had known Derek Ledford since he was a little boy, but never before asked to meet with him.

"Well, Adriel, I hear that you have been involved in some excitement over the last few days."

"Yes, Father. We stood on the edge of the War, but missed the real excitement."

"You returned before the Confederates got there?"

"Yes."

Father Ledford paused and then asked, "You mentioned to me on Sunday that you were bothered by the injustice in the world and wanted to hear what I had to say."

"Yes. It's become a nagging thought."

"I've thought of the injustice and suffering in the world many times. I've preached a few sermons about it; but, I've no easy answers. Nobody has. Nobody will until the Kingdom comes, if these questions are at all relevant when Christ comes in power."

"What does the Bible say?"

"That's a good place to start, so I'll begin there. In Luke 18, Jesus tells a story about a persistent widow who kept coming to a wicked judge to ask for justice against her adversary. He refused time and time again to grant her justice until he became weary of her tenacity. The parable is about persistent prayer. Since the wicked judge grants justice to the woman, will God not do the same to those who cry up to him day and night? Jesus says that God will give justice to His elect speedily.

"The problem is that we do not see such speedy justice. Almost nineteen centuries have passed without remediation. The wise, along with many other folk, still ponder the question of God's justice. Some people don't believe in God because of the unresolved question of theodicy, that is, reflection and discourse on the problem of the lack of justice in the world that God made.

"The parable is about faith and prayer in the midst of the injustice of the world. Keep faith and keep praying is what Jesus counsels us to do. Faith says that in the end God's justice will win the victory.

"In Matthew, Jesus quotes Isaiah 42, where God's chosen servant is said to be the one to proclaim justice to the nations and bring it to victory. Jesus is this servant that will bring all to fulfillment. God knows our suffering and the injustice we suffer. His own Son experienced these things. He was an innocent man, unjustly executed. God will be victorious over all evil in the world. This is what we believe.

"But, it has not yet come in its fullness. Why? Perhaps there is no God. You and I, though, believe in God. That there exists no God cannot be the solution for us.

"Elsewhere in Matthew, in what Saint Augustine calls the Sermon on the Mount, Jesus instructs us to love our enemies; for, God makes the sun rise on the good and the evil and sends rain on the just and unjust. Here, Jesus does not explain why injustice exists in the world, but tells us how we are supposed to act toward those who hate us. Even the evil receive gifts from God so that they may live.

"From the New Testament, all we can say is that we must

pray and keep faith and act justly toward others until God brings justice to victory. The Book of Revelation is about the suffering of the saints, a terrible injustice at the hands of the state, and God's final intervention and victory over all evil."

Adriel asked the priest, "But, what about now? Is there no victory over evil now?"

"Victories do occur. Evil people are punished for their misdeeds, as the Book of Proverbs indicates. But, no final victory has yet been achieved; no consistent pattern of the punishment of evil has been perceived. We must wait. This is hard. Job tells us that God's ways in this matter are opaque; Ecclesiastes borders on despair yet holds to belief in God.

"We must choose which way we shall go. We Christians are called to believe in God through Christ. Or, to put it another way, we must be caught up in the Holy Spirit through the mighty Word of God and believe what He has promised in spite of the injustices, sufferings, and miseries of the world. To do this takes tenacity and patience."

"How does this War fit into what you have said?" asked Adriel.

"The War is a consequence of our national sin of slavery. We live in a moral universe, set by God, where personal and communal sin is punished, sometimes; but, in other cases God's vengeance is not so apparent. Why this is so? We don't know. This is where the problem of justice lies, that is, in the sometimes, not all of the time.

"The youth of the nation are in a crucible. Many are not returning home, lying in their graves; many are maimed for life; many soldiers live in emotional anguish; and, some are bitter. I don't mean to say that all the youth of our nation are being punished for this particular sin; but, they all are caught up in the national sin that can take as its booty anyone. Noble sacrifice for a just cause is also part of the mix. Sacrifice for the welfare of others provides a justification and explanation of suffering."

"Father, the world is unjust, then, isn't it?"

"Adriel, the injustice and suffering of the world is mostly due to our having fallen into sin. God hasn't yet delivered us completely from our own sin and the sin of the world. We must live on and remain faithful to God, who has promised us deliverance from evil. 'Deliver us from evil,' we pray."

Adriel spent the afternoon thinking about his discussion with Father Ledford. It was only the beginning of his struggle with a baffling and often unjust world.

CHAPTER NINE

THE SUMMER OF LIMESTONE AND LIMESTONE KILNS

It was during the summer of 1863, when I worked in Mr. Alden's quarry, that I became discontent with the world and myself. My carefree youth, under the protection of my parents, entered a time of care laden adulthood. I was asking questions I had not asked before. I wasn't getting a lot of answers.

    – A Wanderer Who Becomes a Pilgrim, *Adriel Peregrine.*

After the Wrightsville Bridge burned and before Adriel returned to school in October, he worked for Mr. Alden in his limestone quarry. Set next to the quarry were five limekilns where some of the quarried stone was reduced to quicklime. The bulk of the limestone was sold for building stone. The quicklime had a ready local market, as did the limestone. A significant part of Massey Alden's wealth was derived from this lucrative mining operation. In those days limekilns were common around the American countryside. In his days of wandering, Adriel would find opportunities to work at a kiln. The summer days of 1863 would help train him in the operation of one.

On the morning of his first day of work, Adriel came down for breakfast sluggish and reticent. During the night he had slept little, because of his worry that he might not do a good enough job at the kilns where he was assigned.

His father reassured him. "Adriel, there's always a starting place when you learn something new. Everyone at the kilns has experienced a first day, first week, and first month. I've asked Jesse Becker, an old hand at the kiln, to take you under his wing." While Sylvan was speaking, his wife, Adriel's mother, was listening intently. She would speak if she thought she needed to.

"I don't want to look ridiculous."

"You've got to earn the workmen's respect. They're very experienced at their jobs and the wise ones remember when they were new at them. Most of them will have sympathy for your situation. There is always at least one who is difficult. They may test you for what mettle you are made of."

"OK, Father. I'll do my best."

Adriel showed up at the kilns on time. Most of the workmen were already there. Jesse Becker approached the young man to introduce himself and to help him along the way as he took up his new job.

Becker was the foreman who had the respect of the other men. He was quite a bit older than the other workers. His skill at the kilns was unchallenged. The men often sought his advice; because, they regarded him as wiser than they. People like Jesse stand out among any group of people. A few men and women walk among us who reflect a preternatural light that doesn't originate with them but abides with them, bright and shining, as they journey through life. They can be found in every state and condition. Christians show forth the light, some more brightly than others.

Becker was the son and grandson of a lime burner and had spent all of his adulthood working the furnaces. He knew his lifelong vocation well. He had helped produce quicklime from the limestone for several uses—plaster, mortar, concrete, and fertilizer, products sold in the local area.

Two teams worked each kiln—one placed the fuel and limestone in the opening at the top, located on the side of a hill; the other drew out the fuel and quick lime at an opening in the front of the kiln. At Alden's quarry, the teams rotated between the two tasks of loading the fuel and limestone and drawing the ash and quicklime from the kiln.

Becker was a man who showed in his features and behavior little of the suffering that he had experienced in his life. He lost his parents young. He and his siblings were raised by an aunt and uncle who had their own health problems. He set out into the world at fourteen from his home in Berks County, Pennsylvania, and always made a living with his hands. Massey Alden's father employed Jesse when he was nineteen. Not long after he acquired his new job, he married a woman of the locality, Laura Groff, who bore him five children.

Becker worked hard to support his family while his wife kept the household, raised the children, and tended a vegetable garden, several chickens, and a cow. The Becker family did not live far from the Peregrines in a more modest cottage than they.

Throughout his life, Jesse Becker, of German parentage, took his family to the local Lutheran Church. Even during his battles with doubt, he went to church with his family: a wife, three boys, and two girls. The Becker's lived with daily hard work, but managed to find joy in each other and their children.

Jesse took Adriel under his wing, showing him the things that make for quicklime production. Despite some barbing from other workmen, Adriel saw himself through to becoming expert in the manufacturing of quicklime. Resentment of the college boy cooled as the men got to know Adriel better. Adriel was a young man who possessed many qualities to win people over, among them being amiability, but especially the mettle he exhibited.

One early afternoon Jesse and Adriel were sitting on the hillside next to the kiln eating lunch, as they habitually did. On this particular day, Jesse mentioned Nathaniel Hawthorne's short story, *Ethan Brand*; because, Adriel expressed to his new friend perplexity about what the unpardonable sin was and if he, Adriel, had committed it. Young people tend to be very impressionable, Adriel being no exception. Adriel mentioned the passage in the Gospel of Mark where Jesus responded to the religious leaders' criticism of Him as an agent of Satan; because, he cast out unclean spirits. Jesus' family was fearful that He was out of his mind. Jesus countered His opposition with the absurdity of their criticism: Why would Satan cast out Satan? Such a kingdom cannot stand. Then He asserted that accusing Him of casting out demons by Satan was the unforgiveable or unpardonable sin against the Holy Spirit.

At this point, Jesse told Nathaniel Hawthorne's story, recognizing that Hawthorne in his story was not giving Jesus' view of the unpardonable sin, but wanting to pursue what the great author had to say to clarify obscurity on a difficult subject. He was a great storyteller, not losing Adriel's attention at any time throughout.

"Ethan Brand was a lime burner who left his work eighteen years before his return home in order to find out the meaning of the unpardonable sin. Finally realizing that the sin could be found by looking into his own heart, he returned home from his wanderings, where he encountered the man who had taken over from him at the working of the kiln.

"Brand, characterized as the wayfarer, discovered that the unpardonable sin dwelt in his own heart, requiring no journey to discover it. It was said that Brand had an association with a demon that dwelt in the furnace that pondered with him the nature of the unpardonable sin. Brand discovered that the unpardonable sin was the intellect's working evil against fellowship with other humans and reverence for God. At the end of the story, Ethan Brand, while tending the lime-kiln fire during the night, cast himself into it. All that was left was his skeleton and the form of a heart, now of lime. Pity and empathy for the human condition had forsaken Brand in his search. The cold intellect had triumphed over matters of the heart."

When Becker was done, the two men sat silent for a while, as if both needed some time to absorb the gravity of the story, though Jesse had read the story before that day. Adriel thought of the wayfarer who in no way was a pilgrim to a holy place, but actually wandered until he cast himself into the fires of hell. Brand's direction was not set toward heaven.

Adriel broke the silence. "Hawthorne may not be a biblical interpreter; but, he does get to the heart of the matter regarding the importance of sympathy for and amity toward human beings and respect for God."

What does the biblical text mean? Those who ascribe to the devil and his minions what is the work of the Holy Spirit are so hardened in heart that they won't and can't repent of their evil.

As Adriel entered young adulthood, he became restless and uncomfortable with the way the world works and how human beings suffer so much from their own sin and folly and that of others. The world is full of human wickedness and supernatural evil. The serious-minded young man was thinking more and more that Macbeth was right about life being all sound and fury, signifying nothing. He yet had a long way to go; but, he was moving in the direction of despair. He would descend into this crucible like limestone into the fire.

CHAPTER TEN

RETURN TO SCHOOL

The war goes on, more men die on the fields of battle and many more die of disease. Many soldiers lie in hospitals lacking one or more limbs. We won a great victory at Gettysburg; but, no end is in sight. Mr. Lincoln bears a great burden. I will join the army when the school term is over and do my part in the fight for freedom.
— Diary of Adriel Peregrine, *October 1, 1863.*

As Adriel prepared to go back to school, Union and Confederate armies continued the hard fight on many battlefields. At Chickamauga, the Union Army of the Cumberland was bested by Braxton Bragg's Confederates. Only the steadfastness of General George Thomas averted a disaster for the Union forces. It was clear that the war would go on for some time.

Adriel returned to school but was making plans sometime after his eighteenth birthday in November to join the army. He would finish the first term and then sign up.

Adriel's first term back to school was rough going. His roommate was not like his good friend, Jake Brenneman, who had joined the army along with a number of Jake's and Adriel's other friends. Adriel and his roommate tried to avoid each other as much as one is able to when living in the same room.

His new roommate was not at all considerate. During the night he would make too much noise, keeping Adriel awake; moreover he was caustic and drunken, breaking house rules until he was caught and thrown out of school. Adriel spent the remainder of the term as the only lodger in the room—a

godsend in his estimation; but, it created the problem of loneliness.

In the depths of the night Adriel often thought of Abigail. His nightmare about her being swept off a clipper ship recurred frequently. He would wake up in a sweat, crying at the loss until he realized he was having a bad dream. Though he hadn't seen her during his time working at the lime kilns, she was still very much on his mind. Through months of living at home, he didn't call on her, though he wondered again if he should tell her of his dream. Abigail made no attempts to con-tact him during these months. He wondered if there was yet a chance for them one day to become husband and wife. How persistent is human hope and delusion!

Adriel took the edge off his discontent and moments of dejection with deep study. During the term he worked hard on his writing style, which showed much improvement and promise, as his professor told him. While interested in being a teacher for the lower grades, he also desired to write fiction and poems.

On weekends when he was particularly lonely, he would write short stories. When he thought the loneliness would overcome him, he met a friend in Uri Brown who lived a few doors from him. Uri stopped Adriel in the hallway and intro-duced himself. From then on, they visited each other and ate together in the dining hall.

Uri's home was not far from where Adriel grew up. He was the son of a Mennonite pastor and his wife, who raised four children. Possessing a golden voice, Uri sang in the church choir *a cappella*, a strong Mennonite tradition that included con-gregational unaccompanied singing. He was also in the Normal School chorus. He was a man of great integrity and taciturn in his manner, yet strong of will to do the right thing. Uri was studying to become a teacher in a Mennonite school.

One afternoon, Adriel, Uri, and some friends from one of the literary societies on campus to which Adriel and Uri also belonged were conversing in the Old Main dining hall right after lunch about a story written by Adriel. These young men and women would befriend Adriel, whose loneliness was fast coming to an end. Adriel's story would end up years later in a collection he entitled, *Tales from the Wooded Hills*.

Adriel told the story, a narrative regarding the imagination, in brief to the gathered literary enthusiasts.

"A young boy, named Daniel, loved to walk in the woods that surrounded the little village in which his family lived. On his perambulations, he would look for the animal life and inspect the plant life. He came to identify the species of many trees, plants and animals. The deer and fox were his friends, as were the frogs and snakes (the poisonous ones from a distance). One day he came upon a most extraordinary sight—a rock formation that looked like a monster or like one of those recently discovered dinosaurs, known then by the name the English discoverer William Buckland gave them—megalosaurus, from earth's distant past.

"He slowly approached it; and when he felt confident that the rocks were not alive, he climbed them. It was the biggest thrill of his young life. Every day afterward he would visit the monster, stand in awe at the figure, and then climb him.

"His imagination carried him away into a world where stone formations turn into living beings. When he walked through the woods, he fantasized that the monster was watching him from the forest or following him, careful not to be seen (hard for a monster to do). He would scare himself, and after the shivers, he would enjoy the thrill. Every time he approached the clearing where it resided, he would delight himself with the thought that the monster was not there; because, he was roaming the forest. Anxious to meet this dweller in the forest, he would repeat a couple of lines out loud:

> *Monster, monster, come to me.*
> *We'll sit at table and have some tea.*

"One night in the summer, when the windows of the house were open, he thought he heard the beast somewhere close to the house. He got up, put his shoes on, and walked out into the night, straining his eyes to get a good look. He saw the bushes rustle and thought he heard the beastly growling of a large animal. When his fear vanquished his curiosity, he ran back into the house where he would be protected by the walls of this fortress and by his parents.

"On one pleasant summer day, he walked, as was his wont, to the home of the monster. On his way he was sure that he heard the sounds of the creature in the forest. Then, he heard it trumpet. After somewhat recovering from his fright, he said to himself, 'It must be that it is alive!' He summoned all the courage he could and continued on his journey. When he arrived, the rock formation was in its usual place. What a disappointment this sight was for Daniel!

"That night he again heard sounds outside the house. He ventured forth but found nothing. Early the next day he ran to the home of the monster, and he was not there! The rock formation was gone."

The gathered company applauded the story. "Publish it," one of them said. It wouldn't be too many years later that he did so with other of his tales.

Adriel was caught up in an imagination-created world. It was not that he shut fast the door to everyday reality; but, he used his fancy to create fantasy that pointed to a larger, richer world that was not the product of a disconsolate mind, seeking to escape the harsh circumstances of life, but an imaginative mind seeking truth in the extraordinary or odd.

What is the fundamental truth of Adriel's story, entitled *The Monster of Stone*? First, it is set against those who would deny a child (and an adult) a world of imagination, or at least starve the imaginative faculty with an insipid world that is reduced to sense experience and logic alone that, though important, cannot span entirely the meaning of truth, but only a small part of it. And even more so, imagination manifests the truth that the world consists of more than swirling atoms and molecules. There exists a world the human imagination grasps that lies outside immediate sense experience. It can tell us many important truths. It is the world of story, metaphor, legend, myth, poetry, parable, epic, and allegory that bring home truths everyday reality cannot. It is often the subject of literature and art. Imagination pertains not only to our emotions and feelings but to the truths that come from a concert of heart and mind. God has provided us with hearts and minds that conceive worlds that often point to the deep realities of life. God sometimes acts in these stories; he always stands behind them as the source of goodness and truth. He is the ground of all meaningful discourse and expression that point to transcendental meaning.

Adriel's story writing and his association with new friends like Uri sustained him during the term. He would have strenuous bouts with dejection, but never such that they lead him into self-destructive behavior—at least, not yet.

CHAPTER ELEVEN

LEAVING HOME FOR THE BATTLEFIELD

When I enlisted, I felt a great relief; because, I had done the right thing, not playing the coward but the patriot. Not long after this glorious day, I hopped onto a train in Lancaster with other recruits to travel to Camp Cadwalader in Philadelphia. From there it was to the front lines in the battle rich Commonwealth of Virginia.

— A Wanderer Who Becomes a Pilgrim, *Adriel Peregrine.*

Adriel's mother and father convinced him to remain in school through the term that began in the spring. Distracted though he was, Adriel did well. Uri remained in school also, but told Adriel that after the term was over, he would go to Philadelphia to seek service in some capacity at Satterlee General Hospital. Through his parents, Adriel found out that Jennie Hallewell was, since June, residing with her aunt in Washington and assisting her in her duties as a nurse in one of the military hospitals. Jennie would have become a nurse herself; but, she was far too young to meet the requirement.

Of what was Jennie Hallewell made? She was outward beauty and strength as well as inward beauty and strength. In the military hospitals, she saw the effects of the battlefield—the loss of limb, the loss of health, the loss of sanity, the loss of meaning, and the loss of life and was able nonetheless to serve the young men who convalesced or died there. Her experience was never published, though she wrote it down. Walt Whitman's (his letters, newspaper articles, *The Wound-Dresser*) and Louisa May Alcott's (*Hospital Sketches*) literary accounts would give the reader some idea of the profound suffering of the War, helped by the thousands of photographs. Jennie saw the young suffer and die, but never lost her compassionate heart and never became cynical or dispirited, though she wept often. She was built of courage, much like the men who fought the War.

Adriel signed up for one year with the 199th Pennsylvania Volunteers. He would train in Philadelphia at Camp Cadwalader before leaving for the lines in front of Richmond. In the fall of 1864, the War continued its grueling march and its relentless slaughter. General Sherman was marching to the sea; General Grant was besieging Richmond and Petersburg.

The day of departure for training camp was not a day of joy for Sylvan and Agatha Peregrine. Adriel was a lot more chipper than they; for, he had been waiting for many months to join the army. The family left early in the morning for Lancaster in a Barouche carriage, along with a driver provided by Mr. Alden. The train was scheduled to leave at 3:00 P.M. Adriel took with him what he could carry in a knapsack.

Talk along the way was spare until they drew near to the city of Lancaster. Both parents shared some moral advice and wisdom, mostly drawn from Proverbs and attempted to be of cheer, while they knew only sadness of heart and distress. As they approached the terminal, the conversation picked up.

"Be sure to write, Adriel," his mom reminded him.

"I'll write, Mom."

"I'll pray for you every day," she responded.

"Thanks, Mom."

"We'll soon arrive at the station, Adriel. We'll wait until the train departs. No hurry. As you know, we're staying in East Petersburg tonight with my sister," said his father.

"Yes, Father. Thanks for waiting. Say hello to Aunt Nettie for me."

The two parents were already grieving for their son quietly in their hearts; for, they knew very well what the casualty counts from both wounds and disease had been over three years of war. The lists were very long. They imagined receiving the bad news by telegram or letter. Many parents were bereft of their sons and would never know another day without grief. Tears would mark the rest of their lives. Southern battlefields had become extensive graveyards for the young—academies of death and destruction. The knell was tolling throughout the land.

Adriel failed to say his good-byes to Abigail. His heart was heavy with the thought that he may never see her again. Acceptance of this fact followed begrudgingly after the realization. His emotional blindness finally turned to reality. He might write to her, but what would be the point? Romance had never been born; friendship was withering.

When the family arrived at the train station, Adriel hopped off the carriage and disappeared into the crowd. Sylvan helped his wife off the buggy with assistance from the driver. Before long, they found Adriel in the crowd. The driver stayed with the carriage. Passengers, families of passengers, well-wishers, and recruits crowded the area outside the terminal. The train station consisted of a rather large rectangular two-story building set next to a pavilion under which trains stopped.

The train would arrive from the west to take the Lancaster passengers to points east. The city of Philadelphia was the goal. Adriel and thousands of other young men would begin their service in the training camp.

In their enthusiasm, with no sobering experience to discourage them, some of the recruits began singing a song of the Union, "The Battle Hymn of the Republic," by Julia Ward Howe, with others joining in. A magnificent voice in the crowd stirred the singing to a great volume. Men and women, many of whom sang in their church choirs, broke into harmony. It was an emotional scene. The song ended with cheers. Then, the people began singing "Battle Cry of Freedom," written by George F. Root after President Lincoln's call for 300,000 volunteers on July 2, 1863.

Adriel's parents found their son in the crowd with a group of other recruits from Lancaster County whom he had met at the time of enlistment. They would join others at Camp Cadwalader who together would soon live each day suspended between life and death in the great cause of the Union.

Adriel noticed that his mother's face was wet with tears. Undeterred by the crowd, he went over to her, looked at her, wiped away her tears, and hugged her. His father, usually not so demonstrative, also began to shed tears for his only child. He embraced his wife with his left arm; and, facing Adriel, looked straight into his eyes. He spoke to him in the imperative. "Come home." He shook his son's hand, took Agatha by the arm, and said to Adriel: "Good-bye for now. Write and come home." That is all he said. They disappeared into the crowd.

As the train was pulling out of the station, Adriel noticed that his parents were sitting in the buggy with the roof retracted, their eyes on the train. Adriel stood up and opened the window. When Agatha saw him, she waved from her seat in the buggy. Sylvan stood up in the carriage, waving both hands. The driver also joined in the farewell. Along with his compatriots, Adriel leaned out the window, shouting and waving spiritedly. His parents caught notice and waved all the more.

The train soon disappeared out of sight. Adriel was at the beginning of a journey whose vagaries he could hardly imagine and whose end he could not conceive.

CHAPTER TWELVE

ON THE TRAIN

When the time was drawing near to join my regiment at training camp, I was, at the same time, both eager and excited and resistant and terrified. How can one sustain such opposite emotions and attitudes? It is most easily possible when one is caught up in such terrible events as occurred in the Civil War, or as some would call it, among many names, the "Great Rebellion" and "The War Between the States."

– A Wanderer Who Becomes a Pilgrim, *Adriel Peregrine*.

The train pulled out of the station for Camp Cadwalader, located in Philadelphia, where Adriel, with many others, would prepare for the battlefield. When he turned to sit down at his window seat, he discovered a fellow passenger who was standing near him in the aisle. After he greeted Adriel, he sat down next to him. As the din of the youths around him died away, the outgoing man who had sat next to Adriel initiated a conversation.

"My name is Michael O'Brien. What's yours?" He extended his arm for a shake.

As the two men shook hands, Adriel told Michael his name and asked, "Where are you from?"

"I'm from right here in Lancaster city. How about you?"

"I grew up in the northern part of the county at Red Oak," Adriel responded.

"Yes, I know where that is. Is your father a farmer?" Michael asked.

"No, he works for Massey Alden on his properties," Adriel said.

"Have you ever been to Philadelphia?"

"Never."

"I was there once. It is something to see. You'll see it soon," Michael said.

"I've never been much farther than Lancaster County. I don't know much about the world out there," an irony considering Adriel's knowledge and imaginative life.

"I haven't been far either, only to Philadelphia. My parents came through there from County Galway, Ireland, with me, a little one. We were fleeing the potato famine, what we Irish call 'The Hard Times.' My grandparents came along with us. They died just a few years ago. Other relatives died in Ireland of the famine. My parents tell me of those nightmare times. It causes me great grief."

"That's really something. I've heard only a little bit about the famine. I was told that a million people died."

"Yes. The greatest toll was in the west and south of the country. My family's from Galway in the west.

"You have quite a story."

"When we got here, Mom and Dad, with many other Irish immigrants, had to contend with prejudice. We arrived in Philadelphia after the riots there against the Irish in 1844. I was born in 1845; we stepped off the ship in 1846. We settled in Kensington. Later we moved to Lancaster. Have you heard of the burning of Catholic churches like Saint Michael's?"

"Yes, I have. My parents told me about it. I'm sorry all of that happened. You and I, though, will be buddies."

"OK, great!" Michael responded.

Silence followed. Michael fell asleep, and Adriel reflected, as he often did. For a while, he took in the beautiful Pennsylvania countryside that caused him to soar in his thinking. He thought of the deep, dark forests that must have existed three centuries before and now the green fields and farms with groves and woods marking the landscape.

Adriel closed his eyes as these vivid pictures came to his mind. And then elfin land appeared before him. As the music began, the elfin women stepped out to dance with their men.

To dance to the tunes of an elfin band,
Her true love took her by the hand.

Under the toadstools and ferns, the inhabitants of the elfin city came out to celebrate the riches of the wonders of creation made from nothing by the Lord of the universe, present everywhere and in all things but not those things, sustaining the whole universe.

Adriel could hear the music as the festivities continued. He drew near and joined in as a spectator, drinking the nectar so well-prepared by the elfin distillers. He sang along to the elfin tunes and then danced with one whom he didn't recognize, though she looked somewhat familiar.

The train coach came back into his awareness. Michael was still sleeping, as were many others. A few were conversing, some keeping their voices low for the benefit of their slumbering comrades; others were not so considerate. The train was moving fast toward Philadelphia.

Adriel's imagination drifted off in the direction of the battlefield. He wondered if he would survive the conflict; and, if he did, what he would do when he mustered out. He observed himself during a battle with bullets whizzing past him and shells exploding all around. His company was surging forward as several men fell to the ground. There was the shouting of orders, groaning, and yelling. He could see the gray line with smoke filling the air in front of him. As his company drew near the foe, he attached his bayonet to his rifle. It was going to be a close fight.

The scene quickly changed. He was lying in a tranquil field, gazing at the sky. The clouds appeared to form an artillery piece, with the rising sun providing the light of the explosion. The peaceful sky turned belligerent. Adriel imagined that he stood up and jumped into a nearby gully for protection. He would most likely be doing this in earnest before long.

Next, Adriel was sitting in the coach, waking up from sleep. He looked over at Michael, who was already awake. "You seem to have had a bad dream."

Adriel responded, "It started well but ended badly. How were your dreams?"

"Not so good either. I was in the middle of a field, the dead and wounded all around me."

"That's where both of us are going, right into the middle of a war and the most bloody, awful one we Americans have ever seen." Adriel would soon become familiar with the implications of his enthusiasm to fight as a volunteer in the Union Army.

The train was now on the outskirts of the city and would soon be pulling into the station. Tightly grasping their valises, both Michael and Adriel were on the edge of their seats.

CHAPTER THIRTEEN

TRAINING CAMP

*Human nature had become, for me, a conundrum. Why was evil
among human beings so rampant in the world? I no longer looked to
my Christian faith for answers. I traveled out into the wilderness to
find them. I found nothing to replace faith to make sense of things.*
A Wanderer Who Becomes a Pilgrim, Adriel Peregrine.

It would be in training camp, as the temptations, routine, and
drill wore on his soul that Adriel continued to question all
that his parents and the church had taught him about God.
This growing skepticism would lead Adriel down paths he
never imagined as a youth.

After Michael and Adriel arrived at camp in a horse cab
that they collaborated to hire and pay for—they had little
money—they were assigned bunks in one of the barracks.
Since it was late in the day, nothing else happened until the
next morning when they were awakened very early. After eating breakfast, drill—the backbone of the day—and other training routines began.

At the end of the first full day, the two men fell into their
bunks completely exhausted. They had no energy to talk to
each other about what had happened; but, during the several
breaks between drills, there was opportunity to meet and converse with some of the other recruits that would become the
199th Pennsylvania Volunteers, also known as the Commercial
Regiment; because, it was organized by the Philadelphia
Commercial Exchange Association. These talkative young

men readily gave their impressions of what would become the training routine.

Adriel wasn't talkative. He spent many days of his youth walking silently through field and forest—for him a training ground for his reticence and restraint. There were many things in camp that one could complain about. Adriel complained little. A faultfinder, either about things or people, he was not.

During this brief training at Cadwalader, tedium was a problem for the recruits, including Adriel. It was then Adriel partook of his first alcoholic drink and many more during his service and afterward. He also caught glimpses of the pornography that circulated in the camp; but, he resisted a first experience of sex from readily available prostitutes. Adriel was drifting off the path.

Future tragedies would encourage a swifter departure from the road that led to beatitude. Where he trod for many years would be a wilderness of spiritual dangers. The landscape was barren, with many hidden perils among the scrubby flora. The serpent was coiled to strike with a deadly bite.

Though Adriel had been steeped in his religious beliefs, his time in the army caused a more tenuous hold on them. They gradually provided less and less the central explanation for his experience. While Father Ledford was very helpful to him when he had posed to the priest those questions that trouble everyone, he was drawn toward an agnostic interpretation of the world and human life, away from a Christian view. God became less and less important in his life during those years of his youth from the War through his employment on the packet ships between New York and Liverpool.

Adriel's and Michael's friendship deepened during those brief weeks before joining the Army of the James on the Richmond-Petersburg line. The two recruits added other friends, a number of whom didn't survive the war. When Adriel and Michael had free time, they would talk about many things, but most especially about what sense their experience of these troubled and apocalyptic times made. There were many things to figure out, many of which were not figured out.

It was during breaks in drills that Michael and Adriel often conversed about camp life, that is, about human nature like Herman Melville does in *White-Jacket or The World in a Man-of-War*. Michael was freer in his complaint about how others irritated him than Adriel. The convergence of thousands of human beings was an opportunity to observe how we behave in groups. For Adriel and Michael this was no academic study or undertaking in abstraction, but was personal and specific as everyday life tends to be. Camp could produce and multiply spiritual disease, as it did physical disease.

One afternoon Adriel and Michael were in the mess, whiling away time before the next drill. They had moved from family reminiscence to topics close to their present circumstance.

"Camp would be a lot more tolerable if we'd all get along a little bit better. The other day an ill-tempered recruit tripped me; because, I angered him over a trifle, or what I thought was a trifle." Michael had become disgruntled with camp life in less than a week.

"I've got one too. I somehow got on the wrong side of a fellow who since has spoken unkind words mixed with much profanity every time he sees me. Maybe I shouldn't take it to heart. I shouldn't let it bother me. We young soldiers are immature. We need more growing up." Adriel too had more downs than ups.

"What is it with us humans? We are perverse in our relationships with one another. We range from difficult to wicked," observed Michael. "I don't want it to be this way; but, it is this way. I know from my Catholic upbringing that I should first look into myself. Where have I strayed? I should confess my sins and be open to God's mending me and leave it at that;

but, I stray from my self-criticism to criticism of others. It's easier and more fun."

"I'm confounded about an explanation. At one time, I was more confident that Christianity gave a clear answer, namely the fall. Adam and Eve transgressed God's command and then everything fell apart. Cain killed Abel. Lamech killed a young man. The earth grew more and more evil. The writer of Genesis says that before the flood, God saw that the thoughts of human beings are always and only wicked. But, my Christian belief is eroding, leaving me with an unsure foundation for an assessment of us humans.

"I was taught that we behave terribly toward one another; because, our wills are inclined toward evil. What is evil without a standard of what is good and evil? Without Christianity I have to find a new ground for my judgments about people and the world. So far, I haven't found it. I do know what I observe. Humans are a mix of good and bad. For now, that's all I can assert, nothing more. What is my standard—what I've been taught and my own personal judgment. Some of what I've been taught, I reject like the biblical account of sin and Jesus Christ as Savior. I don't accept the authority of the Bible anymore. I've found nothing to replace it, no higher authority. I guess I, in some ways, depend on the faith of my forebears without believing as they did." Evident was the fact that Adriel had not yet completely given up his childhood religious training, but was well on the way. He wished to forget the Christian dynamic of God's good creation—fall—sin in the world—justification in Christ—final salvation in the Kingdom of God. Yet, his moral sense was yet dependent on judgments that come from Christian belief.

Joining the army was opening a much wider world for both men, each of whom was well-protected, or as protected as one could possibly be, in their growing up. Now they were in a large mix of other human beings with a lot to observe and bad habits to pick up, not that they didn't also contribute their flaws to the mix. Army discipline was meant to suppress the flaws for the greater good of the regiment so that it could do more effectively the hard work it had to do; but, the flaws didn't disappear.

Both young men were deeper thinkers than most of those around them. Both had been nurtured in their Christian churches, though different, yet shared many similarities. They knew their catechisms that included the remedy of forgiveness for their transgressions. Michael was more traditionalist, not having rejected his religious legacy as Adriel had done.

They got up and returned to drill. The remaining days of training in camp were growing short. Soon, they would be in the line before Richmond, the capital of the Confederacy.

CHAPTER FOURTEEN

ON THE LINE BEFORE RICHMOND

The stars looked down upon the dead with no sympathy or heart-break. When it rose, the sun shared the sentiment of the host of heaven. But, in households throughout the country, a multitude of tears have fallen for the dead men, both North and South, who took up a cause they thought noble and just. For the North it was the preservation of the Union and, a little later, also the emancipation of an oppressed race. For the South it was states' rights and protection of a way of life.

– Essays on the Late Rebellion, *Adriel Peregrine.*

Behold the slave ship in turbulent waters rendered by the English artist J. M. W. Turner. The painting was of the infamous incident when, because of lack of drinking water, a captain threw scores of slaves overboard into the deep. Not too long afterward, the United Kingdom prohibited the slave trade. Then, in 1833, the United Kingdom ended slavery in the Empire. Now, Michael, my comrade in arms, and I were fighting side by side to keep our country in which, though the slave trade was ended by stipulation of the Constitution in 1808, slavery still existed in several of the states.

– *Adriel Peregrine, Art and Literature and the Civil War*

The Picket-Guard
"All quiet along the Potomac," they say,
Except, now and then, a stray picket

Is shot as he walks on his beat to and fro,
By a rifleman hid in the thicket.
"Tis nothing—a private or two, now and then,
Will not count in the news of the battle;
Not an officer lost—only one of the men
Moaning out, all alone, his death-rattle."

— Ethel Lynn Beers

The *Philadelphia Inquirer* reported that on October 1, 1864, the 199th Regiment moved out of camp and marched through the city to their embarkation point after stopping at a refreshment saloon to the cheers of the crowd for Lincoln and Johnson. The recruits were now soldiers in blue headed for the field of battle. Adriel's heart was in his throat as danger and adventure drew near. He tried to train himself away from these physical symptoms, but was not successful. He attempted to envision what the battlefield might be like. But, all the speculation in the world would not prepare him for the reality of war.

The 199th crowded into the train, a sea of blue that flowed into and took up the space of every car, becoming a river headed for a southern battlefield. Each man wore a dark blue coat and light blue pants—the uniform of the volunteer— while regulars wore dark blue coats and dark pants. Add to these a blue kepi hat. The volunteer soldiers were equipped with a knapsack, haversack, blanket roll, cartridge box, cap box, canteen, a bayonet in a scabbard, and a Springfield rifle.

When the unit arrived in Washington, they boarded transports that brought them to Deep Bottom Landing, Virginia. They took their place on the right wing of the Army of the James in front of Richmond at the New Market Road. The regiment was, for a while, part of the 10th Corps, First Brigade, First Division; and, then the 24th Corps, First Brigade, First Division of the Army of the James. The unit would spend the winter on picket duty, construction, and training.

Adriel's loneliest and most dangerous times during the period before the 199th marched south to Petersburg were when he was on picket duty. The pickets were set out in front of the camp in no man's land to watch for the enemy. The Confederate lines were not far in front of them. To escape being killed, they needed to use caution and cover.

At night, visibility was almost non-existent, requiring the soldier to keep especially alert. Failure meant death at the hands of the enemy or execution by the military authorities for sleeping while on picket duty. In a famous case, William Scott, known as "The Sleeping Sentinel," from a Vermont regiment, was convicted of sleeping on duty and sentenced to death. Lincoln commuted his sentence. Scott had taken a comrade's place the night before, so that he was exhausted during duty the following night.

On some nights when on picket duty, Adriel heard gun shots from fellow guards that represented either a false alarm or the stirrings of the Confederates or fire from Confederate snipers. Throughout the winter months, Adriel avoided being killed during this duty.

One moonless night when Adriel was on the picket line, he thought he heard sounds of movement not far in front of him. He raised his rifle, prepared to shoot. A shot was fired that grazed him on the neck. Immediately, he returned fire, followed by a thud on the ground. When he touched the spot on his neck, he discovered that he was bleeding; but, the bullet had not entered him. How badly he was bleeding he didn't know. Out of his coat pocket he took a handkerchief that he was very glad to have on hand. He sighed with relief that he was so fortunate. It was the first time he fired a shot in the field. He couldn't see well enough to judge whether he had killed or wounded someone.

All the while he kept alert for other assailants. Who knows but that a squad of soldiers was approaching his position? Adriel tried to make out moving silhouettes in the darkness.

The fires of two camps gave some light, but not enough for certainty. Adriel held his gun tightly, ready to pull the trigger in an instant. Over the next hour Adriel heard two more shots fired along the line.

Adriel couldn't wait for sunrise. The hours seemed interminable. He was exhausted, but remained alert until the breaking of a new morning. Despite his growing religious skepticism, he recited many prayers. The sun advanced above the horizon, and Adriel was alive. The bleeding had slowed to an almost complete stop. Later, he learned that his mates along the line also survived the night.

Directly in front of him, about twenty yards away, was a corpse. Adriel was tempted to see what he had done, but knew better. Snipers were an ever-present threat.

Adriel was sure that the young man dead on the ground in front of him had left behind loved ones, maybe a sweetheart, whom he intended to marry, and would be mourned. Would his body be taken home? Or would he be buried in a grave in the field where he was killed? During the Civil War, the cry of grief was the greatest in the history of the country up to that point. No war produced the number of American dead like this war. The Revolutionary War, the War of 1812, and the Mexican War were minor actions on the basis of the number killed and wounded. The soldiers on both sides of the conflict were Americans.

Adriel was finally relieved. To make it more difficult for snipers, he returned to camp crouching and alert, though he was exhausted. During his return, when several bullets whizzed by him, he hit the turf. When the picket detail got back to camp, a night of silence turned into outbursts of joy.

Adriel encountered Michael as he was returning to the shelter tent they shared. In the field, each soldier was issued half a tent that he carried with him to be matched by another soldier to make a complete tent for them to sleep in.

"You're back! It's so good to see you, Adriel. They didn't

pick you off. What's with the blood?"

"I almost took a bullet."

"Lucky man."

"Yes, I am. Someone else isn't. I killed a man during the night," Adriel responded with remorse.

Michael took a moment and then said, "I don't yet know what that's like; but, I'm also sure that it's very disturbing. It's happened thousands and thousands of times on the battlefields of this War, and will probably happen many more times before it's over. Come away from the horror and rest. It must have been a long, long night, far too long."

CHAPTER FIFTEEN

IN THE LINE AT PETERSBURG

. . . we band of brothers.　　　　*– Henry V, William Shakespeare.*

The air was miserably cold; the wind often howled; the snow fell and blanketed the earth with its white chill; the cold rain fell that made mud and more mud except when the ground froze; the land was short of green; the sky was gray much of the time. In their huts the soldiers struggled to keep warm.

The winter was long and dreary for Adriel. There was too much time to think and try to figure out and put in order all the new experiences that came his way. He couldn't let drop or forget most of the things that kept tugging his shirt sleeve.

Unfamiliar places, new people, the vagaries of army life, and widely contending viewpoints in abundance contrasted with his upbringing in a quiet place among family and friends. As intent as he was on joining the army, Adriel often longed for the fields and forests of home.

Even in his growing skepticism, Adriel remembered the steadfast dignity and solemn beauty of the parish church of Saint Jude Thaddeus, its sandstone walls and stained glass, its ringing bells and great red entrance door that represented the shed sacrificial blood of Christ. Saint Jude Thaddeus was a country church without those monumental characteristics of a Notre Dame de Paris or Salisbury cathedral, but quite imposing to the lad, Adriel Peregrine. His fond memories and present doubts represented, in part, the conflict raging inside of him.

In the midst of the cacophony of war, he could hear the Anglican chant and the hymns, the voice of the rector praying over the sacramental elements, and the Our Father recited by the congregation. His mother made sure he took along with him to Cadwalader his Bible and *Book of Common Prayer*, still in his knapsack, yet unopened from September through March.

On a summer day he would approach the church and lay his head against the cold and rough wall, as if it were the soft shoulder of his mother. He would put his hands on the sandstone, not noticing its rough quality. For him the stones had a pleasant smell. It's as if they exuded a sweet scent like frankincense, the smell of which he remembered from church. Father Ledford had introduced incense into worship under the influence of the Oxford Movement. The stone also reminded him of God's firm, steadfast love that moves not from its purpose.

He drew from the stone a mystical quality that took him to heavenly places. When he was an older youth, after he had read *The Divine Comedy*, he would imagine that he was with Dante, Beatrice and Saint Bernard in the high heaven, beholding the divine vision and caught up in "The Love which moves the sun and other stars." (Dante, *Paradiso*, trans. Henry Wadsworth Longfellow)

The red door for Christ's shed blood.
The solid stones for God's steadfastness to save.
The stained glass for the light of God.
The bells for the Gospel proclaimed.

These were words he wrote down and saved when he was a young teenager. But, his faith was growing cold, a fact with which he was uncomfortable, yet he seemed unable to alter its downward course. Nonetheless, he spoke several times to the chaplain of the regiment, Joshua Janeway. He told the pastor about his reaction to killing a Confederate soldier. He wanted reassurance that killing in war was justified. He remembered his friend, Uri Brown, a member of the Mennonite Church, who was serving in Satterlee Hospital, Philadelphia, rather than fight in the war. He also told the pastor about his declining faith. Chaplain Janeway looked directly into his eyes and said, "Christ will be with you through everything. I know; because, He is everywhere, loves his people, and promises not to let go, even if you let go of Him. Only in death will he let go of those who do not believe. Remember this if you cannot any longer see the pilgrim path. Throughout your life He is there to show you the way back. Pray that you may turn around."

On March 28, 1865 the 199th Regiment moved south toward Petersburg, where they fell in line for the final assault that forced General Lee to flee westward and, finally, surrender at Appomattox. The regiment was strangely silent as the men marched swiftly on foot to their new destination. The rumor was that soon a break in the thin Confederate line would occur. They would be at the heart of it all. Most would live; some would be wounded; some would die.

When Adriel was on duty north of Richmond shortly after Lee's surrender at Appomattox, he wrote a long letter to his mother and father, describing the events he witnessed and participated in from Fort Gregg to the end of the war

April 20, 1865

Dear Father and Mother,

I hope all is well with both of you. I think about you often and look forward to coming home soon. I have not forgotten the peace of our cottage, of riding Bunyan, and of the trees and fields of home that must be greening as spring begins its rich decorating for the summer.

Since my last letter, my regiment has moved after months of siege from outside Richmond down to Petersburg to Appomattox Courthouse and then to Richmond again, where we are now on

guard duty. The order had gone out on March 28 that the 24th Corps was to move south to the vicinity of Petersburg under the command of General Ord, who had replaced Benjamin Butler in January.

As you know, the army of the Potomac and the Army of the James have been laying siege to Richmond and Petersburg for many months. More recently, our regiment came on to the siege line after a short march and the crossing of the James River by a pontoon bridge constructed by our amazing engineers.

We formed in the line of battle against a place called Fort Gregg, south of Petersburg. The Confederate line was thin and on the verge of breaking. We attacked this gun emplacement and overran it. It was during this battle that my good friend, Michael O'Brien, was killed while attempting to scale the breastwork. He is buried on the battlefield. I hope someday his body will be transferred to a cemetery for the Union dead. I grieve for him with a great sadness. I've written to his parents who live in Lancaster. In this world true friends are few. I lost my best friend and a friendship that grew quickly during difficult and dangerous times.

We pursued Lee across Virginia to a little place called Appomattox Courthouse after engaging the Confederates at Rice's Station. Our 24th Corps, of which I'm a proud member, confronted the Confederates as they came over a ridge. Soon after, Lee surrendered to Grant in a house owned by Wilmer McLean, who had previously lived in a house that stands on the Bull Run battlefield.

I am now stationed at Richmond. Our unit expects to be discharged soon. I'll send you a telegram with details when the time comes.

For now, I send my best to both of you. I look forward to seeing you soon.

Love,

Adriel

Adriel also sent a letter to Michael's parents.

Dear Mr. and Mrs. O'Brien,

My name is Adriel Peregrine. I write to you disconsolately at the death of your son, Michael. He was my best friend and, I know, your beloved son. We trained together at Camp Cadwalader in Philadelphia and served in the same company.

Our regiment was charged with attacking Fort Gregg at Petersburg, Virginia. We ran together across a wide field to the earthworks. As Michael was climbing the breastwork, he was shot and killed. After the battle, I made sure that the grave dug for him there included identification of his person. A small wooden marker designates the place of his burial. His name, regiment, and company have been placed on it. I also included identification on his body in the grave itself. I would not have him buried in a mass grave. Hopefully, he will be reburied in the future.

Michael was a brave soldier and a man of faith. He told me before the battle that if he were killed, I would be sure to write to you. At that time, he expressed his faith and was confident that God provides a place of beatitude after death. He wanted me to let you know that he loved you very much and did not want you to despair—all will be well in Christ.

I will keep you in my thoughts and prayers during this difficult time. May your burden be lightened by the love and mercy of Christ.

Yours sincerely,
Pvt. Adriel Peregrine

Adriel remembered the day well when he recovered Michael's body from the watery ditch before the fort and then surmounted the wall into Fort Gregg. He never forgot his friendship with a man whose faith endured to the end.

CHAPTER SIXTEEN

SICKNESS STRIKES

A sick bed is a grave, and all that the patient says there is but a varying of his own epitaph.
— *John Donne*, Devotions upon Emergent Occasions

It was during his time in the Richmond area after the surrender that Adriel showed symptoms of dysentery. He was treated in camp for a few days, and then sent by train to Washington's Harewood General Hospital.

When Adriel came down with dysentery, his condition had already weakened from his emotional state of mind and lack of sleep and nutrition. During the early days of his illness, he was barely on the living side of death. He was attended faithfully day and night by dedicated nurses and doctors. Not long after Adriel arrived at the hospital, Jennie Hallewell and her aunt began playing a major part in providing for his needs. They found out by telegram about his condition from Adriel's parents, who were informed by letter by a company mate to whom Adriel gave their address as he sickened. The Peregrines got the aunt's address from the Hallewells.

By the standards of Dorothea Dix, Superintendent of Army Nurses, Jennie was far too young to be a nurse; but, she managed to serve Adriel and some others at Harewood under the supervision of her aunt, a nurse on the staff of the hospital. During her service, Jennie roomed at the home of her aunt in Washington. Thousands of women worked in what was then a man's calling. She took a small part in what was the beginning of a great change in women's role in medicine.

When Jenny arrived at his bedside, Adriel was exhausted from his ordeal. Jennie took his hand in hers. He heard his name and her name, "Adriel, it's Jennie, Jennie Hallewell." Then, he fell fast asleep and dreamt.

In a vision, he saw Virgil and Dante walking through the Sixth Circle of hell. He knew this, for in his dream he saw the Roman numeral VI. He was following them not far behind. Adriel thought that they didn't know he was there until Virgil turned around and asked him, "Quid mihi et tibi convenisset nos? Tu scis Latine?" Adriel knew Latin from high school and normal school. In English, the words translate, "Why have you joined us? Do you know Latin?"

Adriel responded, "Intellego," meaning, "I understand." Then, Adriel said, "Nescio cur hic sum," meaning, "I don't know why I'm here."

Dante then asked Adriel, "Visne me scribere te in hunc Cantum?" translates as, "Do you want me to write you into this Canto?"

"Non atus alius," meaning "No. Not at all," was the response.

At this Adriel awoke in a sweat and sat up in bed. He was exasperated by his dream. Was he in hell? No, the large room had too much light and its residents didn't have the look of the damned, or what he thought the damned might look like.

He was more alert than at any time since being admitted to the hospital. He found himself in a barracks-like structure filled with sick soldiers. He tried to remember what happened to him, but only came up with the fact that his regiment was on guard duty in Richmond. He forgot that he had contracted dysentery. Jennie had already left for the day.

The following day, while Adriel was looking at one of the two entrances to the long room, he saw a familiar figure coming towards him. As the young woman approached him, familiarity became recognition. His heart leaped as Jennie Hallewell greeted him.

"Adriel, I'm glad you're sitting up."

"Jennie!" he cried. He hadn't remembered that the day before she had called out to him. His illness and distress made her a welcome sight.

Jennie had a lovely face that beamed joy, kindness, and gentleness. She showed that beauty, the Spirit's gifts, and studiousness can exist side by side without detriment to one another. She was a good student and would shortly go to the Normal School to study to be a teacher. She was becoming a remarkable woman.

Outward beauty is sometimes reflective of inward. In other instances, it hides an inward ugliness or evil, as physical homeliness may also hide inward fairness. Jennie's appearance reflected an inward comeliness. She was a sinner like everyone else; but, she didn't possess the disfigurement of evil that is set against the will of God. Her life was taken up at that time with service to wounded and dying soldiers. She didn't need to be anywhere near a battlefield; but, she chose to devote much time to help in a small way in alleviating the massive suffering of the War. She saw what Louisa May Alcott and Walt Whitman saw. She was made of steel in her ability to experience what many couldn't tolerate.

There, in that great hospital of the Civil War, she stood before her friend of years who didn't know the treasure he beheld because of an inordinate obsession with another woman who didn't love him. She was gold Adriel overlooked. She was treasure he had not yet found.

"What an amazing turn of events that we have encountered one another." Adriel was very glad to see her, but uncomfortable in her presence.

"Why am I here? I don't remember."

"You contracted dysentery. You almost died."

"Dysentery? Have you been visiting me all the time I've been ill?"

"No, but I've been here visiting in the hospital for over a year. Just the other day, we were informed by telegram from your parents that you were here."

"What a coincidence that I was brought to this particular hospital." Jennie thought, *maybe not a coincidence.* "What horror you must have been through."

"Times of fright mixed with the dirt and discomfort of camp life. I lost a good friend at Petersburg."

"Sorry to hear that."

"But, the Union's saved!"

"Yes it is after a great slaughter. The country will never forget the sacrifice. Adriel, what are you going to do when you get home?"

"I'm going to take a long walk through the countryside, gaze at the clouds, and get a dog."

"Speaking of home, your mother arrived by train late yesterday."

"She has! How long have I been here?"

"Over two weeks."

"Over two weeks! They were lost to me."

"But, you came through, Adriel." Jennie couldn't hide her affection for him, nor did she try to hide it.

In *Devotions for Emergent Occasions*, John Donne said that a man's words on his sick bed are like an epitaph. Adriel thought and thought again about what these words mean. While perplexed, he illustrated the words in what he said next.

"Jennie, my faith in God wavers. I'm losing the way I've trod my entire youth." It surprised Adriel that he said these words. They seemed to have come out of nowhere. Yet Jennie and he had been fellow travelers. They attended the same church and had spoken together of spiritual things. Even in their childhood, they were interested in matters of faith. The conversation on that day in Harewood General Hospital was simply the taking up of an old conversation about God and the meaning of life.

"I don't like your saying such things, Adriel. It brings sorrow to my heart. I wish I could be an encouragement to you to hold on to what is so dear and priceless."

"I've fallen off the edge with nothing to hold on to. I've found no way to save myself. I don't believe God Himself can save me."

"Do you mean that? Adriel, let me help."

"There's nothing you can do."

Jennie began weeping softly, hiding her eyes from Adriel. When he noticed, Adriel said softly, "Weep for me, Jennie. You've been a good friend. I need your tears." And thus, Adriel's epitaph may have been written here: "Weep for me. I lost faith in Christ."

CHAPTER SEVENTEEN

AGATHA BRINGS BAD NEWS

My world collapsed and broke into a million pieces. Nothing could put it back together, not even God. Later, I was told that world ending events for an individual have the possibility of containing some good. I didn't believe this.

– A Wanderer Who Becomes a Pilgrim, *Adriel Peregrine.*

On that same day, another woman came down the hall to see Adriel, older than Jennie, with the wisdom that years can bring, but for many people never comes. Agatha Peregrine had traveled from Lancaster by train to see her ailing son after Sylvan and she had received by letter the word of his illness. Agatha made haste to Washington with the prospect of Adriel's dying before she arrived. Sylvan remained behind to keep watch over the homestead and his many duties for Massey Alden. He agonized about the plight of his only son and child in his quiet way.

When he recognized his mother, Adriel wanted to cry out, "Mother!" but held his tongue so as not to make a scene among his hospital mates. Seeing him awake, Agatha quickened her pace while Jennie stood up to greet her. His mother embraced him with tears, and then Jennie. "How wonderful it is to see you alive, Adriel!"

"It's so good to see you, Mother. Is Father OK?"

"He's fine. He stayed home to tend to things."

Jennie gave her seat to Agatha, who protested only a little. Agatha held her son's hand as Jennie looked on. She knew some very bad news that Adriel didn't yet know.

"I'll give you two some privacy to catch up. I'll be back in a little while." Jennie went away to visit another patient while Adriel's mother was preparing herself to tell him the bad news.

"Adriel, I have some news to give you." Adriel knew from his mother's demeanor that it was bad news. His heart began to bang against his chest. His mouth went dry.

Agatha hesitated to give him the bad news and then forced herself to speak. "Abigail Dunlap was killed three days ago." Agatha dropped off into silence, anticipating a strong response from Adriel.

Adriel placed his hand on his face and wept. Without saying a word, Agatha took his other hand and pressed it against her cheek. She whispered to him softly, "I mourn with you."

He thought to himself, *the dreams are true.* He looked at his mother. "The weight is too heavy. How did she die?"

Agatha didn't want to answer this question.

Adriel repeated more emphatically, "How did she die?"

"She was found on the Dunlap farm lane. She had been strangled. Conrad Kraybill, the manservant, has signed a statement that he witnessed Abigail running out of the house with Caleb following her. That night when the Dunlaps returned from a social gathering, they happened upon the body." Adriel felt like he had swallowed his own heart.

Adriel cried up to God, whom he felt to be less real than any time before. He heard nothing, though over the next few days he lifted his face to heaven. The silence was no surprise to him. He thought of himself as crying into nothingness; but, he cried anyhow as if God was listening to him.

Agatha had more news. "Caleb Landis is in the county jail, awaiting trial for the murder."

When he left for the service, Adriel was at odds with Caleb over Abigail; but, he remembered how much they had been good friends. His immediate reaction was that Caleb was being wrongly accused. He had no basis for this judgment except his knowledge of Caleb's character.

"I must get home as soon as possible."

Jennie had learned of Abigail's death and Caleb's incarceration from Agatha. The news saddened her greatly. No consolation from Jennie would soften Adriel's fierce grief.

CHAPTER EIGHTEEN

RETURN HOME

*Death is an ocean of unconsciousness from which we cannot be
retrieved, nor do I wish to be.*
   – Diary of Adriel Peregrine, *written at a time of his growing
skepticism. July 20, 1865.*

The 199th Regiment was mustered out on June 28, 1865. Adriel
was in the hospital until July 1. Having received word in the
hospital that his unit had been dissolved, he made preparations to return home as soon as the doctor would permit.

Adriel said good-bye to Jennie in an awkward conversation. "Adriel, I know that you'll be leaving tomorrow for home.
Is there anything I can do to help you get ready?" Jennie was
hoping for continued contact with Adriel, even if only by letter, since she would remain in Washington for an undetermined time. Adriel would return home and forget her. Letters
would not be arriving for either of them from either of them.
Adriel would forget her; Jennie would remember him. Her love
for Adriel didn't subside. She was either foolish, obsessive, or
insightful. She was certainly in love with him.

"Jennie, there's nothing you can do for me. Thanks for all
you've done." He was packing his uniform and a few other
items soldiers carried on campaign while speaking to her. His
mother had brought him clothes he could wear on the train.

Adriel and Jennie said their final good-byes. She gave him
an embrace and turned to continue working on the ward.
Adriel watched her as she spoke to a patient a few beds from

his. His thoughts were not of love, though he was fond of her and could even regard her as a friend, as he had in the past, especially after their meeting in Harewood General Hospital, where he came to appreciate her care and concern.

Adriel's mother arrived in the ward for the journey home. She greeted Jennie and gave her a hug. She had hoped for a deepening relationship between the two young people that didn't happen because of Adriel's disinterest. A cab, awaiting them outside the hospital, hurried them to the New Jersey Avenue Depot, where Adriel and his mother boarded the train for home.

As the train was rolling west toward Lancaster from Philadelphia, Adriel was looking out the window as his mother crocheted next to him. Much was on Adriel's mind as he reflected on the war; his future; and, most of all, the death of Abigail. He had thought of Abigail as Romeo had thought of Rosaline before he met Juliet. "The all-seeing sun ne'er saw her match since first the world begun." His thoughts continued to prevent him from loving one who loved him.

He had known for a long time that Abigail wouldn't be his love; but, he had great difficulty in coming to terms with the fact of its unrequited nature. He thought of his premonitory dreams about her death, which struck him as quite amazing since he didn't think of himself as soothsayer, mantis, or seer. He then thought of how he must go and see his old friend despite his anger at Caleb's becoming Abigail's young man.

In the lane where Abigail's body lay, the constable found one of Caleb's cuff links inscribed with his initials, CJL, given to him by his parents on his last birthday. His footprints were imprinted on the muddy lane. The evidence pointed to Caleb as the murderer. Adriel decided he would conduct his own investigation to prove Caleb's innocence.

All the way home, Adriel could think of nothing but

Abigail's death. How could this be? How horrible a turn of events! What a nightmare to dwell in his consciousness! Early in his young life, he had become a cynic. Youthful joy had been pressed out of his life.

CHAPTER NINETEEN

THE ROARING FIRE

My ardor is a fire I hope will burn my entire life.
— Preface to Tales both Tall and Short, *Adriel Peregrine.*

With a heavy heart, Adriel returned home after almost a year of being away. Disease and loss took a great toll. The victory of the Union was not foremost in his mind. He was exhausted in mind, heart, and body. When he arrived with his mother, he slowly walked to the front door, fearing that he would fall to the ground from the dizziness he felt. He managed to enter the house without doing so. He greeted his father with a weak handshake and then asked if it were all right if he went straight to bed. For most of the next week, that's where he remained. A few times he came downstairs to join his parents at dinner, but with a reticence his parents had not heretofore known.

One morning, with resolve, he got dressed and went downstairs to where his mother was making breakfast. His father was sitting at the kitchen table. Adriel spoke out a weak, "Good morning."

"Adriel, it is good to see you downstairs so early. We were beginning to worry about you." Agatha came over to the table with a plate of pancakes. She set them on the table. "You two need to eat all of these with a little help from me. If you want more, I would be glad to make them." She sat down with them and shared in the feast.

Sylvan looked at his son and said, "Adriel, how are you?"

"I feel better than when I first got home. But, all week, Abigail's death has been preying on my mind. I intend to do my own investigation. I don't think Caleb committed the murder. He didn't have it in him to do such a thing."

"I agree, but what can you do? The evidence points to him."

"I don't know what I can do except I must try to do something. I'm going over to the Dunlap farm to look around a bit."

"Dunlap may not want you snooping around."

"I'll take the chance of being detected. I can't stand the thought of two senseless deaths. They'll hang Caleb."

"Adriel, what're you planning to do now that you are home?" asked his mother to change the subject of the conversation.

"I'm going to ask Mr. Alden for my old job back for the summer and then return to the Normal School in October."

"That sounds good," his mother replied.

"Today, I'm going to ride Bunyan around the countryside with special attention to the Dunlap farm."

"Will you be home for dinner?"

"Yes, I think so."

"Good to have you home, Adriel, and alive."

"It's good to be home." Adriel finished breakfast and went to the stable to saddle up Bunyan. He took a ride through the countryside. He exhilarated in the breeze hitting his face and the sun shining gloriously on him. He hadn't felt such freedom and ecstasy since before he left for the army. It helped lighten his despair. He then set himself in the direction of the Dunlap farm.

As he approached the lane where the murder occurred, Adriel dismounted and walked the remaining distance. He intently looked along the road but found nothing. No one on the farm seemed to notice what he was doing. For most of the rest of the day, he continued riding through the countryside. All his thoughts were focused on the horrible event that occurred on the lane Abigail and he had strolled along so many times.

Before Adriel was aware of it, the day had passed as the sun was approaching the horizon. The Pennsylvania countryside was deepening into long shadows as the birds sang their vespers, the diurnal populations headed for their shelters and the nocturnal population of the forest began stirring. The evening star was the first to greet the approaching night. When he noticed what nature was doing around him, he rode back home and fell into bed without dinner after he tended to Bunyan.

Adriel dreamed of that same clipper ship off which Abigail had been swept. This time she never appeared; for, the ocean of death had claimed her. With the death of Abigail, an unrequited love, and Michael, his brother in arms, he thought it might be well for him to be swept overboard after them into the ocean. How well he knew the turbulence of the sea. How well he knew the turbulence inside his own soul.

Mr. Alden gave Adriel his old job. Most of the men at the lime-kilns, too old for service in the army, had gained respect for Adriel, now a veteran and remembered to be a good worker. They gave him a hearty greeting as if it were the return of the conquering hero. Knowing of his grief about Abigail, they expressed their condolence.

With his stories, Adriel often provided lunch time entertainment. The workers knew from experience that Adriel was a great story teller. So, one day at lunch they asked him to tell one as he had done before.

Before he went into the service during the time he had worked for Alden, Adriel had been building a cabin in the woods, not far from his parents' home. Mr. Alden had given him permission to build it on his land. When he returned home, he had thought of finishing what he had begun, but had not gotten to it. The cabin gave him an idea for a story; Pontiac Rowbottom gave him an idea for a character.

"A young man, named Reuben Birdwhistle, set out in the woods to build a cabin for himself. While working at a carpentry shop near his parents, he built what was to become his home. Regularly, he took a buckboard load of supplies that he bought or received as gifts from his employer to the site and worked to sunset in the summer and fall season.

"With Reuben's skill and dedication of time, the structure rose quickly. After he put on the roof, he began staying overnight in his little retreat in the woods. The nocturnal sounds of the forest were vivid since the cabin didn't yet have windows. He listened until, deep in the night, he would fall deeply asleep.

"One night in the fall, he heard rustling close to the cabin. He thought it might be a wild animal examining this thing that was rising in its realm. He got off the bunk and, helped by the waning light of the fire in the hearth, slowly moved toward the door. He listened carefully. Then, he moved to one of the glassless windows in the front of the cabin to see if he could catch a glimpse of what was making the noise. Because the moonless night was so very dark, Reuben could not see much of anything.

"When he heard sniffing at the door, Reuben walked back to it. As he stood there, an animal came leaping through the window from the porch. His heart leaped into his throat as he reached for his gun, leaning against the wall next to the door. As he aimed, he realized with the help of the fire in the hearth that he was about to shoot a dog. He put his rifle down; the dog sat next to the fire looking at him with hopeful eyes that said, 'Please, let me stay.'

"The dog then came toward Reuben, wagging its tail. Knowing the dangers of rabies, Reuben wanted to be cautious, but couldn't. He extended his hand and stroked the dog's head. He gave her what was left on his plate from dinner, which she quickly consumed.

"This dog of many breeds became his dog. He had no idea how it happened to be in the woods, nor did he spend much time speculating. Leaper was her name now, whatever it was before.

"Leaper would go with Reuben to work and return with him to the cabin in the evening. During the night she would lie next to the roaring fire, the warmth of which gave comfort to both man and beast.

"One day, while Reuben and Leaper were in the woods, not far from the cabin, collecting tinder for the fire, Leaper caught a glimpse of a human form moving from tree to tree. She ran toward the man, catching Reuben's notice. 'What is it?' he asked. Reuben tried to keep up with the dog with little success. When he overtook his dog, he found her growling at an emaciated man with a long beard in ragged clothes pressed against the trunk of an old oak.

"Reuben greeted the old man, assured him that he posed no danger, and then asked him if he needed any help. The old man hesitated and then asked for some food in a timid and tremulous voice. Reuben bid the man, whose name was Micajah, meaning: Who is like Jah, or Who is like the Lord, to follow him to his cabin. He was somewhat wary of this forest-dweller, but not enough to deny him food. Leaper didn't growl on the way home—a good sign of the stranger's harmlessness and friendliness. Dogs have a sense of the presence of good and evil that humans often don't detect.

"The old man put on his backpack, containing his only possessions, and came along. They said little on the way, while Leaper ran into the woods and disappeared and then re-appeared.

"When the little party arrived at the cabin, Reuben invited the old man into his house, where he prepared food for him. After eating heartily in silence, Micajah told his story.

"'I'm from a far-off town where I taught in the local schoolhouse. About a year ago, I lost my only child after my wife died but a year before. I went completely mad, not knowing for days where I was and who I was. Friends cared for me during this time. As soon as my health was restored, I struck out to wander the world with no goal in mind. I ended up here, poverty-stricken and alone. I had become a hermit without religious affiliation and, for that matter, without God. I thought I would try living off the land with little success. You found me desperate.'

"'Why are you a hermit?'

"'I couldn't stand the idea of being in the company of others until desperation set in. You found me in my straitened circumstance. Why I couldn't tolerate human company has for me only one explanation. The irrationality of anger led me to become a hater of God and humanity—hate toward God for his indifference; and hate toward humanity for its cruelty. But, now you've helped me. As I was playing the hermit, my neighbor lent me a hand. It seems that there exists kindness in the world—a fact I overlooked.'

"'What kindness I've shown comes from the mercy of God.'

"'Of God I have nothing to say. He is for me a distant figure, no longer real in my life. I don't know Him. I didn't set out as a pilgrim, seeking truth and solace, but as a wanderer. I wasn't headed toward some holy place or God Himself, but toward nothing, as life is nothing.'

"'For me that's a devastating view of the world.'

"'It's what I've come to. I can't help it, or so it seems. I've been a teacher for many years. I have looked into the bright faces of my students and thought of the many years ahead for them that will bring disillusionment unto bitterness and cynicism.'

"'I regret that you're going through such a struggle.'

"'I'm glad to have someone to talk to. Thanks, Reuben.'

"'You're welcome to stay here for a while.'

"'Perhaps for a few days.'

"That first night on an old cot that Reuben used before he

built a bed, the old man slept deeply by the roaring fire and dreamt dreams of the forest with many of its residents looking on. He was walking an old beloved dog through the woods on a night of the full moon. The moon shone through the leafless trees, some of its light flooding the forest floor.

"Micajah and his dog were walking to a destination—a cabin that he had bought as a summer retreat. There waiting for him was his wife, sitting next to the hearth. When he emerged from the "Weald of Dreams," as the forest was called, into the clearing, he could see the cabin lit up by the fireplace. When he entered, all the joys of the focus—hearth and family—met him, as did the heat and light of the fire.

"He woke up in the middle of the night with a feeling of felicity and gladness in his heart. But, quickly he realized that he had been dreaming. His joy evaporated to become lament and distress.

"Next morning, after a breakfast of eggs, bacon, and bread, the two men, with Leaper accompanying, set out for town to get more supplies to complete the building of Reuben's woodland home. When Reuben was at work, Micajah continued the construction. After seven days of persistent work, the job was done. On the night of the seventh day, they celebrated with a feast accompanied by the best local beer. They ate before the fire, sharing with Leaper the good food. The two men talked well into the night as Leaper, in her sleep, snored with ardor.

"On Sunday morning, Reuben woke up late, which for him was 8:00 o'clock. When Reuben noticed that Micajah was not on his cot before the dying fire, he called out to him but got no answer. He quickly dressed, went to the front cabin door and yelled for him several times with no answer.

"When he returned to the hearth, he noticed a short note pinned to a log ready for use in the fireplace. It read:

Dear Reuben,
*   I have very much enjoyed staying with you over the past*

month. I came to realize personally what John Donne meant in his sonnet, No Man Is an Island. *Though we may never meet again, I shall always remember you. During my time with you, I have felt closer to both God and man. This is a blessing from God through you.*

I didn't have the heart to say my good-byes in person. I didn't want to weep so as to make a fool of myself. Please forgive me.

Farewell and Godspeed,
Micajah

"Reuben, with Leaper, went searching for his newfound friend and helper. Half a day later, very close to home, he found Micajah's body with a knapsack and falcon-headed walking stick in a hollow with trees all around. Reuben called to him, then approached his body. He discovered that he had lost his friend. Reuben surmised that Micajah must have died suddenly.

"He brought Micajah back on his buckboard to his newly finished cottage. After Reuben informed the authorities, the local priest buried Micajah the next day behind Reuben's cabin, using Micajah's own *Book of Common Prayer* that Reuben found with his Bible in his friend's knapsack. Micajah had lost his faith but still carried with him these books.

"Leaper was the only member of the congregation besides Reuben. Around the open grave, the body placed in its resting place in a coffin built by Reuben, stood the priest, Reuben, and Leaper.

"Later, Reuben placed a marble marker at the grave, incised with Micajah's name with the biblical inscription, 'The voice of the Lord divides the flames of fire. The voice of the Lord shakes the wilderness;' (Psalm 29: 7-8a KJV). Reuben arranged the obsequies in accordance with Micajah's last note to him that indicated a restored faith.

"Leaper was restless all that night, as was Reuben. Things

were not as they should be, for a quickly made friend had become a good friend, and now he was gone.

"Weeks later, Reuben walked back to visit Micajah's grave. The spot that had been nothing but overturned dirt was now replete with flowers of a most beautiful aspect and sweet scent. It was as if Micajah's body had lent to the luxurious growth. Reuben thought he saw flames above the grave. What preternatural event had he encountered?"

The men remained silent as they absorbed the story that Adriel told. They thought of their own losses of family and friends, and felt the sorrow that never goes away, but trying their best not to show their grief. After they thanked Adriel, they went back to work.

Adriel's story expressed a faith he no longer affirmed. Yet, he wouldn't change it. He would keep the original manuscript in a safe place for future reference. He asked himself, *how could I know in the midst of the vicissitudes of life and the changes in the self where my heart would be years hence?* He didn't trust in himself any sort of constancy. If God existed, He could be the only constant and faithful reality in creation. It was as if he refused to believe he would always be a skeptic. He believed certain things about the God of the biblical witness, even if he didn't have a firm faith in His existence.

CHAPTER TWENTY

THE GHOSTS OF RED OAK

The ghosts were out one moonlit night
That gave a drunk an awful fright.
His true-blue horse conveyed him home
Where all the night he heard them moan.
– Adriel Peregrine sang these words to himself and his closest
friends for a good laugh.

As the summer waned, Adriel was drinking more and more. His habit had begun in camp while he served in the Union army and increased as the days and weeks went by. Now at home with the murder of Abigail constantly in his thoughts, he followed a strict regimen of hard drinking, dedicated to the god Dionysius.

Against the wishes of his worried parents, he would frequent a tavern in Manheim, not far from home. Some days Adriel would find his way into town early in the evening after work, but not find his way home until the middle of the night. On Saturday nights he might not get home until the sun was well above the horizon. You would find him sleeping along the road with Bunyan's grazing or standing near him. His drinking led to many confrontations with his father, who threatened a number of times to throw him out of the house, but never did.

One Saturday night, Adriel was coming home very late. The moon was full. He hesitated as he was about to pass the graveyard next to Saint Jude Thaddeus Church. His vision was affected by his drinking; but, he was sure that he saw the ghost of Abigail wandering among the graves and conversing with other ghosts! She came toward him with arms uplifted, appealing to him more than once to help her. "Adriel, Adriel, I'm drowning in the sea. Come and help me. Don't forsake me." Then, all the ghosts chanted a refrain, "Help her, Adriel, help her." With a chill that kept traveling up and down his spine, Adriel hastened the short distance home. When he arrived there, he fell off Bunyan, picked himself up, ran to the house, falling twice on the way, and leaped up the stairs. Then, with enough sense remaining, he realized that Bunyan was out front untended. He went outside, looked around for the company of specters, and, when confident they were not in the vicinity, led Bunyan to the barn.

Later that night Adriel woke up to the sound of moaning. He thought it was the ghosts in the cemetery and not the spirits of alcohol. An odd fact about his experience was that Abigail was not buried in the cemetery of Saint Jude Thaddeus. She was buried in a family cemetery miles away and had belonged with her family to a local Presbyterian Church. She must have been a guest of the cemetery residents. Adriel asked himself, *who knew that ghosts extended hospitality?*

The next day, Sylvan waylaid Adriel in the kitchen. "You made a lot of noise late last night."

"I was out with my friends and lost track of time."

"Maybe you should heed the time so that you don't wake your parents."

"I'm an adult. Why must I give you an account?"

"Because family members are accountable to each other," Adriel's father replied with some vehemence. "You know that."

"OK. I'll be more careful."

"Please do. You're causing your mother and me great distress."

Adriel's encounter with his father didn't discourage him from carousing that same Sunday night. He avoided church that morning as he had since he returned from the war, both because he was indifferent in his belief and didn't want to encounter Jennie, who had returned from her service in Washington to attend the Normal School in the fall.

It was only after his carousing, as he was returning home, that Adriel realized he must again pass the graveyard. He decided to shun the immediate vicinity for a more roundabout way home. He rode close to the quarry, taking a path that led to a spot between the cemetery and his house. A dense line of pine trees shielded him from a view of the cemetery. As he was contending with tree limbs, he heard a sigh in the gentle breeze. He looked up and saw the outline of a person who soon defined herself as Abigail Dunlap. Adriel was quite drunk, but was of the firm conviction that what he saw was real. His belief, he thought, seemed to be substantiated by the uneasiness of his horse, though the horse had caught sight of a bobcat on the Peregrine property that he, in his drunken state, was unaware of. Bunyan wouldn't move from the spot, so Adriel got off and tried to lead him with a problem similar to that of Balaam. Finally, he got Bunyan to follow him home.

Adriel settled Bunyan in his stall and then went into the house, where, for a while, he watched the dying fire in the living room fireplace. His parents were already in bed.

In the following days Adriel neglected to go to the tavern and made sure he wasn't passing the cemetery at night. He didn't want any longer to deal with the early-hour or late-hour ghosts that lodged next to Saint Jude Thaddeus Church; nonetheless, there would be a time when he would encounter them again.

CHAPTER TWENTY-ONE
THE DRY DESERT

I am like a desert owl of the wilderness, like an owl of the waste places.   *– Psalm 102: 6 ESV.*

After his decision not to travel in the middle of the night, Adriel was very thirsty in the following days, a problem solved by a co-worker named Lemuel, who brought drink for after-work delectation. Lemuel had to be careful so the boss didn't detect his possession. Adriel and Lemuel would go into the woods and have a party every day. Then, they would both stumble home, where Adriel often had a confrontation with his father, and occasionally with his mother.

As the days followed one another, Adriel asked himself, as did the preacher in Ecclesiastes, "What profit hath a man of all his labour which he taketh under the sun?" (Ecclesiastes 1: 3 KJV). He thought all things were vanity.

His parents wished for him to talk to Father Ledford; but, this suggestion didn't receive his favor. He stayed away from church; he stayed away from the rector; and he stayed away from Jennie. He was only slightly aware that Pontiac Rowbottom had remained in the area, living in a broken down shack in the vicinity.

The news from Lancaster about Caleb Landis was that he would surely be convicted and sentenced to hang. Adriel was conflicted. He was very angry at Caleb that Abigail had become Caleb's fiancée. At the same time, he had the terrible feeling that Caleb didn't perpetrate the deed. Adriel was angry with Caleb and also sympathetic toward him.

As he was preparing to return to the Normal School, Adriel heard word that Caleb was condemned to die. After he arrived at the Normal School, he received a letter from his mother informing him that Caleb would be hanged in the Lancaster County prison a week hence. His heart felt no joy, instead a sickness that infected the depths of his soul.

Adriel imagined himself walking and walking in a land where there existed no God of heaven and earth and no human presence. He was alone. He could no longer see the road that he had once trod, the Way of the Pilgrim. He was like an outcast with an ostracon in his hand; but, he was a self-exile who inscribed his own name on the pottery.

CHAPTER TWENTY-TWO

FROM NORMAL SCHOOL TO THE DELAWARE CANAL

Once a good friend, Caleb Landis became a rival for the affections of Abigail, though when I woke up later from delusions I accepted the fact that she didn't love me. My anger at him burned hot—a destructive ardor. It was necessary for me to work in great earnest to cool my disappointment. My thoughts of vengeance were transformed into reality through the instrumentality of the state. According to Paul, God authorizes the state to function as the arm of vengeance. But, I wondered, then, if a terrible miscarriage of justice was about to occur. My heart cooled before Caleb's death. I went to visit him in prison. I'm so glad I did this. My regrets at my vengeful attitude continued for many years. Only God's compassion led me away from destruction for this and other reasons.

– A Wanderer Who Became a Pilgrim, *Adriel Peregrine.*

He who curbs not his anger will wish that undone which vexation and wrath prompted, as he may haste with violence to gratify his unsated hatred. Anger is short-lived madness. Rule your passion, for unless it obeys, it gives commands. Check it with bridle—check it, I pray you, with chains.

– Horace, Epistles, Book 1.II.62ff *Loeb Classics, vol. 194, translated by H. Rushton Fairclough.*

. . . I say to you that everyone who is angry with his brother will be liable to judgment. – Matthew 5:22a ESV

1865 was the year of the War's end and the assassination of President Lincoln. Andrew Johnson became President, which eventuated in his impeachment and near conviction because of conflicts over executive and legislative power with Congress, especially regarding the reconstruction of the South.

Adriel worked at the limekilns, drank with his buddy after work, trudged home early in the evening, and occasionally went out drinking with friends at night—such was his routine; such was his life; such was his despair. On Sundays he went to the woods instead of church where Christ was found in the Word and Sacrament. He no longer felt the joy that comes from the resplendence of nature, experienced through knowledge of Christ from whom, writes Paul, comes all things. Yet, he extracted from these walks as much as he could to keep him from complete grief and despondency.

When fall came, Adriel returned to the Normal School to complete his studies so that he could teach. He rented a room in the home of an elderly couple close to campus. After his stint in the army, he didn't want to live again in close quarters in a dormitory. He had also become somewhat of a nonreligious hermit. He would go to class; study in his room, and drink there too, but didn't do much of anything else. He asked his landlords not to enter his room. He would keep it clean himself. He didn't want them to find the bottle that he kept in his desk drawer. He had enough control over the drinking that he could keep up with his studies, though his loneliness could have set him on a steep downward spiral. It is amazing that some people who over-drink can do so and yet fulfill demanding obligations. Adriel was one of them. He was able to discipline himself more than he had back home; because, he truly wished to succeed at school.

Seldom did Adriel go home over the weekend. He made no effort to renew old friendships. He knew that Jennie, whom he made a special effort not to encounter, was taking classes to become a teacher. He was always on the lookout to avoid her, though he encountered her occasionally. When they did meet, he exerted great effort to keep their conversations to a minimum.

While at school, he decided, after much conflict and consideration, to visit Caleb Landis at the county jail. He was angry with him on account of Abigail; but, at one time, they had been the best of friends. Adriel remembered their friendship fondly. His anger had cooled as it often does in us. It is unruly, unpredictable, often overpowering, destructive, and dangerous. It also can become a burnt out cinder. **We often do great damage to others armed with our wrath, what Horace calls "a transient madness (*ira furor brevis est*)." Jesus regards it as tantamount to murder—a breaking of the commandment.**

Adriel had a deep, sick feeling that Caleb wasn't responsible for the murder. Such a terrible thing as homicide was completely out of character for his longtime friend. Despite his spiritual problem, that is, turning his back to God, Adriel hadn't wished death upon an old friend. His waxing agnosticism and weakened conscience still depended on a Christian moral sense. There was nothing to replace it except ethical nihilism.

On a Saturday in late October, Adriel journeyed into Lancaster. It was a bright day with the fall sun shining through a multitude of yellow and red leaves many of which were falling like rain on Adriel, traveling in an open carriage, to his destination. The beautiful day belied the darkness descending on Caleb.

Adriel hardly noticed the beauty around him because of his preoccupation with his mission—to visit a condemned man, a young condemned man. O, what depth of sorrow motivated him to this service! How powerless he felt about preventing the tragedy! His investigation of the murder had produced no fruit.

Adriel felt a deep sickness about what would happen—an innocent man, once a friend, hanging at the end of a rope in the prison yard of the Lancaster County Prison. Even alcohol didn't dull Adriel's dread of the day that was fast approaching.

After admission preliminaries, Adriel was escorted to Caleb's cell. When he saw Adriel, Caleb sprang up from his bunk. Not caring whether Adriel was going to yell at him, Caleb rushed to the opening door of his cell to greet Adriel. After these two old friends embraced, Caleb invited Adriel to sit on his bunk.

"I'm so glad to see you. I've thought of you time and time again." Caleb paused and then said, "I didn't kill Abigail. I'd never do such a thing."

"I believe you, Caleb, and I wish I could do something to make a difference in your situation. Is there anything?"

"I've been convicted, as you know. I'm scheduled to hang next Monday."

"That's horrible!"

"Yes, it's horrible. I dream every night of the trap door on the gallows opening under my feet. I wake before it reaches bottom. I'm very afraid. My parents are in shock. My mother can't stop crying. I receive a letter from them almost every day. They visit often."

"I feel bereft of sense over this," responded Adriel.

"Adri, I'm afraid." Adriel had not heard this name in a long time.

"Caleb, I'm in grief for you and will pray for you. I'll ask God to deliver you." What Adriel said to him at this moment seemed so terribly inadequate, trite, and, most of all, hypocritical to him. He was ashamed of himself. He was surprised he even mentioned God, so little did he regard Him. At the same time, Adriel knew that Caleb needed this comfort.

Caleb didn't feel the same way; for, they were the most comforting words he had heard recently. Tears appeared in his eyes and trickled down his face. Adriel couldn't help but heave and choke down his sadness and remorse.

"Do you want me to say anything to your parents and brothers and sisters?"

"Tell them I love them. Tell them I didn't do this and that

someday I'll be vindicated." At that moment, Adriel resolved that he would be the means of Caleb's vindication. When he got home from school, he again would take up the investigation.

"I'll do this and seek justice if it takes me my entire life."

"I'm grateful, Adri." At that moment the guard came to inform Adriel that his time was up. Adriel rose from the bed, as did Caleb. The former friends embraced with tears in their eyes. Adriel then turned away in deepest sorrow and departed, looking back in great distress.

Caleb William Landis was hanged the following Monday after Adriel's visit. Adriel read about it in the Lancaster newspaper. All of the formalities of an execution were followed within the confines of the castle-like prison structure. His family stood not far away from the prison, weeping for their condemned son and consoling one another, believing to the last that he was innocent.

At the end of the two terms at the Normal School, Adriel received his certificate for teaching. He returned home with no idea of what he would do. At that time, he had little interest in teaching, though he had spent much effort in becoming a teacher.

The weeks at home were characterized by great conflict with his father. He spent much time out of the house, following leads about the murder. He was reluctant to seek out Mr. Dunlap; for, he felt he wouldn't receive a hearing. He knew that Dunlap's workers had already been interviewed by the authorities. Nothing came of this.

With his lack of success in finding Abigail's murderer and his conflict with his father, Adriel decided to leave home and take up work somewhere else. He found a job on the Delaware Division of the Pennsylvania Canal in Mexico, renamed Uhlerstown, working for Michael Uhler at his limekilns, an industrial process with which Adriel was very familiar. Uhler was a successful merchant on the canal, producing several products, including lime and baled hay, and transporting them on his fleet of boats. Adriel was hired on the spot because of his extensive experience at the Alden limekilns. Despite his drinking, Adriel worked hard at his job.

The Canal extended from Easton to Bristol near Philadelphia, with coal from regions north as its primary commodity. It had been built in the 1830s before the railroads had gained traction. Despite eventual railroad competition, the canal was in operation into the twentieth century.

Adriel lived in one of the houses built for Uhler's employees, but spent little time there. One could often find him in the tavern at the Uhlerstown Hotel. Drinking with friends and acquaintances had become the mainstay of Adriel's social life. Encouraged by the deaths of Abigail, Michael, and Caleb, Adriel had found a good excuse for his drinking. His loss was great, especially for a man that had not yet reached his mid-twenties. During his war service he had seen death all around him. He witnessed young men dying of disease or torn apart on the field of battle. *What was life but death?* he would ask himself. He had no faith in the Christian belief that death becomes life. It was as if his life were draped in black.

Several months into his employment, Adriel was given the opportunity to travel to Philadelphia on a canal boat. It would be his first time in Philly since the war. He looked forward to the trip.

CHAPTER TWENTY-THREE

THE DELAWARE DIVISION OF THE PENNSYLVANIA CANAL

What gain has the worker from his toil? I have seen the business that God has given to the children of man to be busy with. He has made everything beautiful in its time. Also, he has put eternity into man's heart, yet so that he cannot find out what God has done from the beginning to the end. — Ecclesiastes 3: 9-11 ESV.

Adriel's work at the Uhlerstown limekilns occupied most of his time outside the tavern. Respect and envy grew around him for his competence at his work. His experience was owed to the time he spent working for Massey Alden back home. It was not long before he was given greater responsibility for the operation of the kiln.

The long working days, heavy drinking evenings, and dream-troubled nights characterized Adriel's life at Uhlerstown. Despite his bar buddies and work associates, he led a lonely life. His parents knew that he was working on the canal, but not much more. He sent one letter near the beginning of his employment, and that is all. On his first and only Christmas in Uhlerstown, one could find him walking alone on the towpath.

*

In the spring, after the canal re-opened, the foreman asked Adriel if he would accompany a load of lime to Philadelphia to arrange for its sale and delivery. Adriel would travel on one of Uhler's barges that carried the material that would be used for plaster and mortar in the big city of over 600,000 people.

On a sunny day, months after he arrived at Uhlerstown, Adriel boarded the canal boat. The word was given for the two mules to begin the trek to Philadelphia. While the mules pulled the craft, Adriel stood on deck in a day-dreamy state. In his reverie he composed a song of the canal.

> *Pull, mules, pull. The day has now begun.*
> *Pull, mules, pull. The boat will make its run.*
> *Pull, mules, pull. So bright the channel stream.*
> *Pull, mules, pull. Old Jacks, we're such a team!*

The mules trod on the towpath that was on the river side of the canal, led by a driver or skinner. On Adriel's barge, a man, both husband and father, worked the tiller, while the rest of the family performed other tasks. At Lock Seventeen, Adriel watched closely as the water poured into the lock to make the water level even with the level of the barge; the upper lock gate then opened and closed after the barge entered. Water was drained from the lock to bring the boat level with the lower channel, and then the lower gate was opened. It was an amazing process. **The elevation drops over one hundred feet along the sixty miles of canal from Easton to Philadelphia, hence the need for locks.**

The Delaware Division began at Easton, where the Lehigh River flows into the Delaware River. A gate yet stands at the entrance to the canal that continues to Philadelphia. From Mauch Chunk, now called Jim Thorpe, along the Lehigh Navigation to the Delaware Division, the canal boats conveyed coal from rich anthracite coal fields, as well as quicklime and hay from Uhlerstown, along with products from other places.

As Adriel stood on the deck of Michael Uhler's boat, he daydreamed, as was often his wont. He was headed again to Philadelphia nearly two years after he entered the Army. He remembered Camp Cadwalader; he remembered marching through Philadelphia with the 199th to board the train and then the boat for the war front; he remembered Richmond, Petersburg, and Appomattox; he remembered his friend Michael O'Brien, ever hopeful and often cheerful; and he remembered Michael's death that occurred right next to him at Fort Gregg. His grief was almost intolerable as he remembered the tragic deaths of three friends, Abigail, Michael, and Caleb. It was so difficult to bear. He tucked these things deeply into his heart, but felt little comfort in so doing.

He remembered his youth—worshipping with his father and mother; helping his father on the Alden property; celebrating the holidays; attending school where he learned fascinating things about the world from his inspired teacher, Joshua Schreiber; and the soaring of his imagination in the brilliant woods and fields of central Pennsylvania where, he then envisioned, the elfin population played. What a wonderful world until the realities of life set in—disappointments, loss, sorrow, and grief.

Adriel didn't experience hardship early in his childhood, mostly because of the care and protection of his parents. But, when he did, he lost his belief that the world had meaning for pitiable human beings. At that time, his expectations of life far underestimated how deeply suffering ran through it.

We all must face the fact that life in this world is not the Garden of Eden before the fall. We must remember that we were thrown out of Paradise and will only know its joys in the kingdom of heaven. Adriel discovered the hard realities of life in his late teens. He couldn't accept this hardship without denying the reality of a caring Lord and hope for the future.

An atheist he wasn't; but, he was no longer a believer in the Trinitarian God of his ancestors. Believing that God existed, Adriel wasn't quite yet a true agnostic. He was certain only that God existed; but, God didn't care about what He created. Perhaps, even this certainty would one day come to an end, leading him into agnosticism, then atheism, from a claim that God cannot be known to that God does not exist.

Adriel had ceased being a pilgrim, becoming a wanderer both in his soul and in the world. He had not learned that the Christian pilgrimage included, but was far more than, singing in church and walking in the woods on a beautiful day. He had read *Pilgrim's Progress*, but had not taken it to heart. The same was the case with *The Divine Comedy* of Dante. Adriel's was an immature faith that didn't stand up to the severity life sometimes brings.

For him no goal or meaningful end for him or anybody existed. This wanderer, Adriel Skylar Peregrine, protested the world, as it was, without having anyone to appeal to who cared, especially God Himself. His growing bitterness and resentment was put afloat on a sea of alcohol and then worse, if this were at all possible.

Adriel was awakened out of his daydream by a thud on the deck of the canal barge. A man had dropped from the camel-back bridge that the craft was passing under. He pushed Adriel to the deck, then, held a gun on Adriel and the steersman. A younger man was holding a gun on the mule driver. The rest of the crew, that is, the captain's family, was below.

The man looked down at Adriel who didn't move. "I've come aboard for some compensation for my efforts."

The man had dark eyebrows and deep brown forbidding eyes. He was exceedingly thin, almost emaciated. He didn't stand quite straight but was slightly bent over, though his jumping onto the deck from the bridge showed some agility. He was passing middle age and had the look of incipient old age about him. He had a deep scar above his right eye. He wore a mask over his mouth and nose. Only his eyes and scar were showing. He was a tough bird.

The man called over to his companion, who at that moment was being assaulted by the driver, called a hoggee, who happened to be a son of the captain. The result was the robber's falling into the canal. At the same time, Adriel tripped the robber holding a gun on him by taking hold of his ankles and pulling his legs from under him, causing him also to fall into the water.

When he saw the straits of the would-be robbers, the driver, without hesitation, continued the journey with his two mules. The steersman had remained at the tiller. Looking backward from the boat, one could see two sorry souls foundering in the water. The older man was trying to help the young man, who couldn't swim, out of the five foot deep water. The captain's family, realizing the boat had stopped moving forward, came out on deck to learn what had happened and, when they did, began cheering the brave men on deck and the young driver. Laughter was everywhere. Captain Mosely MacDonald, steering at that moment rather than his sixteen year old son who often had the duty, held firmly to the tiller as the boat continued its journey to Bristol and Philadelphia

CHAPTER TWENTY-FOUR

SIGHTSEEING

*And behold, the woman meets him, dressed as a prostitute, wily of
heart.* — *Proverbs 7:10 ESV.*

*With this book in his hand, a man will be enabled to shun those low
dens of infamy and disease with which this city abounds, as a true
and authentic description of the grade of each house is here briefly
given.*
— A Guide to the Stranger or Pocket Companion for the
Fancy Containing a List of the Gay Houses and Ladies
of Pleasure in the City of Brotherly Love and Sisterly
Affection, *Philadelphia, 1849.*

*Jesus said to them, "Truly, I say to you, the tax collectors and the
prostitutes go into the kingdom of God before you. For John came to
you in the way of righteousness, and you did not believe him, but the
tax collectors and prostitutes believed him."*
— *Matthew 21: 31-32 ESV*

Through seventeen locks the canal boat traveled the remaining distance to Philadelphia. At New Hope, four locks, including a double lock that allowed two boats to enter at the same
time rather than one, stood on the watercourse.

Before it reached Bristol, the boat stopped for the night,
because the locks were closed from 10:00 P.M. to 4:00 A.M.
The captain provided a place for Adriel to sleep where addi-
tional travelers were accommodated. The captain's family had

permanent quarters below deck.

The next morning the barge arrived at Bristol where it was towed by tug to Philadelphia. After doing the business he was assigned, Adriel found a place to stay at what had been known as the Man Full of Trouble Tavern. After checking in, he roamed the town to see some of the historical sites, including a visit to the site of Camp Cadwalader.

Adriel remembered the rigors of camp life, the drills, the campfires, the card playing, and departure to Virginia. He remembered the battle at Fort Gregg and the burial of Michael O'Brien by the company after the battle. Like thousands of young men, Michael's bones lay in the earth near the place of battle. Adriel learned later that Michael's body was re-buried in Poplar Grove National Cemetery.

Adriel visited Independence Hall—its earlier name was the Pennsylvania State House—where the Declaration of Independence was signed, and the Constitution was drafted for the consideration of the several states, spending some time walking around the dignified old building. His war service represented his contribution to the preservation of the Union whose ground are these two documents. He could hardly tear himself away from the hallowed precincts.

Later in the day, Adriel stopped by one of the many taverns in Philadelphia to have dinner. His original intention was then to go back to Man Full of Trouble Tavern for a night of rest after a rigorous day of walking that left him limping from a blister on his foot. But, he was tempted to visit a "gay house" where he would spend the night with a *fille de joie*, a prostitute. With the help of *A Guide to the Stranger*, a manual for finding the safest houses of pleasure in Philadelphia, he visited an assignation house in the neighborhood of Ninth Street.

The pretty woman he spent the night with was gracious and refined in her manner. She who came to Philadelphia from the countryside was one among the thousands of prostitutes in the city. He was satisfied with his decision and expended his youthful vigor half the night.

During his service in the War, Adriel avoided frolicking with prostitutes, partly because of the danger of venereal disease; but, after he left home for the canal, he didn't use such restraint. During these years he knew little about the genuine love of a woman. It was only later that he became acquainted with the true nature of love. For now, sex was simply a response to an urgent physical need.

The next morning, Adriel opened his eyes to find that the young woman was still asleep. He stared for a while at her beautiful face. He wondered what brought her to this way of life. He got up and dressed. He realized that all he knew about her was that she was a farmer's daughter whose name was Maggie. They bedded together for reasons other than love—she for a living, he for pleasure.

Long afterward, when he would think of the years of his youth and his many transgressions, Adriel remembered from the New Testament Jesus' willingness to reach out to the prostitutes and tax collectors. Jesus wouldn't have hesitated to approach Maggie and others to call her into the kingdom. He hoped that perhaps she and other women he had been with had left life on the streets behind and accepted the dominical invitation. He wished them well, yet knew that tragedies met many of them along the way. He also knew that Jesus was there among them with the invitation He first extended in His ministry.

Adriel didn't wake Maggie. Their business had been concluded. He went downstairs, speaking to no one, and stepped outside. There was a bustle on the street as morning activities in the big city were in full swing. Adriel found a place to have breakfast; and, after checking his pocket watch, he decided he would be in time to attend Christ Church.

CHAPTER TWENTY-FIVE

RETURN

The body is not meant for sexual immorality, but for the Lord, and the Lord for the body   *— I Corinthians 6:13b ESV.*

On Sunday morning, before Adriel left Philadelphia to return to Uhlerstown, he attended a service at Christ Church, an old colonial parish in Philadelphia of the Church of England and the American Episcopal Church. Why did he make such an effort? He had heard about the old parish when he was a student. He was more of a curiosity seeker than a worshipper, though he did love the Anglican chant.

Adriel's attendance was in stark contrast to his activity the night before. The irony was not lost on him. He entered the sacred precinct not as a worshipper but as an aesthete. He loved the beautiful, whether it was art, music, literature, or women.

Since the Service of Morning Prayer had already begun, Adriel slipped unobtrusively into a back pew. After hearing, not reciting, the confession with the congregation, he listened to the absolution with skeptical and doubting ears. He felt no difference in his mind and soul between the before and after of this liturgical rite except for an appreciation for the aesthetics of the words of *The Book of Common Prayer* and of the church.

During the Service, Adriel was struck by the bright light of a spring morning streaming through the plain window glass. The blend of light and song gave a resplendent aspect to the place.

The congregation sang the psalms and hymns with vigor like he remembered from home. He listened to the voices rather than sang, not wanting to be too much of a hypocrite. He shed some tears; for, he wasn't yet a contented unbeliever. Adriel noted the warning in Psalm 95 not to harden his heart, but his heart was hardening against the God of his youth.

Early training of a child in morality leaves an influence that's difficult to efface. An adult, so trained, must usually deal with a strong sense of obligation that controls him from devising and perpetrating the wrong. Sometimes, this power works; sometimes, it doesn't. Strength of mind and heart that would have hindered Adriel from doing what was sexually immoral failed. He felt some small measure of remorse for his action; but, it didn't lead him to avoid repetition. The hold of his Christian education from parents and church may have provided him strong encouragement to do what is right. His departure from the faith of his ancestors made it easier to defy the command that extended to a lack of true repentance. Without the power of the Spirit to affect a willing obedience, Adriel was bereft of moral fortitude. The powerful force of a young man's bodily desire conquered matters of conscience.

One could write off Adriel's behavior as one of those slight mistakes of youth or not an error at all. But, in the Eleventh Homily of the Church of England, the writer, Thomas Becon, comments about adultery and fornication, ". . . this vice has grown unto such a height, that in a manner among many it is counted no sin at all, but rather a pastime, a dalliance, and but a touch of youth: not rebuked, but winked at; not punished but laughed at."

In I Corinthians, Saint Paul warns against becoming one with a prostitute. He writes that a person cannot be one with a prostitute and one with Christ. Adriel decided to be one with a prostitute, a practice that turned out to be habitual over the next few years.

Guilt is not always a bad thing. It's not always overween-ing. It's the mechanism by which we know that we have bro-ken a sacred command and have violated holy ground. The solution for doing the wrong is confession and absolution. One should add reparation, if it applies.

Adriel left the church just before the service was over. He found his way to one of Uhler's barges for his return home. On the afternoon of his return, he walked into the tavern of the Uhlerstown Hotel to do some drinking. When the sun set, he was still there.

CHAPTER TWENTY-SIX

A NOT SO OLD ENEMY

*Life presents some extraordinary surprises. One afternoon, I con-
fronted one in a tavern along the Delaware Canal.*
    – A Pilgrim Who Becomes a Wanderer, *Adriel Peregrine.*

One late afternoon, after working all day at the kilns, Adriel
was at his usual watering hole at the Uhlerstown Hotel with
some of his fellow workers. "So, Adriel, please tell us about
your trip to the big city," requested Eli, a veteran of the
Uhlerstown kilns.

"Well, early on, two men tried to rob us."

"Good start." Lewis was a bit tongue in cheek in his humor.

"They found themselves in the drink." A surge of laughter
followed Adriel's remark.

At that very moment, two men walked into the tavern
and sat down at a table across the room. Adriel could see them
from where he sat. Though they were wearing masks at the
time of the attempted robbery, Adriel believed that the new
customers were the robbers.

Adriel looked at the two men whom he suspected to be
the culprits. Noticing Adriel's attention, though brief, the
older man looked back at him with a sneer, an indication of
mutual recognition.

Adriel mumbled to his two fellow workers, "You may not
believe this; but, the men across the room are the robbers."

"It can't be so! What a coincidence this would be," said
Lewis. "There were several robberies in the local area while

you were gone. Maybe these guys committed them."

"I didn't know this until now. I'll bet it was these same people," responded Adriel and then changed the topic back to Philadelphia as he kept an eye askance on the two he suspected. The others at his table, knowing what he was doing, played along.

"I saw the sights of Philadelphia. It reminded me of the days I was training there. Among other places, I went to where Camp Cadwalader was located. And I stayed at a place once called Man Full of Trouble Inn, and now B. Naylor's Hotel." Adriel didn't tell the men that he was with a prostitute. He wasn't a braggart about such things among his friends. He was careful to maintain propriety about such matters.

"Man Full of Trouble Inn. There can't be such a thing," Eli responded with disbelief.

"No. I'm not lying. I guess the name is descriptive of the lives of many people who have bunked there, or of the owner, or all people. Everybody has some trouble in life, some more and some less. Do you know the old spiritual, 'Nobody knows the trouble I've seen? Nobody knows the sorrow?' I was in a music store in Philly where I came across a book of spirituals entitled *Slave Songs of the United States*, just published. I bought it and brought it home. The slaves surely knew the sorrow. Their sorrow was the most important reason I joined the army. Adriel played the guitar and banjo and was always looking for music to play and sing.

Eli and Lewis were too old for the army, but enthusiastically supported the Union cause. "We're proud of you, Adriel."

"Well, I wasn't looking for a compliment, but appreciate what you say." At that moment, the two robbers got up to leave.

Despite his lightheadedness from drinking, Adriel had enough presence of mind to know he had to do something about the two bandits. He summoned the resolve to walk over to them to challenge them. As he drew closer, he noticed the scar above the older man's right eye. The two men stood and faced Adriel as he moved closer to them. Adriel stopped some distance from them and said, "You tried to rob the barge I was on the other day." The older man pulled a knife, a weapon a step down from the gun he had the other day. Adriel backed away as the two men turned to flee. Lewis and Eli stood behind Adriel and followed him out to apprehend the culprits. In the struggle, Adriel and his co-workers prevailed. The knife scathed no one.

Later, numerous items of value were discovered in the men's saddle bags. They had a large amount of cash on them. Adriel became the hero of the hour. The news of the incident spread throughout the area from Easton to Philadelphia.

Despite Adriel's growing dissipated life, he retained a commitment to justice in his heart. He felt that the lack of justice in the world and of a just God had to be compensated by his own and others' zeal for what is right. Justice and the maintaining of it was a human matter with no help from God.

Adriel had seen many things, including terrible things, and much more was to come in his life. Filled with many dangers, the world was anything but a safe place. Of course, Adriel knew this from firsthand experience. His awareness caused him to react with bitterness and resentment, as if some higher power had not sufficiently regarded his views on how the world should be run. His talk with Father Ledford didn't convince him that justice would ultimately prevail.

Adriel preferred utopia to heaven. The utopia he preferred was one of his own description, not necessarily conforming to others' preferences. One of many differences between the two is that utopia is for this life only, and heaven for life after death, though a relationship with Christ begins before death. The heavenly life has its inception now in this life, to be perfected in the life to come. Another is that utopia is human-made; heaven is a divine reality and gift in which we participate. He no longer believed heaven existed. It is neither a reality nor a gift. Only humans would be able to build the perfect society; but, they hadn't accomplished it yet. Adriel and all the living had experienced neither utopia nor heaven. The final word, in his estimation, was that the drudgery of the world ends with death, and death speaks the final word!

As the summer months went by, Adriel was becoming restless, for he had the heart of a wanderer and a vagabond. One warm summer night, he decided, after much previous consideration, to travel to China to work aboard one of the clipper ships that had caught his imagination when he was a boy. This journey would take him around *Tierra del Fuego* at Cape Horn and across the Pacific to what the Chinese called the Celestial Empire, or in Chinese, Tianchao.

CHAPTER TWENTY-SEVEN

FAREWELL TO THE DELAWARE CANAL

Life is a mystery. I don't understand it, nor do I think I ever will.
— Diary of Adriel Peregrine, *August 10, 1867.*

Adriel had decided to leave his job at the kilns at Uhlerstown to travel to China, where he expected to find employment on a British or American clipper ship. He had saved a little money during his stay at Uhlerstown that would see him through until the first pay day in the Far East.

On a bright Sunday morning several days before his train would leave for New York, Adriel decided to take a walk on the canal north of Uhlerstown. He would go on the towpath north toward Easton, at least as far as the Narrowsville Lock. Adriel had picked a beautiful summer day for his excursion.

The canal corridor is a world of its own, separated from the wider world by the river and the bluffs. The Delaware River flows south through the bluffs to the Delaware Bay and into the Atlantic Ocean. The Delaware Division of the Pennsylvania Canal flows along the river from Easton, where it begins and connects with the Lehigh Navigation, to Philadelphia.

The canal corridor was a place of industry and commerce. It begins yards from the river except at such places as Uhlerstown, where it bends away and follows close to the course of the bluffs. Coal was the black gold that was hauled on the Lehigh

Navigation and the Delaware Canal from the anthracite fields of northeastern Pennsylvania. Other products like building stone, quicklime, agricultural products, and lumber were also transported on the barges.

The Delaware River Valley consisted of a combination of beautiful natural scenery and the infrastructure of the canal with the industries that collected around it. As he was saying his farewell, Adriel took into his mind and heart as much as he could of the unique region in which he had worked for almost a year.

The day was warm with a gentle breeze blowing. One could hear the chatter of the leaves as the wind sough through the branches, as if both boughs and leaves desired to have a conversation with Adriel. The same as when he was a child, Adriel was willing to have a conversation with the natural elements, including any bird or other animal. Anyone coming upon him might think that he was talking to himself.

Adriel felt a certain peace that had escaped him since he entered the army two years before. Even the fledgling agnostic needs relief from the dreariness of unremitting world-weariness. He looked up into the sky, which he had failed to do for so long, and saw a few puffy clouds floating by in a field of summer bronze-blue.

Along the way, Adriel rested on a patch of green and lay in its lush embrace. He looked up at the sky with full attention. He thought that it would be better if all of humanity would do the same more often in order to become aware again of the beauty and immensity of nature. The world beckons us to a closer inspection of its wonders. This wonder was about all that remained of Adriel's faith-filled childhood. He was a skeptical aesthete.

Adriel's religious faith had drifted from the specific revelation of Christianity to a hazy belief that God may exist—that was as far as he would go. What is God like? He claimed to know very little. Is He the creator? Yes. Does He care for His creatures? Not much. What he did affirm at this point in his life was that human beings are part of a much greater whole whose author, if there is one, dwells in mystery that he, for one, could not grasp. At this time, he didn't believe he would ever understand or figure out the larger purposes of life. He wasn't at ease with this view; but, he felt he had to live with it.

A little later, Adriel watched a barge go through Lock 19. He never lost a fascination with the whole process. The barge was heading north toward Easton. He observed the lock fill with water, and the gate open up to the higher elevation. In less than a week, the vessel would be returning south on the canal with a full load of anthracite coal.

Adriel spent a short time walking on the towpath itself until he sighted another barge headed his way. He crossed the camel back bridge at Upper Black Eddy, just north of the general store, where he stopped for some food to eat along the way. He continued north for a while longer, then sat down to have lunch.

On his trip back to Uhlerstown, Adriel attempted to write a poem with partial success,

> *The clouds float by; the river flows.*
> *Stored riches now the barge-mule tows.*
> *All things are drawn to the final goal.*
> *What does it mean for body and soul? . . .*

CHAPTER TWENTY-EIGHT

TO CHINA

Here is the sea, great and wide, which teems with creatures innumerable, living things both small and great. There go the ships, and Leviathan, which you formed to play in it.

– Psalm 104: 25-26 ESV

On the day of his departure from Uhlerstown, Adriel boarded one of Uhler's barges to Philadelphia, where he caught a train to New York. In New York he would seek passage on a clipper ship to China as a crew member.

When he arrived in New York harbor, Adriel sought out his transportation to the Far East. He was impressed by the magnificence of the American tea clipper, *Leviathan*, that he boarded to seek employment. Though he was not an experienced seaman, he was hired for the journey. He would learn along the way skills that would carry him through his time on board sea-faring vessels.

Clipper ships were noted for their great panoply of sails and their sleek design. They predominated in trade between India and China and on other trade routes. Only with the introduction and growing use of steamers, already having begun with Robert Fulton's invention in 1807, were clippers superseded.

Among other things, clippers were employed to exchange Indian opium for China tea, a remarkably popular item, and other products like silk and porcelain. While opium had earlier been illegal, including its importation, at the time of Adriel's journey to China, it no longer was. In fact, it was grown in China itself. The United Kingdom had fought two opium wars, in part to protect the opium trade. The problem was the devastating effects opium would have on those who were smoking or eating it.

The Chinese emperor was hard-pressed to rid his country of this problem, as it was destroying many of his people; in fact, the problem was not solved in the time of the Qing (Manchu) dynasty, the last imperial dynasty, or afterward during the Chinese Republic. Though not his original intention, Adriel would get involved in the opium trade and in smoking opium.

Adriel boarded the clipper, where he had an opportunity to speak with the captain who hired him for the journey. He would be a sailor "before the mast," that is a common sailor who would be quartered in the forecastle. The ship would sail three days hence on a long journey that would take it around Cape Horn in South America to San Francisco and then across the Pacific to Hong Kong. With the experience he acquired on the long voyage to Hong Kong, Adriel would be able to find a job on other ships if he were so inclined.

Except for a mishap that almost caused Adriel to fall from the rigging of the foremast, a plummet that would have cost him his life, the trip to Hong Kong was uneventful; in fact, boredom, and sometimes even world-weariness, was an ever-present threat on board ship.

In those dull moments, Adriel would try to imagine what the new British colony of Hong Kong was like. The island city that began as a fishing village was acquired after the First Opium War between the United Kingdom and China by the terms of the Treaty of Nanking. The village, a trade center, was growing from town to the large city it is today.

One day, as Adriel was standing on deck, looking out over the sea, his mind began to wander. The ocean was on that day pacific, as it was when the explorer Magellan named it. The sun shone down, spreading its golden rays onto the water, where they were shattered into shards of light. A slight breeze caressed his face with its tender ministrations.

Adriel thought of the power and majesty of the sea as the Bible describes. The Lord God created the sea and all the fishes therein. He split it open for the Israelites to pass during their escape from Egypt. He made the sea obey him and gave the great sea monster, Leviathan, for food. Christ brought the sea to stillness in a storm and saved Peter from the waters. Adriel had learned these texts in church and Sunday School; but his remembrance was no longer part of a living faith.

Adriel passed on to other thoughts of his mother and father and of the people he had known at home. He had not written to his folks since the first months working on the canal; for what reason, he didn't know. He thought of his father's directing the management of the property of the Alden estate. He thought of his mother cooking at the stove and knitting him a hat for winter. His thoughts didn't draw him home.

A mate of Adriel's came up and stood next to him. Jim Yarrow was a storyteller whose tales, sometimes about himself, often conveyed legendary material. Legends are based on actual extraordinary events and persons, told in wondrous stories, like the lives of the saints. These stories contain truth, embedded in the imaginative. Jim was not a braggart but simply a lover of storytelling, mostly in an exaggerated sort of way. He was the master of hyperbole.

Jim had been sailing on clippers for twenty years. He hoped to end his time at sea after this last voyage to resume his carpentry on land instead of at sea. His flight to the sea was inspired by curiosity. He had been on many ships in the tea and opium trade, but avoided the use of opium. He stuck to whiskey in taverns of the ports the ship visited.

Jim said to Adriel, "How are you doing, old boy?"

Adriel responded, "Doing OK. I'm a little bored and a lot looking forward to docking." At that time the *Leviathan* was in the middle of the Pacific Ocean.

"It won't be too long. Give it twenty days."

"Quite a while."

"It's a long trip. I'll keep you occupied with some of my stories. I'll try to fill your imagination with what I have witnessed."

"Let's see you do that. If anyone can, you can."

"Here's one. Do you have time?"

"I don't go on duty for two hours."

With the din of the crew in the background, Jim told his story. "Several years ago, I took a hike in the hills above Hong Kong. Along the way, I met up with a Chinese man sitting on a rock that partially blocked the path. His head was resting on his breast, and his hands were folded as if in prayer. The man didn't look up right away. Then, he slowly lifted his head and stared at me as if I were an intruder on his meditation, and yet there was pleading in his eyes. I couldn't pass him by without a word. It took me a while to find the words as we gazed at one another. His clothes were tattered and his feet were bare. By his wrinkled face, I judged him to be old.

"When I recovered my senses from the surprise of encountering such an unusual figure, I told him my name and asked for his. He told me that he was Leong Xiuqing. Years before, he had fled from his home province, where he lived with his wife and seven children. During the Taiping rebellion, Leong Xiuqing's family was wiped out by elements of the Qing Dynasty imperial forces sent against the rebels. He managed to flee to British-held Hong Kong. At the time I encountered him, the rebellion had not been fully repressed. He was a symbol of the devastation caused by both sides during the time of the Taiping Heavenly Kingdom.

"The suffering on his face, a map of China's many ills,

evoked pathos in my heart and soul. His body testified to the many days he went without food. He told me that he took up opium smoking, at least when he had some money, to ease the pain of his misfortunes and now is addicted. Without friend or family he was alone in the world, wandering the streets of Hong Kong in a daze. Homeless, he slept in the streets. He found odd jobs. He begged for food when he had no money, which was often, mostly because of his opium use. He was a man without hope. His grief is numbing to the imagination.

"I gave him what food I had brought along. I told him I would pray for him whom, I found out, was a Protestant Christian, not of the Taiping sort. Then, I took my leave with reluctance as I felt somehow I was abandoning him.

"Down the path from my encounter, I turned to witness the horrible sight of an individual casting himself from a great height. I concluded that Leong Xiuqing committed suicide. The rest of the day I felt pangs in my head and stomach and didn't sleep that night, or many nights to come. I had recurring nightmares about him and the circumstances in which he lost his family and friends.

"A year later, my ship returned to Hong Kong. I felt compelled to hike up to the same spot where I had met Leong Xiuqing. As the rock on which he sat came into view, I thought I saw, to my amazement, that it was the same man I had encountered a year before. I grew dizzy at the sight. When I got to the spot, he had disappeared. Was it an apparition, or was I so beside myself that I only imagined his presence? I don't know and will never know."

"This really happened?" Adriel asked skeptically.

"Yes, indeed, it did, though, I think I may have been seeing things when the man came hurtling down to his death," Jim replied. "I was in a disquieted state of mind."

"It is a disturbing story." Adriel thought that when he got to Hong Kong, he would visit the spot Jim was talking about. "Could you tell me where this place is? I might visit it."

"I would be glad to," was Jim's response.

Adriel knew what was happening in China before he arrived there. His motive was to travel as far as possible from home and, for a while, to be close to the events of which he had heard; but, how long he would stay was uncertain. It was his teacher, Joshua Schreiber, who had been in the Orient with the navy, who was the inspiration for his own interest.

The *Leviathan* was drawing close to Hong Kong; but, before arrival, the ship was hit by a monstrous storm—so much for a pacific ocean. No one who hasn't been aboard a ship can know what fear is engendered by such a storm on the open water. Adriel thought he was sure to get dumped overboard by the angry deep. During the tempest, a man was lost, consumed by the sea's endless appetite. When the storm had passed by and the sea came to rest, the men on board cheered for their deliverance and mourned for the loss of a brave sailor.

Adriel came through the storm alive and well. He had a sense of gratitude, but didn't know who to thank except other crew members for their skill and bravery. He wouldn't consider thanking God, for thanksgiving to the deity was not a consideration since his life became one of roaming far from the Way. But he did write a song that he sang when he played his guitar.

Mighty rolled the awful waves
Over our imperiled ship.
Steady were the on-deck braves.
"Mates, hang on with firmest grip."

Storm clouds came with dreadful speed.
Wind and dark ran with the squall.
Sailors lifted up their beads.
"Mates, let not the rage appall."

"Overboard," went up the cry.
Willis, swallowed by the deep,

Caused no tear from earth or sky.
"Mates, please mind the loss and weep."

Don't forget the lowly tar,
Bringing to each hearth and home
Wonders of strange lands afar.
"Mates, fare well on seething foam."

After several months out from New York, the *Leviathan* dropped anchor in Victoria Harbour, Hong Kong. Adriel weighed his options during his stay in this burgeoning city, a European outpost in China. He had said farewell to his shipmates whom he knew he wouldn't see again; for, he planned to sign with another ship, headed for London.

CHAPTER TWENTY-NINE

THE SEA VOYAGE TO LONDON

Like unto ships far off at sea,

Outward or homeward bound, are we.

Before, behind, and all around, Floats and swings the horizon's bound,

Seems at its distant rim to rise

And climb the crystal wall of the skies,

And then again to turn and sink,

As if we could slide from its outer brink.

Ah! It is not the sea,

It is not the sea that sinks and shelves, But ourselves

That rock and rise

With endless and uneasy motion,

Now touching the very skies,

Now sinking into the depths of ocean.

Ah! if our souls but poise and swing

Like the compass in its brazen ring,

Ever level and ever true

To the toil and the task we have to do,

We shall sail securely and safely reach

The Fortunate Isles, on whose shining beach

The sights we see, and the sounds we hear,

Will be those of joy and not of fear!

– The Building of the Ship, *Henry Wadsworth Longfellow*

Adriel decided to sign on with the British clipper *Sea Wind*, about to leave for London with a shipment of tea, silk, and porcelain. Before departure, he spent two days in Hong Kong, going on a drunk to make up for the dryer season on board the *Leviathan*. Yet, he managed to get onto the ship in time.

The *Sea Wind*, with its cargo, departed on the third day after Adriel's arrival on the *Leviathan*. Tea was the big item that in earlier days caused a great imbalance of payments that drained silver from the United Kingdom to the advantage of China. The imbalance was reversed with the importation into China of Indian opium, which in the early days was a monopoly of the East India Company, a trade in which Adriel would be implicated to his serious disadvantage.

The ship sailed down the coast of China to the islands through the Sunda Strait between Java and Sumatra and then across the Indian Ocean around the Cape of Good Hope at the tip of Africa and north along the African coast past Gibralter to London. Over three months would be required to complete the trip.

Adriel applied the skills he had learned on the *Leviathan* that kept him in good stead with the captain and first mate. He had come to have a great affection for the sea, seasoned by fear and respect for its cantankerous moods. When not working on deck or otherwise, he would spend some time looking out onto the watery vastness both during the day and at night.

One night, when not on watch, Adriel was standing on deck while the *Sea Wind* was passing south of the island of Mauritius in the Indian Ocean off Africa, an area known for its brilliant night sky. He was lost in wonder. The sky was luminous with starlight, shining in contrast to the dark deep of the ocean. Lost in his vision, he heard voices singing "All Praise to Thee, My God, This Night," a hymn tune by Thomas Tallis, and words by Bishop Thomas Ken, that he sang with the congregation at home. For a moment he wished he could believe in God as he had in the past, that the prophet Amos writes, made the Pleiades and Orion; but, he could not—too many questions, too much suffering in the world, and too many disappointments and tragedies for him.

In the ancient world, the sky was an object of worship, reflected in the fact that the planets are named after ancient gods and many stars and constellations after ancient heroes. The Greeks called the highest heaven the empyrean, a place of fire as the word denotes. According to ancient belief, the empyrean was the residence of the divine. Christians also locate heaven in this region, at least, as a metaphor for His glory and majesty; for, God is everywhere.

Adriel was viewing the heavens of the southern hemisphere, south of Mauritius and Madagascar. In that sky is a constellation called Phoenix. The Phoenix is a mythical bird who is said to be immolated and to rise out of the ashes every thousand years or so. In the Christian letter of *I Clement*, this mythical bird's death and rebirth is likened to Christ's death and resurrection. Adriel could identify the constellation and thought again of the faith he had rejected. What could he do but go where his heart directed him? And yet, whether one believes in Christ or not, one's belief or disbelief is never secure. While one is alive, there's always the possibility of rejecting or confessing Christ. His agnosticism was always on the edge of belief, and belief is always on the edge of unbelief. Such is the spiritual struggle in this life. This he clearly knew.

Along the west coast of Africa, the *Sea Wind* passed the region where most of the slaves were acquired from Africa for importation to the Americas. On the coast, Europeans received slaves from interior tribes. In school Adriel heard stories of horrendous conditions for these forlorn people, many of whom died in transit. In 1807, the Parliament of the United Kingdom banned the slave trade in the British Empire. Adriel had the firsthand experience of fighting for the emancipation of the slaves as a soldier in the Federal army. In America, trading was ended in 1808; slavery was eliminated by the 13th amendment in 1865.

*

The *Sea Wind* was at anchor in London for a number of days for repair and to on-load cargo for the return trip to India and then to China. Adriel spent his time taking in the sights of London and walking so much that he got blisters on his feet as he did in Philadelphia. He visited Westminster Abbey where the monarch was crowned, and many famous English were buried including kings and queens. He stood in the nave, running his eyes over the masterly built medieval stone church with embedded resplendent stained glass. Such man-made beauty brings the faithful, but also the unfaithful, into the realm of the numinous. At the end of the day, he joined some of his shipmates at one of the many pubs in London. They toasted a grand and ancient city and their own safe arrival in the metropolis.

Because of his sore feet, Adriel rested the day before the ship weighed anchor. The next day, he limped on board to help with final preparations for departure to India and China.

CHAPTER THIRTY

FORECASTLE TALK

When I traveled on the Sea Wind, I had many discussions with my ship mates. We talked about a multitude of subjects. I will never forget those hours of good feeling, even with the occasional disagreements among the participants.

– A Wanderer Who Becomes a Pilgrim, *Adriel Peregrine.*

For Adriel the days fled swiftly along the passageway of time. When Adriel was on duty, he was assigned many tasks, accounting for much of his perception of the rapid flow of the hours, days, and weeks. On a clipper ship, the crew didn't stand idle. Off-duty he would spend time looking out over the sea, but also palavering with his mates and reading Melville's novel, *Moby Dick, or The Whale,* that he had brought with him from America. Sometimes, the talk became more serious, as when Adriel participated in a conversation about trust.

Adriel's duty for the day was over. He headed for the forecastle to rest a while. When he entered, a discussion had just begun. Three of his mates were talking about trust. The reason they were having such a conversation had to do with the experience of Jefferson Kynaston, an American, who, like Adriel, signed on with the *Sea Wind.*

Jefferson, with his Yankee accent, said, "I was in business with another man from my home town in Vermont. We owned a very profitable general store. Before I went off to war, my partner and I made an agreement on how to handle the business while I was away. He was too old for the military;

I still qualified for service, but barely. I was over forty years old. When I returned home after the war, I discovered, to my shock, that he had stolen both the business and my wife. I was more hurt about his stealing the business. Our agreement was not in print, not co-signed by a witness, and not handled by a lawyer. I allowed him to use my money for the business. Nothing was left when I returned. Like a fool, I trusted him.

"We'd been friends since we were boys. Though I was not young, I went off to sea, taking a ship from Boston town. I had to get away from the disaster he caused. I thought of killing him, but decided he wasn't worth my being hanged or going to prison for a long term.

"So here I am on the *Sea Wind*, serving on a British ship with British mates and a few Americans and Chinese. I don't trust any human being any of the time. I don't even trust Adriel, though he is probably better than most people I've met. Tell us, Adriel, what do you think?"

"I agree with Jeff. I don't trust human beings on any matter. I don't even trust myself. All of us, at one time or another, have been untrustworthy. We're untrustworthy; because, we're humans, and humans are weak. At one time, I believed that the explanation was that our original father and mother, Adam and Eve, had fallen into sin in the Garden of Eden. Now I have no real explanation except that's the way we are. We all suffer a miserable lot among those whom we should be able to trust. No one's trustworthy. I once thought that God was reliable and true. Now I don't believe much in God. He may exist, but who can be sure? I'm not sure. I don't trust you, mates, and I don't want you to trust me."

Young English sailor, Walker W. Walker, known as Walk on the ship, cursed with an odd name given him by drunken parents, responded to Adriel. "I want to be able to trust someone. I never trusted my parents. They almost always reneged on their promises. I didn't find it any different in the world when I was trying to make my way on my own. There are people who have motives that serve their own interests with no concern for the welfare of those around them. It usually has to do with money. I've found that men and women are alike in their untrustworthiness. If I ever found someone tried and true, I'd be very surprised. I guess another's trustworthiness can only be proved over a period of time; I've found most individuals untrustworthy in a short period of time that didn't require me to wait and see very long. I too have failed people. We humans put self-interest first."

Shadrach Jones responded with an objection, "But, if we don't have any trust in others, how can we survive? We must be able to trust people to live. I guess we're forced to take our chances."

Adriel responded, "Yes, Shad, we must take the risk of trusting others in order to live, and some people we can trust more than others. On this ship, the same applies. We depend on a person's character, and there are many bad characters in the world. And, you know, none of us here are perfectly reliable. We've lied, and we've failed. No one is perfectly trustworthy, not even the best of wives and husbands in their relationships."

"And some have gone as far as betrayal, especially Judas," Shadrach added.

Adriel wondered how the teachings of Jesus could be in any way practical. Humans were not capable of the good conduct he calls us to exhibit. One would have to be an unfallen angel.

That day, the conversation continued on other subjects, including affairs of the ship. Other talk on important matters of living would occur as the ship glided fast toward Calcutta, where opium would be loaded as cargo. And then, of course, there was the banter of seamen. One of the subjects of this talk was the Civil War. Shadrach and Walker served in the Army of Northern Virginia under Lee. Jefferson served under Grant. Like Adriel, they too were at Appomattox on April 9, 1865.

As another day was ending on the *Sea Wind*, an exhausted Adriel went sound asleep in his berth. In the middle of the night, Adriel woke up, as he often did. He stared into the almost quiet darkness of the forecastle, where the snoring was soft. When he was awake at night, he would think about many things. His first thought was of his decision to come aboard the *Sea Wind* as a member of the crew. He knew beforehand that the merchant ship would be transporting opium to China as well as much valued goods from China. How did his conscience sit with this fact? He had made a decision with rationalization before he signed on; but, the decision still caused him some discomfort.

Then, he thought of home. It was never completely out of his mind. How were his mother and father? He even thought of Pontiac Rowbottom, the wanderer. What was he doing now? He thought of his three dead friends. His heart, though, was still in his wandering, and he had wandered far, all the way to the other side of the world. Now, he was on his way back to China via Calcutta.

He thought of what he would do with his brief time off in Hong Kong. He would have to hike in the hills above the settlement where Jim Yarrow met Leong Yang Xiuqing. He looked forward to returning to the burgeoning settlement that was the new British colony. Then, he fell off to sleep until the bell sounded for him to go back to his duty.

Adriel had a dream that night that caused him some consternation. He was swimming out into the open sea, always looking back to make sure he could see the beach. Once when he looked back, he could no longer sight the land. He turned around in the direction that he thought he should go. Still, the shore was not visible. He began to panic as extreme tiredness came over him. Some creature skirted him along his leg. He hoped it wasn't a shark or other harmful denizen of the deep. Then, in the near distance, he saw what looked like an untended rowboat. He gave his last strength to achieve the craft. When he reached his destination, he crawled in with no trouble, marking that two oars were resting on the seats. He sat for a moment in the boat, overcome with relief; for, he had been overcome with fear. As he took the oars in his hands, the shore appeared to him. He rowed safely home. Adriel awoke as he heard the bell's announcement of the next watch.

CHAPTER THIRTY-ONE

TEA AND OPIUM

Deep calleth unto deep (Ps. Xlii. 7). The abyss of misery calleth upon the abyss of mercy; the abyss of sins calleth upon the abyss of grace. Greater is the abyss of mercy than the abyss of misery. Let therefore deep swallow up deep. Let the deep of mercy swallow the deep of misery. Have mercy on me, O God, after Thy great mercy; not according to the mercy of men, which is but small, but after Thine own which is great, yea which is immeasurable, which is incomprehensible, which infinitely surpasseth all sins, according to that Thy great mercy wherewith Thou didst so love the world, as to give Thine Only-begotten Son, John iii.16.

– Girolamo Savonarola, Meditations on Psalm 51 and Part of

Psalm 31

The *Sea Wind* was nearing Calcutta, the port through which opium was sent to the Celestial Empire. The poppy was harvested in Bengal, a region up the Ganges River, and brought down to the city for export. Merchants would bid on the product, eventually to make huge profits. Over time, the use of the drug in China had grown rapidly.

Before he signed on to the *Sea Wind*, Adriel had accepted the idea of involvement in this trade. It was not only the United Kingdom but also the United States and other nations that were involved in the trade; but, the United Kingdom was the primary trader. Adriel had not thought through where this decision would take him. He would find out before long.

The *Sea Wind* always had a destination; but, Adriel's travels represented wandering; no long-lasting goal was ever in his mind. He was most unlike the pilgrims in the Middle Ages who traveled to the Holy Land or some other holy site like Santiago de Compostela in Spain or Canterbury in England or Jerusalem. It was clear that he was not on the path to the Celestial City like the pilgrim in John Bunyan's *Pilgrim's Progress*. He had no direction except where at the moment he decided to go. For a while he would travel on the *Sea Wind*, then sign on to another ship or find employment on land.

Adriel's temporal wandering indicated a vagrant spirituality, that is, no God, no ultimate destination, no spirituality at all except a sort of self-fabricated Buddhism in which God had no role, and a nirvana-like extinction defined the ultimate human end, yet without the discipline Buddhist practice requires. Adriel was not a practitioner, but an observer. Unlike Israel, whom the Lord guided, he had no one to lead him. He was really no different from many people. His spiritual vagrancy created a larger and larger void in his soul.

The vanities collected and burned by the Dominican monk Savonarola of Florence have remained with us, as they did with Adriel. Adriel would indulge himself, increasing his misery and forgetting God's mercy. He would continue to be an avid customer and consumer of the world's vanities. He would find them everywhere in his wanderings and be infected with them and corrupted by them. How long would the misery last? Until death? Would there be no relief from the delusion?

As the *Sea Wind* sped toward Calcutta in fair weather, Adriel tried to imagine what the city was like. He knew it was a busy port on the Hooghly River under British control and a major depot for trade in opium. The poppy was grown primarily in

West Bengal, contiguous to the city. Factories prepared the product for export from Calcutta. Thence, it was transported to China, where the opium and some other products would be sold for tea, silk, and porcelain. The opium trade from India fed and encouraged the appetite for the drug in China and elsewhere. Opium dens cropped up in such cities as San Francisco, London, New York, and, of course, the bustling cities of China, including Canton (Guangzhou), not far from Hong Kong.

Adriel had thought much of Bill Yarrow's story about the Chinese in misery whom Bill encountered on the path. He knew enough to be aware that this mysterious man who consoled himself with opium represented the misery of China. He decided he would take that same hike if he could find the way. He had a curiosity and appetite about strange happenings. It was part of his view that the world was a magnificent oddity and mystery with many wonders, even if it was without a god.

CHAPTER THIRTY-TWO

A SURPRISING ENCOUNTER

If the serpent bites before it is charmed, there is no advantage to the charmer. — *Ecclesiastes 10:11, ESV.*

As she arrived at her destination, the *Sea Wind* passed many other ships—large and small; native, British, American and from many other nations. Sampans, junks, clippers and a multitude of others filled the harbor of Hong Kong.

The crew was finishing its tasks, anxiously waiting for the moment when shore leave was granted. The ship would tarry in port for repairs and off-loading chests of opium. Adriel anticipated an interesting time in a city with which he was unacquainted.

The first thing Adriel did with his leave after some rest was to take a brief tour of Hong Kong. Included in his interest was the mountainous region that overlooked the city. He was curious to find the spot where Bill Yarrow encountered the Chinese man who had lost his family in the Taiping rebellion. On another day, he would take a hike to find the spot.

Adriel found a room the day after the ship docked. He had asked some of the veterans where they had stayed when in the city in the past and chose this particular place. On the day after his tour, he set out for the hills of Hong Kong, which gave a magnificent view of the city. Adriel wished to enliven his imagination by beholding the panorama of city, hills, and harbor. He would enjoy a few days on *terra firma* before returning to the restless sea.

It was a day of clear sky and glistening ocean. The day was warm and humid; but, during his afternoon hike, the breeze was refreshing. The work on the ship at sea increased Adriel's fitness. As was his wont, when walking, Adriel walked fast. Occasionally, he would stop to take in the view.

How resplendent is the world! From his perch he saw nature and human civilization contiguous and on display. The sea, in its incursion in the harbor, bore many ships—mercantile, naval, familial, and otherwise—on its back. The hills were green in contrast to the whitish buildings of the city down below. The noise of the city was unheard in the quiet of the hills, as if it were without inhabitants.

Adriel looked for the large rock on which the Chinese man sat. At a certain point, as he was walking down the same path as Bill did some time before, he thought he saw the rock from a distance with someone sitting on it. His breath was shallow, and his eyes were wide open. As he approached, the figure disappeared. When he came close to the location, he stopped and stared at the rock for a few moments, trying to imagine what Bill Yarrow saw. He decided to sit on the rock and eat some of the food he brought along with him. After lunch, he resolved to continue his excursion.

As he continued on, he heard rustling in the tall grass on the one side of the path. Startled, he quickly stood up. Before he could move away, he was face to face with a white striped black king cobra with head flared. Its underside was of light color. Adriel froze where he was, as the snake hissed and swayed. His heart was flinging itself against his chest; his breath was shallow; and his stomach was tight. He ran through his options, deciding to fling himself to the ground as far from the snake as possible. When he did this, the snake struck, but missed. Not knowing the location of the serpent, he lunged forward from the ground, running as swiftly as he could. He didn't look back until he thought that others walking along the path might be endangered. He turned around and walked toward the rock to investigate whether he could sight the snake. It was nowhere to be found; but, Adriel's survey was obstructed by the tall grass. While remaining alert, he waited for the next hikers to warn them of what he saw, then continued down the path.

Adriel's lively imagination led him to wonder if the snake was the embodiment of the soul of the forlorn Chinese man, Leong Xiuqing, living out his karma. A form of Buddhism had existed in China for over fifteen hundred years. Like the Hindus and Jains, Buddhism taught the doctrine of reincarnation, the belief that the soul returns to live in another body, not necessarily human, what is called *samsara*. He imagined that the Chinese man had returned as the snake and was taking out his grief and anger on human beings, though king cobras tend to be shy and non-aggressive in most instances. Of course, such behavior, according to Buddhist teaching, will slow down his final entrance into Nirvana, an indescribable state of bliss that amounts to an extinguishing of individual consciousness.

As he proceeded down the path that overlooked Hong Kong, he heard a yell. He turned toward where he had been and saw an object plunging down the mountain, just as Bill had described. Could this be Leong Yang Xiuqing? When he unlocked the door of his room, he was in a state of perplexity. He thought maybe his imagination took him too far, or maybe not?

CHAPTER THIRTY-THREE

THE OPIUM DEN

Our self-interest often pre-empts our concern for our neighbor. We prefer fame, power, and money over dedication to the needs of the other. In the endeavor to follow Christ's command, it is not that we deny essentials to ourselves, at least in most cases. The pursuit of fulfilling many of our desires is often on behalf of excess and wrong.
    – A Wanderer Who Becomes a Pilgrim, *Adriel Peregrine.*

The opium on the *Sea Wind* was unloaded for distribution in China. The Chinese Empire forbade the importation of opium in 1799; but, legalized it in 1860 as one of the terms of a treaty with the British. At this time there existed also a significant native production of the drug. Many Chinese were in the habit of smoking. Its importation gave the trade balance advantage to the British that before the opium trade the Chinese had possessed.

Indian opium, the trade that was first monopolized by the East India Company, now carried by numerous traders, was packed in chests. It found its way to China through many ports opened up by the treaties that were concluded after two opium wars between China and the United Kingdom. Adriel fit into this large picture through his being of the crew of the *Sea Wind* on which was transported the dear and dangerous cargo.

Though it had its medicinal benefits—laudanum, a mixture of alcohol and opium, was in common use—opium also posed a threat to the welfare of any nation, but especially China.

Many writers pointed out its dangers; many church leaders opposed British policy.

At the time of Adriel's association with China, the devastating Taiping rebellion had recently ended (1864). The Qing (Manchu) Dynasty that managed to defeat the rebels was an offense to many Chinese and would end with the founding of the Republic in 1912. So much trouble was occurring and was ahead for China.

Adriel was curious about opium and its effects. He had already made alcohol too close a friend. So, being of a mind to experiment to see where opium use would lead, he decided the day after his unusual and dangerous experience in the hills to patronize an opium den. He had no trouble finding one in the city.

Adriel entered a den that was by no means run-down, as one may imagine. Opium dens ranged from seedy to elegant. At the time, opium was not the monopoly of one social class or another. There he was met by the owner who, discovering that Adriel was new to the practice, explained in English how to use his facility. The proprietor also provided all of the utensils on a tray and the opium required by the customer.

A smoker reclined on a mattress where was set a tray that included a lamp that heated the opium located in a pipe so that it could be smoked. The pipe consisted of a bowl, saddle, and stem. The saddle connected the bowl to the stem, made in this case of bamboo. The bowl was the location where the opium was heated over the lamp. Reclining was necessary in order to heat the drug. Usually, a companion smoker would be reclining next to another smoker.

Adriel was set up for his first experience. The use of the drug had the benefits of relief from anxiety and euphoric feelings. The same happened to Adriel not too long after he started drawing on the pipe. After a while, he put the pipe down and lay on the mat, enjoying a pleasant feeling undisturbed by stress.

In his reverie, Adriel imagined himself in a peaceful place

where he was walking amidst the deep green of the forest. All around him he began to hear the sounds of melodious music. The folk of the woodland were singing wonderful songs in both word and note. He rehearsed a poem he had written when he was yet home.

"Come out and meet me by the tree.
Come out, beloved, and dance with me.
We'll hoof away till sun has set,
And all our woes at once forget."

"The moon will rise in splendor true,
This night her fullness in our view.
Her brightest shining in the sky
Midst lavish, scented late July."

Titania with King Oberon still
Danced as the light crept down the hill.
The merry pair were holding hands,
When they went off to keep the banns.

And so the two are quite content,
And rule their realm with just intent.
Each summer on the holy night
The forest deep is quite a sight.

Adriel's imagination took him from earth to sky. He saw some clouds passing by and bright blue sky above them. He felt a profound sense of well-being. His anxiety and stress seemed more under his control than he had ever known before.

As his thoughts returned to the den, he began to take note again of the environment around him. The room was neither run-down nor opulent, but it was well-maintained and clean. His companion, to whom he spoke few words during the session and whose name he did not know, was intently smoking his pipe. A Chinese woman came over to him to see how he was doing. She was attended by a beautiful young woman whom Adriel guessed was her daughter. Adriel tried to hide the fact that he couldn't keep his eyes off her by seeming somewhat distracted and aloof.

Later, when he felt like he was capable of handling himself, he got up. As Adriel walked to the entrance of the establishment, he noticed again the high level of activity. A large number of people were lounging and smoking their pipes. Attendants were assisting some of the customers. The unique smell of opium was in the air.

Adriel's first experience smoking opium was a pleasant experience. What awesome and fabulous musings did he have! For a while, he felt such a sense of peace until he came back to the daily reality. He knew the possible dangers of the drug; for, he had spoken many times about it with his mates who had the experience. But, he was driven more by the alleviation of anxiety and euphoria the drug produces than by its perils. He would henceforth use the drug he helped bring into the Chinese Empire. He assured himself that he could control his use of it. Would the drug wreak havoc on those who encouraged the use of such a toxic substance on so many people? Adriel had a superstitious fear that his involvement in the trade would rebound on him with a vengeance; but, this thought didn't deter him.

On the following day, Adriel checked with the ship's captain about the schedule of departure of the *Sea Wind*. He had decided to sail the triangular trade yet once more--some manufactured goods and silver to India, opium to China, and tea to London.

In two days Adriel would sail. In the meantime he made another trip to the opium den. He wished to introduce himself to the lovely daughter of the proprietor, hoping to overcome his own native shyness. The daughter was not present on the day he returned.

The time came to sail. Adriel was set for another voyage in

his wanderings. He would return to Hong Kong for the sake of the beautiful face he saw in the opium den; but, he could not dare to say where he would be a year later.

CHAPTER THIRTY-FOUR

THE IMAGINATION

Having a well-formed imagination does not necessarily mean that one is an impractical dreamer who denies what is right in front of his face at the expense of his and others' welfare. A truly imaginative person can make the distinction between the reality of the everyday world and flights of fancy and give to each its due space. He is to be pitied who has no ability through the imagination to look into the vast realms of the human mind and of the world that help one understand and appreciate what is, especially the human universe of meaning. Imagination deals with the great themes of human existence in legend, fairy tale, fable, mythology, epic, fantasy and so on. Elves under the toadstool can mean a lot more than one may first think.   – The Art of Art, Adriel Peregrine

The work on a ship is hard and dangerous. The sea is unpredictable and ready to swallow a sailor at any moment. Its hunger is insatiable. In ancient Near Eastern myth, the sea was viewed as an opponent of the god of order. It represented chaos—a constant threat to humanity. According to these ancient stories, fortunate for humankind are the victories of the conquering god over the raging sea.

In the Old Testament the sea is depicted as strong and restless; in fact, it is sometimes portrayed as a sea monster, similar to Babylonian and western Semitic myth; but, with the notable exception—as a creature it is no match for the one God, Creator of heaven and earth. Psalm 74 tells us that God defeated Leviathan and the sea monsters. In the beginning

God brought light and order out of chaos and darkness. The Lord parted the sea to save Israel from Pharaoh and his host. In the Scriptures, no doubt is left about what the outcome of the battle has been or will be. The essential difference between ancient Semitic myth and the Hebrew Scriptures is that the God of Israel has no equal, nor is the contention with cosmic forces really a contest. God is omnipotent and will, inevitably, win the battle. Adriel doubted this.

In Matthew, Jesus calmed the sea on which there was a great storm. The Greek word used to describe the storm on Lake Galilee is the same word for the earthquakes of the end time, as found in the Book of Revelation. Again God triumphs over the forces of chaos and destruction. Adriel doubted the reality of God's victory.

Adriel no longer regarded himself as a member of the faith community worshipping the One God in three persons. At the time of his wanderings, he couldn't appreciate God's power over the forces that work contrary to human welfare; because, he didn't believe that God had such power, if there was a god at all. He was not at all sure that anything in the world could oppose chaos and evil, the real powers in the world. Humans were far too weak to be an effective force for good against evil, including the evil in themselves.

Adriel had a respect for the sea. It could be ruthless and even seem diabolical. But, it also made his imagination soar. When he looked out onto it, as the clipper *Sea Wind* glided swiftly on the waves, he reached for and possessed the sensibility that highly regarded the splendor of the world. In his thought he kept side by side, though in contrast and in tension, the sea's hostility, as well as its grandeur, preferring one to the other according to his mood. The sea caused him to think more of its grandeur than its danger, though he was riding on its often untamed, fierce, and raging surface. The Scriptures say that God keeps the sea within its limits (Job 38). Adriel had no confidence that God had such power in the world.

Adriel sang to himself a song of the sea that he composed:

I stand upon the wooden deck
To watch the gentle, soothing sea,
While on our lengthy ocean trek
To bring the folk the Chinese tea.

I stand upon the wooden deck,
And fear the angry, raging sea,
That it would bring our ship to wreck.
O, fragile mortals all are we.

I stand upon the wooden deck,
And must to all my heart confess,
"The sea remains at no one's beck.
Its ear is deaf to our distress."

And so, when he had time, as in the past, he would stand at the rail of the ship and imagine the world as a place of mystery, where many things were hidden and some things eventually revealed, but not all, including the world's ultimate mystery, what it really was at its core.

On a particularly calm day, when the ship was sailing in the South China Sea on its way to England, he thought of the young Chinese face in the opium den that captivated him so much. She bewitched Adriel, even though he knew nothing about her, not even her name. Such is the power of first impressions, especially of those things that are beautiful and yet unknown.

Adriel called her *Meinu*, the Chinese word for beauty. Included among the *Four Great Beauties of China*, she would be the fifth. He had read much; and so, he read into his imagination much. But, the following story, entitled *The Painted Skin*, written by Pu Songling long ago, told to him in Pidgin English by two Chinese sailors on the ship, gave him pause about first impressions.

A man named Wang met a poor young girl along his way. He took her to his study, where he had sexual relations with her. Wang's wife was concerned that the young woman may have run away from a prominent family she had been serving; but, Wang didn't agree to cast the girl out. Later, a Taoist priest whom Wang encountered noticed, to his amazement, an evil aura around him. Wang was incredulous that the beautiful young girl could cast a curse on him. When he returned home, Wang discovered that the beautiful young girl was a demon. The thing was attending to a painted pelt of a human being. The creature put on the pelt and became the beautiful girl. The demon killed Wang; but, it turned out that the Taoist recommended a madman of the village who provided the means to bring Wang back to life.

Was *Meinu* a demon in disguise? He was such a fool for thinking of her in a romantic way. Here he was in the middle of the ocean, months from London, months on the return to China. *Meinu* was an instance of his imagination going awry. But, he would go again to the opium den, called *The Sign of the Dragon*, and see if she were still there. He would get around her mother so that he could talk to her and befriend her if it so worked out. Of course, he didn't know if she was married or about the other circumstances of her life. He would find out. Adriel had become somewhat bolder than when he was younger.

In most part, the imagination was a friend to Adriel. In his visits to the forest he would spend hours dreaming up scenes, people, and creatures in his mind's eye. He was not the sort of dreamer who was so lost in his dreams that the reality of the everyday world was an outsider in his life; but, indeed, he was a dreamer. Opium is what would take him into unreality.

Human beings are explained through more than biological processes; the drama of life is more complex than a mechanical device; and time is richer in meaning than the ticking of a clock. Even in his agnostic days, Adriel believed that the world was larger than the physical, that it contained a spiritual element even if there was no God.

Siddhartha Gautama (Buddha) had no time for the gods, but experienced the assaults of Mara, the evil demon, and his host, when he sat under the Bodhi tree at Bodh Gaya, a town in Bihar, the same province out of which came opium, before his enlightenment. Does transcendent evil exist without transcendent good?   Are we left alone to face wickedness? Adriel avoided any attempt to answer such questions.

Adriel believed there were realities in the world transcending the physical, but was not clear of what they were. His imagination provided some substance to their existence. His ideas were half formed; he lacked certainty about many important things. What then is the world? What is it made of? And who made it, if any greater reality at all? His loss of God led to peregrinations in the wilderness.

Buddha was not concerned about such questions. He focused on the human capacity to escape desire and suffering; but, Adriel was unsettled about these enigmas and would continue to be. While in the Far East, Adriel studied Buddhism in its Theravada form, in which are found the central teachings of the Buddha himself—the Four Noble Truths, the Noble Eightfold Path, and the release into Nirvana, attained by a very disciplined meditation and the following of the Dharma, enshrined in the Four Noble Truths and the Noble Eightfold Path, taught by Buddha. The goal was that by following the Dharma one was released from the suffering of desire into the state of Nirvana, thus avoiding reincarnation into another physical body. Buddha taught that one's release from the wheel of suffering and attachment occurred only by one's efforts, not by the help or grace of the gods or God, though some forms of Buddhism regarded Buddha as a savior figure who would lead his followers by his great compassion to release from the cycle of suffering. These spiritual teachings offered Adriel a way to higher spiritual things without God, though thoughts of God and questions about Him at times intruded into his consciousness. His heart and mind were unsettled about the big questions of life. They always involved God whether he believed in Him or not. Moreover, Adriel never became a convinced Buddhist.

Adriel learned these Buddhist principles from a sailor from Ceylon whom he encountered in Hong Kong and a Chinese sailor on the *Sea Wind* who practiced the Chan (Zen in Japanese) form of the religion. His wanderings exposed him to many ideas and ways of looking at things that, at home, he would never have entertained.

Adriel turned from looking at the sea and headed for the forecastle. He would be on duty in a few hours. During the night, while on duty, he would look up at the stars and muse about many things.

CHAPTER THIRTY-FIVE

TO LONDON AND LIMEHOUSE

Dorian winced and looked round at the grotesque things that lay in such fantastic postures on the ragged mattresses. The twisted limbs, the gaping mouths, the staring lusterless eyes, fascinated him. He knew in what strange heavens they were suffering, and what dull hells were teaching them the secret of some new joy.
— The Picture of Dorian Gray, *Oscar Wilde.*

The *Sea Wind* sailed west of Gibraltar on the final leg of its journey. On a windy day, she entered the Channel and sailed to the mouth of the Thames. After docking at London, the crew attended to certain duties and then took leave. Some would visit their families whom they had not seen in so long. Others would find their way according to their interests. Adriel found a room in town in the same establishment as before and drank with some shipmates that same evening into the late night.

A few days after the ship's arrival, Adriel decided he would investigate Limehouse at the East End of London, north of the Thames, where sailors gathered. What he was really looking for was an opium den where he could again indulge himself in the joys of the trance that the first time led him to more vivid imaginings. He craved more of this experience and the feeling of ease that came with smoking the substance.

Limehouse was the location of limekilns whose product was used in the pottery industry. It is here where sailors from different nations converged and where a small community of Chinese lived.

Adriel found Ah Sing's opium den in Limehouse, where he would spend some time and money. While in London, he became more familiar with the drug, meaning that he actually spent much time and money. He bought his own pipe that became a close travel companion. He hoped to achieve a sense of peace and visionary experience while smoking, as he did the first time.

His host greeted Adriel and showed him a place to recline and smoke. He spent the day, losing a sense of time. When he left, the sun was setting. How he found his way back to his room was a mystery to him, for his mind in its tranquility was elsewhere than finding his room in an unfamiliar place.

What he remembered most from the musings of that day was one in particular where he was walking in a thick forest. He encountered who he thought was a young woman obscured by the shadows. She walked forward into the sunlight; but, he didn't recognize her.

"Who are you?" he asked. She didn't answer.

"Who are you?" he asked again. She didn't answer, but walked closer to him.

"Who are you?" he asked emphatically. She didn't answer, but stopped and looked at him.

"I'm your love. You don't yet know who I am; but some day, not too far into the future, you will. She walked back into the shadows, and there was silence.

After some moments of perplexity, not resolved, Adriel continued on until he came to a large rock formation onto which he climbed; and, seeing when he reached the top a pond of crystal clear water circumscribed by the rocks, dived in, knowing somehow that it was deep enough. In fact, it was so deep that he entered into a world of strange and exotic sea creatures arrayed in the most unusual hues and odd shapes. He felt that he was no longer in the pond, but in an outlandish ocean. Suddenly, he was faced with an immense, dark creature with untold hideous eyes that was about to consume him when he woke from his drug-induced slumber.

As he came out of the trance, Adriel could feel the lessening of euphoria and the rising of anxiety that was already working its power in his stupor during the encounter with the dark creature. He focused his eyes on the ceiling where, dancing and frolicking on its surface, were these same deep-sea inhabitants that he had seen in his dream. Eventually, they dissolved and the ceiling again became a desert, emptiness uninterrupted by anything whatsoever.

Adriel found his way home; he knew not how. The next morning he awoke, not sure where he was, a soon-passing amnesia. He realized that he was in the room he had rented.

The *Sea Wind* was now scheduled to depart in three days. Adriel planned to remain in Hong Kong when he returned there. His attractions to the new colony were opium and the young Chinese woman at *The Sign of the Dragon*.

CHAPTER THIRTY-SIX

RETURN TO HONG KONG

Ah, love, let us be true
To one another! For the world, which seems
To lie before us like a land of dreams,
So various, so beautiful, so new,
Hath really neither joy, nor love, nor light,
Nor certitude, nor peace, nor help for pain;
And we are here as on a darkling plain
Swept with confused alarms of struggle and flight,
Where ignorant armies clash by night.
– Dover Beach, Matthew Arnold

The day the *Sea Wind* sailed was an auspicious one. The sea was choppy; the sun was hot, but cooled by the sea breeze. The crew was in good spirits as the ship sailed down the Thames and entered the channel. They again wondered at the beauty of the cliffs of Dover, a symbol of England to so many people. Adriel also thought of the recently published poem of Matthew Arnold, *Dover Beach*, that laments the waning of faith.

As he performed his duties, Adriel looked across the water to the sturdy, white chalky face of the precipice that served as a welcome and farewell to London and fair England. *Dover Beach* spoke of a joyless world where old certitudes had passed away. His certainty had dissolved before tragedy and doubt. Did he yearn for days of yore when he would gaze up into the welkin and know that God was active in the world and would win the final victory? He longed for a life that made sense and had meaning. He, in fact, ached for the cohesiveness that comes from belief in God. Without Him all things shatter into little pieces, sharp fragments of despair. Adriel's life was headed for greater and greater fragmentation. Before long, nothing of earlier spiritual certainty and aspirations would be left in his heart and mind. Unlike some others, he didn't exalt in this age of disbelief. Accompanied by tears, he despaired of the age of faith like so many Romantic poets and other writers. Alcohol and opium provided some meager compensation for the loss.

As he stood on deck, looking up at the canopy of heaven, Adriel saw a falcon soaring high above. With the help of a spy glass that he had bought in London, he took a closer look at the bird. It was a peregrine falcon with its dark eyes, blue-gray back, and white underside. He recalled his encounter with Pontiac Rowbottom, who leaned on his walking stick with the brass falcon atop. Pontiac was a wanderer, so was the falcon, and so was Adriel. The falcon had more purpose than Pontiac and Adriel in their wanderings.

The peregrine falcon has very acute eyesight. It can see a long distance, a good representation of the visionary that can see things many cannot see. Adriel was a sort of godless visionary. Especially in the induced-by-opium state, he saw things, but not that convinced him of heaven; but, more likely, to point him to hell. He had again met up with Dante in the poet's turning to him as Adriel followed him and his guide, Virgil, through the precincts of hell.

Again the Cape, again the Indian Ocean, and again they arrived in India to load opium, the wonder drug of calm and imagination. British India again serves as mother to all of those nurslings of *dopium*. This shipment would find a home among the millions of imperial China.

The imperial Chinese flag with its blue, five-clawed dragon

on the yellow field is symbolic of power. The banner was an irony; for, China in the nineteenth century was beset by rebellion, European incursion, and opium addiction. It was weak, not strong. It was a nation on the path of invasion and sedation.

Adriel lived in the midst of this decline and knew from inside some of the suffering of the Celestial Empire to which he contributed. For him there existed the contradiction of sympathy and antagonism. He was now returning to this place, though actually to the British possession of Hong Kong, where he would live for some time and come closer to destruction.

The *Sea Wind* was passing through the Malacca Strait between Malaysia and Sumatra, drawing nearer to Hong Kong as it entered the South China Sea. It was in the strait that the boatswain, Giles Collicott, died of what the ship's surgeon diagnosed as a heart attack.

Giles' body was committed to the depths of the sea. The men, who greatly respected Giles, soberly attended to the funeral rites. The Service was given from the 1662 *Book of Common Prayer*. The chaplain read from Psalm 90 that reminded the congregation that humans are grass that quickly withers; but, God is everlasting. Then the priest recited the prayer of committal: "We therefore commit his body to the deep, to be turned into corruption, looking for the resurrection of the body—when the sea shall give up her dead—and the life of the world to come, through our Lord Jesus Christ, who at his coming shall change our vile body, that it may be like his glorious body, according to the mighty working whereby he is able to subdue all things to himself." The boatswain then was cast into the sea wrapped in canvas and weighted, the Union Jack left behind. Silence enveloped the ship as the men remembered a fine man and leader. He wouldn't be forgotten.

Adriel had a special reason to honor Giles. In Calcutta he was on an opium trip when Giles burst into the opium den to bring him back to the ship that was about to leave port.

Giles had gotten special permission from the captain to do so. Fortunately, Giles knew where Adriel was doing his smoking.

"Come on, Adriel, the *Sea Wind* is about to depart to China."

"We're going to China?" Adriel responded.

"Yes, that's our intention, and you need to be on board, or you're in for a lot of trouble."

"I don't think I'll make it."

"You're going to have to, mate."

Giles pulled Adriel off the mattress and struggled with him to keep him on his feet back to the vessel. The other smokers, if they were alert enough, were amused. Adriel's opium pipe was left behind in the establishment where he had been smoking—an object of veneration for another smoker.

When the two men arrived, the crew was about to weigh anchor. The appearance of the two caused laughter among the mates and a grunt of disapproval from the captain. Adriel received extra duty on the way to Hong Kong. Though a good seaman, because of his failing, he had to endure for a while the snickers of the crew.

CHAPTER THIRTY-SEVEN

THE SIGN OF THE DRAGON

*Oh, just, subtle, and powerful opium! That to the hearts of nega-
tive and wealthy alike, for the wounds with a purpose to in no way
heal, and for "the pangs that tempt the spirit to rebellion," bringest
an alleviating balm; eloquent opium! That with thy mighty rheto-
ric stealest away the purposes of wrath; and to the guilty man for
one night time givest again the hopes of his adolescence, and hands
washed natural from blood; and to the proud guy a brief oblivion for
Wrongs undress'd and insults unavenged . . .*
– Confessions of an English Opium-Eater, *Thomas De Quincey.*

Adriel was counting every day to their arrival in Hong Kong.
His addiction was developing so that it was becoming harder
to go without. During his last trip on the *Sea Wind*, he was
restless at night and discontent and jittery during the day,
though he performed his duties well. He possessed some laudanum to get him through.

When the ship docked, Adriel took leave of the *Sea Wind*
for the last time, informing the captain that he no longer
desired to serve aboard her. He would find a job in Hong Kong
as a stevedore on the docks.

Adriel found the same room in Hong Kong that he had
rented before. That same day he was hired on the docks and
immediately began work. At the end of the day, he walked
over to *The Sign of the Dragon*, first to discover whether *Meinu*
was still in residence with her parents.

Adriel's infatuation had not cooled during the long months

at sea. He thought much of the beautiful young woman who served her parents in one of the opium dens of Hong Kong. The fact was that he knew little about her; but, he was determined to get to know her. He had not been in love since the death of Abigail. His fare had been the prostitutes in the various ports where the *Sea Wind* docked. With *Meinu* he would declare his love. He thought nothing of the marriage practices of the Chinese or any of the barriers that might exist for him.

Adriel thought that he had changed very much during the months he had been involved in the China trade—more independent, able to manage his affairs in a competent way, and successful in his being on his own. Though he had been away from home during the War and then on the canal, it was only now he felt confidence. He was a world traveler, earning his own way as a crew member of a great clipper.

Adriel didn't take notice of the fact that he was becoming more dependent on opium. While he managed long periods with very little of it, as was the case when he was at sea, he thought obsessively about it on his return to Hong Kong. The smoking began in Hong Kong, continued in London, and now would be a part of his life's purpose again in Hong Kong. He intended to remain close to a source of supply. At sea it was almost impossible to engage in the practice of smoking it. In the colony, where the supply was sure, opium would become a virulent addiction. Already, he had spent a good portion of what he earned on this "Chinese tobacco," but managed always to pay his bills. When he returned to the colony, he would buy a new "dream stick." He left his pipe behind in Calcutta in the bustle of getting back on the ship. It was to be seen whether or not he would succeed in remaining financially solvent.

Opium, for Adriel, was a replacement for God, though nothing near equivalence is possible. The true God is constructive; opium, a false god, is destructive. Shattered fragments were all that remained of Adriel's youthful faith in God. What was important to him as a child and youth had become, in most part, a memory of an Adriel he no longer knew well. He felt no need for a God who had failed him. Abigail was dead. Michael was dead. Caleb was dead. The suffering he and many others had experienced in the War, he was not able to reconcile with a belief in God. God was a useless concept that he had put aside, placing Him on the edges of his life where He could do no harm (except God can't be marginalized). God may or may not exist. Adriel became indifferent to deciding which. His moral behavior had slipped greatly, but enough remained that he was seen as a reliable companion among his shipmates. His frolic with prostitutes and his opium smoking and alcohol drinking didn't stand out among the crewmen, many of whom engaged in the same things. Only at Calcutta did he attract snickers from the men because of his nearly missing the departure of the *Sea Wind*. He had not descended into criminality, or at least not yet. So far, he was able to come up with the money to feed his habit, but with nothing to spare.

Opium is a very hard master. It is a god without mercy. It requires a believer's full devotion. All other gods must serve this supreme idol. If a devotee fails in his service to the god, opium will strike back, inflicting a special sort of physical illness due to withdrawal. Feeding the god causes a terrible spiritual malady that works its darkness in the depths of mind and soul and also produces physical affliction that can eventually kill the user.

It was on the second day of his arrival in Hong Kong that Adriel patronized the opium den. He stood outside the establishment for several minutes before deciding that he was prepared to enter. His heart was beating fast in anticipation of meeting *Meinu*. Adriel was approached by the mistress of the establishment, who showed him to a mattress where he would smoke. With him he had his brand new pipe. He stealthily looked about for *Meinu*. "She is not here," was her mother's response to Adriel's casual inquiry. He had to swallow his disappointment so that he didn't reveal it to her mother.

Adriel would come another day to introduce himself. What he knew about the family was nothing. He had been to the den twice before. What he would find out is that the name of the young woman was Meili, remarkable in that his name for her, *Meinu*, meaning beauty, is related to her actual name, meaning beautiful. She was Cheung Meili, born in Hong Kong to natives of the island. Her father, Cheung Yun, had been a fisherman, a profession pursued by generations of his ancestors, before he decided to open an opium den, much more profitable than his inherited calling. Yun was an astute merchant, expanding into other business concerns in the community and participating in the opium trade itself. Her mother also, whose given name was Ting, was a native of the island. The couple had not been far from their home during their twenty years of marriage except for the occasion when Yun was a crewman on one trip by boat on the Grand Canal to Beijing to deliver goods for a friend of his father's.

Hong Kong was a sparsely settled island of the Chinese Empire. After the Chinese loss to the British in the First Opium War, Hong Kong became a colony according to the terms of the Treaty of Nanking. In 1860, when Meili was eleven years old, Yun invested some small savings in an establishment of the colony. Like many people involved in the opium trade, he justified his participation with the thinnest rationale. He convinced himself that people wanted to smoke, that the drug was not harmful, that it had beneficial uses, and that it had been a Chinese habit for a long time, especially among the upper class.

Yun had his rationale ready at hand if challenged. He involved not only his wife and daughter, but also three sons. Meili worked every day in the den. She herself had not partaken of the drug.

After work the next day, Adriel went to the den. On this occasion Meili was helping her parents with the many customers. Meili's mother showed him to a spot where he could smoke. The mattresses were placed on wooden structures set off the ground. A fellow smoker on the same platform as Adriel had fallen sound asleep. Adriel found his place, bought his opium, and arranged the items that Ting brought to him on a platter. As he began smoking, he looked for Meili, who happened not to be in the den at the moment. Soon after, she reappeared from a doorway in the back of the large room.

In his drug-induced state, Adriel furtively watched Meili seated playing the pipa, a Chinese lute, held vertically and singing a traditional Chinese song, words Adriel couldn't make out. Even if he could, he didn't speak or understand Chinese. Meili's voice was beautiful, as she was beautiful. Every once in a while, she looked at him with a smile.

Adriel put his pipe down and fell asleep. In his dream, Meili and he were walking hand in hand in a garden. The sky was blue. The pond was green with lily pads and also with colorful flowers on them. The buildings were in an elegant and monumental style. The statuary was of the finest quality, especially the rearing dragons with fearsome aspects. If Adriel had ever seen the old Summer Palace in Beijing before it was destroyed by the British, he would have said that much of his dream took place there.

The sky was deep blue; the garden was a rich green. The landscape was so lovely that Adriel gasped in his sleep. Lovelier yet was Meili, who was wearing a full length, red, silken dress with lotus flowers from neck to ankles, holding a fan in her hand. In the midst of the garden, she joined other women in a traditional Chinese dance attended by the playing of the pipa. It was a magnificent Chinese artistic rendering.

Adriel woke up after darkness had fallen. His companion had left the establishment. Meili came over to him to inquire of his needs. Her English was nearly perfect; for, she had gone to a good British school in Hong Kong that her parents could well afford. Her Chinese education was supplemented by a tutor, who, among many other things, taught his talented student the art of Chinese calligraphy.

"Mr. Peregrine, are you in need of anything?"

Drowsily, Ariel responded, "No, I'm fine." It was the first time Ariel had spoken directly with Meili. He was somewhat caught off-guard. He recovered to ask, "What time of day is it?"

"It's nine o'clock in the evening. You've been here for many hours."

"I must get home. I'll return tomorrow." Adriel stood up, but was unsteady on his feet. When Meili took him by the arm to steady him, he looked at her with gratitude for her kindness and with wonder that they had met. He stumbled to the front door. He treasured the touch of Meili's hands on his arm.

"Don't you want to stay a little longer?"

"No, I'll be all right," he said with little confidence. Adriel wandered home, arriving there an hour later. He fell into bed and dreamed of the paper dragon dance, an ancient practice of the Chinese that was believed to bring good luck, but not for Adriel in his growing habit. The paper dragon, along with the human dancers, turned into a real fire-breather, missing him only because he was able to leap out of the way. The beast chased him over a bizarre landscape reminiscent of "The Triumph of Death" by Pieter Bruegel, the Elder. He didn't know if in the future he would be able to avoid the fire, otherwise known as opium.

CHAPTER THIRTY-EIGHT

UNREQUITED LOVE

I live upstream and you downstream,
From night to night of you I dream.
Unlike the stream you're not in view,
Though we both drink from River Blue.
When will the water no more flow?
When will my grief no longer grow?
I wish your heart would be like mine,
Then not in vain for you I pine.

– Li Zhiyi, Song of Divination

Feeling ashamed of his behavior, all the next day Adriel thought of what transpired in the opium den the night before. He resolved to return to the den that night but to smoke less. Adriel knew that Meili had seen the odd behavior of smokers many times, though this thought provided no consolation to him.

The day went torturously slow. Adriel was tired and had gotten a tongue lashing from the foreman for being late. When the day was over, he dragged himself home and fell into bed, not waking until early the next morning. He was disappointed at missing his intended visit to the opium den.

The next day was also torturously slow; because, Adriel anticipated a visit to *The Sign of the Dragon*. He barely remembered what he did that day, for his mind was on other things.

Adriel had fallen in love with a Chinese. He didn't even know her. She could be painted skin as in the story by Pu

Songling, a demon in disguise. He knew in his heart that his feelings on these matters of love were probably immature; but, he didn't care.

Adriel arrived at *The Dragon* early in the evening. Yun was there with several assistants, serving a large crowd. When he entered, he could only hear a murmur among the guests, though the room was full of people. Many were in a stupor; some were whispering to their neighbors. As he entered, eyes turned to him and then turned away. Everyone was inspected as they entered to determine whether friend, enemy, or neither.

Adriel was led to a spot next to an American sailor. With a face filled with a sort of ecstasy, the seaman ignored Adriel, finding his pipe to be enough converse for him. Again, Adriel engaged in *da yen*, the "Big Smoke," but more cautiously than before, using his own "smoking pistol" or *Yen Tsiang* or opium pipe that he acquired after his return to Hong Kong. Though he had smoked less, Adriel was in a drug-induced reverie, less intense than the previous visit.

Adriel's dream began with a vision of a beautiful green meadow encircled by lush hills with grazing sheep. In the distance he saw a shepherd who, to his squinting eyes, looked like Jesus with a crook in his hand. His heart was full of peace and joy. He felt a soft breeze on his face with the faint smell of frankincense on its breath. He then heard the congregation of Saint Jude Thaddeus at Morning Prayer, singing the 100th Psalm using Anglican chant. He envisioned himself standing between his mother and father in the pew they always occupied during services, his mother holding his hand and bearing the Prayer Book in the other. He was a small child. The rector in his cassock, surplice, and tippet was standing in a pew of the choir, holding his Prayer Book and singing with a strong, delightful voice. Adriel looked over at a stained glass window with Christ the Shepherd standing with his crook among the sheep and holding a lamb in his arm. The sun shone through the window, making bright the rich colors of red, blue, and green. The white of Christ's robe glowed with a special brilliance. The white of the sheep matched the Lord's tunic.

The vision faded and what succeeded was a scene in hell—that recurrent scene of Adriel's walking behind Dante and Virgil. Dante turned to him and said, "Where would you like to be, here or elsewhere?" Adriel didn't answer. Then he was awake. Nothing much had changed except that his neighbor was no longer there.

Adriel looked around the room. Meili was not there. He would have to come another day, and he would be ever hopeful that he might have an opportunity to introduce himself to the beautiful one.

The next day was Sunday. Adriel decided to walk around Hong Kong to become more familiar with the city. He went down to Victoria Harbour to begin his tour. Ships filled the harbor, their masts with furled sails, appearing as a city of incomplete buildings. The dock was quiet early on the Lord's Day. Some early risers were strolling along the waterfront, among them being the Cheung family. Meili was walking between her mother and father. She was the first to catch sight of Adriel. A smile came to her lips. Adriel returned her smile with his own.

"It's good to see you on such a fine Sunday," were Adriel's first words as the parents nodded silently in recognition of his presence. He felt awkward in the presence of Meili, but held his own in the conversation.

"It's a pleasant day and pleasant to meet you here. I suppose you're getting to know Hong Kong," Meili said in her musical voice.

Adriel responded, "Yes, I've just gotten back from a voyage to England and India. I want to settle here for a while."

Yun and Ting were silent as Meili replied, "That's delightful." The parents were protective of their daughter, who was engaged to marry a young Chinese of Hong Kong, a fact unknown to Adriel. As was mostly the case, the marriage was an arrangement of the parents. They wished no intruder into the arrangement. Perceptive, especially when it came to his daughter, Ting saw in Adriel a possible rival suitor. Being also perceptive, it wasn't hard for Adriel to detect suspicion toward him. He didn't think that he had revealed his interest in Meili; but, the face often shows what one is not aware of manifesting. Maybe Ting noticed Adriel's watching with interest Meili perform her duties in the opium den. However unobtrusive, a person can expose much that one is not aware of.

"You'll like Hong Kong, I think," Meili answered. Yun took Meili by the arm as a sign that it was time to go.

Meili, an obedient child, said to Adriel, "Would you like to walk with us?"

Hesitant because of the parents' coolness, Adriel at first didn't respond. Then, he said, "I'd love to; but, I must follow my itinerary so that I can get around better. Thank you for the invitation." Adriel's lame excuse was meant to hide his anxiety at the thought of accompanying the family.

They parted; but, as Adriel took his several hour tour, he could think of nothing but his brief conversation with the Cheungs. Did he make a fool of himself? Of course, he didn't; but, when the stakes are high, that is, the affection of Meili, he could think of himself as acting like a fool without at all acting like one.

In Adriel's eyes, Meili was polite but remote. Adriel had no idea how much or little she loved her husband to be, not that this mattered in an arranged marriage. He regarded her as a sweet flower, beautiful to the eyes and fragrant as osmanthus. He loved her from afar without knowing her, as Petrarch with Laura and Dante with Beatrice.

CHAPTER THIRTY-NINE

THE DRAGON IN THE CHALICE

In the beginning was the Word, and the Word was with God, and the Word was God.
                                        – John 1:1 ESV

So Jacob called the name of the place Peniel, saying, 'For I have seen God face to face, and yet my life has been delivered.
                                        – Genesis 32:30 ESV

The feelings which make a man call an object sublime are not sublime feelings but feelings of veneration.
                                        – C.S. Lewis, The Abolition of Man

Adriel continued his tour after meeting up with the Cheung family. On Garden Road, he came to the Anglican Cathedral of Saint John the Evangelist. When he had been in Philadelphia, he couldn't resist entering Christ Church on a Sunday. The same was true in Hong Kong with the cathedral. When he entered the building, the congregation was worshipping. He took a back pew and did not join in, but sat, knelt, and stood when the congregation did. His was an aesthetic appreciation. He enjoyed the visual art, the music, and the words without believing what they meant and proclaimed.

As the service proceeded, Adriel took in aspects of the magnificent holy place. The walls were white. The woodwork of pews, pulpit, lectern, and other furnishings in their dark finish contrasted with the walls. The stained glass behind the altar was splendid in its many beautiful hues, representing the crucifixion of Christ with the Virgin Mary and Saint John standing under the cross as described in the Gospel of Saint John. "It is finished," Christ said before he died, according to the account in this Gospel. He had completed his work that would bring salvation to the people of the world.

Despite his agnosticism, Adriel knew joy in his heart and mind because of the surroundings. He detected in himself a feeling of exaltation at the sublime environment he found himself in, as he did during his long walks back home. Can one know the sublime without believing in God? The sublime can be known to some extent without a firm belief in God, or, more specifically, in the Trinitarian God of the Holy Scriptures. A mountain or waterfall or beautiful sunset or the appointments of a church can draw an individual, no matter what his belief, into ecstasy or terror or both. The experience is all the richer and truer when one realizes that the sublime is a representation of the highest order of being—the Lord God who can cause terror or joy, perhaps even both at the same time.

After the service, the dean allowed Adriel to make a closer inspection of the stained glass windows, including those in the chancel. Among the windows was one of Saint John the Evangelist holding a chalice with a dragon coming up out of it, representing poison in the cup.

The window represents an old legend, told by Jacobus de Voragine in his *Golden Legend*, of John's being tested by the priest of Diana in Ephesus. If John would drink from a cup of poison and live, the priest would become a Christian. First, Aristodemus, the priest, gave the poison to two condemned criminals who died after they partook of it. John then drank and lived and also brought to life the two dead criminals. The result was that Aristodemus became a Christian and later a bishop.

Among others, the Spanish painter Alonso Cano depicted John holding the poisoned drink in the chalice. John is looking down at the chalice held in his left hand containing the threatening dragon arising from the cup, while with his right hand he is in the act of blessing it, thus neutralizing the poison.

In another window of the cathedral, John bears pen and book, representing his authorship of the Gospel, with an eagle standing next to him, the primary symbol of the evangelist. The brass lectern of the cathedral represents the Word of God delivered to the people, shown in the symbol of an eagle, the very symbol of Saint John. In the legend, the apostle remarks that the eagle flies highest of all the birds; thus, it has the best view of the sun. Saint John's Gospel soars to the greatest visionary height. The tradition is that John also wrote Revelation that narrates a vision of heaven from the throne room of God and what was soon to take place with the coming of Christ.

In the afternoon Adriel returned to the rock where he had met Leung Yang Xiuqing. He listened for a rustle in the grass, and then looked out over Victoria Harbour at the motley collection of vessels. He thought to himself that he would one day build a sampan with a sail, emblazoned with a dragon on it, to while away hours in the harbor, dreaming of the sky and sea and a ship laden with the treasures of human love. Meili would be traveling with him; she would be the most valuable treasure.

CHAPTER FORTY

THE NEXT DAY

An opium smoker am I.
Why don't you give it a try?
— Adriel in a tongue-in-cheek cynical mood

On that Sunday, Adriel never made it to *The Sign of the Dragon*. Instead, he partook of a few drinks alone at a tavern not far from his room. He felt an intense loneliness like he had never felt before. He lacked the company of shipmates he left behind when he forsook the *Sea Wind*. Far from home and almost completely alone in his wanderings, he felt an oppression that drove him further into addiction. Off hours, if he was not in a tavern, he was in an opium den, that is, *The Sign of the Dragon*. His dragon was not one of good fortune, but one of curse. Its hot breath had not yet consumed him, but it did singe him.

The sun was very hot in the desert where shade was as precious as gold. He wandered alone, attempting to fend off demons that had been assailing him since the War. He was an anchorite of a merciless religion, that is, no religion at all.

But, if one were to relent in this judgment a bit and take a broader view of religion, one could say that Adriel's faith consisted of a worship of beauty. When Adriel beheld fair scenes of land or sea, he would imagine that he breathed in what he saw into his heart and soul and let it reside there for his spiritual nourishment. Even one who has no confidence in the existence of God requires some sustenance for the spiritual aspect of his being. Rather, one must be aware that the spiritual in the human is not an aspect but the very ground and foundation of his existence.

Adriel's religion had become idolatry, a worship of the creature rather than the Creator. It was not pantheism that described his belief. For it to be pantheism, Adriel would have to have a definite conception of God. What he believed about God was that he had no certainty of His existence. His belief was one that rested its confidence in beauty. "Ah, such a beautiful painting." And that's where it begins and ends. He was of the congregation of worshippers known as aesthetes. *Objets d'art* were gods, not symbols pointing to the true God. They were idols coming from the hand of humanity, worshipped but not worthy of such esteem. The wise man says, "But that which is made with hands is cursed, as well it, as he that made it: he, because he made it, and it, because, being corruptible, it was called god." (Wisdom of Solomon 14:8 KJV) For beauty to be true to itself, it must be a servant of the one and only God.

Adriel's spirituality was a sort of polytheism, with opium as the supreme deity and beautiful objects of the world as representing the host of other gods.

The next morning, Adriel awoke early to the first stirrings on the street below. He threw on his clothes and set out to get an early breakfast before work. He stopped at a little shop for a bowl of chow mein with bean sprouts, cabbage, carrots and a few pieces of chicken. He stood there as he consumed his rich Chinese meal.

After a walk around Government House, Adriel went off to his day of work at the docks. His labor was grueling, involving the lifting and moving of goods onto or off the docked ships; but, it provided adequate compensation, an inordinate portion of which went to Adriel's habits. He managed to pay his rent and eat, but barely.

That day, Adriel often watched the sun out of the corner of his eye; because, he was anxious to spend the evening at *The Sign of the Dragon*. Once in a while he checked his pocket watch. He would skip dinner and hurry to the place where he could smoke *chandu*, opium for smoking, to chase troubles away and befriend those around him. His recreation was largely what was called "chasing the dragon." Food and tea were also offered to the customers. He hoped to be served by Meili.

When Adriel arrived at the den, he was greeted by Ting, who showed him a place to recline and provided all the essentials for the smoke except the pipe. As was her habit, she fussed about this or that in both English and Cantonese. His companion lying next to him was an interesting sort. He appeared to be Chinese. Adriel noticed that his hands were rough from work. Wrinkles formed a road map on his face that revealed age, care, and sorrow. The man had a resemblance to the one he saw on the heights above Hong Kong. Adriel nodded to him, not knowing if he knew any English. He could speak a few words of the Cantonese dialect, but only enough to order food, say hello and good-bye, and express displeasure in slang.

Adriel prepared his pipe and began his smoke. His companion was watching Adriel take his first puffs, while he was taking some of his own. Both men looked reflective as they drew on their pipes. Both would soon be in the cloud that is opium.

The man said to him, "You seem very much to enjoy this pastime. I too am one who appreciates such finer things."

Adriel hesitated as amazement came over him that the man's English was so good and his hands were so rough. He had the hands of a peasant, but the speech of a cultivated individual. "Yes, I get comfort from the smoke." A multitude of thoughts raced through Adriel's mind as he tried to explain to himself the incongruity he perceived.

"So do I. I've seen a lot and for a brief time want to forget."

Adriel decided to probe for the man's story. "I'm Adriel

Peregrine." Adriel paused to allow his smoking companion to give his name. The man said nothing, so Adriel asked, "What is your name?"

The man looked at Adriel and said, "Qing."

Adriel immediately thought of the man he met in the hills above Hong Kong, whose given name was Xiuqing. A very unsettled feeling came over Adriel. The man's physical appearance bore some likeness to the one whom he encountered in the hills of Hong Kong. But, his good English seemed to belie peasant origins.

Qing explained that he had fought in the Taiping army and fled to Hong Kong at its defeat, just as did the mysterious stranger he and Bill Yarrow met in the hills above Hong Kong. He now worked as a gardener for a British family that lived in town.

Qing was cautious in how much of himself he revealed. He feared that imperial officials were after him. He had been a commander in the Taiping army. Many Chinese were killed during the almost fifteen year conflict. He was attempting to avoid adding to the statistics. In his flight he lost contact with his mother, father, brothers, and sisters. His wife had died in childbirth; his children were either dead or scattered. He had worked a prosperous farm in Jiangxi Province and studied for the civil service exam that he had no opportunity to take in the tumultuous events in his home province.

"I spend my days working and my evenings smoking. You'll find me here most days. The pipe takes the edge off my anxiety and apprehension. My employer doesn't mind; in fact, he has made much money in the opium trade," commented Qing.

Silence fell on the two as they continued contentedly to smoke. Meili came into the den to assist customers. While conversing with Qing, he attempted to keep sight of her without seeming disinterested in his partner in the smoke or attracting Ting's notice.

"Until recently I served on a ship that was involved in the

trade. I've smoked opium here, in London, and in Calcutta, and will probably do the same on some other continent," Adriel said with a smirk.

"I see no better substitute for cares and worries. I didn't smoke it when I was in the Taiping army; for, it was greatly discouraged. When I arrived here, I took up the habit."

Meili got closer to where Adriel was smoking. He anticipated her inquiring on whether he or Qing needed assistance. The moment came. "Do you gentlemen require anything at present?"

Qing took the pipe out of his mouth to say, "I'm fine, thank you." Qing observed the two as he drew on his pipe.

"May I speak with you later?" Adriel was almost as surprised he said it as Meili was to hear it, though what Adriel didn't know was that she had some interest in him despite her commitment to another man through family arrangement.

"We can't here." Her parents kept a close eye on their young marriage-age daughter. Commitments had been made, and they planned to have them fulfilled.

"On Sunday, meet me at Government House at noon."

"I'll try. It will be hard to get away, but I'll try." Meili then slipped away. Adriel looked at Qing, whose face had gone from smirk to smile.

"I love her and don't even know her. What do you think of that?"

"Not strange for most young men. It may even apply to young women. Appearance is everything. If they are thinking at all, they believe the heart is reflected accurately in the appearance. Young ones don't have a knack for plumbing the depths of a personality. Your love will be put to the test. You'll learn soon whether, in this instance, love proves true."

CHAPTER FORTY-ONE

THAT EXTRAORDINARY SUNDAY

Adriel woke very early on that Sunday morning before the sun rose over the placid ocean to shine on the not-so-placid British colony of Hong Kong. It seemed a dream that Meili was willing to meet him. In the early hours before he got up, he speculated about why she was so interested. Was she discontent with the marriage arrangement that could not be far from being fulfilled? Did she want to escape the restrictive life she was living in her family, and what would be the case with her new husband? Did she seek an adventure with a young man from the West? He didn't know; but, he would find out. He did know from observation that her parents kept a close watch on her and that, at least in public, she had great respect for them. But, his fixed regard was of a limited nature; he knew only what he learned in the opium den.

Adriel had a great deal of time before his meeting with

Meili, so he spent time walking around town. He was nervous about the meeting and feared she would be waylaid by her parents so that they wouldn't meet at all. He'd make certain that he was not late for the agreed upon time of noon. Meili's family traditionally took a walk on Sunday morning. Adriel kept a sharp eye out for them in fear that he'd encounter them.

Adriel looked out over the harbor at the bustle of ships—sampans, junks, and European clippers and steamers. He turned his head toward the highest point on the island called *The Peak*. It looked so serene from where he was standing; but, not far from there, he had seen or imagined a man jumping to his death. Few places close to human habitation provide quiet and rest for the human traveler. He understood the desire of old Hindus who wished to escape to the forest. In his young adulthood, he experienced a wonderful tranquility when he walked the fields and forests of his home in central Pennsylvania. How he longed for the peace of such a place as he had known. And yet, he felt compelled to continue his wandering in order to forget the War and the tragedies he had already known as a young person. Opium smoking was added to help in his forgetting.

Would Meili be willing to roam with him? His smoking couldn't possibly repel her. She worked in the opium den of her parents. Yet, he was able to ask himself honestly if he would be a good husband as a drug and alcohol user. He rationalized that he would be able to do this.

With young heart and body, Adriel also wished to be in love. He didn't think much about the conflict between a life of wandering and married life. Ignoring this problem, he wished that Meili would be the fulfillment of his hope; but, he was apprehensive of the challenge of overcoming what would be parental opposition.

When Adriel checked his pocket watch, it was 11:30. Though it wouldn't take long, he decided to head toward Government

House. There he waited fifteen minutes beyond the hour, acceding to a deep misery. Then, as he was about to give in to despair, he saw her come toward him. She was wearing the traditional Hanfu dress, a white blouse and dark blue skirt. The blouse was decorated with red camellias that represent beauty to the Chinese. Her black hair fell down her back; her face was a vision of beauty, what seemed to Adriel to be without defect. What Adriel didn't see were her bound feet—practiced on girls during the Qing dynasty, especially in more affluent families. Small feet were regarded as beautiful. The painful binding of feet was seen as the way to attain this beautiful feature—a perverse thought!

Adriel walked toward Meili as she walked toward him. She hesitated for a moment, as if the moment was more than she had anticipated, and then hurried toward him. Adriel kissed her on the cheek. He took her hand and began to walk with her toward the harbor. It was remarkable that they were hand in hand despite the fact that they really had not yet become well-acquainted.

Adriel said to her, "I've been wanting to meet you for a while. Thanks for coming to me." They didn't have to introduce one another or give their names; because, they'd been aware of one another since Adriel settled down in Hong Kong.

"I too have felt the same. I've left the house without permission from my father. I hope he doesn't discover that I'm gone. I'll be severely punished. I'm already engaged to be married to someone."

"I don't mean to get you in trouble. I wish no harm to come to you."

"I had to take the risk to meet you."

"I'm glad you were willing to do so. I've thought of you much without knowing you well. I've engaged a sampan to tour the harbor so that we can talk for a while."

"This is good; but, I must be home in two hours, or my parents will surely discover my absence."

"It will be difficult for us to meet. Perhaps I should confront them with what we're doing."

"They wouldn't understand. They'd be very angry."

"Then when shall we meet again?"

"I don't know. I don't know what's possible in my situation. It'd be risky, yet again, I so much desired to meet you."

Meili's quandary caused Adriel some pain. He feared that this would be the first and last time they'd be with one another, except when Adriel visited the opium den.

In the harbor Adriel found his man and climbed into the sampan, helping Meili with his strong hand. They took seats under a tarp stretched above their heads to shield them against the sun. The owner of the boat propelled the boat with a *yuloh*, a single oar placed at the stern of the boat.

That day was resplendent with sunshine, giving a sheen to the surface of the water. The boatman weaved in and out of the many boats and ships anchored there. Then, the boat broke out into open water. Sampans would not stray too far from land, for they were not built for the deep beyond the sight of land. They typically hugged the land.

Adriel and Meili had much to say to each other in very little time. They told each other about their lives and their hopes. Meili wished to flee the life of a traditional Chinese woman; Adriel wished for a companion and wife, as Meili wished for a husband, but not the one chosen for her.

While they spoke to one another, Meili willingly allowed Adriel to hold her hand. All the while Adriel's heart was thumping in his throat.

As the boat returned to its anchor, Adriel asked, "When can we meet again?"

"I don't know. I'll speak to you again when you come to the opium den."

"I'll be there tomorrow," Adriel responded.

When they returned to the dock, Adriel escorted Meili as close as he deemed safe to Meili's residence. Fearing that someone from the family may be watching, neither Meili nor Adriel kissed the other there. At the time they had disembarked Meili kissed Adriel on the cheek, knowing that it would be indiscreet near home. Adriel watched from a distance as Meili slipped into a narrow passageway that led to the family apartment behind the opium den. Before she vanished into the house, she looked back at him.

CHAPTER FORTY-TWO

A CLASH OF TRADITIONS

The face is the beacon fire of the human heart.   – Adriel Peregrine

No one obstructed Meili as she hurried to her room in the living quarters of her family. She didn't know if anyone detected her absence, but feared that she was already found out. She freshened up and made sure nothing on her person would give away her midday tryst.

Meili wasn't expected to help in the den until the next morning. That evening she joined her parents for dinner. If they knew anything, they didn't let on. But, Meili's brother looked at her with a knowing smile, as if he knew of Meili's defiance, at least her absence from home for hours. He, in fact, had seen her depart from the back door of the living quarters. He would not tell; for, one day he also wished to be unshackled from the rigid traditions of his ancestors, though for him, as one of male gender, the oppression was not nearly so weighty. He sympathized with Meili's plight.

The next day, Meili began work at the usual time, and Adriel arrived to smoke at the usual time. They watched each other out of the corner of the eye. Meili approached him a while after he arrived, so that she didn't seem too anxious to see him.

She whispered, "Where shall we meet, and when?"

He answered, "If you can again get away on Sunday, let's meet at the same place and at the same time."

"I'll try."

Meili's mother was watching the two as they spoke to one another. She didn't hear what they said, but suspected that something was going on that she would not approve of. Never before had such suspicions about Meili arisen in her heart. She resolved to keep a closer eye on her daughter so that she could stop any nonsense. The Cheungs wouldn't suffer shame as the result of silliness from a soon-to-be-married daughter to one with whose family arrangements had been made. The shrewd mother never gave the impression that she was closely observing the young people.

That next Sunday, the couple met at the same place in front of Government House and spent time in the harbor riding on a sampan. As the boat approached the opposite shore at Kowloon, Adriel placed his arm over Meili's shoulder. When she kissed him on the cheek, he turned to kiss her on the lips. It was an enchanted afternoon.

"I love you, Meili," said Adriel, an inexperienced enthusiast of love whose only other love was love at a distance. His time with prostitutes didn't count for romance.

"I love you too, Adriel; but, I fear that our growing love will end with separation. How can we go on? My parents will not approve and will be very angry."

"Perhaps we could flee from this place and start a new life elsewhere?"

"I love you very much," she said. Meili was conflicted about what to do.

"Please consider what I'm saying," Adriel beseechingly replied.

"I'll think about it. I'll have to decide soon, for my parents are going to discover my disobedience."

Adriel had no plans about where to go and what he would do to support both himself and Meili. Young romance often offers the distortion of extreme optimism that doesn't count the cost of love. They couldn't stay in Hong Kong—too many chances of encounter with the family and friends of the

Cheungs. Adriel thought that if they decided to marry, they would have to leave Hong Kong.

That night Meili again had dinner with her parents. What she didn't know was that Mrs. Cheung had discovered her absence from the house. Instead of berating her, Ting decided to continue to watch closely. Neither the mother nor the father asked a question or made a comment that would raise suspicion. Their faces showed no emotion that would reveal their mistrust of Meili. Meili's brother kept concentrating on his food, but couldn't help revealing in his face some of the awkwardness he felt, knowing what Meili had done.

Ting would wait for the next time. Mother and father would watch and watch and have someone follow their daughter. Then, they would set things straight so that the family's honor would not be compromised or the traditions broken. The ancestors would be proud. Meili would have to return to her senses and again show filial respect. Her obligation included marrying the man picked out for her through arrangement.

While Ting was the first to be suspicious, Yun would direct what they would do. Ting would exert her influence on her husband.

Meili tried very hard to act as if nothing was happening. Her face, though, showed discomfort that her parents noticed.

Adriel was back in his room writing poetry about his new love. Though the next day was one of hard work, he kept awake most of the night. Romance can add strength to the body and the soul.

These are the lines of a requited love.

Yellow Camellia
The camellia is a beautiful flower.
In its gilded petals, a subtle power,
Conveying the balm of healing love
Like that descending from heav'n above.

For the third time, Adriel and Meili met at Government House. They walked all over town, stopping only to get something to eat. As they sat at a table, they talked about their predicament.

"I'm not sure that they know what we're doing; but, they soon will, one way or another," Meili said with an expression of pain on her face.

"We must decide to leave Hong Kong," Adriel said with vehemence. Meili could read great disquiet in his voice.

"I love you, Adriel; but, I can't leave my family."

"I see no alternative; you go with me or stay here without me. Please, come with me. I'm not meaning to be cruel to your parents or anyone else; but, I know of no third way."

"I'll let you know my decision the next time we meet."

Adriel put his hand to Meili's cheek and stroked it. She shed tears at the possibility of losing him—salty tears that soaked his hand. In Meili's face, Adriel beheld the look of both pain and love, two things that most often go together between a man and a woman. Meili was torn between family and the love of a man.

CHAPTER FORTY-THREE

ADRIEL'S GREAT LOSS

Her mother and father had strong suspicions about Adriel and Meili. On the lookout, her mother assigned a house servant to follow her to find out what she was doing. He witnessed the two embracing and walking off toward the harbor. He trailed until the lovers arrived at the waterfront, and then he returned straightaway to report back.

Adriel and Meili had a wonderful time on the water. They talked and laughed, hugged and kissed. The boatman kept to his oar, acting as if he were alone in the boat, except for the smile on his face. He took the couple to Kowloon and back. At the end of the afternoon, they walked toward Meili's home, where the parents were waiting.

Gladsome was Adriel's smile. Since his childhood, he had not remembered being so happy. But, in his mind was also the thought of the possibility of loss. Meili could be taken from him by parents steeped in Chinese tradition. Yun and Ting would not allow their plans for their daughter to be undone. As Adriel walked Meili home, his happiness fell into the background, and his anxiety came to the fore.

With a kiss Adriel sent Meili back to her parents. He

watched her as she walked down the street to her parents' opium establishment and wondered if Meili and he could free themselves from this place. Adriel could think only of freeing Meili from her parents that would allow him to marry her; but, he put aside the problem of his addiction to the "dream-stick" and alcohol that would destroy both their lives.

Later that same day, Adriel decided to visit the opium den to have a smoke in an attempt to discover what may have happened when Meili arrived home. As he had done many times before, he entered the den to take a place on an opium mat, preferably where he habitually smoked. When he entered the room, he saw Ting at the very back. He waited much longer than usual to be served. Finally, Ting came up to him and looked him in the eye, very cross in her demeanor. With a broken opium pipe she had acquired in the back of the establishment, Ting suddenly began beating Adriel on the head. Adriel ran out of the building with Ting in pursuit, speaking in Cantonese. Adriel didn't stop until out of sight of Ting and the opium den.

Meili's parents knew of their tryst. After Meili returned from her meeting with Adriel, her parents locked Meili in her room after a sound verbal thrashing and a few blows. She was to marry him who was chosen for her.

Adriel contemplated rescuing Meili from her situation, but decided otherwise. By some reckless act, he could make her life miserable. He had little money and no permanent home. What did he really have to offer her? Nothing. He was beginning to think a little less about himself and more about her. With a surprising maturity, he decided to leave the colony without attempting to take her along. He wasn't sure that she would go with him anyhow. His heart was broken; his despair was deep. He wept and wept. What did he have but himself and a little money in his pocket for the time he spent in the opium trade and in Hong Kong on the wharves? Adriel again would take up his wandering, though he would head closer to home; in fact, he would pass near home to another part of the world.

Adriel descended from happiness to despair. After work he spent his time in another opium parlor and at various taverns around town. He thought of suicide, but backed away from doing the deed. He decided to return to America, so he bought a ticket on a steam vessel for San Francisco.

The day before he left for California, Adriel walked down the street where the opium parlor was located. He stood some distance from it for a long time. Only when the sun was setting did he return to his apartment, where he packed his things for the trip.

As Adriel lay in bed with the sounds of the street importuning his attention, he thought of his great loss with concentration and determination. He thought of Orpheus' loss of Eurydice and, in his dream, he imagined standing at the cave entrance bereft of his beloved. For him his deprivation was like the darkness and despair of the underworld. No one could have consoled him, nor did he have anyone to do such. He imagined that perhaps he would bump into Meili and gain her assent to go with him. They would cross the Pacific as a happily married couple. He looked for her every time he was on the street before his departure. She didn't appear.

CHAPTER FORTY-FOUR

TO YOKOHAMA

"It is a long way off, sir."
"From what, Jane?"
"From England and from Thornfield: and ____"
"Well?"
"From you, sir."

— Charlotte Brontë, *Jane Eyre*

On the morning of his departure from Hong Kong, Adriel rose early. He placed the final items in the one bag he was taking. Laudanum and his opium pipe were also included. All the rest of what he possessed, he had given away. Dressed in his best clothes, he ventured out for breakfast and one last view of his beloved's home. The steamer was leaving port at 1:00 P.M.

After breakfast, Adriel wandered over to the street where the opium den was located. He stood at an intersection and observed intently the front of the establishment so that he lost track of time. When he looked at his pocket watch that came with him in his travels from his days on the canal, he realized that the time was drawing nigh for him to board the steamer.

With a heart heavy with sorrow for losing Meili and regret that he didn't try harder to gain her as his wife, he walked toward the harbor where he would board ship—an iron hulled propeller-driven steamer with sails named the *S.S. Lewis and Clark*. The S.S. abbreviation represented "Screw Steamer," meaning that the mode of propulsion of the ship was a pro-peller driven by steam, a new technology that changed travel on the high seas.

Adriel almost missed the *Lewis and Clark*. He ran out of breath to the ship, where he was informed of the location of his sleeping quarters in steerage on the lower deck. When he got there, he beheld bunk beds lined up in a large area. Until he reached land, any privacy needs Adriel had would have to take a back seat. He had been at sea often during his wan-derings and, thus, was not surprised at the accommodations for third-class passengers. The same as other crew during his travels, he had slept in a hammock in the fo'c's'le, or forecas-tle, the raised upper deck before the foremast. He cast his old haversack on his bed and then returned to the deck as the ship was leaving the harbor.

Adriel said his farewell to Hong Kong from the passenger deck. What he didn't know was that Meili was on shore sur-veying the ships in the harbor, lamenting his departure from Hong Kong. She didn't know what ship he would leave on or when exactly he would leave; but, she knew that he would soon be gone from the colony and her life. Perhaps he was already well on his way across the Pacific. She was saying her own farewell to her love whom she would never see again. Tears streamed down her cheeks. Her heart was broken in two.

Meili hired a sampan whose oarsman took her into the middle of the harbor on the way to Kowloon, where she jumped out into the water and disappeared to the protests of the boatman who had no chance of rescuing her. Later that day, her body was retrieved on shore by some British sail-ors who reported her death to the colonial government. The day following, her parents, inquiring of the police about their missing daughter, were told of her death by drowning.

Meili was lamented by her parents, family, and friends. They blamed Adriel for all the misery they felt. He was the demon who took life from their daughter. Adriel felt the grief of separation but not of loss in death. He stood on deck looking out over the sea, oblivious of the tragic conclusion of their relationship. Adriel would never know of her suicide.

That night as the *Lewis and Clark* made its way to Yokohama, Adriel dreamt of walking alone through a bamboo forest like he had seen in Guangdong, the province that borders Hong Kong. Light from the sun pierced here and there through the thickness. He approached a beautiful Chinese lacquer table set at the side of the path with the appointments for opium smoking, including a bamboo opium pipe that looked much like his. Suddenly, a young woman with looks similar to Meili came out of the forest and handed him the pipe. Not knowing whether her smile was unfriendly or friendly, he took the pipe from her hand. She disappeared back into the forest. He asked himself what never occurred to him before, was Meili aware of the dangers of his addiction, or didn't she think or know of the possible consequences of his habit? It was hard for him to believe that she was completely unaware of the possible consequences with all the time she had spent in her parents' establishment. Was she the demon hidden under the beauty of a young woman? He shuddered and denied the possibility. In any case, her concern would have made no difference to Adriel's usage of the drug.

Adriel had taken with him on board his pipe and laudanum. No privacy existed for steerage passengers, making it difficult for Adriel to smoke, so he made sure he had a substitute.

Some Chinese passengers were on board, seeking employment in the United States. Like their compatriots who also had traveled across the ocean on a ship, they were fleeing war—the Taiping Rebellion had taken a heavy toll—and poverty. Many Chinese had been employed in the California gold rush and the construction of the transcontinental railroad that began operation in May 1869. Adriel would be buying a train ticket to cross America on the very same line from Sacramento to

Omaha, Nebraska, from its beginning to its end, then beyond by train to New York City, where he would seek employment on one of the passenger steamship lines to England.

As was often the case when Adriel was traveling by ocean craft, whether clipper or steam ship, he would spend much time on deck looking out over the vast expanse. He thought of Odysseus wandering for ten years before arriving at home. He thought of himself wandering and wandering, not knowing when the end of his peregrinations would come. Only he would know when that time came.

The *Lewis and Clark* steamed into Yokohama harbor, where it would remain for all the next day before crossing the Pacific. With opium he bought in the city, Adriel spent the time smoking his pipe in a room he rented on shore. The proprietor smelled the sweet savor, but seemed indifferent.

CHAPTER FORTY-FIVE

WANDERING

Tell me, O Muse, of that ingenious hero who travelled far and wide after he had sacked the famous town of Troy. Many cities did he visit, and many were the nations with whose manners and customs he was acquainted; moreover he suffered much by sea while trying to save his own life and bring his men safely home.

– The Odyssey, trans. by Samuel Butler.

Like Odysseus, some people wander because of adverse circumstances (the will of the gods). After ten years of war, Odysseus wished to get home to his country and wife; but, obstructions prevented him. Others wander or drift to find opportunity, pecuniary or otherwise, like the gyrovague, the monk looking for his next meal without dedication to God and the community. Yet others, like the children of Israel, wandered in the desert as punishment because of God's anger against them for their sins. And yet others simply wish to wander like the wandering that takes place in their own minds. They have no goal and no purpose. They wish to forget the pain of their past. This last instance matches the primary reason for Adriel's peregrinations.

Adriel wandered here and there, looking for emotional relief from the void he felt with a spirituality that discounted God and placed all the effort and responsibility for redemption on himself alone, a sort of works-righteousness. He drank and smoked opium, both activities giving him temporary relief, a sort of ephemeral and addled deliverance.

Meili lightened his heart; her loss was devastating; but, at the same time, he reflected as he crossed the Pacific, if she wasn't wittingly or unwittingly one of the sources of his continued decline. She didn't pursue him with opium; but, she did serve him with it. Her refusal to come with him was largely due to her unwillingness to leave home, which also meant her unwillingness to leave behind the opium culture she was immersed in. Was she a siren calling him to his destruction? He came to realize that opium and drink would take him to the bottom of the abyss; but, he couldn't give them up. So, deeper he went into the darkness.

As Adriel stood on the deck of the *Lewis and Clark*, he thought about his next endeavor. After getting off in New York City, he would seek a job in the packet trade, ships on a regular schedule going to and fro from New York and London or Liverpool. Thence, who can tell?

CHAPTER FORTY-SIX

TO AMERICA

When I saw San Francisco from the ship, I had the feeling that I was about to visit a foreign country, so out of heart and mind in so short a time had been my homeland.

> – A Wanderer Who Becomes a Pilgrim, *Adriel Peregrine.*

When Adriel met the captain of the *Lewis and Clark*, he found a fellow of very similar experience to himself. Cornelius Bythesea had been a sailor for over thirty years. Four years earlier he had been made captain of the *Lewis and Clark*; but, during most of his time at sea, he was on the crew of a clipper ship, importing opium into China and exporting tea from it. The captain had many stories of unloading Indian opium off shore from the clipper onto ships that would smuggle the drug into China.

The captain chanced to encounter Adriel shortly after the steamer left Yokohama. When, in their short conversation, he discovered Adriel's experience at sea, he invited Adriel to his cabin for a drink. Not being a man who could tolerate periods of quiet and reflection, the captain obviated melancholy by often having people over to his quarters. It was two days later that Adriel conversed with Bythesea.

"Come in, Mr. Peregrine. I'm glad to meet you. Thank you for joining me for a drink."

"It was gracious of you to invite me."

The captain invited Adriel to sit on a wicker chair. "What would you have, port, sherry?"

"Port, please."

The captain poured them both some port and handed the glass to Adriel. After he sat down, he asked, "So you were in the opium trade?"

"Yes, I spent all of my time at sea in that trade."

"And I too spent much of my time trading opium for tea."

"Yes, I know the trade well," Adriel said with some regret in his voice.

"Did you have any dangerous adventures?" The captain was going to relate a story that he took every opportunity to tell others. His desire was backed up by his ability.

"Let me tell you a story about pirates. As you know, pirates have been a big problem along the Chinese coast."

"I'd be glad to hear." Adriel too had encounters with these sea thieves.

"Very good." The captain put down his drink and began his story.

"I began my adventures on the high seas like you, at a young age. When I was small, my family left England for the United States where we settled in Boston. When I was nineteen, I served on a coastal ship for a brief time that engaged in trade with New York, Boston, and Charleston. Then, I decided I needed more excitement and adventure, so I went to sea on an opium clipper. I soon experienced the excitement I sought.

"Along the coast of China near Canton, a *lorcha* approached our ship with guns firing. We fired back when we saw little chance of outrunning them. The pirate ship kept its distance but continued to follow us. We hove to and fired again, doing damage to our pursuer. He kept coming at us and succeeded in coming alongside our ship. Anticipating an attempt to board, the boatswain, in all the commotion, had distributed small arms during the chase.

"A fight commenced on the deck until we overcame the pirate crew. I had my hand in on it, killing two of the thieves. The captain of the *lorcha* and the crew members who survived were forced to surrender. We detained them in the brig until after we sold our opium. Then, we took them to Hong Kong to the authorities who handed them over to the Imperial Government. As with the pirates, the government was not very pleased with us. We too sold opium.

"These pirates and others attacked the merchants trading along the coast and took the loads of opium they were intending to smuggle into the country. Some crewmen on both sides always got killed in the scuffles.

"After many years of trading in China, I had learned the language fluently with some help from studying it during my free time on the ship. The pirate captain and I conversed in Chinese when I was sent to him to glean information about his activities. My first two brief visits were met with silence; but, on the third try, the captain spoke with great caution. During our exchange he told me little of his operations in hopes that he would find a way out of his predicament to return to the sea and his notorious profession. He was not repentant for his life.

"He was the son of a farmer from Hunan Province. Despising his parents and their way of life, he left home at an early age. In Shanghai, he got a job on a ship employed in the Yangtze River trade and also worked for some time on the functioning parts of the Grand Canal that was sorely in need of repair. The moral corruption—opium, loose women, crime—that he found along the river and canal attracted him until one day he joined with a group of freebooters. They stole a ship to engage in their illegal activity. For two years they sailed up and down the coast attacking opium clippers and other ships. Some Chinese pirates commanded fleets; but, Zhao Hai possessed only one boat. Despite this, the pirate mounted up a fortune, mostly on the opium trade. On board the boat, he took with him opium, women, and crime.

"Success was theirs until they met us, who sent them into the hands of imperial officials. The imperial government had been for a long time making a strong attempt to discourage piracy along its long coast. The pirate captain's fate was an example to others who continued to flout the government or were thinking of a life of maritime larceny. It came to pass that the captain of the *lorcha* and two of his crew were tried and sentenced to death by beheading. The others of the crew were punished with less severity.

"He said one thing that has stuck in my mind since I met him. Though a rough and coldhearted man, he was known for his generosity among poor and orphan children, especially in Canton. He was known to give money and necessities to destitute families. He was a sort of Robin Hood, taking to sea to rob others, but giving some back to those who were in dire need. The people in Canton whom he helped must miss him very much. You may be able to imagine the suffering of the poor. I'm sure you've seen the unsightly face of poverty in the Far East.

"Human beings fall very short of any standard of perfection. Was Zhao Hai evil? Some would say that dealing in opium is evil, perpetrated by evil people. Such a view would make you and me evil, for we have spent much time trading in opium. Neither Zhao Hai nor we could offset the evil with anything good we have done.

"I would have it that opium is not evil in its use as a reliever of pain. Many Chinese and those of other nations use the drug for this purpose. Maybe, some people should stay away from it, but not everybody. Admittedly, it can be addictive. It is then that it becomes harmful. I'll admit that my conscience has been somewhat relieved since departing from the trade. I guess I have great reservations about the trade and use."

Adriel told the captain about his experiences on an opium clipper. He knew that the Chinese Empire had attempted to stamp out the opium trade and its use; because, the Imperial Government thought the stuff was destroying many people, which, in fact, it was. But, at the same time, opium had been used in China for quite a while and has been cultivated more and more in China itself. Many rationalizations for its use were available

Disturbing thoughts about the opium trade pre-occupied Adriel for the rest of the trip. But, it wouldn't prevent him from continuing his habit of opium smoking. The battle of overcoming it would wait for another day and place, beyond America in the land that was promoting the opium trade. As he traveled across the Pacific, he was committed to his habit with the enthusiasm of a fanatic. His own body was the temple of the fierce god.

Adriel stood on the deck of the ship when land was sighted and San Francisco came into view. He would soon be traveling across half the country on the new transcontinental railroad and then further by train to New York, where he hoped to be employed on a packet steamer. Adriel hadn't seen the shores of America for several years. His emotions were a mix of anxiety at what the future may bring and relief that he had made it through so many dangers to return to his native land

CHAPTER FORTY-SEVEN

GOLDEN GATE

To this Gate I gave the name of Chrysopylee, or Golden Gate; for the same reasons that the harbor of Byzantium (Constantinople afterwards), was called Chrysoceras, or Golden Horn.
    – John C. Frémont, Memoirs of My Life and Times

John C. Frémont, the well-known American explorer, described the terrain around the entrance into San Francisco Bay, giving the channel of water and surrounding land the name of Golden Gate. The sea there is very treacherous, its danger consisting of turbulent water and fog.

As the *Lewis and Clark* passed through the Golden Gate, Adriel's thoughts were directed to his favorite vice. In San Francisco he would have some days to enjoy smoking Aunt Emma in his dream stick, that is to say opium in his pipe.

As soon as Adriel got off the ship, he found quarters in a somewhat respectable part of town. The next day, he was off to do a little serious smoking in the netherworld of a Chinese laundry—clean wash and dirty habit. The accommodations were below those that he was used to in Hong Kong in the den where he met Meili; but, it didn't matter to him. He brought his pipe with him and acquired the rest of the implements in the establishment. While waiting for his train to leave from Oakland Long Wharf, he engaged in the Big Smoke. He was startled by the tourists who came through to slake their curiosity; but, remained intent on the task at hand.

Adriel had four days before his train would leave from the Wharf; but, the question was, did he have enough time? He had gotten behind on his smoking of opium. So, on the first day in the den, he spent eight hours before returning to his lodging that he found that night with some effort. He reverted to a state of utter placidity and composure. For all he cared, his train could already be entering Nebraska, poised to arrive in Omaha.

Sleep, unconsciousness, nothingness, oblivion, and then images and dreams. Adriel lay there for hours with no fear and dread. He sailed in the clouds over land and sea. As he looked up and around he saw figures and pictures of one sort or another—sailing on a clipper ship; sitting in a sampan with Meili; riding Bunyan on a dirt road in the countryside; and walking down the Dunlap farm lane with Abigail. He ascended to consciousness and re-entered the den where the many conversations sounded like a hum. His edginess had been calmed by the long smoke. During the entire trip across the Pacific, he had little opportunity for the habit except for some swigs from a bottle of laudanum.

It was late November in San Francisco. The evening was cool, but not cold. The sky was clear and dark before moonrise that night. Adriel found his way, stumbling to his room where, when he finally reached it, he collapsed into bed until late the next morning. The sun was some distance from the horizon when he finally walked out of the rooming house to engage in a walking tour of San Francisco. He delayed his travel east in order to take in some of this new bustling city. Eventually, he found himself at water's edge on the bay at Fisherman's Wharf, looking over at Alcatraz Island with its Federal installation. He then walked next door to Chinatown, where he got breakfast and spent another day "Chasing the Dragon."

At the den, Adriel got into a conversation with an American

who also had spent many years as a crewman of a clipper ship. "I too spent time in Hong Kong. The opium was good; the women were better."

"Horace, you may've been in Hong Kong at the same time I lived there," Adriel replied.

"I was there for two years up to the early part of this year."

"I was there until recently. We were walking the same streets." Adriel was astonished. And then he asked with some trepidation, "Did you ever patronize *The Sign of the Dragon*?"

"Yes, I did. A pretty Chinese girl helped her parents with the business."

Adriel thought that his head at that moment was emptied of its contents, so lightheaded did he feel. "I knew her also. I'm surprised we hadn't encountered one another though you look somewhat familiar to me."

Sensing from Adriel's inflection that his acquaintance with Meili was more than that of buying and selling opium, Horace asked, "It sounds as if she was very special to you."

Adriel was surprised by his perceptiveness. He didn't know that he gave himself away.

"I loved her."

"Why did you leave her?"

"Her parents had arranged a marriage that they insisted she fulfill. She didn't want to; but, she also didn't want to leave home. Filial piety is a big thing among the Chinese. I know she loved me, but not enough to leave with me. She must've also feared the unknown. She had only known Hong Kong."

"She didn't seem to like working in the den; but then, what else could she have done? She was working for her parents. Maybe your smoking was a discouragement to her," Horace replied.

"I never thought of that. She never said anything, and I never asked her about it. She seemed to be content with providing me the drug." Adriel took a long draw on his pipe, chasing the dragon right into his cave.

"Even thinking about quitting is something I avoid. It's too hard a thought for me and an impossible task. I've been smoking for ten years, and I don't plan to quit."

"I, for only a couple years, yet I couldn't do without it. I guess I have loved Aunt Emma more than anything else, and I too don't plan to quit." Adriel was a determined devotee.

"We both belong to that distinguished club known as opium addicts."

The two of them looked at each other soberly.

CHAPTER FORTY-EIGHT

ON THE WAY TO OMAHA

A man who cannot tolerate small misfortunes can never accomplish
great things.   *– A Chinese Proverb.*

Adriel picked up a prostitute on the street on his way home
from the opium den and sneaked her into his room in the
middle of the night. They spent most of the night making
love. When he woke, the woman was gone, and so was his wal-
let. His initial panic was calmed by the thought that, as a pre-
caution, he had hidden most of his money in the room that,
fortunately, the "daughter of joy" didn't find.

On that last day in San Francisco, Adriel again took in
the town. It was a western American town with a population
looking for adventure and riches. Twenty years before, James
Marshall discovered gold on the property of John Sutter. The
gold fields were not far from the city in the foothills of the
Sierra Nevada along the South Fork of the American River.
His train would pass close to these fields near Sacramento that
made some rich and others disappointed and poorer. Like others, the Chinese followed the gold and then the tracks of the
transcontinental railroad. They were good workers and mas-
ters with explosives that bore the tunnels of the railroad built
by the Central Pacific extending 690 miles from Sacramento
to Promontory Point, Utah. The Union Pacific built from Omaha
to where the two roads met. The Chinese weren't admired for
their accomplishment; they were underestimated and over-
performed.

*

Money was also to be made in trade with the Far East and in supplying the multitudes that converged on the city that, shortly before, was a desolate place. The Chinese found a niche with restaurants, laundries, and other businesses, including, in some instances, opium dens. They were a significant work force in farming and performed other menial services.

Adriel left early the next morning with his few belongings and five bottles of laudanum, a mixture of alcohol and opium that one could buy in many retail establishments. He was not going to be caught without a good supply of the narcotic.

He boarded the steamer to Oakland and arrived at the new installation of Oakland Long Wharf, where he caught the train. The overland train had just been completed the same year Adriel took it east, that is, in late May 1869. The country was now connected from the west coast to the east.

The first stretch of the railroad, run by the Western Pacific, took Adriel to Sacramento. From there, he traveled on the Central Pacific, first through the Sierra Nevada Mountains, Sierra Nevada meaning "snowy mountains." Through many tunnels, built mostly by Chinese labor, the train moved onto the flat, dry wilderness of Nevada to Promontory Point, where passengers disembark to get onto the Union Pacific for Omaha and Council Bluffs.

That first night Adriel was in his berth, passenger seats made into a bed, looking out the window into the darkness. He struggled to find among his bedclothes his remedy and panacea. When found, he took a good swig, swilling his laudanum with great relish. He also ate some of the food that was left over from dinner. The train stopped three times in the day for passengers to dine.

Adriel thought of the day just past. The mountains were

majestic, and the train was a marvel as it traveled along uninhibited by the great wall of the Sierra Nevada through which the Chinese bore. The astounding expertise of the engineers, the daring vision of the investors, and the bravery and skill of the workers combined to make for the tremendous accomplishment of the transcontinental.

In the early hours of the morning, before the sun rose, Adriel woke up, thinking of the remainder of his trip. Through the mountains, through the desert, and through the prairie, he would fare toward Omaha and Council Bluffs, towns located along the Missouri River. At Promontory Point, passengers would change trains from Central Pacific to Union Pacific.

Adriel again thought of home since he would come close to it to get to New York City to acquire a job on a packet to England. East of the Mississippi he would change trains a couple of times to get to the metropolis. Going home to him was not a good idea because of his opium smoking and drinking. Before he left home, he had had several confrontations with his father over his drinking. He habituated a certain tavern in town where he had gained a reputation for drunkenness. Several times the constable brought him safely home late at night. His father didn't relish meeting the officer at his front door in the middle of the night.

The next day on the train, as it steamed toward the dry lands east of the Sierra Nevada, he overheard two of the neighboring passengers speak of current events. The first item was about the Cincinnati Red Stockings, the first ever professional team that traveled to San Francisco to play baseball. Part of the trip was traveled on the transcontinental railroad. In their first season they won every game. As he looked out the train window, he listened carefully to details about the Red Stockings' first professional season. His two neighbors also talked at length about the election of Ulysses Grant, which they thought was grand. What a year 1869 was—baseball, the transcontinental railroad, the election of U.S. Grant, and women's suffrage in Wyoming.

After thinking about the Cincinnati baseball team with the excitement that goes with it—he loved baseball and remembered playing the sport with his army buddies as they whiled away many hours in camp—Adriel's mind drifted to many other things. He settled on thinking about riding a horse across a dry plain, stirring up the dust as they proceeded—a sort of land-based wave—as he approached a lone figure waiting for him to draw near. Adriel recognized—he didn't know how—that the rider was a chief of the Shoshone. The man wore an elaborate headdress, a clue to his status, and carried with him a decorated lance. The Shoshone spoke to him in English rather than his Uto-Aztecan Numic language. After greeting Adriel, he told him that he was in deep sorrow for what the railroad had, could, and would do to his people, that is, assist in destroying their way of life. Though Adriel thought the railroad a good thing for the country, he also lamented the harm it would do to many tribes of the West. Thus is the plight of the aborigine when he meets those of higher technical knowledge and expertise. The train was nearing the Rocky Mountains when Adriel met a fellow veteran, Hugh Gray, who was traveling in the same car. His friends called him Blue, playing on Hue for Hugh and his last name Grey. To them he was Blue Grey. From 1861, Blue served in the war in a cavalry unit that had seen action in places like Chickamauga. He was with Sherman in the general's march to the sea. After the war, Blue joined the regular army, serving in numerous places, including Fort Laramie, Wyoming, where he was then stationed.

He was returning to the Fort from a visit to San Francisco where his parents had resided for over a year. His father had died suddenly, so he received leave to go to the funeral. The railroad got him there in three days. The two men had dinner together at a stop along the way. During that brief time they shared war experiences.

Blue related to Adriel his time in the army since the War.

He was stationed at Fort Laramie, protecting a portion of the Oregon Trail and fighting the Sioux until the Treaty of Fort Laramie between them and the United States. The Treaty would be broken when gold prospectors entered the sacred land of the Sioux in the Black Hills.

Blue got off the train at Fort Laramie on the North Platte River; Adriel continued on his way to Omaha. He spent his time thinking, as he often did, about what he would do when he arrived in New York City. There was always room for opium smoking.

CHAPTER FORTY-NINE

MAKING SENSE OF IT ALL

We desire truth and find within ourselves only uncertainty.

– Blaise Pascal

"What sense can one make of the world?" Adriel asked himself once again this question that he asked many times before as he gazed out the train window taking in the western Nebraska prairie. He had attempted to put the question away for good, but was unsuccessful; for, such a question is not amenable to a firm, unequivocal answer. Time and time again, life's meaning nagged at him. A definitive answer to the enigma was not possible.

The conundrum of life's meaning leads to the conundrum of death. Why does death exist? The Bible gives an answer in connecting sin with death, of which the opening chapters of Genesis speak, and Paul elaborates in Romans. As a skeptic, the Bible was not for Adriel an explanatory basis. When one is young, the enigma of death is often not pressing; but, it was for Adriel. He thought we live only to die into nothingness. He was dust, and to dust he would return. The return to the elements was the end of the story for everyone. Macbeth was right—life as we travel to "dusty death" signifies nothing. It is a tale told by an idiot full of sound and fury (Shakespeare). Opium helped Adriel cope along the way to the finale of dust and ashes.

*

As the train moved toward Omaha, Adriel daydreamed about the tall grass prairie of Nebraska. It helped him leave behind thoughts of meaning and death. He saw himself walking through the tall grass under the dome of the sky that on the Midwest prairie was so large, not having the obstruction of innumerable trees. He could smell the sweet scent of the vegetation, reminding him of the fields at home that he used to walk through. It was in that place, far from the soil of his growing up, so quiet, so silent of the human voice, but rich in the sounds of bird and insect that drew him to a world of meaning. And, then, the wind, so at home on the prairie, began to blow with a strong voice, calling him not to forget hearth and home.

Adriel walked up to the top of a hill as hills go on the prairie. There he looked out over the great expanse, turning so that he viewed it in all directions. The wind blew in his face, carrying with it a song of the grandeur of nature. In his reverie he joined in, shouting a poem into the wind.

Prairie wide, prairie long,
Here's my joyful, exalted song.
Bobolinks, yellow and black,
Voices are full, nothing lack.

Prairie wide, prairie long,
Here's my joyful, exalted song.
Rising sun, setting sun.
Brilliant blue till day is done.

Prairie wide, prairie long,
Here's my joyful, exalted song.
Sunflower yellow, sunflower bright
Painting land to my delight.

Prairie wide, prairie long,
Here's my joyful, exalted song.

Prairie wind blows up a roar,
Knocking at the old barn door.

Adriel didn't repeat the last verse, for it was praise of the Creator. Adriel came back from his daydream when the conductor passed through to announce arrival at Omaha.

CHAPTER FIFTY

BACK EAST, THEN ENGLAND

*I have arrived in New York City to begin a new stage of my life. I
have no idea what to expect, but I know what I want to do.*
    – Diary of Adriel Peregrine, *December 1, 1869*

Adriel bought tickets for his trip from Council Bluffs to New
York City. It took three days to arrive in the city, where he
rented a room in the same boarding house he stayed in when
he first came there after setting out from the Delaware Canal.
He got a job with a passenger ship company, providing service
between Liverpool and New York.

As he waited for the departure of the packet ship on
which he would work, Adriel found an opium joint on Mott
Street in Chinatown. He spent most of his time while in New
York in this place. It was more desirable to Adriel to smoke
opium rather than drink laudanum, which he had been doing
for many days on his journey across the country.

One thing Adriel most appreciated was the way opium
seemed to clear his mind, only seemed, and granted him a
euphoric state. He enjoyed this altered state of consciousness
that transported him from the chaotic thoughts and feelings he often experienced. When sober, he tried again and
again to prevent the mental and emotional anarchy and turbulence from flowing like a raging river through his brain;
but, he couldn't, no matter what strategy he followed. Most of
the content of these thoughts consisted of material from the
copious dark content of the human psyche, his psyche.

Adriel found himself becoming lonelier if this were possible. No woman to love, no close friends, no old mates on ship, no anybody but himself described his circumstance. He'd never known such loneliness in his life, though he had known loneliness more than once. Meili helped soften his feelings of isolation. He could have gone home; but, he didn't want to for a number of reasons. Opium would be difficult to acquire; he would have to depend on laudanum. He didn't know how his parents would receive him home. He didn't know what he would do when he got home.

It was in New York that Adriel began to show acute symptoms of his alcohol and drug habits. Along with the euphoric moods, Adriel struggled with depression when sober. Other signs of his use, including nausea and vomiting, were evident; but, depression was the leading problem. At night time, he would often have bad dreams. The recurring one was walking behind Dante and Virgil in hell. He began to feel that they would leave him behind there, even though he didn't believe the infernal region existed. He would be bereft of a guide to free himself from the abyss. The only one who could rescue him from it was the One in which he didn't believe. Adriel decided to reduce his intake of the substances—a very difficult thing for him to do.

Adriel joined the crew of a propeller-driven passenger steamship that ran between New York and Liverpool. After arriving in Liverpool and taking a room in a boarding house, he headed for an opium joint that a fellow sailor told him about. On a later trip, when he had a few extra days off due to repairs on the ship, he decided to go by train from Liverpool to London's Limehouse district to visit, as he had done before, Ah Sing's opium den.

*

The ship's captain had become concerned about Adriel on the return to New York and warned him, just before the ship left again for Liverpool, that he could see that Adriel's judgment was less trustworthy; and, that if Adriel didn't do something about it, the captain would have to relieve him of his duties and put him ashore. Adriel was permitted to return to Liverpool as a crew member. During this trip, he made a strenuous effort to do his duty and succeeded in reducing his intake of the drug. He did well enough that he could continue on the crew, but decided to go to London and not return to the ship. Adriel planned to work on the canal and docks in Limehouse, London, where he would be close to Ah Sing's. He worked loading and unloading wares from ships to canal boats.

Adriel traveled to London by rail with a fellow crew member, Aubrey Baxter. When the time came, he would send Aubrey back to Liverpool while he remained in London. Aubrey knew nothing of what he intended. Both men were looking forward to the opium smoking they intended to do in the metropolis.

The train departed from Lime Street Station. Adriel and Aubrey passed the time enjoying the English countryside and conversing about this or that. They had become acquainted working together on the ship. Adriel's loneliness was somewhat mollified by his work on the steamer.

Aubrey was talkative, but quiet talkative. He had a very pleasant tidewater accent that was anything but loud. His mild manner and good looks assured him of female interest. He hoped to marry a Virginia girl but corresponded only with his parents, brother, and sister. One thing that bothered him was his opium-smoking habit. He got into smoking while serving on a ship in the East Indies.

Aubrey had come from a family who worshipped in the

Episcopal Church, like Adriel's. His ancestors landed at Jamestown in 1609 and made a living growing tobacco. During the Revolution they sided with the Patriots; in the Civil War they were Confederates who held dear their southern identity and black slaves. As a child, Aubrey played with slave children and even developed a friendship with one of them. He didn't know where Kitch was. He lost contact with him after the war; because, Kitch went west to seek his fortune on the range as a cowboy.

Their serving on different sides didn't prevent Adriel and Aubrey forming a friendship. Aubrey said that when they both retired from serving on the sea, he would invite Adriel down to his home near Williamsburg, Virginia. Before the Civil War his family owned a plantation, but because of the devastation and adverse economic environment moved to a humbler farmstead. One of their emancipated slaves stayed on with the family as an employee while also working some land of his own.

After Adriel and Aubrey disembarked, the two sailors rented a room and then proceeded to Ah Sing's, where they began their first day of smoking. Many hours later, they stumbled through the streets of the East End to their room, calm but unsteady. They slept till late and, then, after eating lunch at the George Tavern in Limehouse, returned to Ah Sing's.

Adriel's life had a certain affinity to the Limehouse section of East London. It was a place where seafarers gathered along the East India docks; Limehouse was named after its limekilns, the working of which was a sometime occupation of Adriel's in Uhlerstown and back home; the Limehouse basin connected the Thames with the canal system, another reminder of Adriel's work history and, of course, it contained within its limits a well-known opium den.

Two days before their train was to leave for Liverpool, Adriel broke the news to Aubrey that he would remain behind. The two seafarers were drinking a pint at the George Tavern when Adriel said to Aubrey:

"I'm not returning to Liverpool."

"What? Why not?"

"I've decided on a change. I'm going to stay in London and work here. I'll be close to the next smoke. That gives me comfort."

"I'll miss you, Old Boy. I must return to the ship. I'm thinking of returning to Virginia soon. Maybe one more trip out, then home. Only problem is that I need to shake this habit. How I'll do that, I don't know."

"Not easy. I've no plans to do that," Adriel replied.

"I guess I could sip it out of a bottle or take some pills; but, I don't think a wife would appreciate my habit."

"I was in love while smoking. She was Chinese, working with her parents in their opium den. I never thought about her approval since she worked in a joint. She wouldn't come with me. I lost her. To this day, I don't know what happened to her. I'll never know. I don't think I'll love again. I haven't had any success."

"I know you well enough. Don't count on never falling in love again, Adriel."

"We'll see," Adriel replied.

Adriel ordered another pint. He didn't want to be hasty with his good-byes. He had so few friends, fewer as he moved further into addiction. His only friends would be those who had the same problem as he—opium, "western sea smoke," as the Chinese called it because of its western origin. A fellow opium smoker is really not a friend, but simply a fellow smoker. The habit brings them together, but is incapable of forging a true friendship.

The two men whiled away another few hours and emptied several more pints. At a late hour they walked to Ah Sing's, where they capped the night with a smoke.

CHAPTER FIFTY-ONE

THIS CIRCLE OF HELL

Hell is empty, And all the devils are here.
　　　　　　　　　– The Tempest, *William Shakespeare.*

At the railroad station, Adriel said farewell to Aubrey with a shake of the hand and a pat on the shoulder. He returned to Ah Sing's, where he smoked for the remainder of the day. The next morning he got a job working in the docks at the Limehouse Basin, where goods were transferred from ships to canal boats. It was work with which Adriel was well-familiar.

Adriel's routine was smoke and work, work and smoke, until smoke became his primary pre-occupation. His attempts at reducing his consumption were desultory. On an early morning, two months after Aubrey's departure, after a night of drink and drugs, Adriel lay on a forlorn back street of Limehouse. Some people walked by unconcerned about his condition; but, one individual did stop.

The stranger called to him, "Son, wake up." He repeated, "Son, wake up." Silence followed. Then, he tapped Adriel on the shoulder. Adriel responded with a groan and some move-ment. The man again said, "Son, wake up." Adriel propped himself up on his elbows and looked up at the old man. In the early morning light, Adriel discerned an elderly man, clean shaven, with lively and friendly eyes. From what he could see on a first impression, he sensed a benign presence intent on his welfare, not a thief.

The stranger bent down to Adriel to speak with him, but

hesitated until Adriel had come more to his senses. "Young man, you've had a rough time of it." Silence followed as Adriel came fully awake.

"Young man, let me help you up." Adriel was able to get on his feet with the help of an older, and stronger, person, a man who himself had been through the agony of addiction. "There, how can I help you?"

"Where am I?"

"You are close to Saint Peter's Church, London Docks, Wapping Lane."

"Why do you think I need help?"

"Yes, my boy, I think you do from my own experience."

Adriel recollected that he had been drinking and smoking a lot in the last few days, forgetting that he had a job on the docks. He looked around to view the squalid surroundings in which he had settled for the night. He felt sick from the night's revels and thought he would vomit.

Adriel looked at the old man and said, "Yes, I think I do need help." The old man led him to a street curb, where he sat down. He sickened and vomited, the old man not letting go of his arm.

Adriel felt a little better. He looked up at the old man and said to him, "What's your name?"

"I'm Louis Hatherton. I live here and have known in my own life what you have known—opium and alcohol."

"How do you know that?" Adriel replied.

"I know it when I see it. I've known it in myself and in others. I've picked others off the street. I've worked with them through the Mission."

"What Mission?"

"We Anglicans have a mission to the people here. We help the poor in spiritual and physical matters. I know a priest who may be able to help you." The man's kindly face struck Adriel as out of step with the ruthlessness that Adriel had known living in Limehouse.

"I don't need help."

"I thought you just said that you do?"

Adriel adjusted his response, "Yes, I need help, but maybe I don't want it."

"That's your choice."

Adriel realized that over the months he had lived in East London, his life had worsened terribly. He had Aunt Emma (opium) and other women (prostitutes) as companions all along. He visited the pubs and drank the toasts. He was often seen by passers-by stumbling down the street in what could be interpreted as a bizarre dance, dedicated to the chthonic deities or, like a *danse macabre*, harbinger of his coming death. Wandering had taken him into more and more forbidding regions of the wilderness. There were no oases, only the arid desert. He began to wish that he would be swallowed up by the wasteland and spit out a corpse to be among the dry bones of the barrens.

Dry and barren is my thought.
Life for me has come to naught.
Peace of mind I ever sought,
Yet my heart with woe is fraught.

"How can he help me? I have wandered and erred."

"He's prepared to speak with you about this."

"Am I under any obligation?"

"None at all, if I know what you mean."

"I'm not a Christian."

"It matters, but matters not. He'll be glad to speak with you. Come with me. I'll introduce you."

Adriel straightened his tousled, untidy clothing, attempting to make himself a little bit more presentable to the priest he was about to meet. He felt some reluctance. He hadn't been in Church since Hong Kong, and then not with an intention to engage in worship. But, his desperation was mounting. Louis took him to a coffee shop for breakfast and then to the

Mission House where the priest resided.

The priest was sitting at a desk in a common room when Adriel and Louis entered.

"Ah, Louis, what've you been up to?"

"Early this morning, I found this young man lying on the street. His name is Adriel Peregrine, an American working in Limehouse."

The priest rose from the desk and came over to Adriel to greet him with a handshake. "Nice to meet you, Adriel. My name is Kenton Frith."

"I thought you might have some time to speak with him. He needs some spiritual counsel. He is an Anglican, or former Anglican, from America who has been traveling and working for several years in various places, including China. He lives now in Limehouse and works on the docks."

"I've some time right now, Adriel."

"Thank you, Father."

"Louis, I'll see you at Saint Peter's later today to talk about the project we are planning."

"Yes, Father. For now, I'll be on my way." Louis shook Adriel's hand and left.

Father Frith invited Adriel to take a seat. He came out from behind the desk and sat in a chair opposite Adriel. Kenton Frith was a tall, thin man with deep, perceptive eyes and a crop of unruly black hair. His eyeglasses gave him the look of a scholar, which he was. He had done well at Oxford; and, in his career, had published two books of theology. He was well-respected among his peers and the people he served in East London.

Frith's commitment to the poor was almost of an obsessive nature that originated in his deep commitment to Christ and His Church, which in England was represented in large part by the Church of England. The Limehouse/Docks area of East London was rife with prostitutes, drunks, and drug users. Along with and including them were the desperately poor whose fathers and husbands eked out a living on the docks and other places of employment. Wages were miserably low. The evils of alcohol and drugs also existed among the people, making a significant contribution to the suffering of the world. Home life for most was hardly existent, and where it was, it was more torment and woe than anything else.

Frith was committed to bringing about the blessings of peace wherever he went. He was committed to the purpose of the Mission to save souls. An effective preacher, he announced the Kingdom of God wherever he had an opportunity in his ministry. Part of his personal sacrifice was to refrain from marriage in favor of a complete focus on his calling.

Now the priest was confronted with a young man who had misspent years of his life and found himself in the deep shadows of addiction that had led to despair. As Adriel sat there, Father Frith was praying that Christ would give him the insight to draw Adriel to the light of salvation or, at least, help him to begin the journey.

"Adriel, it's good to meet you. Please tell me something about yourself."

"I've been a wanderer. I haven't seen my parents during this time. I grew up in central Pennsylvania, trained to be a teacher, and then entered the army during the Civil War. I lost a good friend, killed at Petersburg. I worked for a while on the Delaware Canal, then boarded ship for the East. I became a crew member for a British ship trading with China. It's there that I acquired the drug habit. Later, I worked on a packet line between New York City and Liverpool. A few months ago, I decided to stay in London to work on the docks, but really to be close to an opium den. Since my residency in London, things haven't gone well. My habit has gotten worse."

"How would you describe your wandering?"

Adriel answered, "What do you mean?"

"Wandering can take several forms. One may wander for the purpose of visiting many interesting places. One may wander purposelessly; because, one has no purpose. One may be attempting to escape and hide from a danger pursuing him. One may be looking for something of which he has no certain idea; and so, he looks here and there in hopes of coming across that which has resided in his deep consciousness, hoping that he recognizes it when he sees it. It is the pilgrim who has a clear destination of much importance. You've not been a pilgrim?"

"No, Father, I've no destination. I've wandered to escape my past with no other purpose. There's nothing before me that I intend to reach. What impels me is what I have left behind. I wish to escape it."

"Adriel, your drug habit is an escape?"

Adriel was surprised that the priest knew of his drug habit with so little information; but, his being on the street unconscious was enough for a priest of such wide experience in East London among the poor, addicts, and prostitutes to know something of the signs.

"I guess it's an escape from emotional pain and the emptiness that I feel much of the time. Several years ago, a girl I loved was murdered. More recently, in Hong Kong, I left another I've loved."

"So tragic. Such sadness. Very difficult for you. But, you must stop the addiction, or you'll die."

"I know; but, I can't stop. The Smoke gives me some relief from the emptiness and sadness I feel. My body shivers at the prospect of going without. My body revolts at not taking the drug. How can I stop?"

"It's not easy, I know. When I was young, before I was ordained, I got into the habit for a short time."

Adriel was struck by this admission. "How did you stop?"

"Determination with the help of a good friend and the priest of my home parish in Leicester."

"How can I stop?"

"I'd be willing to serve as your mentor, Adriel. Louis will

help, and also some others who have had the same experience as yourself. You must, however, consider your relationship to God. There is no healing of this 'sea of troubles' without the Lord playing a part," the priest said without hesitancy.

"Father, when I was a child, my mother and father were faithful at church and, most likely, still are. We belonged to a little Episcopal Church called Saint Jude Thaddeus back in Red Oak, Pennsylvania. But, for many years I have seldom seen the inside of a church. I'm not sure I believe in God."

"The Lord is important for all of life and certainly for being delivered from addiction. We must talk about this, Adriel. Our mission here in East London is centered on saving souls. You can't do without God. With no repentance and faith, there is no deliverance from our idols and slavery to them. I want you to think hard about this. Will you?"

"I will try; but, I doubt there will be any success."

That night Adriel was very restless. He dreamt again, as he had done before, of walking through hell with Virgil and Dante. This time he heard the shrieks and cries of the damned. He was alone in the "darkness visible," as Milton describes hell, and yet all around him was the inhuman wailing of a fallen and unrepentant humanity.

Adriel awoke from the dream crying out, "Is God merciful? I can't find Him. Where is he?" He realized that all the devils of hell seemed to be in his room, tormenting him with thoughts of damnation.

CHAPTER FIFTY-TWO

THE HABIT CONTINUES

When in London in the Limehouse district, I struggled day and night with my addiction, but kept falling deeper into despair and further into dependence on alcohol and opium. Before I met the priests and people of the East London Mission, there was not even a contest. I enjoyed my habit. Where was God? I had forsaken Him, and He had forsaken me. Nay, I discovered later that He had not abandoned me to my own "devices and desires."

— A Wanderer Who Becomes a Pilgrim, *Adriel Peregrine.*

Adriel decided to take Father Frith's advice to make every effort to free himself from both alcohol and opium. He knew he couldn't do it alone and was doubtful he could succeed even with many friends in the Mission surrounding him. Opium is seldom outdone in its power over and attractiveness to the habitual smoker. As he had done for quite a while, Adriel continued to carry opium with him. If he couldn't find an opportunity to smoke, he would drink it out of a bottle.

After talking with Father Frith, he continued his habit, but with the attitude that someday he might sunder himself from its destructive course. Adriel's health was compromised by his drinking and smoking, a fact that made it difficult for him to engage in the very physical nature of his employment on the docks. Adriel sought out and succeeded in getting another job. His days were filled with working at the docks on the Thames in less strenuous work and helping in the Church of England Mission in East London, while he continued to struggle with his addiction. During this time, Adriel was compelled to think about his own life like he had never done before.

One afternoon found both Adriel and Father Frith sitting in a pew at Saint Peter's, London Docks. Out of his frustration and emotional upheaval, Adriel had a pressing question for Father Frith. Unable to sleep properly, he woke up that day with a sick stomach. His dreams that night were altogether unpleasant. He needed to speak with the priest, whom Adriel found at Saint Peter's.

Saint Peter's was the first church established by the Mission. The beautiful interior of the Church surrounded the two men sitting there with its rich stained glass and brick interior. It radiated the light of the holy God.

"I've had great trouble trying to free myself from the drug. I'm sick when I'm taking it and sick when I'm not taking it. My misery is increasing rather than decreasing. I feel as if I'm going to die." Adriel placed his face in his hands as he leaned against the pew in front of him. He tried to swallow his tears, but was unable. He heaved up a cry of despair, followed by a flow of tears. He couldn't control the shaking of his body.

Adriel very seldom cried, except when he was young and often wept tears of joy at the beauty that surrounded him when he walked over "holt and heath" back home. He hadn't called the place of his birth and upbringing home for many years; but, now he was doing so. When he gave in to his emotions on this day, he surprised himself with their vigor.

Father Frith spoke to him in a soft voice as Adriel wept. "Adriel, your friends and I won't forsake you. We'll be at hand to do what needs to be done. But, there's someone left out that you need to include." The priest paused to give Adriel an opportunity to answer; for, he knew Adriel was quite aware of his reference.

"I've not approached God for many years. I've doubted his

existence, thinking that when I approach Him, I'm drawing near to nothing."

"You can't emerge from the labyrinth unless you follow him. There's no other way out. Without God, the Minotaur will consume you."

"Where do I meet Him? Where do I see Him? The world is empty of Him. I may wish Him to exist; but, my wish doesn't make it so."

"Adriel, God doesn't usually display Himself as He did at the Red Sea or the Resurrection; but, He can and will in certain circumstances. God's presence and action are usually hidden, as we find in the Holy Eucharist. In Communion are the outward visible signs of bread and wine, while the inward part is the true body and blood of Christ. God's working. You must open your eyes and see. In this world, God's glory is not often seen directly, nor do we see Him face to face. But, He is here among us. Open your eyes and heart and see. Tell me again, what has caused your skepticism?"

"I've had many disappointments, lost many friends, and seen many terrible things. I was a soldier in the Civil War, only serving for a little over a year; but, I saw more blood than I ever want to see again. I lost a friend in the War and suffered the tragedy of a friend murdered, and one falsely accused of the murder and hanged for it. Disillusionment was my experience's legacy. Drinking and smoking were aids in forgetting."

"I'm sorry that you have known such grief. But, I ask you again, why such a forsaking of God?"

"I've told you, Father," Adriel said with some irritation in his voice.

"The reason I ask again is that some people who've known such grief as you haven't rejected God."

"I don't know," Adriel said with greater irritation. He wondered if the priest had any sympathy for his plight.

"Adriel, without God there is no hope of ultimate justice and every chance of long-lasting bitterness in your own heart.

Worse than the suffering of any human being, including your own, is unrectified and unredeemed suffering. Christ tells the story of the persistent widow who demands justice from the unjust judge. In Luke, Christ says, 'And the Lord said, Hear what the unjust judge saith. And shall not God avenge his own elect, which cry day and night unto him, though he bear long with them? I tell you that he will avenge them speedily. Nevertheless, when the Son of man cometh, shall he find faith on earth?' (Luke 18: 6-8 KJV) You've given up faith in bitterness. Bitterness had driven you in your troubles, hasn't it?"

"I've tried to hide it; but, whether successful or not in my dissembling, I have grown more bitter in my heart and mind."

"You feel anger. Do you feel guilty?"

"Lots, I couldn't save my friends. I failed because of my inadequacy or my indifference or my complacency."

"Do you think rejecting God will resolve these thoughts and feelings?"

"So far, nothing I do has resolved anything. But, the drug and the bottle have given me temporary relief. Using them is like entering a world of peace and acceptance by mouth that has little or nothing to do with the heart and mind. The heart and mind are willful, stubborn, and persistent."

"I see that you have some wisdom. Open your heart to God and see what happens. Be honest with Him about your sin that He's already very well acquainted with, but also remember that repentance and faith can heal you."

"I'll think about it, Father." Adriel was attempting to put off the priest.

"In the meantime, keep up your work among us. I've heard good reports. And seek me out when you need to."

"I will."

Father Frith bade farewell to Adriel, who remained in the church for a while longer. Adriel tried to pray; and, when he tired, he left the building and went to the local pub for an evening of drinking and partaking of a bottle of laudanum he always kept with him. By these means He imbibed no peace, only a further sinking into despair. Later, he would discover that peace is neither a liquid nor solid, but a state of mind and heart, assured by a relationship to the Lord.

234

CHAPTER FIFTY-THREE

THE POSSIBILITY OF CHANGE?

I am, and again I am.
What I was, I am.
No change in these many years
Despite my abysmal fears.

– Adriel Peregrine

Adriel felt as nauseous as he ever had in all the time he drank and smoked. When he woke, he could see morning shadows formed by the rising sun coming through the windows. He squinted to make out the images he thought he could see—monsters at daybreak. They disappeared with his greater clarity and only shadows remained. But, his mind was not clear. He had fuzzy memories of the night before. What he could put together was a rousing time, followed by a sick stomach that led to vomiting in the street. Somehow, he found his way home, but he knew not how. Perhaps a drinking buddy helped him.

Adriel lay there, wondering if he could stand on his two feet, when there was a knock at the door. He didn't answer, hoping that the caller would go away. Again, someone knocked on the door. No answer came from Adriel. The third time, the knock was accompanied by a voice: "Adriel, it's Louis. I've come to bring you to church at Saint Peter's. Father Frith asked me to stop by to invite you to come with me."

Adriel groaned and then answered, "Louis, I'm sick. I can't go with you."

"Let me in. We can talk."

Adriel stumbled to the door. When he opened it, he was greeted by his friend who had pulled him off the street while on an opium excursion. He looked at his visitor with bleary eyes. He was fully dressed in rumpled clothes. When he had gotten home earlier that morning, he dropped into bed. He supported himself on the door jamb, otherwise he would have fallen. Then, he looked at Louis with eyes half-focused.

"Adriel, get cleaned up, and then we'll go to church."

"I'm sick."

"I believe you, but let's get breakfast and sit and talk for a while. The Eucharist is two hours from now. You may feel better by then. I'll wait for you at the coffee house here on your block."

"All right," Adriel said reluctantly.

Louis left for the little hole in the wall café while Adriel straightened himself up. Adriel was tempted to go in the opposite direction and stay away from his room until he was confident that Louis was gone from the neighborhood; but, he was drawn to the shop where Louis was waiting for him.

When Adriel arrived, Louis was sipping tea. A plate of sweet cakes rested on the table. The room was filled with early morning chatter from various tables where neighborhood folk were sharing the latest news of East London and that from further up the river at the Palace of Westminster and its environs and of the daily issues and problems their families were facing. When Louis saw Adriel enter, he waved to him to come to the table. Adriel found his way to where Louis was sitting.

"I'm so glad that you decided to come," Louis said as Adriel sat down.

"I almost didn't. I was afraid to."

"Why, Adriel?"

"I was afraid that I would have to give up the habit along with the fact that I was feeling sick from last night's carouse. I always get sick when carousing and getting little sleep."

"How do you feel now?"

"Sick, but glad I'm here, now that I'm here."

"Good. How about tea or coffee?"

"I'll have coffee. I can't eat."

"I understand." Louis ordered coffee for Adriel. After Adriel had taken a few sips, Louis spoke to him.

"Adriel, you know my story with drink and the dream stick. I went through hell to get where I am, but not without the Lord and good friends who wished me well. You too can do the same."

"I don't think so."

"Adriel, rely on the true God whom you knew as a child. He'll be your 'refuge and strength,' as the Psalmist says. I've been free of the curse for ten years. I would never go back to the thralldom of my former life. For me it took friends, will power, and God."

"I don't believe a person can change. People don't change. They travel in the same rut all their lives."

"I've changed and found meaning in Christ and the mission on his behalf in East London and Limehouse. Come with me to Saint Peter's this morning."

"I'll come, but don't expect any transformation. I'm lost. I can't find my way. I'm erring, wandering, and have gone astray. I see no path to anywhere, let alone to God."

"It doesn't have to be this way. You can change. Many people in various circumstances have been redeemed. You loved God as a child. You told me so. You can love Him again. He loves us now, in the past, and will in the future."

Adriel placed his hands on his face. Tears extruded from between his fingers. His face was awash. He tried to regain composure; for, he was in such a public place. Except for Louis, no one seemed to notice what was going on.

Louis himself was overcome, shedding some tears as he remembered how hard it was and how dark it became during those difficult days of his own. He looked down for a moment, wiping away his own tears, and then looked up again to see Adriel looking back at him.

"May I tell Father Frith about our conversation?"

"Yes. I'm ready for church."

Louis smiled. "Let's go."

CHAPTER FIFTY-FOUR

CHURCH AND THE MISSION

Jesus said to them again, "Peace be with you. As the Father has sent me, even so I am sending you." — John 20: 21 ESV.

O what their joy and their glory must be,
those endless Sabbaths the blessed ones see;
crown for the valiant, to weary ones rest;
God shall be all, and in all ever blest.

Now in the meanwhile, with hearts raised on high,
we for that country must yearn and must sigh;
seeking Jerusalem, dear native land,
through our long exile on Babylon's strand.

— O What Their Joy, *vss. 1 and 6, Peter Abelard,*
trans. John Mason Neale.

Adriel's life was changing, and he was changing with it. It all began on that Sunday he went to the Holy Eucharist at Saint Peter's with Louis Hatherton. They arrived shortly before the service began. Louis found them a pew near the back of the sanctuary in an almost full church and pulled out a kneeling bench to pray. Adriel knew the custom, but was not sure he wanted to do the same. He decided not to kneel, but sat down with some discomfort in his heart at the kneeling man next to him.

When the two men entered the church, the organist was playing the prelude. In those moments before the procession began, youthful memories of church came to his mind—the beautiful music; the elegant and fervent prayers of *The Book of Common Prayer*; the hues of the sanctuary blending into a rich brilliance, lighted by sun, candles, and oil lamps; his mother's hand on the back of his head, as she sang the opening hymn with the congregation; and the people and animals in the stained glass enlivened by the penetrating rays of the sun. His attention came back to the service at Saint Peter's as the congregation rose and began singing, "O What Their Joy" (tune, O quanta qualia) by Peter Abelard and translated by John Mason Neale.

Adriel heeded the service, wandering little in mind during it. He often gazed at the crucifix above the entrance into the chancel. Despite Louis' urging, Adriel didn't take Holy Communion. They had not talked about reception of the Sacrament before the Service. When the liturgy ended, Louis and Adriel walked into the sunlight that seemed brightest that day, compared to any other. They had lunch at a little place along the way.

"Adriel, why didn't you take Holy Communion?" Louis inquired.

"I still am not sure I believe, and I don't deserve it with my burden of sin."

"I hope a time will come soon when you will be able to take it. Remember that you come to the table, not as a righteous or perfect person, but to have your sins forgiven and your joy restored. Remember what is expressed in the service, 'We do not presume to come to this thy Table, O merciful Lord, trusting in our own righteousness, but in thy manifold and great mercies.' We don't make the Sacrament; God does. He promises to be with us. All that we bring is repentance in which God is working."

"Louis, all of this makes sense. I must cry out of the depths, hoping for a renewed faith. I'm not optimistic."

"I will pray that this may happen."

As they drew near Adriel's home, Louis suggested that he

see Father Frith soon.

After speaking with Louis, Adriel felt more confident that with the help of Father Frith and his friends, he could abandon his habit; but, he also felt the dread of how difficult things would be and how easy it would be for him to revert to his old ways. Adriel was fighting a battle within himself about his habit. "*I can quit. I can't quit. I can change. I can't change. I'll live. I'll die.*"

Later that week, after working at the docks, Adriel met with Father Frith.

"Adriel, your week has not been good?"

"No." Adriel shook his head and let out a sigh.

"Well, I hope you're not going to give up. I hope that you'll keep working for the Mission and go to church."

"Yes, I'll do these things; but, as I told Louis, I don't know if circumstances will ever change for me—I don't know if I can change. Confusion has been part of my life for so long. The drug has certainly not given me clarity. I was under some sort of illusion while taking the drug that I possessed clearness of mind. I was actually in a fog. My confusion about myself and my life is greater now than when I was younger.

"All of us Christians sometimes fight confusion. The only thing really that gives us some stability in this regard is our relationship with God. As the Psalms say, "He is our Rock and Strength." I must rely on the I AM."

"I'm not sure when I look into myself whether I'm deceiving myself or getting it right. I really don't know who I am. Whoever I am, I am always the same without change—the same lost and wandering person. I don't think I'm making any sense. Will I always be so confused?"

"God knows who you are, and He can change your heart and mind. God knows you at any and every moment when you are deceiving yourself and when you are getting it right; because, He knows you better than you know yourself. Read Psalm 139. Every day pray, even if you don't feel like it, even if you are not convinced God exists. Don't relent. Will you try to do this, Adriel?"

Adriel paused to think over what he might be committing himself to. The silence was about to become awkward when he said, "Yes" to Father Frith.

Over the remaining months Adriel lived in London, helping out in the Mission and going with Louis to church every Sunday. At first, nothing seemed to change in him; but then, he noticed a growing sensibility of the presence of God—in the Liturgy, in reading the Scriptures that he pursued under the direction of Father Frith, and in the events and people around him. One Sunday, to the delight of Louis, Adriel went up to the altar for Holy Communion—the first time in many years. Something very good was happening to him, something specific, a relationship with God that he hadn't known since the days wandering in the woods of central Pennsylvania and attending church with his parents.

The decisive experience was one day while working for the Mission during the early evening, he chanced upon a woman of the streets. As she came up to him, he became disquieted, wondering if he would give in to temptation as he did many times before during his wanderings.

Adriel looked into her face and saw for the first time not only the salaciousness, but also the affliction and sorrow. What story is being worked out by this woman of the street? It began with poverty and neglect and continued with the cruelty of those who had taken advantage of her. This is not to say that she didn't have any responsibility. She did. Many women like her roamed the streets of East London with similar stories, looking for their next customer, of which there were many. She hoped Adriel would agree to a transaction. He would not. He asked if he could assist her in some way to relieve her distress. She looked at him incomprehensibly.

It was not a week later that Adriel came upon a crowd of people surrounding something or someone on a narrow back street. He found a place in the crowd and, to his amazement, the body on the ground was that of the prostitute he encountered the week before. She had been assaulted and killed. Another life full of adversity ending in tragedy. It was then, as Adriel walked away from the scene, that he decided that Christ who taught among the tax collectors and prostitutes and brought them to faith would be his Lord too. He continued his church attendance unfailingly during the remainder of his stay in London.

CHAPTER FIFTY-FIVE

INSULA SACRA

To Bishop Aidan then, upon his coming, the king appointed his episcopal see in the island of Lindisfarne, where the bishop himself desired it to be. Which same place with flowing and ebbing of the tide is twice every day environed like an island with the surges, twice joined on the mainland, the shore being voided again of the sea waves; and so following humbly and readily in all things the advice of the bishop, the king set himself very diligently to build up and enlarge the Church of Christ in his realm.

– Bede Historical Works, *Harvard University Press, Cambridge, translation by J. E. King Bede,* Ecclesiastical History of the English Nation, *Book III, chapter 3*

The day came when Adriel decided it was time to leave London for the island of Lindisfarne. For some time, he had inquired about the Holy Island. One of the priests whom he knew had been there. Adriel also read about it. When he learned that he could work in the limekilns located on the island, he made a final decision to travel there. He would spend an undetermined time on the Holy Island as a retreat for his renewed and regained faith. In the slums of London, he saw Christ at work among the priests and people. In one of the many forlorn parts of the world, Christ was served by those He serves. During that year Adriel became aware that Christ could be found in the most hopeless places in the world, invented and cultivated by humans.

The day Adriel left for Lindisfarne, he said his good-bye

to Father Frith and a few co-workers who gathered to wish him well. Tears were shed, for a close bond developed among those who worked in the difficult and desperate environment of East London. The ministry and mission drew these disciples close together. Adriel would never forget his association with Father Frith, Louis Harrington, and others. Working and living in this forlorn place was the occasion of his return to the Way of the pilgrim.

The journey to Lindisfarne marked the end of Adriel's wanderings and the re-introduction of his pilgrimage. After the war his restless despair was the motivating force behind his travels that led him to England and China, back to America, and then to England again. His wanderings represented a circumnavigation of the globe. With his return to Christ and the Christian faith, he had resumed the pilgrimage that began when he was a young man at home. No longer did he imagine himself disconsolate and lost in a dry wilderness. He now lived in a country that flowed with nourishing streams; but, he could still look out over the wilderness that he had left behind, a place of temptation and damning sin. The road he resumed would be hard, as Jesus says; but, it would lead to life with Christ from now to the fulfillment of the kingdom. The question would be, would he remain on that road?

Opium had the striking ability to hold a person down and strangle him when great efforts at freedom were not attempted. The mistake that Adriel could make would be to relent in his efforts.

On the way by train and foot, he thought about many things that were not new to him, but that he saw, since his renewal, from a different perspective. Especially, he perceived once again God at work in the world. In all the confusion of life, he knew above all else that he belonged to the Lord and was a person among the people of God's pasture. He experienced a deep sense of repentance for all of the misdeeds, wrongs, and transgressions in his life over the past several years from the time of his service in the army and before. He remembered in the presence of God the use of opium and his drinking to excess, the lost amnesiac days, the blackouts in his room and on the street, his cavorting with prostitutes—his reckless behavior. And even at the moment he reflected on these things, he was not immune from temptation. He had to struggle to keep away from the pipe and the bottle. And his youth, in its exuberance, was a constant erotic potion to draw him to the delights of the flesh. He had seen in his dreams Dante and Virgil touring hell and heard the invitation to remain in that infernal place, not posed as a temptation, but as the consequence of how he was living his life. He never accepted that offer, but was, at the same time, far short of Dante's ecstatic vision in heaven and steeped in the obsessions that are hell.

Adriel recalled his sense of meaninglessness during what seemed like interminable years, and yet again, like yesterday. The heavens were a solid, indestructible surface with no possibility of a descent of the divine, the antithesis of the Baptism of Jesus when the heavens break open, the Spirit descends, and the Father speaks. He couldn't say those words, "Come down, O love divine." His heart pumped the poison that iterated and re-iterated the sheer nonsense of living.

He hadn't been able to brave a bold confession of Christ in the face of a nineteenth century world of unbelief and skepticism. He read the English translation by Mary Ann Evans (George Eliot) of Ludwig Feuerbach's *The Essence of Christianity* while in England. At that point in Adriel's life, Feuerbach's atheism aided in pulling him down into a destructive pit. But, it had been his own views leading to the infernal regions that would not cease to haunt him until now.

*

After getting off the train in Berwick-upon-Tweed, Adriel found a room for the night. The next morning, after buying some food at a local grocery, he started out on his journey along the coast to the island. During a glorious day in July, he walked over the stony coastline, on cliffs, and sandy beaches and stopped for a while to see Saint Cuthbert's Cave. It took him five hours to arrive in Lindisfarne in the early afternoon when he could get across to the island on foot before high tide. At times during the day the island is connected to the mainland; at other times, it is an island.

He wished he could have spent more time at Saint Cuthbert's Cave, but was pressed for time because of the tides. Adriel visited the cave where, as the story goes, the monks hid Saint Cuthbert's body during the threat of a Viking invasion of the Lindisfarne community in 875. Early accounts like that of Bede's tell of the saint's life. He had been the Prior of Lindisfarne.

The walk to Lindisfarne was an inspiration for Adriel. The North Sea stretched out in its dark blue-green immensity to the horizon—as flat as a wide plain on this calm July day. It could, in a storm, transform into a hilly or even mountainous terrain. On one of the cliffs lining the English coast between Berwick and Lindisfarne, he viewed the salty deep—he, amidst grandeur, a speck in an expanse. He felt as if he were a figure in a Chinese painting where he was miniature in magnitude. Adriel peered out as far as his sight would take him and, then, beyond sight through his imagination with which he was much gifted. He could see Odysseus sailing on the "wine-dark sea," wandering, though his fervent intention was to get home after many years at war. He thought of Israel Potter, Melville's wanderer, living in exile for fifty years.

Adriel was alone, leaving behind his friends in London and approaching a place where he had never been. He knew that there were fellow travelers along the way as there were in London; but, with his departure in this transitional time, he had nobody to confide in or to be confided in. Except for the thought of the communion of saints and of God Himself He felt alone on that remote seacoast looking out over the North Sea. His loneliness was accompanied by the knowledge that there existed a great host of witnesses of which he was a part. The Lord had given him the gift of community even when he was solitary.

Adriel came to a point where he could see in the distance Lindisfarne Castle on the Holy Island. His excitement was intense in anticipation of dwelling and working on this sacred ground. It would be but a little while, and he would be there.

CHAPTER FIFTY-SIX

A PLACE TO STAY AND A PLACE TO WORK

I cannot describe Lindisfarne without tears coming to my eyes. It is a small, modest island; but also, a green patch of ground amidst blue sky and blue-green sea that counts as especially sacred ground because of the monastic foundation that Saint Aidan had established there. Remnants of that monastery and of later but old construction still exist. After an extraordinary experience in the midst of the ruins under a full moon, I re-dedicated myself to Christ and His service. — Diary of Adriel Peregrine, May 11, 1871.

Adriel was exultant as he walked across the causeway that connected the mainland with the island during low tide. He felt a lightheadedness that was not borne of anxiety but of joy. He breathed in the salt air deeply and was aware of the sea breeze soothing his face. He hoped that Lindisfarne would represent in a most definite way a break with his erring past and a return to a life of repentance, from wilderness to Way of Holiness, from erring to ruing, and from despair to hope and joy in God's grace and mercy.

When he arrived in the village, Adriel came upon the Crown and Anchor Inn, where he inquired about renting a room for the long-term. The proprietor directed him to an unassuming stone house on the neighboring street where a widow had put a notice in a window to lease one of her small rooms. Regarding him a "good lad" after interviewing him over tea and scones, she let the room to him.

The next day Adriel was hired at the limekilns. The foreman was impressed with Adriel's description of his experience and took a liking to him. It didn't take long for Adriel's experience and skill to become evident. After some testing, Adriel's fellow workers warmly received "their Yankee" into their company. The work was hard, dirty, and hot; but, it would supply Adriel with the funds he needed to remain on the island for a while.

On his time off, Adriel explored Holy Island, as it was often called. He had learned that monks under the leadership of Saint Aidan settled the island in the seventh century and continued their mission from there to northern England until the pagan Viking attack of 793. Bloody destruction and theft of valuable monastic property was the result of the assault. The monastery was restored some three hundred years later, but fell into disuse during the suppression of the monasteries by Henry VIII. What Adriel saw were the ruins of the monastic establishment from the time of the Norman foundation.

On a night of the full moon, when Adriel had a difficult time sleeping, he decided to get dressed and walk to the ruins that lay just south of the town. He had had a dream that he was back home in Pennsylvania. He was walking up toward his parents' house that stood back behind the church he attended as a child and young man. As he turned the corner to the house, he saw his parents standing along the stone wall that separated the church and cemetery from the road. They waved and called to him; but, in the next scene, they had disappeared. Adriel felt alone and without family or any prospects of enjoying the fellowship of those he had loved. The church bell tolled a mournful "passing" bell that indicated the death of someone in the congregation, perhaps his own parents. He woke with a start, tears in his eyes. He knew then that it wouldn't be too long before he would return to America. It was the first time in years that he thought sympathetically of his parents, from whom he departed in anger and who had been angry with him.

He quietly left the house so as not to disturb his landlady. He walked to the Priory, located at the edge of the water. The moon shone on the stones and remains of the ancient monastery. He walked into the midst of them, quite visible because of the light of the full moon. It was as if he were in a painting of Felix Kreutzer, an artist of Adriel's time who painted many wondrous, moonlit landscapes.

Adriel stood there admiring the moonlight on the venerable ruins. He strained his ears, thinking that he could hear the voices of a choir singing a hymn translation from the Latin by John Mason Neale, a prominent English high churchman. It was a hymn he often sang at Evening Prayer in London.

From all ill dreams defend our eyes,
From nightly fears and fantasies;
Tread under foot our ghostly foe,
That no pollution we may know.

Adriel heard a rustling beyond the ruins and his sight. He shuttered at the prospect of some unwanted encounter or immediate danger. All again became quiet, and he thought nothing more of it. As he continued on, Adriel felt that he was making friends with the moonlit night and had no reason to fear any danger. The Lord was with Him.

Adriel looked out at the North Sea to the west. The ocean sparkled with the reflected light of the full moon with a bright path that came across the water to him, as if he were being invited to take a walk on the deep, with which he had become so familiar over the last several years, to a place where he had not been before. The place would be a transcendent city inhabited by a blessed people, where the senses took in all that was good, the mind was clear, and the heart replete with love.

The dancing light reflected a joyous earth receiving a special gift from the moon in honor of the former's greater dignity.

Adriel got down on his knees with head clearer and heart fuller than he had known in many years. At that moment, he yearned for the divine Love to bend down and embrace him. He prayed the words of Bianco da Siena, whose fine verse was translated by an English priest, Richard Frederick Littledale, appearing in *The People's Hymnal*, published a few years before.

Come down, O Love divine;
Seek thou this soul of mine
And visit it with thine own ardor glowing;
O Comforter, draw near;
Within my heart appear
And kindle it, thy holy flame bestowing.

After praying for some time, Adriel stood up, walked over to a ruined wall of the old priory, and sat down on one of the stones. He could see Saint Cuthbert's Island, lying just off Lindisfarne. It is said that to this island Saint Cuthbert used to go on retreat to pray. The Anglican parish church of Saint Mary the Virgin was right next door to the small island. To the south, Adriel's vision was obscured by a natural wall called the Heugh.

For the longest time Adriel sat there, looking west and watching the moon slip toward the western horizon. He imagined the monks that lived there before the Viking attack singing Gregorian chant, praising the Lord with both heart and voice. He thought he heard them chanting. He strained his ears again, as he had done earlier. He was convinced he heard them. He wondered if he was deluding himself. Then, he decided he would enjoy what he heard, ceasing to wonder if it was his imagination or a detachment of the heavenly choir.

In those early hours of the morning, Adriel heard a voice reassure him that his life was in God's hands and that the

Lord would use him as His servant. Just months before, Adriel would've said he was talking to himself. At that moment, he was inclined to say that he was being spoken to, not by just anyone, but by God Himself. He rested content with that assumption. No final determination can be made outside one's own judgment; but, it was clear to Adriel that not all things have a naturalistic explanation.

The moon was descending toward the horizon over the land. The light was breaking in the east over the sea. It was time for Adriel to return home for the work of the day. Adriel got up and walked through the ruins to return to his room. It wouldn't be long before he would be headed for the lime-kilns. Before work, he wanted to make an entry in his diary. Despite spending several hours in the ruins instead of sleeping, he didn't feel tired; in fact, he felt refreshed by the vitalizing wind of the Spirit.

CHAPTER FIFTY-SEVEN

DIVINE PRESENCE

When Adriel arrived home, his landlady, Luella Chatburn, was already busy in the kitchen. She didn't seem surprised when he walked in the door. In fact, she heard him leave during the night and watched him through a window, walking down the street toward the ruins. Her assumptions were right. He was restless and couldn't sleep because of his spiritual struggle and spiritual consolation. He needed to take a walk. Without any effort she fell back to sleep. Luella was a woman of uncommon perception. In several weeks, she had come to know the "good lad."

Every Sunday Luella and Adriel would walk together to church for worship. The young man and the old woman made a picture of loving grandmother and devoted grandson. As in Proverbs' description of the worthy wife, she possessed wisdom, dignity, and strength. She was one who feared the Lord. From her, Adriel learned much about how to be wise and even how to sew on a button or mend a tear. It was in this context that Adriel thrived during the months he lived on the Holy Island.

Adriel would often stop by Saint Mary the Virgin Church to sit in a pew to think, reflect, and pray. It was on one occasion that he, while sitting there alone, had an extraordinary experience. The figure of Christ in one of the stained glass windows seemed to break out of its setting and come alive. He said to Adriel the simple words that he spoke to Matthew, "Follow me," and that is all. Adriel was nothing short of flabbergasted while he sat in this extraordinarily peaceful place.

When his calm returned, he considered the Gospel text from which the two words came and realized how much the passage applied to him. It was then, after Jesus invited Matthew to follow him, that the Lord shared a meal with Matthew and tax collectors and sinners, causing the religious leaders grief. Jesus' response was that the well do not need a doctor, but the sick; that God desires, not sacrifice, but mercy; and that the Lord does not call the righteous, but sinners.

Adriel realized so very clearly that he was one of those reclining at table with Jesus. His life had been a sinful excursion; but now, it was again a peregrination involving both faithfulness and repentance for sin. For him, God was real, trustworthy, and replete with a love that transcends all human notions of love.

The priest of the parish came into the chancel through the sacristy door. He acknowledged Adriel with a nod of his head and then proceeded to do what he had intended, preparing for the next day's Sunday Service. Rather than break the silence, his presence only added to the sanctity of the sacred precincts as he went about his duty.

Adriel thought, "Follow me." I must follow him throughout the rest of my life. The Lord has given me the opportunity and power to leave destruction and participate again in His great reconstruction project that began with the fall. I have come to a holy place. And soon I'll return home to continue my life as a disciple of Christ, a pilgrim, no longer wandering, but in mind and heart walking the sacred Way as a believer in the Way.

Adriel had rededicated himself, though at times he felt almost desperate at the loss of alcohol and opium. He was not drinking or smoking; but, he was tempted.

CHAPTER FIFTY-EIGHT

THE STRUGGLE CONTINUES

Let holy charity
Mine outward vesture be,
And lowliness become mine inner clothing—
True lowliness of heart,
Which takes the humbler part,
And o'er its own shortcomings weeps with loathing.
— Bianco da Siena, trans. by Richard F. Littledale

A week later Adriel dragged himself home from the local pub very drunk. Some of his co-workers convinced him to go along with them. By the time the pub closed, Adriel had had many drinks. It was a wonder that he found his way home. Late at night, he stumbled into the house and then fell; he picked himself up and then fell again. Luella made haste out of her room to Adriel. As best a small, old woman could, she helped him to his room, where he fell into bed. That was the end of it for that night.

The next morning Adriel woke up and stared at the ceiling for the longest time. His mind was blank. He could remember what had happened, but as if it had been a dream. He knew that Luella had helped him get to his room. He felt bewildered and humiliated at what he had done. How could he face his landlady? He couldn't go with her to church on this Sunday. Then, a knock came at his door. Adriel didn't answer.

"Adriel, it's Luella. Are you there?"

He answered with a weak, "Yes."

She responded, "You need to get ready for church."

"I can't go today."

"Why?"

"I've got a headache."

"No wonder, dear. You'll feel better if you go with me to church."

"No, not today."

"I'll wait for you. Let's not be late."

Adriel didn't answer but felt compelled to get ready to go, though he had no idea why except out of loyalty to a woman who had been a good friend to him. Probably, it was the respect he had for her. Though he felt very low, he hated to let her down. He sat up and groaned, got out of bed, and dressed himself as his head pounded in protest at the previous night's behavior. The throb kept saying to him, "Don't go."

Adriel walked into the kitchen, where Luella was sitting at the table finishing some tea. She looked at him and said, "Good lad, you look horrid. What possessed you to get drunk?"

"I was with co-workers. I joined the crowd."

"Sounds like a bad idea."

"It turned out to be."

The two of them walked the short distance to Saint Mary the Virgin Church. On the way there was a reflective, not spiteful, silence. Worship lifted Adriel's spirits enough for his unquiet heart to feel the soothing effect of God's presence. During the service he looked over at Luella, who was closely following the service. She held *The Book of Common Prayer* gently, but firmly in her hand.

Adriel had come a long way since his departure from Hong Kong. He didn't want to lose what was gained, but wondered if he had the strength to follow the path set out for him. Then, he thought: *God has won for me this new freedom. But, I'm so weak. My shortcomings are so great. I'm but flesh and blood, alienated from God. I'm Adam outside the Garden. What am I to do? I fear I'll drink again or worse. Will I ever know the peace of God? I cry to you, O Lord, out of a deep need. I truly am not worthy to gather up the crumbs under your table. Help me to do better.*

That day Adriel didn't fail to take Holy Communion. When the service ended, Luella looked over at Adriel and said, "I'm glad you came along this morning, Adriel. When we're at our lowest, we need the Lord the most. I guess we always need God the most."

"You've been a great help to me—a reminder of what's important in this life."

She replied, "We learn the hard way, but we learn. Praise to God." Luella then turned to a friend, seated in the pew behind her, who sought her attention. Adriel sat back down in the pew, thinking of what may come. He feared he would relapse into the horror that he had known so long. He prayed there as worshippers around him were speaking to one another before departing—a typical friendly ritual of any church. For Adriel, though, the sounds of talking and laughter receded as he thought of the times to come, the temptations, and the struggle that would persist throughout his life. At the same time, he hoped that God would attend him in all the trials he'd have to face and keep him under His everlasting wings.

Realizing that Adriel was deep in thought, Luella stood there for a little while before she placed her hand on his shoulder and gently squeezed it. Adriel came out of his reverie and walked Luella home.

CHAPTER FIFTY-NINE

FAREWELL

And so the yearning strong,
With which the soul will long,
Shall far out-pass the pow'r of human telling;
No soul can guess his grace
Till he become the place
Wherein the Holy Spirit makes his dwelling.
— Bianco da Siena, *trans. Richard F. Littledale*

Adriel was standing on the hill where stood the Lindisfarne Castle, built in the sixteenth century for the defense of the Holy Island. He looked out over the calm sea, remembering his past as a sailor and imagining the future when he would travel over it to home after many years away. As he reflected, he could hear the clamor of the seagulls and smell the fragrance of the sea. He thought of Abigail and Caleb and the tragedy they suffered. He thought of his comrades in the War and his schoolmates at the Normal School. He thought of Meili and wondered what happened to her. He still wept for both Abigail and Meili and the friends he lost in battle. He thought of Jennie, whom he knew loved him; but, he didn't have the same affection for her. And then, he thought of his parents. He didn't know if they were still alive or, if they were, whether they ever thought of him.

For two months since his night of drunkenness, Adriel kept sober. He was within arm's reach of a drink. In the name of conviviality and friendship, all he had to do was go along with some fellow workers after the day's work had ended. He resisted this temptation with considerable effort. Luella provided him encouragement that made a difference. He was indeed her "good lad." He had helped her in so many ways that made her life as a widow easier. Now, her son planned to move back to the island with his family so that Adriel didn't think he was abandoning her.

It was time to depart for America. He felt this pull deeply in his heart. He would send a letter ahead to his parents informing them that he would soon be returning. They didn't know if he was alive or had died in some forsaken cranny of the world; for, he hadn't written to them in years.

Adriel pondered many things on that promontory of the Holy Island; then, he soared. The solitude, the sea breeze, the ocean surf, the bright sunlight, and the blue sky with white puffs of cloud sailing effortlessly in it encouraged an ecstatic sensibility that he imagined had taken him up into the third heaven like Saint Paul.

Adriel thanked God that he was being healed of the sickness of his soul. Adriel pledged that he would never indulge in pipe or bottle again. He knew, though, that the battle was never over. The void in his soul that led him to addiction in the first place was filled with the radiance of God, sometimes not as bright as at other times. Sojourn on the island was the culmination of where his life had been headed during the last year, not without setbacks.

Adriel looked across the inlet to the Priory ruins and St. Mary's, then turned his vision to the village. He took in as much as he could for the sake of memory, not wanting to forget all that the Holy Island had meant to him. It would be difficult to say good-bye to Luella, the men he had befriended at the kilns, and members of Saint Mary the Virgin. During his stay congregants had embraced him with Christian hospitality. His tears testified to the difficulty of his leaving; but, he knew in his heart it was time to return home.

On his last Sunday, Adriel, as always, attended church with Luella. The sermon was about following the way of Christ. He heeded the words carefully. Holy Communion filled Adriel with a vivid sense of the body and blood of Christ. He thought that on this same day his parents were receiving Communion at Saint Jude Thaddeus Church, far away but close to his heart and mind despite the long years of alienation and separation. The Prayer of Thanksgiving in *The Book of Common Prayer* says that in Holy Communion we are assured that, "... we are very members incorporate in the mystical body of thy Son ..."

He made his farewells to the people with whom he had become acquainted and shook the rector's hand at the door for the last time. That afternoon, he packed a few items. On his departure, he didn't walk back to Berwick; because, Luella's son, Aubrey, would take him to the station.

Years later, Adriel was sitting in his cabin in front of a blazing fire in the hearth. This time, when the Holy Island came to mind, he was moved to write a poem. He pulled up his writing desk and began to compose with a respectful smirk.

The Holy Island of Lindisfarne
The island green, the heavens blue;
North Sea of blue and greenish hue.
The tide goes in; the tide goes out.
When it's coming, give a shout.

Adriel chuckled to himself that he was so clever; but, it wouldn't do. The poem had to be of a more exalted quality. So he tried again.

CHAPTER SIXTY

DEPARTURE AND RETURN

O Lindisfarne, O Holy Isle,
Retreat of peace to reconcile
Both erring heart and mind
Through Jesus, Lord so kind.

– Adriel Peregrine

Adriel took the train to Liverpool, where he boarded an American packet to New York. From there, he boarded a train for Philadelphia, then to Lancaster. During the trip he could think of little else than how he would be greeted at home. In his heart he knew that he had been the prodigal son. Would he be welcome with open arms as the penitent or spurned as the knave he had been? He feared rejection, not wanting to be an outcast in his own family, which included the brothers and sisters and their families of both his mother and father. Since his leaving, he knew nothing of the lives of his friends. He had not communicated with anyone at home since his departure for the canal. Perhaps those who knew him assumed he was dead; at least, he was dead to them.

Each mile closer to home on sea or land increased his disquiet. He thought of all that had happened and anticipated what the future would be. Contrition about the past and apprehension about the future filled Adriel's days. He would distract himself by reading books he had bought in Liverpool, including *20,000 Leagues under the Sea*, recently published.

*

The day came when Adriel was traveling on a mainline train for Lancaster. Soon he would be home after five years of wandering. Soon he would discover whether he was welcome or not. On the chance that his parents would meet him at Lancaster station, he sent a telegram to them from Philadelphia.

As the train pulled into the station, Adriel's heart was pounding so that he was quite aware that he had one. As the train slowed, he strained his eyes, looking for his parents. He didn't see them. When the train stopped, he grabbed his haversack, a companion during and since the War, and got off. He disembarked and then scanned the crowd. When he didn't see them, he thought his heart stopped. Then, out of the throng appeared his father. When their eyes met, his father moved toward him and extended his hand. Adriel did the same.

The first words out of his father's mouth were, "Welcome home, Son."

Adriel responded, "It's good to be home, Father. Forgive me for what I put you through."

His father placed his hand on the back of Adriel's neck and looked straight into his son's eyes. Adriel knew that it meant "Yes." "It is so good to know that you are alive and not dead, as we thought. Your mother and I despaired for you."

Adriel entreated again, "Forgive me, Father."

"Son, I can speak for both myself and your mother. You are forgiven. Let's go home." And to Adriel's amazement, his father embraced him with vigor. Sylvan remained apprehensive that Adriel had not left behind his former habits, but was willing to take a chance that he had.

"Yes, let's go home," Adriel sighed.

The ride home was silence, with interludes of quiet conversation. Adriel told his father something of his five years—of his work and addiction, of his conversion and days in London and Lindisfarne. He didn't mention Meili; because, it was too painful for him. Maybe he would relate the sad story at a time in the future.

Sylvan updated Adriel on what had happened since his departure. Both of Caleb's parents had died, probably due to heartbreak. Adriel was cut to the quick about this news. He resolved himself to take up the investigation that he had forsaken when he left home. His father also let him know that the new constable in the township was his roommate at the Normal School. Jacob Brenneman was married and taught in a one room schoolhouse in the township, as well as serving as constable. When Adriel learned this, he decided he would ask Jacob for help in finding the murderer. Adriel's anger rose as he thought of what happened to Abigail.

Later that day, father and son arrived home. Adriel had an odd feeling of both familiarity and unfamiliarity. It was the old homestead in which he grew up, but hadn't seen in five years. Considering the distance from home and the events that took place at that distance, more than five years seemed to have passed in Adriel's life.

Inside, Adriel's mother was waiting for her son's return. She was sitting in the chair she used to rock Adriel to sleep in when he was a baby. Her nervous energy was partly consumed by the crocheting project, a blanket for Adriel, she had been working on. When she heard the sound of horse and buggy, she jumped up out of her seat and went to the front door. She paused, knowing what she wanted to do next, but not doing it. Then, she summoned the resoluteness to open the door, unsure of what she might hear, see, and feel.

Adriel was standing alone facing the front door with his haversack slung over his left shoulder, while his father was unhitching the horse in the barn. Mother and son were staring at one another. Adriel stood there with a visible change in his face from tense to smiling. He couldn't help the transformation; for, he was overjoyed to see her. She was gladdened by his arrival as she stepped toward him. They embraced without a sound as they shared tears that moistened shirt and dress. Neither mother nor son wished to let go.

"I love you, Adriel."

"I love you, Mom." They walked into the house to await Sylvan. The house had the scent of love. Mom was cooking dinner. She would soon have to look in on the food to prevent its burning, but not at the moment.

"Sit down, Adriel; you've had a very long journey."

"Yes, five years' worth," he replied.

"You must tell your father and me all about it." Agatha wanted to ask if drinking was still a problem; but, prudence prevented her from doing so at this early date. She would broach the subject later. She didn't know Adriel had had a problem with opium. As he told his father, he would also tell her about his struggle.

Sylvan came into the house as mother and son were sitting in the front room. Without a word, he sat down.

Somewhat awkwardly, Adriel began the conversation. "I'm very grateful that you're willing to have me home. I wasn't pleasant when I left, and you don't know what you're getting into now."

"We're glad that you're home and alive! For so long we didn't know one way or another whether you were dead or alive," his mother struggled to say while weeping.

"I'm so sorry for how I treated you. I'll do better if you'll let me stay for a short while. I intend to settle and work here." Adriel couldn't keep the tears back. They streamed down his face in a flood. They were silent tears without the thunder and storm that the voice could contribute.

"You may surely stay, Adriel, if you'll refrain from your former behavior," his father replied.

"I will, thank you."

Adriel gave his mother and father a description of his last five years. Hours later, they shared together a meal of his favorite food his mother had prepared for his return home. He hadn't eaten such in the five years that he was gone—chicken pot pie and baked corn—a delicious dinner that lacked the color green. For dessert there was cherry pie with cherries picked from Sylvan's own trees he tended on the homestead. They had been canned by Agatha.

Adriel was at home. Of this fact, he was very glad.

CHAPTER SIXTY-ONE
THE LORD'S DAY

The woods are still;
The morning bright.
The land bedight
By nature's skill.

The church bells ring;
The organ plays.
The people praise
Our holy King.

— Adriel Peregrine

The Peregrines went to church as they always did on Sunday. This time, for the first time in five years, Adriel accompanied them. The people welcomed him back warmly. At Morning Prayer the chants and hymns swelled; and, Father Ledford preached a wise and discerning sermon. He greeted Adriel heartily at the door, but not with great surprise; for, Adriel's parents had told him that their son was headed home right after they received the telegram. The priest invited him to stop by the church so that Adriel and he could catch up after all the years. Adriel was quite willing, agreeing on the very next day for a visit after seeing Mr. Alden for a job.

Adriel had seen Jennie Hallewell in church with her family and, though he had no romantic interest, wished to speak with her as an old friend. She was startled to see him, having received no intelligence that he had come home.

They embraced. Adriel said, "Jennie, it's so good to see you. I hope that you've been well."

Jennie felt disconcerted and overjoyed by Adriel's presence. She had loved him for years, refusing a suitor in hopes of seeing Adriel again. She knew that her hope was unrealistic and immature. With good reason she was afraid that she would unwittingly reveal her disposition toward him; for, she knew that he had no interest in her. She didn't want to look foolish; but, she also yearned for his love.

"I've been well, Adriel. I live at home and teach school in our township." She exerted great effort to appear without strong emotion.

Adriel wondered why Jennie wasn't married. She was pretty, intelligent, and kind. But, he didn't wonder why he hadn't courted her. He had been so preoccupied with Abigail that Jennie somehow didn't come into view as a possible mate. At times he wished to avoid her; because, he knew that Jennie had some affection for him. He'd been away for five years. He had thought of her little, and Abigail much—Abigail who had been murdered and lay in her grave all these years. Meili was his love for a small portion of that time. He had satisfied his youthful desire with prostitutes whom he used and didn't love, a fact of which he was not proud after his return to the faith of his youth.

"Do you have time for a walk so that we can catch up after all of these years?" Adriel asked.

"I would love to," Jennie responded, hoping that she didn't seem overly enthusiastic. She was surprised by his invitation.

Adriel and Jennie begged leave from their parents and started out for a time of re-acquaintance. The late October Lord's Day was bright with the sundry colors of the season adorning the trees and ground. The two walked out into the fields below the church, bathed in the bright sunshine of that resplendent, warmer than usual October day. Adriel was taking Jennie to woods of no great size where he often walked in his youth. A path extended through it and seemed like a world of its own. It was there that he received inspiration for writing a number of poems. It was there that he had met Pontiac Rowbottom.

They walked together, but not hand in hand, through the recently harvested fields of corn, hay, and wheat. The ground smelled of such sweetness that Adriel thought of the remains of the harvest as incense filling the space of an enormous church. He closed his eyes and took a deep breath with mouth wide open, held his breath until it looked like he was struggling for oxygen, and exhaled with much noise. Jennie looked at him and laughed, with Adriel joining in. If there was any tension between them before, it was broken by Adriel's demonstration.

Adriel looked at Jennie as they both laughed joyfully at being alive on this fair autumn day. He looked at her again with more serious intent, a reconsideration that actually had been working on him since he boarded the steamer for home.

"Jennie, I've been many places and done many things, some not so good." Adriel felt that, in some sense, he was making a confession to one whom he had always trusted as a friend, but never loved as a sweetheart.

Jennie looked at Adriel. "Adri, I can imagine you've been in some dark places; but, I also know that you can be as good as any man can be in this fallen world. I remember you before the War. You possess a sinful heart like all people; but, you are not evil-hearted. There's a difference. The Spirit of God has filled you." Jennie was thoughtful—a thinker of matters temporal and eternal. She never stopped reading, nor would she. She was a denizen of the town library, a sprite haunting the stacks.

"I can expect from you nothing but gentleness and kindness." Jennie's appearance, words, and manner were gentle but strong. She was not a pushover. Adriel loved these things about her and wondered at that very moment why he hadn't noticed her before now. Such represented to him the mystery and unpredictability of human emotion and romantic love.

There they were about to enter the woods at the edge of the fields of fall, facing one another. Adriel, forgetting his natural timidity, stepped toward her and took her hand. He realized, as if it were a sudden revelation, that he loved her. How odd it seemed to him. He realized that she had always loved him since that awakening at the coming of age, and even before then, and he didn't see it, or ignored it.

Adriel gently pulled Jennie toward him and kissed her on the cheek and then on the lips. She didn't resist him; in fact, she had been waiting for the moment for a long time. When he took a deep breath, he could smell her sweetness; she was frankincense. She embraced him, placing her head on his breast. He lifted her head and kissed her on the lips again. He held her with one hand on her chin and one in a tight embrace. For the longest time, they were in each other's arms. Adriel took her by the hand and led her to a favorite tree where he had sat to read and while away many summer days, exploring his imagination in lands uncharted and fantastic. They sat down and refrained from talking for a few minutes as they absorbed their newfound love for one another.

The hours went by as they caught up with each other about their lives after years of separation. They lost track of time; and, when they again became aware, the sun was about to descend below the hills. They hurried home, stumbling through the fields and laughing away.

CHAPTER SIXTY-TWO

IN THE CONFESSIONAL

Take heart, my son, your sins are forgiven.   – *Matthew 9: 2b.*

The next day, Adriel went to see Mr. Alden, with whom he had a favorable conversation despite Alden's irritation with Adriel's treatment of his parents. Adriel's recent history, of which he knew little except some of the shenanigans Adriel pulled before he left for the Canal, didn't prevent Alden from giving the young man a job at the limekilns. Adriel described his work on Lindisfarne with which Alden was impressed; his work Alden knew very well. Adriel would again be in his good graces.

In the afternoon, Adriel, with some dread and much sanguine expectation, paid a visit to Father Ledford in the vestry, a room where vestments and sacramental vessels are kept and also meetings are held, including the place where the governing board of the church, also called the vestry, assembles for its business. When he walked into the church, no one was present. As a result, he became more apprehensive. A few minutes ticked by—the sound of the clock seemed to get louder by the moment, and the wait seemed much longer than actual time—before Ledford entered the room.

"Ah, Adriel, sorry I wasn't here to greet you. Good to see you. Come on in."

With great relief Adriel followed the priest into the vestry. He took a seat when offered and waited for the priest to open the conversation; for, with the shame he felt because of his former waywardness and his long time respect for the pastor, he was committed to the priest's taking the lead and hesitant in expressing himself.

"Adriel, it's so good to see you after all this time. I've prayed for you often. I know a lot has happened, including some things that are not so good. Why don't you update me on your life over the past years?"

Adriel hesitated because of his embarrassment. Then, he said, "Father, more than anything else I come to you as a penitent. My life over the past six years has been erring and wandering. I denied God and got twisted up in alcohol and opium. I had been a frequenter of prostitutes, a man burdened with the seeking of sexual pleasure. It started during the War and didn't cease until a short time ago in London with the priests of the Society of the Holy Cross. To them I owe a great debt of gratitude."

"They are a dedicated group. I've adopted some of the perspectives and practices of the Oxford Movement. They have been very good for the church. I've read tracts of the Movement, especially those of John Henry Newman. Edward Pusey and John Keble also have contributed. I have the tracts in my library if you would like to read them. But, now, the matter at hand is your relationship to the Lord. Tell me more about what's happening with you."

"I've been in confession with a priest I admired while serving in East London. After leaving the sea that had been my life for so many years, I served in East London with the Anglican mission. The situation with the people is desperate—poverty, disease, alcoholism, and drug addiction. There I learned to come out of myself and to draw out gifts of the Spirit that showed me how to serve. Father Frith—that is his name—granted me absolution even though I had a relapse since. I know that God is merciful. I come to you primarily as another opportunity to confess my sins and receive forgiveness."

"I'm so glad you have. Remember, Adriel, that when a sin

is forgiven to one who is penitent, the sin is truly forgiven. Don't doubt it."

"Father, I have because of how far I've gotten off the path." Adriel turned red, but felt he needed to be honest with the priest. "I was without God who changes people like me and every penitent. His mercy and grace finally overwhelmed me. I realized that no matter what, God is there to receive us back.

"While in England I decided to leave London and go to Lindisfarne, the Holy Island. There I stayed for quite a while. I found a job in the limekilns."

"Yes, fair Lindisfarne—the home of Aidan and Cuthbert. And, God be praised. You have known how 'deep, broad, and wide' is the love of God. You've been in the clutches of hell and now have returned to the road leading to the Promised Land."

"I've had dreams of following Virgil and Dante in hell. More than once, Dante turned to me and asked me if I wanted to stay in that dark, God-forsaken place. The answer was always, 'No,' and the dream was always a nightmare."

"Do you dream this dream anymore?"

"No. Actually I have dreamt more recently of Saint Bernard and Beatrice in the highest heaven of whom Dante writes."

"Good. Adriel, I'm glad you're home and safe and again traveling the road of the pilgrim."

"Yes, one of the things I had to do was reconcile with my parents, whom I hurt very much. They were open to this. We still have much to do in building trust. I want to show them that I can be trustworthy, a virtue not common in this world."

"How important that is. I'm glad to hear it. Making amends is part of repentance."

"I've much yet to do. I've not resolved the whole tragedy of Abigail and Caleb. I must pursue some course to resolve this matter. Something's not right about it. I don't think Caleb murdered Abigail."

"The court was pretty certain of his guilt, and now he's

dead. What do you think you can accomplish?"

"I want to prove that Caleb was innocent and that someone else, yet unknown, killed Abigail."

"You're setting yourself up for an arduous task; but, I understand why it is so much in your heart and mind."

"Father, I must come to peace about this tragedy."

"I understand. I'll pray for you. I don't know how, but if there is any way I can be of assistance, let me know."

"I will."

"Now would be a good time for confession."

"I think so too."

Adriel was nervous about what he would tell Father Ledford in confession about his past while on his wanderings. The story was filled with Adriel's moral failures he was ashamed to reveal to a priest he had greatly respected. He thought to himself: *I'll look so small in his eyes. He will have contempt for me. Then, he thought that his pride was interfering, as it so often can with everyone, with his spiritual welfare.* He prepared himself to confess before heaven, whose God already knew, and his own spiritual mentor the sins of his youth. He recalled the Psalm of David, "Remember not the sins of my youth, nor my transgression; According to thy mercy remember thou me for thy goodness' sake, O Lord." (Psalm 25; 7 KJV) At the behest of the good priest, Adriel knelt at the prayer desk and made the sign of the cross as he repeated to himself, "Out of the depths have I cried unto thee, O Lord." (Psalm 130: 1 KJV)

CHAPTER SIXTY-THREE

PONTIAC ROWBOTTOM

So long thy power hath blest me, sure it still
Will lead me on,
o'er moor and fen, o'er crag and torrent, till
the night is gone,
and with the morn those angel faces smile,
which I have loved long since, and lost awhile.
– John Henry Newman (1801-1890)

On the night before Adriel's return to the limekilns, he was very restless and couldn't sleep. He wasn't sure why. He peered out of his bedroom window and saw the crescent moon. He was astounded; for, never in the twenty-four years of his life had he seen such a sight despite all the places he had been. It was about to set in the west between two trees that seemed to frame it. The thin, waxing crescent was orange in color, giving a numinous quality to its appearance. Even on the high sea he hadn't seen such a sight. He addressed her as Selene and Cynthia and Artemis and Diana, all classical allusions to goddesses in whom he didn't believe but on whom he relied for poetic symbolism and imaginative inspiration. He sat down on a chair next to the window. He couldn't keep his eyes off the moon. Soon he fell asleep. When he awoke, the moon was gone. The spell was broken; but, memory of the beauty of this creation of God remained with him. He then got into bed and slept well.

Adriel could tell that this day would be extraordinary, and

it certainly was. As Adriel approached the limekilns, he beheld a man whose appearance reminded him of someone whom he had known, but couldn't remember who he was. The man was of medium height with a grey beard. He wore wire-rimmed glasses and dressed in overalls and a checkered long sleeve shirt. He had on a jacket and wore a broad-brimmed hat on his head.

Pontiac recognized Adriel. "Adriel, it's Pontiac Rowbottom."

Adriel then recognized this old acquaintance and realized how much he had changed. The worn lines of grief and suffering remained; but, they were transfigured by his blue eyes sparkling on either side of his nose. His mouth was not drawn down in a frown; it was turned slightly up in the promise of a smile.

"Yes, it's been a long time. How are you, Pontiac?" Adriel drew close to him and shook his hand.

"I'm better than when you saw me last. I decided to settle here. Mr. Alden gave me a job and permission to settle on a parcel of his land." A dog emerged from the woods and ran up to Pontiac. "Oh, yes, I also acquired a dog. Her name is Annie." The dog came up to her master, who stroked her, then came sniffing at Adriel.

Adriel bent down and petted Annie, who was wagging her tail. "You're a good dog, Annie." The dog was a two year old, sleek little terrier that helped Pontiac hunt in the woods he lived in. Adriel had wanted to get a dog for years while he was away, but didn't because of adverse circumstances. He thought to himself, *Maybe sometime soon.*

"Do you work here?" Adriel said.

"Yes, Mr. Alden saved me from certain disaster. I've been working here for over five years. I decided to wander no longer. Because I'm slowing down, he's going to give me another job on the estate."

Adriel replied, "I also decided to stop wandering. We need to get together," he said, "soon."

"How about tomorrow? After work, we can ride over to my place."

"I'd like that. I'll bring some food from home that we can share together."

"I'd like that." Pontiac smiled.

That day, Adriel became re-acquainted with some old friends whom he met when he first worked at the kilns. They were glad to see him. Over lunch they talked about old times. When Adriel asked, they updated him about the Dunlaps, who had not fared well over the years since their daughter's death. Mrs. Dunlap had become a recluse, sitting for hours in her upstairs bedroom, looking out over the land with no explanation but the paralysis of unresolved grief; Mr. Dunlap had become morose. Every Sunday, the Dunlaps would visit Abigail's grave at the small cemetery on their farm property. Even in foul weather, unless it was pouring down raining, they would walk the short distance to the plot. Other members of the Dunlap family were also buried there. The tombstones were testimony to the history that extended back to the beginning of settlement in the area. The older grave markers were worn so that one could no longer read the names, birth and death dates, and any Scriptural verses or other text or maxim.

The next day after work, Adriel and Pontiac rode off to Pontiac's retreat in the woods. On the way, Pontiac revealed to Adriel something that astounded the young man. As they rode side by side with Annie in front of them—for she knew where she was going—Pontiac said to Adriel, "I'm taking you to a very familiar spot."

"I was wondering about that. I've walked this way many times."

"After you had been gone for a while, Mr. Alden allowed me to occupy your cabin. I finished it and moved in. I hope you're not angry."

"How could I be? I wasn't here so I wasn't using it. I'm

anxious to see what you have done." Adriel and Jennie hadn't entered the woods on that Sunday; thus, they knew nothing of the completed cabin.

Pontiac was relieved that he had not angered Adriel. When they entered the woods, Annie barked, knowing she was soon home. As they came up to the cabin, Adriel stirred inside as he remembered those days of youth before his wandering. He was glad that Pontiac could settle here, ending his own wandering after the death of his wife. Both wandered; both had ended their wandering and found peace—as much as can be found in this world before the coming of heaven's concord. Adriel was discovering that peace was not in the drug, but in Christ.

Adriel was impressed with what Pontiac had done to the cabin. Pontiac made for himself a comfortable abode with many windows looking out into the forest. He observed the abundant and diverse wildlife that passed him.

The structure was sturdy, as Adriel had made it. Inside was a large room with a fireplace. A few chairs, an easy chair, and a large table decorated the interior. Many nights, especially in the cool and cold weather, Pontiac would sit by the fireplace and fall asleep, dreaming of many pleasant things, infrequently of fell things. A small kitchen and two separate rooms, one in which Pontiac slept, completed the design of his retreat. He called the place "Deer Run," for deer came through the property every day. His place was truly in what he called "a little wilderness"-- a place of abundant wildlife and thick with plant life that exists under towering trees—ferns and moss and sundry other greenness. Annie and he would search for truffles and, sometimes, Pontiac would find arrowheads from a long departed Neolithic people.

At the door of the cabin, in a rack, stood his walking staff with the falcon on top, the same one as he held when Adriel first met him. Pontiac walked many miles through the countryside with Annie. His wandering on the land was not erring. In his heart and mind, he knew the direction he was taking—to the City of God. He would sing, sometimes at the top of his voice, songs that would lift his spirits.

Above the trees the falcon calls.
The hov'ring bee partakes the bloom.
The forest floor with green growth strewn.
God's comely, well-trimmed halls!

The two men sat down at the long table to a substantial lunch of bread, sliced beef, tomatoes, and cherry pie prepared by Agatha Peregrine. Pontiac added some cooked truffles and milk he had stored in the spring house he had built. Pontiac provided the hot and cold; Adriel the in-between. Annie, who lay under the table, would be a beneficiary of the feast. She patiently awaited her share she knew wouldn't be long in coming.

Pontiac placed the truffles on the table and sat across from Adriel. On the first day at the kilns, Pontiac and Adriel had some time to talk. Adriel had given him a short history of his wanderings.

Pontiac said grace, then, after a moment, commented, "Well, this looks like quite a feast, thanks to your mother."

"And to you," Adriel replied.

"Well, here we are, two wanderers, now on the right path."

"For me, it took a long time to return," said Adriel.

Pontiac told Adriel that after Adriel had gone to work on the Delaware Canal, he decided to remain in that quiet, bucolic spot of Red Oak where Adriel had grownup. He got a job with Mr. Alden and finished Adriel's cabin. Later he acquired Annie from a local farmer. He joined Saint Jude Thaddeus church. He had made many friends and was respected by those around him. Children would hail him with great respect, "Mr. Rowbottom, good morning," or "Mr. Rowbottom, good day," or "Mr. Rowbottom, I hope all's well with you on this fine day."

He would typically respond, "Blessings on you, Little One or Ones." Though he lived in the woods without next door neighbors, he was a neighbor to the people of the area, and they to him. Everyone seemed to know him and enjoyed his company. A blessed life he was leading and would to the day of his death. He was grateful that he'd been delivered from a deep, dark bitterness at the loss of his wife to life directed by the light of God.

"You remember how I was when you first met me years ago, a bitter old man bent on self-destruction."

"I'm glad you, but especially my parents, didn't see the nonsense of my last five years. God saw all of it and had mercy on me. The angels must have rejoiced," answered Adriel.

"You and I are now on a different path, the Way. I hope we can offer each other support so that we don't stray. I no longer want to be out in that terrible dry and deadly wilderness ."

Adriel replied, "We travel together as friends."

Pontiac said, "We travel together as friends." And they shook each other's hand.

"Peace, brother in Christ."

"Peace, brother in Christ."

"I thought of you, Pontiac, over the years as I wandered, wondering where your wandering had taken you."

"It took my mind and soul to some very dark places. At times I thought that an army of demons was assaulting me. I had a difficult time warding them off. I later discovered that God was fighting on my behalf. I eventually would've been overcome. When I realized again God's goodness and mercy, I attended Saint Jude Thaddeus and then joined."

"Oh, I didn't see you on Sunday."

"I was sick and stayed in bed."

"Sorry to hear this."

"It lasted only a day."

"Good."

"I've gotten much out of being a part of Saint Jude Thaddeus.

I keep my Prayer Book next to my Bible."

"God has been good to us, Pontiac."

"I try never to forget this. Yes, we aren't lost any longer out in the desert's scorching heat."

"God has shown us the way. How lost we humans can get! How deep our sin reveals how deep God's mercy is! I can meditate on this all day, but only skim the surface of the astounding wonder it is. In this life I could never come to the end of it."

"You say it well, Adriel. May we fix our minds on the bounty of God's lovingkindness."

"We are lost and are found."

CHAPTER SIXTY-FOUR

NORMAL ROOMMATES

*After years had gone by, I encountered my college roommate in
the community I grew up in. It is amazing how persons, long gone,
return as we grow older.*

    – A Wanderer Who Becomes a Pilgrim, *Adriel Peregrine.*

Adriel often focused on the wooden eagle with outspread
wings that served as the foundation for the lectern Bible in
Saint Jude Thaddeus Church. The eagle was finely made by an
expert woodcarver who once lived in the community, but had
for many years resided in the church cemetery until the day
of resurrection.

From the time Adriel was small, he was fascinated with
the representation of the noble bird. He learned much later
that the eagle in church stood for the Gospel, taking wing
to the people in church and beyond. It also was a symbol for
Saint John, author of the fourth Gospel, that soars in its verses
to a great heavenly height. In one of the stained glass windows, the eagle stands by the seated saint as he writes his
Gospel. The eagle is one of the four creatures, mentioned in
the fourth chapter of Revelation, that came to represent the
four Gospel writers.

On the next Sunday after Pontiac's and Adriel's meeting,
Jennie was sitting with Adriel and his parents in a pew, to the
dismay of her parents, who thought Adriel was a dangerous
man. Hearsay had magnified stories describing Adriel's waywardness. He murdered someone; he was a pirate; he was fab-
ulously wealthy from the booty; he had a harem of women—

all untrue. Jennie was not discouraged by the rumors. She loved Adriel and wouldn't give him up for anyone or anything except the Lord Himself. More than anyone else in the community, she knew the true story and sympathized with his struggle without approving his past behavior. She would risk hardship and disappointment and the disapproval of her parents with whom she yet lived to be with one whom she had loved for so many years—an unrequited love until the present.

During the service, Jennie thought of that great symbol of the Gospel, not able to get her mind off it, though she had seen it time and time again over so many years. Before the service began, as the organ played the prelude, Adriel explained to Jennie the significance of the eagle, something she wondered about, but never asked anyone who might know the meaning. As was her habit, she listened to Adriel intently. She imagined the eagle flying up to the ceiling, disappearing into the roof, reappearing in the sunlight, and ascending into heaven after winging over the land with the message of the Gospel, called kerygma.

Adriel wrote this poem sometime later:

The brazen eagle stood upon the sphere
With wings outspread in readiness for flight,
Upholding on its figure words of light,
The faithful come with solemn hearts to hear.

As sacred text was heedfully proclaimed,
A fiery burst obscured the avian perch
And caused a gasp inside the crowded church.
Stained glass was then by brilliant light inflamed.

So high it flew above the thirsty land
To rain upon the earth God's greening Word,
Descending on the globe from strand to strand.

The Gospel that has many people stirred,
Saint John as witness wrote by his own hand,
Whose hallowed symbol is that very bird.

After church, Adriel and Jennie took a Sunday walk, as they had done the week before. This time Adriel took Jennie into the woods where Pontiac's cabin was located. When Adriel knocked, Pontiac answered the door. He was expecting them. Over tea and biscuits the three conversed until late in the afternoon.

Adriel walked Jennie home, but took leave before they approached the front door. Jennie's parents were not welcoming of the young man. Adriel knew it would be a great effort to win them over—a problem he'd had before with the Dunlaps and then the Cheungs. *Omne trium perfectum*—everything coming in threes is perfect. Well, for him bad things had come in threes, in this instance, the disapproval of families of the women he loved. *Was there something very wrong with him?* he asked himself. In the first instance, the woman didn't love him and the parents thought he was too low on the socio-economic scale. In the second instance, the parents had plans for their daughter in an arranged marriage. In the third instance, he bore with him a bad reputation. In the last case, he was the most culpable. He knew that when a reputation is tarnished, it is hard to restore.

After a month at home, Adriel decided it was time to do something he had wanted to do for a long time—investigate Abigail's murder. He had been certain from the time of the murder that Caleb Landis was not the culprit. Finding the evildoer was, now that he was home, a compelling mission for Adriel. He would not be going on any long trips. It was the murder that was one of the primary factors in his leaving home after returning there from his war service.

Adriel had heard that Jake Brenneman, his roommate at teachers' college, was the constable of the township. Jake was also a teacher in one of the many schoolhouses in the township. Jake's wife and three children lived with him in the locale of Red Oak—the settlement in which Adriel grew up and again lived. The Brenneman family attended the local Lutheran Church.

One day after work, Adriel decided to visit Jake, whose residence was known to Adriel from a description given him by a neighbor. Jake lived two miles from the Peregrines. As he approached the front door, Adriel heard the sound of children's voices. He knocked, but there was no response. Then, he knocked again, a little louder. As he was about to knock yet one more time, the door opened. It was Jake. He looked at Adriel with a perplexed expression, not sure if he knew the man at the door. Then, a rush of recognition led him to cry out, "Adri!" Jake had heard that Adriel had come home, but had not visited him because of his busy life as constable, school teacher, and father.

"Yes, it's long lost Adri."

Jake heartily shook his hand. "Please, come in."

Adriel entered the Brenneman house to the sound of children. Jake's wife came into the hallway where the two men stood. "My wife, Amelia. Amelia, Adriel Peregrine, of whom I have spoken."

"Nice to meet you, Mr. Peregrine."

"To meet you, the same. It is great now to have met my roommate's wife."

The three children who were playing upstairs came down out of curiosity about what was happening. They stood in a row at the bottom of the steps and quietly gazed at this new person in their house.

Jake explained, "Children, this is Adriel Peregrine. He was my roommate in teachers' college. Their faces showed perplexity, though their father had told them about his days preparing for teaching. "Say hello," which they quietly did. "Now you can go off and play," which they quickly did.

Amelia said, "You two will want to catch up after all these years. I'm on my way to the kitchen to make dinner. Please stay, Adriel."

"Thank you. Are you sure it's no trouble?"

"Not at all."

"Well, then, Adriel, we have some catching up. Let's go to my little office."

Adriel followed Jake to the back of the house. There Jake often installed himself to prepare for school and keep up with his responsibilities as constable. "Take a seat."

Jake sat on his desk chair. "So, tell me, what has been going on with you?" The two men updated each other on their lives.

"Jake, I came to see you for two reasons. The first is I wanted to visit my old roommate. We have much to catch up on. I'd like to know about your war service, and I can tell you mine. The second is something that has been bothering me for a long time; the death of Abigail Dunlap. Do you know any-thing about this case?"

"I've read about it in our records. What a sad thing."

"I want to solve the case."

"According to the courts, the case has been solved."

"I know; but, I believe that there yet remains a murderer out there. Would you help me with this?"

"You're convinced it was someone else?"

"I'm convinced."

"What you want to do would be unofficial."

"That makes no difference to me."

"I'll help out where I can. But, I can't officially re-open the case."

"Good. I don't want to interfere with the law; but, I do want to catch the killer."

CHAPTER SIXTY-FIVE

FINDING CLUES

I am determined, more so than at any other time, to find Abigail's killer. I always believed that Caleb was innocent. I have had to resist murderous thoughts regarding the offender, even though I don't know who he is. Most of the time, I have been successful in my determination. – Diary of Adriel Peregrine, *November 10, 1871.*

Adriel began the very next day to investigate the death of one whom he had loved. He really didn't know where to start, but finally decided to start with the Dunlaps. He was sure that the Dunlaps wouldn't be open to talking about their daughter's death; but, he had to attempt an interview with them anyway. So on one Saturday in November, he walked down the farm lane to the Dunlap mansion. He was thinking about knocking on the door, but lost courage as he neared the house. He stopped at a place close to where Abigail's body was found. Years ago, he was led to the spot based on information he had gathered when he first attempted to find the murderer. At that place, the house was hidden from view. On the chance he would find something significant, even after all these years, he kept his eyes on the ground. He looked back and forth on that section of road for the longest time. The sun was under a cloud and then burst forth from it. At that moment, his eyes caught a gleam at the edge of the road. He went over to look at it more closely. Bending down, he picked the object up. On close examination he realized that he had found a tie pin with an emerald embedded in it. It was not an inexpensive piece of jewelry. Adriel stuffed the object into his pocket. It could turn out to belong to the murderer.

That night Adriel couldn't sleep. For the longest time, he stared at the ceiling. Then, he stared out the window and back to the ceiling again. When he decided it was impossible to return to sleep, he got out of bed and looked out the window, as was his wont when he couldn't sleep. He thought he saw someone walking toward the house. He squinted his eyes to give himself a clearer view. It looked like a white mist in human shape, just like the one he experienced a long time ago. The form seemed a likeness of Abigail. Adriel decided that his distress had made him vulnerable to hallucinations. A shiver ran down his back.

The next morning he was heavy with sleep; his back hurt, and he suffered from nausea—the cost of a sleepless night. He was determined to do everything he could to find the one who put an end to Abigail's life and was also responsible for the death of Caleb Landis. His ghostly experience encouraged in him an even greater commitment to the cause. He would investigate no matter how long the process took.

Adriel met with Jake to tell him what he had found in the farm lane. The constable showed interest in what Adriel discovered, but thought that the arrest of another individual as murderer was remote, especially after such a long time. He had looked over Caleb's case and found that there was considerable evidence against him.

"Adri, we need a lot more evidence. Whose is the pin? How did it get there?"

"I know. But, I'm going to pursue this possible lead. If it goes nowhere, I'll start over."

"That seems reasonable."

"I want to speak with the Dunlaps. But, so far I haven't built up the nerve to go to them. They may be unreceptive to the idea that someone else committed the murder."

"Well, if you want to go, I support you. Let me know what you find out."

"I will."

The next day, Adriel was walking down the Dunlap's farm lane again. This time, he was determined to speak with the parents. At the door Conrad Kraybill greeted him. His face declared his dissatisfaction that Adriel was the one knocking.

"Yes, what can I do for you?" Conrad said in a grave, almost fierce voice. Adriel realized that getting around Kraybill was going to be very difficult.

"I'd like to speak with the Dunlaps."

"On what business?"

"About their daughter's death."

"They don't wish to discuss this matter."

"It's important."

"Nothing is as important as protecting them from curiosity seekers."

"I'm not a curiosity seeker."

"Nonetheless, I can't allow you entrance."

Adriel was about to protest when Conrad shut the door in his face. He'd have to find another way to speak with Hamilton and Katherine Dunlap. He decided on one Sunday to attend the Presbyterian Church, where the Dunlaps were members.

Adriel came into church late and sat in the last pew. He saw the Dunlaps sitting several rows from the front. It was difficult for him to concentrate on the service as he was thinking of what he was going to say to Abigail's parents. *Would they allow me to speak with them? But, I must ask them some questions. I must find this fiend who murdered her. Abigail is dead; Caleb is dead. Their blood cries to heaven.*

Just before the end of the service, Adriel slipped out of the church and got on his horse, Bunyan. The Dunlaps didn't notice Adriel's presence. As the Dunlaps departed in their buggy, Adriel followed behind. On the road he caught up with them, who were taken aback by his presence.

"Young man, you startled me." Hamilton pulled on the reins to stop. "What can I do for you? It must be urgent for you to take such measures." Hamilton looked at Adriel and then realized who he was. "You're Adriel Peregrine."

"Yes sir, I am. I need to talk to you about Abigail's death, though I know it must be very hard to talk about it at all."

"I'm not open to speaking to you about this."

Adriel decided he needed to get right to the point. "I don't believe that Caleb Landis was the murderer."

The impact of this statement infuriated Hamilton and completely unsettled Katherine. "How dare you make such an outrageous claim?"

"Please, I only want to ask you a few questions."

The buggy lurched forward; but, Adriel kept up with it. "Give me just a couple minutes," Adriel yelled. "Please."

Hamilton stopped the buggy and looked over at Adriel with an expression of incredulity. "Your boldness exceeds even what I've believed about you." Hamilton had no idea how inaccurate his statement was. Adriel tended toward circumspection, not boldness.

"I'll not let this go until I'm sure of who murdered Abigail." Adriel's circumspection was accented by an occasional hardheaded determination, especially with respect to the murder of Abigail. He wanted justice and revenge, both of which were to be in the hands of the state. He would make the discovery; the Commonwealth would prosecute, judge, and sentence.

Hamilton relented out of weariness. Since Abigail's death, he lived in a state of fatigue. Nothing in the world enlivened him. "Well, though I object to your intrusiveness, I respect your commitment to the doing of the right. I'll give you a little time at my house. Come tomorrow evening."

"Thank you, sir."

CHAPTER SIXTY-SIX
AT THE HOME OF HAMILTON AND KATHERINE DUNLAP

I felt extraordinary relief when Hamilton Dunlap invited me to speak with him about the murder. I really expected to be rebuffed and refused. But, I believe that the Dunlaps suspect that something is amiss. They are giving me a chance to prove my conviction.
— Diary of Adriel Peregrine, *November 13, 1871.*

Adriel had been in the Dunlap house for Abigail's graduation party many years before. He had not gained entrance before or since until now. Conrad Kraybill answered the door. His expression revealed a dislike, bordering on hatred, for Adriel. He couldn't contain himself; for, he didn't have the self-control to hide his hostility toward Adriel. Adriel noticed the butler's demeanor, but kept his focus on solving the murder, not his anger.

"Yes, Mr. Dunlap is expecting you." Adriel kept a close eye on the butler, including his cravat, which he noticed was secured with a tie pin—similar to the one he found.

Kraybill showed Adriel into Dunlap's study. He opened the door and signaled with a wave of the hand for Adriel to enter. He departed with heavy footfalls.

"Come in, Adriel, and have a seat." Dunlap was sitting in a chair examining a book. He stood up and looked at the young man with a gravity that was customary for him. He then shook Adriel's hand. Both men took a seat.

"Now, how can I help you?"

With great conviction and some apprehension, Adriel said, "Since Abigail's death, I've felt the certainty that Caleb didn't kill your daughter. I believe the person who did is still out there. I'd like to find the murderer. I came to you to ask some questions that might help in the discovery."

"Abigail's mother and I have tried to put this tragedy behind us as much as one who has lost a child to a violent crime can. You've come to open wide the wound of this calamity."

"That's not my intent. I simply want justice."

"Your justice causes us suffering, distress, and uncertainty."

"My desire is that Abigail's murderer be found."

"I believe he's been found."

"Could I ask you a few questions? That's all I ask."

"Yes, you may; but, let's not belabor what's dreadful to us."

"What happened the night Abigail was killed?"

Dunlap hesitated as his eyes watered. He felt as if he were going to explode. His chest felt so congested he could hardly breathe. Then, he managed to speak. "Katherine and I went to a reception in town. We left Caleb and Abigail at home."

"Was anyone else in the house?"

"Our butler, Conrad Kraybill; our two sons; and a maidservant. Our sons were upstairs in bed. The maidservant was upstairs also and testified that she heard nothing. It was late."

"What did Mr. Kraybill hear just before Abigail ran out of the house?"

"Caleb and Abigail were having an argument in the parlor. He only heard the loud voices, but not the words. He entered the room to see what was wrong. He testified that Abigail told him that all was fine and thanked him for his concern. Kraybill then left. Soon afterward, he testified that Abigail stormed out of the house through the front door."

"Caleb left too?"

"Yes. So Kraybill testified. Then, Caleb killed Abigail on the farm lane. It may have been unintended; but, he was hanged for first degree murder. We found her body on the lane as we were returning home. You can imagine how terrible it was."

"I can't know like you know; but, I can imagine the horror. Did you notice anything unusual or outstanding?"

"The coroner indicated that Abigail was not raped. Her mother and I noticed she had bruises around her neck and on her arms. She was strangled to death. This was the determination of the doctor and coroner." Hamilton began to weep, placing his head in his hands. "This is really unbecoming of me."

"Mr. Dunlap, I'd do the same." Dunlap looked at Adriel with an expression of gratitude. "What was the disposition of the body?"

"It was dark; but, it looked like she had been dragged some distance. Perhaps the killer was attempting to hide the body in some clumsy way because of his distraction, as if he were not thinking clearly."

"What did you do after discovering her?"

"I stayed with the body while Katherine took the buggy home to enlist help. We had Conrad ride over to the constable to inform him of what happened. The constable wired the coroner, who joined him at the murder site. After a brief investigation in the dark, the body was taken to the coroner's examining room, where he determined the cause of death. Abigail was then taken to the funeral home."

"Did you notice anything else that night?"

"Well, Conrad was dressed differently when we left the house earlier that evening; but, I thought nothing of it. He was fastidious in dress. If he dirtied clothing during the day, he would change. We have a laundress, so he had the luxury of very clean clothes. Our laundress used to complain about him."

"Did you see the clothing he had been wearing that night preceding the murder before they were washed and pressed?"

"No. I never thought about it. I was grieving for Abigail. I thought of little else."

"When did they arrest Caleb?"

"That same night. He had scratches on his face, neck, and one hand. He said he got them from walking through a thicket on his way home. His injuries were used as evidence against him."

"Did everybody on the property have an alibi?"

"The three hands were together playing cards in one of the lodgings in the back of the house; but, the foreman, Conrad, and the maidservant were not in the company of another, as far as I know."

Adriel reflected carefully on what Hamilton Dunlap told him. He narrowed the possibilities down to the foreman and Conrad Kraybill. Yes, the butler may have done it. But, Adriel had no solid evidence against anyone. In any case, there was plenty of evidence that the murder was committed on the lane. The returning home of the Dunlaps probably prevented the murderer from succeeding in his effort to hide the body.

Adriel concluded that it would take much effort to reveal what really happened. He hoped Jake would help in this endeavor. It was two days later that he met with Jake to fill him in on what he had discovered.

The days went by toward Christmas with little progress in Adriel's investigation. Abigail's death filled his mind, so he wished that something would soon break to give him clarity and direction. In the meantime, he worked, read, saw Jennie, and prepared for the great Christian feast.

CHAPTER SIXTY-SEVEN

WINTER DARKNESS AND CHRISTMAS LIGHT

Music on Christmas Morning

Music I love—but never strain
Could kindle raptures so divine
So grief assuage, so conquer pain,
And rouse this pensive heart of mine—
As that we hear on Christmas morn,
Upon the wintry breezes borne.
Though Darkness still her empire keep,
And hours must pass, ere morning break;
From troubled dreams, or slumbers deep,
That music kindly bids us wake:
It calls us, with an angel's voice,
To wake, and worship, and rejoice;
To greet with joy the glorious morn,
Which angels welcomed long ago,
When our redeeming Lord was born,
To bring the light of Heaven below . . .

– Anne Brontë

The celebration of Christmas in Red Oak included dinner parties, church attendance, Christmas trees, thoughts of Saint Nick, but especially thoughts of the Christ child. The Peregrines immersed themselves in the joy of the season.

296

The Peregrine family attended a party at the Alden's, then a late service at Saint Jude Thaddeus. Pontiac went with them to both. After the service they all went back to the Peregrine's for a Christmas toast. Adriel accompanied Pontiac home where, on their approach, Annie began to bark from inside the house. After saying his farewell, Adriel rode home in the cold winter night.

He was bereft that night of Jennie except from a distance at church. He would look over at her, hoping not to be detected by her parents. After leaving Pontiac he passed by the Hallewell house so that he could, at least, sense her presence from a distance, terribly inadequate though it was.

The heavens were illuminated by a waxing gibbous moon almost full. Adriel was thinking about the glory of Christmas; but, dark thoughts about Abigail's murderer intruded into his mind. Adriel had discovered long before that there were times when he seemed powerless to control his thoughts, even when he applied an effort. He would chase them away momentarily, and then, they would return. The persistent thoughts most often happened to be the negative ones.

When he arrived home, he entered into the light that embraced him with a warm greeting. The wood in the hearth was burning bright; the candles on the tree were lit; and the oil lamps were aglow. Adriel greeted his parents who were in the back kitchen, partaking cookies Agatha had made and Christmas cheer, a concoction Sylvan had made. Adriel would stick with the non-alcoholic punch.

"Welcome home," his parents said in unison. "How is Pontiac?" The question was wrought with concern. Pontiac's health seemed to be slipping. He had lost his former strength. Fortunately, he was now working on lighter tasks than the kilns. Mr. Alden assigned him to his mansion, where Pontiac kept things in repair. Adriel was very concerned about his old friend, but could do nothing except offer to help around Pontiac's place. Pontiac took him up on his offer. Every Saturday afternoon,

Adriel would ride over to help inside and outside. He would also spend time playing with and walking Annie. Agatha sent Adriel there with prepared food for the week. Adriel wondered if it would not be better if Pontiac moved closer to Red Oak where others, including the Peregrines, could be of more immediate assistance, especially if an emergency should arise. Pontiac politely declined. He had grown very fond of his cabin in the woods. He called himself "The Man under the Trees." Only a few books stood on a shelf in the cabin. One was the Bible; among the others included several volumes by Nathaniel Hawthorne and *Walden, or Life in the Woods*, by Henry David Thoreau.

"Pontiac is doing fine, as far as I can tell," Adriel said in a fretful tone.

Agatha poured a glass of punch for Adriel, who joined his parents at the table. They conversed about many things, but mostly about the wonder of Christmas. They asked Adriel for a story as they had done heretofore on certain special occasions.

Adriel began: "There was a timberman who lived in a small cottage deep in the woods. He made his living by cutting down trees that he took to the nearby sawmill. He worked very hard to make the trees ready to haul with his wagon and two horses. Because of his industry and frugality, he never lacked what he needed. The only problem was that he was very lonely. He had no one with whom to share his life. He had no family. He had no wife. His parents were dead, and his brothers and sisters lived at a considerable distance. He was shy around others, and befriending was a great effort for him. Especially at Christmas he felt alone except for the company of his faithful dog who followed him everywhere.

"Lewis would spend the sacred holiday like he had for many years—by the fire eating food he had made. He was a good cook—a skill he learned after years of living alone. His dog, Elwood, also appreciated his master's skill.

"One day, just before Christmas, Elwood and Lewis were riding home in the wagon. Snow was falling lightly, covering the ground with a thin carpet of white over the forest floor. All of a sudden, Elwood's ears perked up; because, he heard voices singing deep in the woods. Then, Lewis heard the same voices. He listened intently to determine if he was hearing things, and, if he were not, where the sound was coming from. He discovered it was coming from the west, where the sun was low on the horizon. Not wishing to leave the wagon and horses behind, he rode off into the woods, hoping he would not get stuck. He followed small glistening stars, hanging like tokens and decorations on the trees that led him to the location.

"In a clearing not at a great distance from the road, he came upon a most amazing scene. A whole choir of men and women, boys and girls, were singing a hymn he didn't recognize, composed by a fourth century hymn writer of great note, Aurelius Clemens Prudentius. The hymn was translated into English by John Mason Neale, a leader in the Oxford Movement.

Corde natus ex parentis, ante mundi exordium
A et O cognominatus, ipse fons et clausula
Omnium quae sunt, fuerunt, quaeque post futura sunt.

"The horses and dog didn't show any fear or agitation. They remained still and attentive, watching the resplendence and euphony of the choir that was dressed in liturgical vesture.

Lewis shared in the wonder, inattentive to time and the surroundings. The choir finished the hymn and then, in a bright white light, disappeared. Lewis stood there motionless, washed in the light of beatitude. He then returned home in the twilight.

"Lewis decided that he was being told something important. He concluded that he was to go to church, where he hadn't been for twenty years. On Christmas Eve, he returned to the church that he had forsaken so long before. He entered the building and sat alone in the midst of an almost full church. During the service the strains of the hymn he heard in the woods in Latin was sung by the choir and congregants in English.

> *Of the Father's love begotten*
> *Ere the worlds began to be,*
> *He is Alpha and Omega,*
> *He the source, the ending he,*
> *Of the things that are, that have been,*
> *And that future years shall see,*
> *Evermore and evermore.*

Lewis took special note of the seventh verse.

> *Now let old and young men's voices*
> *Join with boys' thy name to sing,*
> *Matrons, virgins, little maidens*
> *In glad chorus answering;*
> *Let their guileless songs re-echo,*
> *And heart its praises bring,*
> *Evermore and evermore.*

That night Lewis praised the Lord and joined again that company that does the same. A few years later, at his funeral, the church was full of the people he knew and loved."

CHAPTER SIXTY-EIGHT

ADRIEL, JENNIE, JAKE, AND PONTIAC

Amen, So Be It.

In the months after Christmas, Pontiac's health steadily deteriorated. The village doctor said it was trouble with the heart. Adriel was concerned about his friend's living alone in the woods; but, Pontiac was not so concerned. He loved the rustic cabin, the tall trees, the wildlife, and what he could see of the sky—all that pertained to the beautiful spot where he had the privilege to dwell. He wished to die in a place that he loved so much. He continued to work for Alden, but fewer hours during the day and week.

After work, Adriel often checked on Pontiac at the cabin. He would stop at home first and pick up food his mother had prepared. Not long before Pontiac's death, Father Ledford visited the old man several times. One time, Adriel was also there. The three of them conversed about life and death.

The three men sat at Pontiac's kitchen table. Pontiac had made tea, and Adriel's mother had provided shortbread cookies.

"What's the latest report from the doctor?" Father Ledford asked.

"It's the same as it's been. I'll not get better, only worse. Right now, some days are better than others. There may be a time when the days will only be difficult. I'm praying that I'll persevere like a good soldier."

"I'm sorry to hear this news. I'll make sure to stop by frequently and pray that you may bear up under this trial."

"I appreciate it. I'll keep coming to church as long as I can. When I can't, you'll bring me Holy Communion?"

"Yes I will, Pontiac," Ledford responded.

"I've been preparing for this last trial since I returned to church. Before that, I tried to suppress any thoughts of death, including the death of my wife that laid me so low. It caused me to leave my home town and wander until I came to this place and found a new home."

"You know you're not alone. God is with you, and so are we of St. Jude Thaddeus Church," the Rector said.

"And I'm glad, very glad."

Adriel was feeling the deep pain of the inevitability of Pontiac's death in the near future. He said to him, "I'll do all I can to help you."

"I know you will, good friend."

"Pontiac, how're you preparing for death? We had talked about the *Ars moriendi*, the way a Christian is to face death," the old man's priest said.

"I've taken this guide seriously. It's been a great help. I have prayed and prayed. I have asked for forgiveness from a loving Father. With some fear of death, I have put myself into God's hands."

Ledford said, "We all have some fear of death; but, we know the outcome of death is not oblivion but life in Christ."

"Of this, I'm sure. My doubts have cooled, and my trust and confidence in the Lord have warmed. I'm a sinner; but, I also know that God wishes to take me under His wing so that I may be His forever. He'll protect me from all evil, as we pray, '. . . deliver us from evil.'"

"You can be sure, and I will pray for you, and I know Adriel and many others will too."

"I have a simple will. I wish for you to keep a copy, Adriel."

"I'll do that, Pontiac."

"The cabin goes to you, as does my dog. Annie." Pontiac looked at Adriel. All Adriel could do was to weep. Tears flowed down his cheeks that caused him some shame at his weakness that was not weakness.

There was silence until, partially recovered, Adriel said, "I'm sorry—a moment of weakness."

"It's not weakness, Adriel," said Father Ledford.

Pontiac patted Adriel on the back. "You've been a good friend, Adriel. I give God thanks for all the people, especially ones like you, whom I've known over the years. I'm not alone. And you know that death in the end will not come out the victor. Sadness shall turn to joy. Wanderers like you and I have returned to the Way." Pontiac turned to the priest, "Father, anything else goes to the church for its mission. I wish some of it put aside for the poor."

"Yes, Pontiac, this will be done."

Later that day, Adriel met Jennie at his parents' house. She had ridden over on her mare, Christiana. He was reluctant to meet Jennie at her home. Despite her parents' disapproval, Jennie persisted in her love for Adriel. She would not forsake him, no matter what difficulties she faced.

The two young people rode over to Pontiac's on a cold March day. Because Pontiac seemed weaker, Adriel invited him to stay with his parents. He declined.

The next day, as Adriel and Jennie approached Pontiac's residence, everything looked as it usually did. They dismounted and walked their horses to the front door. Adriel knocked. There was no answer but the barking dog. Adriel knocked again. Again, there was no answer other than Annie's barking.

"There may be something wrong," Adriel said to Jennie. "I'm going to go in. I doubt that Pontiac's somewhere. He's been too weak and sick."

The door was unlocked. When they entered, Annie, with

great excitement, greeted Adriel and Jennie. Adriel petted the dog and told her how good a dog she was. With Annie following, they went to Pontiac's bedroom and opened wide the partially opened door. In bed lay the old man. Adriel called out to him. There was no response. Adriel approached the bed and called him again. There was no response. Then, he went to Pontiac's side and touched his arm. It was cold. He bent down to discover if Pontiac was breathing. He was not. Adriel turned to Jennie, who was beside him and said, "Pontiac is dead."

Jennie embraced Adriel and said, "I'm so sorry, Adriel. He was a good friend. I know how much you'll miss him, and I too will miss him."

Adriel buried his face in Jennie's shoulder. For a few moments, she held him tightly. And then he turned and covered Pontiac's face. The dead man's eyes were already closed. Adriel prayed a short prayer.

Adriel and Jennie left the room hand and hand with Annie following. Adriel looked down at Annie and said to her, "I guess you're mine now." She wagged her tail as if knowing what he said.

Outside, Adriel said to Jennie, "I'll go into town to inform the undertaker about Pontiac's death. Hopefully, he will come out today to pick him up. He will build Pontiac's coffin. Hopefully, all should be ready by tomorrow or the day after. I'll be here when he comes."

"I'll go with you, Adriel."

"We'll stop by the rector's to let him know so he can plan for the funeral. We need to let Mr. Alden know too." They rode away with Annie following.

Two days later Pontiac was buried from Saint Jude Thaddeus Church. He was laid to rest in the church cemetery that occupied the grounds right next to the church building. Adriel,

Jennie, Agatha, and Sylvan all attended. Jennie sat next to Adriel. The church was filled with people who had known Pontiac and loved him. Father Ledford preached a strong sermon on the inevitability of death, the appropriateness of tears, and the reason for joy—the resurrection from the dead. Death is real but overcome in Christ. Both confidence in Christ and deep sorrow informed Adriel's mourning. As the bells of Saint Jude Thaddeus tolled for Pontiac, Adriel remembered Donne's poem:

Each man's death diminishes me,
For I am involved in mankind.
Therefore, send not to know
For whom the bell tolls,
It tolls for thee.

A lunch was served at the Peregrine's. It was then that Adriel had a conversation with Jake Brenneman, who attended the funeral. It had been a while since they had talked. During the time Adriel was pre-occupied with Pontiac. But, his private murder investigation had not been forgotten.

"Have you learned any more about Abigail's death?" Adriel asked Jake.

"I looked at all the information pertaining to the murder and trial. I found nothing that surprised me."

"It looks like this case is very cold," lamented Adriel.

"Yes. We'll have to be patient, working with the few clues we have. The tie pin could be a lead."

"I've been thinking a lot about it. I asked Dunlap if it were his. He said it wasn't; but, he said it could be Conrad Kraybill's. This does not mean he killed Abigail. He could have lost it at any time."

"True. But, I'd focus on him."

"I will."

CHAPTER SIXTY-NINE

THE CABIN

Midway upon the journey of our life
I found myself within a forest dark,
For the straightforward pathway had been lost.
The Divine Comedy, Dante Alighieri, trans. by Henry Wadsworth
Longfellow
Dante's opening to La Divina Commedia I retained in my thoughts
throughout my wandering around the world. I could not cast it from
my consciousness.

   – A Wanderer Who Becomes a Pilgrim, *Adriel Peregrine.*

Pontiac gave Adriel the cabin that Adriel had almost finished before he left for the army. Adriel decided to move into it. Henceforth, he with good dog Annie would build a life there and from there. He hoped before too long he and Jennie would be married and share this peaceful place. Anticipating a family, Adriel already had plans to enlarge the space.

The first time Adriel entered the cabin after Pontiac's death, he noticed his friend's walking stick with the head of a falcon on it. It stood in a stand next to the door. Adriel marveled that he had not seen it until that moment. We sometimes see things at an opportune time and miss them time and time again otherwise.

Adriel remembered Pontiac's having the staff on his person when Adriel first met him in the very woods that surround the cabin. The peregrine falcon represented to Adriel the wanderings on which both Pontiac and he were engaged after tragic events in their lives—the death of Abigail and the death of Pontiac's wife. These falcons migrate long distances, hence their name, which includes peregrine. They have a goal—their breeding grounds. Unlike the falcon, both Pontiac and Adriel had been wanderers with no goal. Yet, both falcon and human had been travelers to far off places. Both men again became travelers to the goal of the Kingdom of God—true pilgrims of the Way.

Adriel Peregrine again became a pilgrim. He had been a wanderer for many years, having gotten off the path and lost his way. He was one who "erred and strayed like lost sheep," as the *Prayer Book* says. The Latin derived word, err, means wander. Adriel Peregrine returned to his pilgrimage. The Lord had brought him back like the lost sheep or prodigal son to the Way. He was lost but now is found. (Luke 15) Peregrine, the wanderer, had become Peregrine, the pilgrim. He was at home in an earthly sense; he was yet traveling in a heavenly sense to the destination of all Christians.

So the pilgrim began making improvements on the house, often reminding himself of the gratitude he owed Pontiac. Adriel would work at the kilns during the day and work on the house in the evening after taking a walk with Annie in the woods. He was usually tired; but, it was the tiredness of accomplishment rather than the tiredness of futility like the labor of Sisyphus. Jennie often came over after school and made dinner for both of them. She would help in the improving of the house. Adriel would escort her home before dark.

Adriel had not forgotten his desire to find Abigail's murderer. He had a repetitive dream that a man whose face he never saw was stalking him. These dreams may have represented his fears without warning him of real danger. But, he took no chances; for, he was susceptible to premonitions that were fulfilled. At night, he kept his doors locked. During the day, when he was walking or riding alone, he would often look behind him. He felt an approaching evil that he could not shake. He took his fears seriously.

One day, before returning home from the kilns, he passed by the Dunlap farm. He was emboldened to ride down the farm lane to see if he could find any more evidence. Mr. Dunlap wouldn't mind. He too had come to believe that Abigail's murderer had not been found and thought Adriel could be the very instrument to solve the mystery. His opinion of Adriel had risen with his hopes that the murder would finally be solved.

Adriel dismounted and walked slowly down the lane with his eyes on the road. What he didn't know was that an individual in the house had caught a glimpse of him and was looking intently out the window. It should be noted that three of Dunlap's workmen who lived on the property were working in the house, renovating a room on the second floor. Adriel didn't notice he was being watched.

Adriel walked up and down the lane several times. He found nothing. He was left with the tie pin he had found earlier. He was sure that the workmen didn't wear ties, certainly not on a workday. With this in mind, he concluded that the tie pin was Conrad Kraybill's. He would pursue this line of thought to see where it might lead without excluding other possibilities.

Three nights later, Adriel was in bed, exhausted from a hard day's work. Annie woke him up, growling like he had never heard before. She would often growl in the middle of the night at animals that passed close to the house. Something else was out there that was not a denizen of the woods, but was one of the dark.

Adriel grabbed a rifle he kept on a rack and cautiously approached the front door. All the while Annie was growling and barking. He stood by the door for a moment. He couldn't have heard anything outside because of the noise Annie was making, though Adriel did appreciate the warning Annie gave. He knew something was not right.

Adriel opened the door and rushed out. Annie followed him, barking and racing out into the darkness. She disappeared into the woods as Adriel called her back. She was not good at obedience. For a few excruciating minutes there was silence. Then, Annie emerged from the woods walking at a lively, but not swift, gait. When Adriel called her, she picked up the pace and came to him. He bent down and stroked her head. "Good girl!" he said.

The next morning, Adriel noticed fresh tracks of a horse on the road that passed near the cabin. He concluded that the murderer was intending to do him harm. All of this was conjecture; but, he was sure that he wasn't far from the truth. For days he tried to figure out what to do next. He let Jake know what happened. Unfortunately, Jake and he came no closer to figuring out the identity of the killer who had the advantage. The killer knew whom he wished to harm; however, Adriel was not certain of the identity of the one who sought to harm him.

CHAPTER SEVENTY

HOW CAN WE BE SURE?

Be still, and know that I am God. — *Psalm 46:10 ESV.*

Before he went to war, Adriel would visit Father Ledford to talk about the Bible and theology. With the approval of the priest, he continued the practice. On that particular day, Adriel wanted to talk to his spiritual mentor about certainty. How can we be sure that God exists?

The two of them sat down in the vestry as was their wont. Father Ledford offered Adriel some tea he had brewed before his arrival. "Yes, thank you."

As he was pouring their drinks, Father Ledford said, "Welcome, Adriel. You told me on Sunday that you wanted to talk about how we can be sure God exists."

'Yes, Father. I believe; but, sometimes I have doubts.'

"I've talked to many people about their doubts. In fact, it has many times been a topic of my sermons. How do you want to start?"

"What I feel in my heart could be a fiction? God in my heart and mind doesn't mean that God is."

"Good start. Let me begin by saying that no one will ever provide a proof or explanation that will prove God for all to see. God is not an object to be placed under a microscope or viewed through a telescope or binoculars or with the naked eye. If we could, He wouldn't be God. We may treat Him as an object; because, that's how we think. We live in a universe of objects, of things, and also of persons. It is easy for us to think of God as an object. We use symbols about Him that are objects, as the representation of Him as the bearded old man. God is present everywhere, knows all, and is all powerful, although this last has been especially contested because of the way the world is; that is, it operates as if there were no God, at least in the perception of some people."

"What is the evidence?"

"Traditionally, theology has spoken of two sources of knowledge, reason and revelation. The human mind is capable of speaking of God using the power of reason. For example, when Thomas Aquinas expostulates on five proofs for the existence of God. Revelation tells of things that are beyond the capacity of reason, for example, salvation in Christ and the Holy Trinity. The transmission of revelation, as recorded in the Bible, is regarded as trustworthy by Christians. The witnesses are reliable. And, then, there is apophatic theology that maintains that God is so high above us that we can only describe Him as what he is not. This approach reminds us of the chasm between creature and Creator. The atheist and non-believer can counter these arguments with their own. It wouldn't surprise you that I think the theist has better arguments. The debate will go on to the end of the world. We Christians have faith in our salvation in Christ. Our belief is an engagement of heart and mind. We are committed to our belief and spurn the nihilism of unbelief. This is as sure as we can get in this world. One way or another we choose either faith or nothingness. That GOD IS indicates the essential truth of the universe."

"This makes sense. It clarifies for me things I've been thinking about. I believe in heart and mind in One who exists outside my heart and mind."

"It's so good to hear this, Adriel. Cling to the Shepherd and the Lamb."

"I will." Adriel shifted topics. "I wanted also to tell you about my search for Abigail's murderer. I haven't gotten too far with this. I won't give up. I must resolve this matter."

"I commend you for what you're doing. I was very disturbed by the trial, and the hanging of Caleb was tragic. The whole process was like a train that couldn't be stopped. Pursue this worthy investigation. Don't let anger grip you by the throat. And be careful."

"I've been very angry, and I'll be careful."

"I was afraid of that. Anger is a natural reaction to what has happened. If it runs rampant, it will destroy you inside. You then become a casualty rather than an overcomer of evil through Christ."

"I'll do my best. I know the Scriptures warn against anger."

"This is good. I too know the struggle with anger. It's a momentous and consequential battle."

Father Ledford ended with prayer. Adriel stepped out of the church feeling refreshment in his weariness. He didn't mention that Jennie and he wanted to get married. He thought he would save this announcement for the next time. Plans were uncertain, mostly because of Jennie's parents' opposition.

CHAPTER SEVENTY-ONE

JENNIE HALLEWELL

So soft and strong, my love is she
Describes my kindly dear to me.
Fair eyes of blue-gray and hair of brown
Her unadorned great beauty crown.

– Adriel Peregrine

Jennie stopped by Adriel's almost every night after school. Often, her mother would be watching for her from a window. They had not softened toward Adriel, to whom they hadn't spoken since his departure for service in the army.

One day she was on her way to the cabin from the school-house. She was alone on the road until about a mile away from Adriel's. Then, she heard something behind her—a trotting horse. Shortly afterward, she surmised that not only was the person behind her but also following her. She was no coward; but, she was alert to possible danger and harm. How did she know this? Adriel had told her of his experience during the night and warned her to be vigilant, wary, and alert. He didn't want her to be afraid, but even more, he didn't want her to be unaware. Adriel was sure that if danger was lurking near his cabin, that foe knew Jennie was his beloved. He must have been watching as she traveled from school to the forest.

Jennie realized that her pursuer was picking up speed. She signaled her mare to gallop, hoping she would reach Adriel before the stranger reached her. She didn't look back; but, when she entered the woods her pursuer had almost caught up to her. Then, there was a gunshot that flew over her head, indicating that he was a bad shot, perhaps. Her antagonist turned back as she drew near the cabin. Adriel was outside mounting his horse when Jennie arrived. Annie was barking up a storm.

"Jennie, what happened? I heard the gunshot."

Jennie jumped breathlessly from the horse. Adriel came to her and embraced her. "Someone was chasing me. I don't know who it was. He was either a very poor shot or wasn't trying to shoot me, just scare me."

"I think it was Abigail's murderer. It was a warning to back away. I'll find him out before he gets us."

"I'm not telling my parents about this."

"Whatever you think is best."

"This way is best."

The two went into the house and ate dinner that Adriel had prepared.

Spring was well underway. It wouldn't be too long before Jennie would spend the vacation time helping Adriel at the cabin and her parents on the farm. The days would go quickly. Her days were full and rich whether she was teaching or helping the family.

While Adriel was gone on his wanderings, Jennie attended the District Normal School and then took a teaching job in a one room schoolhouse not far from her home. Joshua Schreiber was still teaching in the school Adriel and Jennie attended. Jake taught yet in another school. Though a preponderance of men taught at the beginning of the common school movement, more and more women were entering the profession. Jennie was one of them. She never shied away from a challenge. In the beginning the children were difficult; but, before long, they learned respect for the young female teacher. She taught thirty children ranging from first to eighth grade.

In that day most women were married around the age of twenty-one or twenty-two. Jennie was twenty-three. She had opportunities to marry, especially in one case; but, she wouldn't because of her love for Adriel. Her parents thought she was being foolish. The most serious proposal would have led to a move up in the socio-economic scale.

Adriel and Jennie wished to get married, delayed by Jennie's parents' hostility and the murder investigation Adriel was personally conducting. They had hoped to be married not long after Christmas; but, matters did not turn in that direction. The future was uncertain, and the present was wrought with adversity and danger.

CHAPTER SEVENTY-TWO

ADRIEL AND JENNIE

O, Shenandoah, I love your daughter,
Away you rolling river.
– Shenandoah, lyrics before 1860

Despite the dark clouds that had accumulated over them, Adriel and Jennie continued as before, improving the cabin and sharing time together. They would work on the cabin when Adriel returned from the kilns after stopping at the school for Jennie; take walks through the woods and fields; talk about the things they would do in the future; and eat a meal together. Adriel always made sure that Jennie got home before dark.

One night, as Adriel was returning home from taking Jennie back to her family, he sensed a lurking presence in the woods. Annie was aware of the same and began to growl at the same time Adriel had misgivings about his safety and welfare. He increased the pace to a gallop and arrived home unscathed.

The sensation of being watched led Adriel and Jennie to take precautions, but didn't discourage them from enjoying the multitude of good things around them. It was now spring between Easter and Pentecost.

On one particular Saturday in late April, Adriel and Jennie were sitting on a blanket enjoying their first picnic for the spring and summer. Jennie spread out a tablecloth and placed all kinds of good things that she had made—fried chicken, red beet eggs, dandelion salad, sweet bologna sandwiches, and apple pie. They ate and reveled in each other's company.

"I would like to set a date for the wedding."

"I agree; but, it's hard with your parents disliking me so much."

"It's time for you to pay a visit to my parents. They were put off by your leaving home and not keeping in touch with your family. Your parents thought you were dead. And, of course, some rumors were flying around."

"I was dead, but not physically. If your parents knew what I had been up to, they'd be confirmed in their opinion."

"You told me about the prostitutes and the opium. But, I know what you had been and what you are now. I loved you when you were away."

"You wouldn't have loved me if you'd been with me."

"Maybe not. We'll never know. But, I love you now."

"I know, Jennie. Your love's meant so much to me. I love you." Adriel bent over and kissed her.

Adriel looked at Jennie and said, "I'll visit your parents and try to mend things."

"Thank you, Adriel. It means much to me."

Adriel and Jennie went back to finishing the meal and then rode throughout the countryside on a perfectly blue and green day. The land was bathed in sunlight, transfiguring many of the common things that make the world—the fields of crops; the lowing cattle; the woods; the modest, but neat houses; the people's working their land; the schoolhouse and church; the playing children; and lovers hand in hand, taking a walk on a fine spring afternoon. Such days prevent only the habitually melancholic from exulting in God's creation.

Adriel and Jennie rode to a little pond on Joshua Schreiber's small farm—a few acres to grow vegetables, raise chickens, and keep a cow, all tended by his wife while he taught school. Adriel had permission to use the row boat. The two young people went aboard, Adriel rowing around the pond for a while until he let the boat drift. Adriel sang a verses of an old song of fur traders on the Missouri River.

"O Shenandoah, I love your daughter,
Away you rolling river.
I'll take her 'cross yon rolling water."
Ah-ha, I'm bound away, 'Cross the wide Missouri.

"O Shenandoah, I long to hear you,
Away you rolling river.
Across that wide and rolling river."
Ah-ha, I'm bound away, 'Cross the wide Missouri.

As he sang, Adriel looked knowingly at Jennie, who then began to laugh. The young couple whiled away the time on the water under the sun in the quiet of the late afternoon.

They rode back to the cabin, Adriel on Bunyan and Jennie on Christiana. When they got there, she spent time collecting moss, ferns, and other plants for a winter garden (terrarium) while Adriel was reading outside under a tree. Annie was lying in a spot of sun under the trees.

Adriel and Jennie realized that the sun was getting low in the sky. As was usual, Adriel escorted Jennie home and then returned to the cabin. It had been a wonderful day, but for Adriel's growing apprehension about speaking to Jennie's parents. He fell asleep, though, thinking of how much he loved Jennie. What a striking change in his former attitude!

CHAPTER SEVENTY-THREE

THE GRAVEYARD

A plot of ground with stony sculpture strewn,
Inscribed with names and dates of those who soon
Will rise to greet their Lord on eighth-day morn,
Accompanied by angel Gabriel's horn.

— Adriel Peregrine

Adriel was making no headway in solving the murder of Abigail Dunlap. Months had passed. Maybe Caleb perpetrated the murder after all. One summer evening, Adriel rode over to the cemetery where Abigail was buried. He didn't dismount. He remained on Bunyan, thinking deeply about the events that preceded and followed the crime. He sat there reflecting on the evidence.

The tie pin, which was all he had to go on, may or may not be Conrad Kraybill's, but it was more than likely that it was. If it were, it could or could not have been lost the night of the murder. Adriel decided to assume the tie pin was the butler's and that he lost it the night of the murder during a struggle with Abigail. How was he to determine if Kraybill was the murderer? He couldn't interview him directly. Kraybill would certainly not accede to being interrogated. Adriel had no authority to do so, and Mr. Dunlap would probably frown on it. Adriel didn't want to alienate Dunlap, whom he worked hard on winning over.

Some tension arose in the Dunlap household as Hamilton and Katherine grew in suspicion of their longtime butler.

Kraybill was stone-faced, revealing nothing one way or another. The Dunlaps were not as successful in hiding their fears and apprehensions.

Adriel also assumed that the pursuer of Jennie and the one lurking outside his home were the same, that is, Conrad Kraybill. What now could he do? He'd attempt to make Kraybill more nervous so that the butler would expose himself as the culprit. Kraybill had already taken aggressive action against Adriel and Jennie, or so Adriel supposed.

If Adriel was right, the murderer would continue to be reckless and aggressive, increasing the danger for Jennie and himself. When he came out of his reverie, he realized the sun was about to set. But, he didn't hasten home. He sat there, expecting something to happen. And it did, at least, in his mind's eye. As the sun sank below the horizon, Adriel thought he saw something at Abigail's grave. It was moving in its proximity. A chill descended his spine. He strained his eyes to determine if he saw what he thought he saw. The apparition brought back memories of a similar sight from previous experience, recent and not so recent. It was in the shape of Abigail Dunlap. Was he casting a mental image onto the external world? He didn't know, and he never would know. Bunyan didn't seem to be aware of any other presence. He was aware that thinking obsessively about the murder and what to do about it, not just then, but also for several previous days, may have made him susceptible to such a vision. It seemed as if Abigail was reaching out, her hands pleading with Adriel. He called out, "Yes, Abigail, I will find the murderer, and he'll be brought to justice." Then the specter disappeared.

Adriel heard thunder from an approaching storm. He decided it was past time to retreat to his cabin, but failed to get home before the rain came pouring down.

When he arrived, Annie was barking inside. He put Bunyan in the little barn provided for him and ran into the house. He was soaked. Annie began licking the water off his pants. He laughed as she did so.

After he lit a fire in the hearth, Adriel changed clothes. It was a warm spring night, but he felt cold. He then sat in his favorite chair in the big room with tools and wood scattered throughout it, testifying to his continuing renovation of his abode. For a while he pondered what he had seen and his commitment to bring his search to a conclusion. The next day he would again see Mr. Dunlap and, thus, set in motion his plan to reveal the murderer.

The storm had stopped; and soon afterward, the unsettling cry of an owl filled the woodland. The owl represents in folklore a dire warning of danger or wisdom. It reminded Adriel of the danger ahead. He asked the Lord for wisdom to face it.

CHAPTER SEVENTY-FOUR

THE FRESCO

Midway upon the journey of our life
I found myself within a forest dark,
For the straightforward pathway had been lost.
Ah me! how hard a thing it is to say
What was this savage, rough, and stern,
Which is the very thought renews the fear.

So bitter is it, death is little more;
But of the good to treat, which there I found,
Speak will I of the other things there.
I cannot well repeat how there I entered,
So full was I of slumber at the moment
In which I had abandoned the true way.

– The Divine Comedy, *Dante Alighieri, trans. by*
Henry Wadsworth Longfellow

On the same night he saw Abigail's apparition, Adriel reflected on his five years of wandering around the world from the Delaware Canal to England, to the clipper ships, to Hong Kong, to the transcontinental railroad, to New York, to London again, to Lindisfarne, and home again. God had been with Him, evidenced by his survival through many dangers along the way, including his abuse of opium and alcohol and his cavorting with prostitutes, an untold number of those unfortunate and degraded, and yet cooperative and guilty women with whom he went to bed. As if his life were charmed, he didn't contract a venereal disease.

Adriel had lost his way. By the grace of God he returned to the path that leads to beatitude. He was lost in the wilderness of which Dante writes at the beginning of *La Divina Commedia*. He was like one of the children of Israel, wandering the desert, before entering the Promised Land, or, like the children of Israel called back from Babylon along the Way made in the desert to Zion. He was walking the Way through a blooming desert with surging streams. Christ offered him the water that Adriel drank for his spiritual refreshment and salvation. He had become again what Jesus describes in the *Gospel of John*:

"He that believeth on me, as the scriptures hath said, out of his belly shall flow rivers of living water. But this spake he of the Spirit, which they that believe on him should receive: for the Holy Ghost was not yet given; because that Jesus was not yet glorified." (John 7: 38-9 KJV)

In the cathedral church of Florence, Santa Maria del Fiore, on a section of wall, one can view a fresco by Domenico di Michelino of Dante with an open book of his great poem in his hand. A representation of Florence is to his left, and Inferno, Purgatorio, and Paradiso are behind him. His right hand is extended toward a picture of hell and its inhabitants. He holds his great work in his left hand.

Dante possessed God-given gifts that allowed him to write *La Divina Commedia*, expressing in high literary art his own journey from the dark wood to the beatific vision. Adriel was on the journey, no longer in the dark wood, but not having attained in reality the vision that surpasses all visions, beholding the face of God in so far as it is possible, even in heaven, for a mortal to experience it. He used his imagination to envision the place of perfect concord.

Adriel had read Dante while at the Normal School. Though an Anglican, he was greatly and positively impressed with all three great sections. It is the journey that ends with the fulfillment of what we crave most—redemption.

Adriel used to have dreams of following Virgil and Dante in hell. Dante would turn to him and ask if he wished to remain in that dark place. He always said, "No." The latest dream he had was in heaven, where he was in the company of Beatrice and Saint Bernard. Saint Bernard said to him, "Do you wish to see the Vision?" Adriel said, "Yes." How gratifying it was no longer to have the nightmare.

For every Christian pilgrim, including Dante and Adriel, the ultimate destination is the kingdom of God. One must pass from death to life in order that our final home can be reached. This life is always a journey, never an arrival. But, death is a problem. The arrival requires one to pass through death, humanity's greatest fear.

Adriel faced this reality on the battlefield—the starkest and most immediate of all places to be so confronted. He saw men torn apart; men killed who had just been vital youths; men dying of disease; men dying in large numbers. Death was all around, and death was close. His friend, Michael, died a moment before victory and days before total victory.

After he returned from his wanderings, Adriel searched to find out if Michael was re-buried. He wrote a letter to the O'Briens, who, in a return letter, let him know that their son rested in Poplar Grove National Cemetery in the vicinity of Petersburg and that they had visited the grave. They thanked him for all that he had done.

As he looked back to that tragic time, Adriel was astounded he expressed to the O'Briens so much of the faith he had forsaken. By the end of the war, Adriel was agnostic in his attitude about God. Was he a hypocrite? On reflection, he thought not. In his view, he felt an obligation to express Michael's faith to his parents, not put out his dirty laundry. And this is what Adriel did.

CHAPTER SEVENTY-FIVE

RECONCILIATION OR ALIENATION

In all the adversity I experienced in my young life, the rejection of Jennie's parents was one of the hardest things that I can remember dealing with. I came to love her and feared that I would lose her. I was in despair and feared I would again partake of those things that would in short time destroy me.

– A Wanderer Who Becomes a Pilgrim, *Adriel Peregrine.*

Adriel was looking forward to his marriage to Jennie. One thing stood in the way of a joyous celebration—the relationship between Adriel and Jennie's parents—James and Esther Hallewell.

On a Sunday afternoon, Adriel rode over to the Hallewells to speak to them about his and Jennie's intention to get married. He was beside himself with anxiety about the visit. He took more time than usual to get from one place to another.

The Hallewells lived on a farm not far from the school Adriel and Jennie attended. Jennie taught in another of the one room schoolhouses beyond the Dunlap farm. Every day she rode over there on her mare, Christiana, named after Christian's wife in John Bunyan's *Pilgrim's Progress*.

As Adriel rode down the lane, Jennie was watching him from the front of the house. When he arrived, she walked over to him. He dismounted, and they embraced one another.

"Adriel, I'm so glad that you've come. I don't know how well it's going to go, though."

"I'm not expecting much. I'll make every effort to do what I can."

The couple walked into the house where they were not greeted by anyone. Adriel remembered the house from when he was a youth.

Jennie led him into a sitting room where no one was present. The couple sat down and waited for several minutes before James and Esther entered the room. Adriel rose and walked over to them to shake hands. By touch and sight he sensed the cold, hostile greeting. He was getting a better idea of what Jennie was dealing with.

"I'm Adriel Peregrine."

"I know. We remember you when you were a schoolboy. You came by every once in a while," James responded. "Please sit down," James invited Adriel.

The couple sat on the settee. Jennie's parents each sat on a chair.

Esther Hallewell had a worried expression on her face. Mr. Hallewell verged on anger.

"Jennie has told us that she intends to marry you, Adriel. But, I'm not enthusiastic, as you already know. I worry that you'll not be a good husband. You left home, didn't keep in touch with your parents—they thought you were dead—and, I hear, you led a prodigal life. I know you had some trouble while still home."

That Adriel led a prodigal life, in fact, was not known by the people of Red Oak except for his indiscretions and missteps while he was home. Regarding his time away, all was imagination and hearsay based on nothing of Adriel's story; but, there was much truth in the rumors, as Adriel would testify. Rumors about his time away were based on his behavior while still home.

"Sir, I admit my life was not exemplary by any means. But,

I always worked to earn my way and changed my habits and behavior before I returned home."

Esther Hallewell said, "We want more for Jennie than I think you can provide. Stability and security would be among those things."

"Mrs. Hallewell, I've worked since I've been home and haven't made for myself a notorious reputation. I don't frequent taverns or any place of ill-repute."

"I wish we could trust you on this; but, we can't." Jennie was about to weep. Tears came to her eyes.

As Adriel was losing patience, Jennie, with tears in her eyes, said, "Mother and Father, I love Adriel and know he would be a good husband."

"Jennie, I think your affection has exceeded your sense," Mr. Hallewell said.

"I wish that you could see something other than faults and behavior that is now long behind me."

"I can't," James Hallewell said emphatically.

"I see that you're not willing to change your minds," Adriel said. Jennie refused to give in to loud weeping and pleading; though, she felt like a storm cloud inside about to pour out rain.

Adriel stood up and said, "I must be leaving now. I'm sorry you feel the way you do." Jennie protested; but, Adriel didn't change his mind. "I'll see my way out." He walked out of the room and advanced to the front door.

Jennie followed him. "Please, Adriel, don't leave."

"I can't convince them to change their minds."

"Please."

"Jennie, I love you; but, I must leave now. You must decide what you're going to do. Take your parents' view or marry me."

Adriel kissed her, walked out, and rode away. Jennie wept softly as Adriel disappeared down the lane.

CHAPTER SEVENTY-SIX

THE FIRMAMENT

And God made the firmament, and divided the waters which were under the firmament from the waters which were above the firma-ment, and it was so. — Genesis 1: 7 KJV

And God said, "Let there be lights in the firmament of the heaven to divide the day from the night; and let them be for signs, and for seasons, and for days, and years. And let them be for lights in the firmament of the heaven to give light upon the earth," and it was so. And God made two great lights; the greater light to rule the day, and the lesser light to rule the night: he made the stars also. — Genesis 1: 14-16 KJV

The meeting with Jennie's parents caused in Adriel a severe crisis. He was tempted to return to drinking that was available and opium that was not quite as available where he lived. He could've gone into town to a local tavern with co-workers anytime he wanted. It wasn't that they were urging Adriel to do so. It was because Adriel was drawn to it. He had to fight temptation with great effort. He succeeded in staying away from what would have surely destroyed him. His renewed Christian faith was essential in the struggle. He couldn't have succeeded as a secular man without Christ, without faith, and without the community of the Church. The skeptical religious tendency of the nineteenth century was not Adriel's tendency after his long time of disbelief.

Adriel was beset by a hidden foe and an absent fiancée.

Jennie had not communicated with him in almost a week. Before his visit to the Hallewells, he saw her every day. He already felt the void. He rode by the Hallewells, but never caught sight of her. He was thinking of meeting her on the road as she came home from school, but hadn't tried to do so.

Adriel's Christian faith held him firm during this difficult time. It was always spiritually refreshing to him when he was out walking or riding in the woods, viewing the sky day or night, or laying in the grass while thinking about many things he loved. Days after his unsuccessful visit, he decided to take a walk to view the stars in the firmament. In those days there was little artificial light to obscure the sky. He decided to walk on the road that led to the Dunlap farm. He looked up to see a magnificent sky. The stars were bright and sparkling. It was an exceptional night for observing the heavens. Adriel was wonder-struck by their beauty.

Adriel thought of human aspiration, always a theme when looking at the empyrean. How many people have looked at those stars from the earliest time? How many noble and wonderful thoughts were conceived during those moments? How many looked up to soften their despair?

Since he attended the Normal School, and even before, Adriel kept up with currents of thought in America and the world. He was aware of the fact that over time, especially because of thinkers like Copernicus, Newton, Galileo, and Kepler, views of the universe had greatly changed. The sky was the same as when Dante viewed it in his time; but its structure was conceived of in a very different way. In Dante's time, all the heavenly bodies rotated in their separate spheres—the Earth at the center, then the Moon, Mercury, Venus, the Sun, Mars, Jupiter, and Saturn. The primum mobile was the cause of all motion. God dwelt in the empyrean.

The sublunary (below the moon) universe was the region

of human strife. Adriel knew from his great experience at a young age the dissonance of the world.

But, on this night, though very difficult for him, he tried to forget his troubles and savor the natural beauty above him. For the longest time he was lost in wonder. He was careless of any lurking danger. When he came out of his ecstasy, he walked home with Annie in the lead and, after he arrived, slept in peace.

CHAPTER SEVENTY-SEVEN

THE ONE ROOM SCHOOLHOUSE

I have come to love Jennie beyond anyone else except God Himself.
— Diary of Adriel Peregrine, *May 5, 1872.*

On Friday after the Sunday of his unsatisfactory meeting with the Hallewells, Adriel decided to take off early from the kilns in order to meet up with Jennie. The foreman understood; for, Adriel was his best worker and was in line to become a foreman himself.

After days without her company, Adriel decided that he would not let bitterness and resentment keep him from Jennie. He was angry with her parents, not with his love. What foolishness it is to punish one who is not responsible for his pain. In fact, what is the sense of avenging oneself on anyone for emotional pain? It could be that the relationship with Jennie's parents would resolve itself if he only exacted from himself some patience and understanding. He came to think that Jennie's parents had every right to be suspicious of him, considering his reputation. He must earn their favor and approval. On this effort he would focus whenever he had an opportunity. For now, he would make sure that Jennie and he were on good terms. He was astounded about how much he loved her after years of avoiding her. How much folly can there be in human relationships! How fickle is the heart in matters of romantic love!

Off rode Adriel to the schoolhouse. When he arrived, school was about to be let out. He stopped on the road in front of the door, anxiously awaiting Jennie.

The children poured out of the school with cheerful voices and came up to Adriel, whom they knew from his previous visits. They had heard of his foreign travels and his exotic adventures. Some of them enjoyed imagining him as a pirate off some oriental coast. The upper grades had learned about China in the geography lessons taught by Jennie. Such new information fed their imagination.

Jennie came up to Adriel, still mounted on Bunyan. The children were jumping up and down and yelling with excitement; for, like on other occasions, Adriel brought candy with him. It was a sea of smiles. Jennie took him by the hand and said, "I'm glad you came by. Wait for me so that we can ride together."

Adriel said, "I'd wait forever for you."

Jennie responded, "You won't have to wait that long, though it takes me time to close up the school." While Jennie was about her duty, Adriel distributed candy among the excited children.

After Jennie closed the building, she retrieved Christiana and joined Adriel. They rode slowly together toward the Hallewell farm.

"I was so worried that we might have shut down our relationship."

"No, Adriel, it has been difficult for me to get away. Moreover, my parents are even more watchful than they were before. The pressure to reject you has become greater. You didn't make a positive impression, nor could you have. I don't think you're going to win them over."

Adriel looked over at Jennie as they walked the horses.

"And I thought I could win anyone over, even the worst enemy." He chuckled; Jennie didn't.

"I don't want to lose you, Adriel. I've loved you for a long time."

"I know. And I love you. I'll think of a way to fix this problem."

"It's not an easy one to solve."

"I've been in a lot of difficult situations. This can't be any harder than they were."

"I hope you're right."

"I'm not going to give up."

"That's the Adriel I know," and Jennie smiled.

"You won't give up either. That's the Jennie I know," Adriel said.

Adriel began singing, "I Dream of Jeanie," but instead of Jeanie, he sang Jennie. She looked at him and smiled, realizing, as no one else in Red Oak knew, that she had won laurels, the crown of her love for Adriel.

Adriel and Jennie parted at the crossroads. She rode to her parents' farm; Adriel turned back to go home.

CHAPTER SEVENTY-EIGHT

WHITSUNDAY

*God, who as at this time didst teach the hearts of thy faithful people,
by sending to them the light of thy Holy Spirit: Grant us by the same
Spirit to have a right judgement in all things, and evermore to rejoice
in his holy comfort, through the merits of Christ Jesus our Saviour,
who liveth and reigneth with thee, in the unity of the same Spirit,
one God, world without end. Amen*

— The Book of Common Prayer, 1662.

El Greco's painting of Pentecost shows the apostles, the
Virgin Mary in blue and red, and other women in ecstasy as
the Holy Spirit imparts His gifts, indicated by flames of fire
resting on each one. In addition, an individual is looking out
from the picture, perhaps the artist himself. What is he saying to us? The Holy Spirit hovers over them in the form of
a dove, the fundamental symbol of the Third Person of the
Holy Trinity. The artist captures the extraordinary mystery
in the event of Pentecost, clearly indicating the divine presence.

The Church of Saint Jude Thaddeus celebrated yet another
Whitsunday, or Pentecost. Seven votive candles, representing
the gifts of the Holy Spirit, stood on the altar. The rector was
clothed in bright red, a symbol of the Holy Spirit and fire. The
choir and congregation sang ancient hymns to the Spirit.

Adriel and his parents attended the service and sat together.
For the sake of peace in the family, Jennie sat with her parents,
though they were aware, because Jennie told them, that she

was still seeing Adriel. Jennie was good-natured and gentle, but not easily overcome when she decided on a way of thinking or course of action.

After the service, Jennie and Adriel had a few moments to converse while her parents and his parents were speaking to friends, but not talking to each other. Her father looked over at them once, but didn't frown, having a constant smile on his face while talking to a good friend. Was something changing that Adriel got a glimpse of?

The young couple decided to ride to the cabin on a glorious spring day. When they arrived, Jennie made tea and lunch for them to enjoy. As they were eating, a rock came crashing through one of the back windows. Annie began barking frantically. The tree line was close to the cabin. Whoever was responsible was easily able to escape without being identified. Adriel came after the culprit for a short while, but had no success in apprehending him.

After Adriel and Jennie settled themselves following the incident, they sat down on the porch with a view of the open space that extended to the tree line at the front of the cabin. Jennie had a note in her hand that she removed from the hurtling rock.

"Adriel, while you were chasing around for the perpetrator, I read the note that was conveyed by the hurling rock."

"What does it say?"

"Curiosity can be a dangerous game." They both looked at the lettering, which was produced carefully to be sloppy.

"Someone is determined to scare me out of my investigation. My top candidate is Kraybill; but, I'm far from knowing for sure," observed Adriel.

"What do you think we should do, Adriel?"

"Well, I regret putting you in danger, but I have. This is the situation: I must continue to keep a protective eye on you and work harder to find this wrongdoer before something tragic happens."

"Be careful, Adriel."

"I'll be as careful as I can. But, at bottom, the circumstances are fraught with danger and the possibility of harm."

CHAPTER SEVENTY-NINE
A SECOND MEETING

It is time, after years of obsession, to solve Abigail's murder. I have decided great risk is worth the achievement of this goal.
— Diary of Adriel Peregrine, May 21, 1872.

Adriel had not come any closer to solving Abigail's murder. With his suspicions on Conrad Kraybill, he decided to meet again with Hamilton Dunlap in an attempt to draw Kraybill once more into desperate action, if he indeed was the one outside Adriel's cabin, the one following Jennie on the road, the one who hurled the stone, and the murderer of Abigail Dunlap.

Adriel wondered how to get around Kraybill. The Dunlaps' butler had served them for years, including standing guard at the front door to protect his employers' privacy and safety. With this in mind, Adriel decided to visit Mr. Dunlap at one of his places of business. Through some research, he found out that Dunlap spent time on Saturdays at his grocery store. Hopefully, Dunlap would be willing again to meet with Adriel. Adriel's objective was to arrange a meeting at Dunlap's house. He wanted to give Conrad Kraybill a chance to overhear and act stupidly. He knew that such an action could increase the danger and encourage the culprit to attempt to murder him.

Adriel entered Hamilton Dunlap's store, very busy with customers. He hoped that Dunlap would be there. At the check-out counter, he asked a clerk if Dunlap was in and if he could speak with him for a moment. The clerk responded that

Mr. Dunlap was pre-occupied with the business of the day, but that he would have someone check to see if the owner was available. Adriel gave his name. Another employee behind the counter was sent to advise Mr. Dunlap. On his return, he said that Mr. Dunlap would see him. Adriel followed the man to the office at the back of the first floor of a three-story building.

When Adriel walked into the office, Dunlap greeted him coldly, because of his pre-occupation with business, rather than distaste for the individual. "Hello, Adriel. What can I do for you?"

"I know that you're busy. I'm wondering if I could meet with you at your home in the near future."

"For what reason?"

"I wanted to talk to you further about my investigation of Abigail's murder."

"Do you have more information?"

"No, but I've got a greater certainty."

"You know who it is?"

"I have a good hunch that I'm convinced of more than ever, but would rather tell you about it when you have more time."

Dunlap was torn between skepticism and hope. "Why can't you tell me now?" Dunlap was on the edge of his seat.

"It may compromise a plan I have for catching the murderer."

"OK. I trust that you know what you're doing."

"Thank you," Adriel said with a cheery voice. He walked out of the office and returned to his plans with Jennie for this day. He was to meet her in town to shop for supplies for the cabin; Jennie was looking for a dress for fall.

On Sunday afternoon, Adriel walked up to the front door of the Dunlap home. He knocked several times before Conrad Kraybill opened the door.

"Yes, Mr. Peregrine," Kraybill said coldly and dispassionately as usual.

"Mr. Dunlap is expecting me."

"Please step in and follow me."

Adriel followed Kraybill to Mr. Dunlap's study, where they had met before. The door was partially open. Kraybill walked in and announced Adriel.

"Thank you, Kraybill. Adriel, please take a seat." The butler left the room and closed the door.

"Well, Mr. Peregrine. What is the business you come with concerning my daughter's death?"

"Thank you for letting me meet with you. I believe that after careful consideration, I know who killed your daughter."

Dunlap leaned forward with intense interest. "Please tell me who it is."

"It may seem odd to you; but, I would prefer to hold that information until I'm certain."

"Then why did you come to me now?"

"I wanted to keep you up to date and assure you again that it wasn't Caleb Landis."

"You have convinced me of that in what you have said." Dunlap was perplexed about the need for a meeting, considering that Adriel didn't have much to add to what he had already told him.

Adriel added, "You'll understand later why I asked for this meeting. Please trust me in so far as I'm determined to find the killer and serve justice. Even if I'm not good for much else, I'll show I'm good for this."

"Adriel, I want the same thing as you do. I know you loved my daughter and would do anything to reveal the evil that killed her."

"I'm so happy that you have confidence in me to bring this enigma to the light of day. I'll not quit until it is solved."

Adriel was counting on the idea that he and Dunlap were overheard, though he didn't know for certain at the time of the meeting. He was hoping that Kraybill was listening at the door. And he hoped it was possible to hear the voices inside the room with the door shut.

When Adriel left the room, Kraybill was at the door to show him out. It was Adriel's hunch that he had been standing there throughout his interview with Mr. Dunlap. As he passed the manservant, Adriel took a look at Kraybill's cravat pin to determine first that he was wearing one and what it was. It was in the shape of a multicolored fly.

CHAPTER EIGHTY

THE LURKING DANGER

The time of confrontation is drawing near. I can sense it in my heart.
When, I don't know. That is the suspense of the situation.
— Diary of Adriel Peregrine, May 22, 1872.

Adriel was worried about Jennie's safety ever since the incident on the road. He urged her to keep her eyes and ears wide open. Adriel would always escort her from school to the cabin and from the cabin home. Jennie's parents knew she was over at Adriel's and didn't know that Jennie's safety was so much at risk; because, neither Jennie nor Adriel told anyone about the peril. Hamilton Dunlap and Adriel agreed not to broadcast recent events to prevent compromising the exposure of the murderer. Jennie didn't dare tell her parents in fear that they would take measures to prevent her from seeing Adriel, and it would be just one more thing they could hold against him. She loved him and would take the risk the danger presented.

One evening, Adriel attended a meeting of the local G.A.R. (Grand Army of the Republic) chapter. He had been active since his return from overseas. The G.A.R. was a fraternal organization of Union veterans of the Civil War. Because he was some distance from his own home town and unit, Jake would attend the meetings of Adriel's chapter every so often. The men would reminisce about army days that were filled with excitement and terror. The organization was also a powerful lobby in Washington for veterans and provided charity to veterans, widows, and orphans. After the meeting, Jake and

Adriel spent some time talking about finding Abigail's murderer.

"I talked to Hamilton Dunlap. He's still supportive of my efforts. The reason I went to him is to attempt to lure Conrad Kraybill into revealing himself. I was counting on his overhearing the conversation."

"That's a little bit dangerous; but, I understand why you did it."

"I think he was listening. He was right outside the door when I left. I don't think that door is soundproof."

"What do you want to do now?"

"Nothing more than wait—wait for him to make a move."

"I guess he might do that. It was probably he who was following Jennie and lurking outside your home at night."

"I'm sure of it."

"What can I do to help?" asked Jake.

"I don't think anything until the culprit is caught. Then, there's plenty you can do to bring him to justice. I have to admonish myself to keep me from an intense desire for revenge."

"Don't take the law into your own hands. As Paul says, God is the avenger who gives the role to the state to punish those who do wrong."

"I've been talking myself out of taking vengeance."

"How successful?"

"I'm sure I'll bring him in if I can. It would be better if you did so; but, he's not after you. He's after me. I'm the bait."

"Be careful, Adriel."

"I'm more worried about Jennie. I don't want to lose her."

"I understand."

"For now, all I can do is wait for him to strike. I think it will happen soon. Where and when, I don't know. I've been carrying a firearm. At this point in the drama, he can't afford to let me live. He'll kill me. He must know how close I am to exposing him as the killer."

"I think that is certain. I'd hate for you not to be here."

"I too would hate not to be here."

As Adriel was going home that night, someone was waiting for him outside of town. The evildoer knew when the chapter was going to meet and what night and time it was meeting. His research was thorough; for, he felt it necessary to kill the only man who could send him to the gallows.

With his owner riding, Bunyan was trotting home. It was already dark, and the road was not well lit. Adriel didn't ride fast; because, he didn't want to increase his chances of an accident. On his mind was his future with Jennie. They would live in the cabin. She would continue to teach, and he would work at the kilns. If she got pregnant, he would apply for the schoolmaster job. It would not be much of a living; but, it would get them by. Maybe, Mr. Alden would employ him for some Saturday work. None of his thoughts about supporting Jennie seemed a challenge; because, he was in love. The young are unaware that love can be arduous; but, most don't care about possible hardship. They see the beloved, and that is sufficient.

On the road Adriel was passing a thicket that led to a hill. Just then, a shot rang out. Bunyan reared; the bullet struck Adriel in the arm. Adriel fell off the horse; got up in great pain; and re-mounted Bunyan, taking a great risk of being shot again. As another shot rang out, Adriel was riding at a flying pace. When he thought he was safe—though he didn't know for sure—he slowed down. His pain was so great that he thought he would fall off; but, he managed to get over to his parents where he would get help for his wound. Only the darkness saved him from his assailant, who seemed to be a good enough shot but not good enough to kill Adriel that night.

CHAPTER EIGHTY-ONE

CONVALESCENCE

Not since the war have I been so close to death. In the war I never received a wound; but, now at home, I am recovering from a bullet wound. Someone really wants to put an end to me, and I think I know who it is. – Diary of Adriel Peregrine, May 25, 1872.

When he arrived home, Adriel was in great pain. He slid off Bunyan, and almost to the ground; but, he managed to keep standing. Adriel's father heard his arrival and looked out the window. He realized that something was wrong. He called out from the open window, "Adriel, are you all right?"

"No, I've been shot."

Sylvan rushed downstairs, flung open the front door, and ran to Adriel's aid. "Take hold, Son." With help from his father, Adriel put his unwounded arm around his father's shoulder. They struggled to the front door, where Agatha greeted them with cloth bandages. She had awakened when Sylvan hastened to the window.

"Adriel." That's all she said.

Sylvan had Adriel sit in a chair in the front sitting room. "Take care of him while I ride over to the doctor's," he shouted to Agatha without realizing it. Sylvan mounted Bunyan, who was yet in front of the house. Fortunately, the doctor was only two miles away.

Sylvan brought Doctor Schilling with great haste. In the kitchen the doctor removed the bullet and patched Adriel up.

"You'll be fine, Adriel." said the doctor. Adriel remembered all of those young men who, during the War, lost an arm or leg. In many cases this radical procedure didn't save them from death.

Adriel remained silent while trying to deal with the pain and not make a fool of himself.

"Good news, my boy," said Sylvan.

"Thanks, Father, and thanks to you doctor," said Adriel.

Neither man said a word. The doctor patted him on the left arm, which was not injured.

"Good night, then," said the doctor. "I'll check on you in a few days. If anything changes for the worse, let me know right away. Sylvan and Agatha, I'll give you instructions on how to dress the wound before I walk out the door."

"Yes, doctor," responded Sylvan. Adriel's mother stood by in great anxiety. During the War, when Adriel was in the service, she worried about him every day. She remembered the long lists in the newspaper. She thought of all those young men in unmarked graves and also those in marked graves who gave their lives for their country to keep it united. Adriel survived the War, unlike hundreds of thousands who didn't. Now his life was almost taken by someone unknown and for an unaccountable reason. She couldn't figure it out. His parents knew that he was looking for the murderer, but didn't know about the several incidents until after the mystery was solved.

Sylvan helped Adriel upstairs to his old room. Adriel asked his father to go to his cabin to retrieve Annie, which Sylvan did first thing the next morning. Adriel was in a quandary on how to tell Jennie.

During that whole night Adriel sat by the window looking out into the darkness. He tried to focus on recent events. Deciding that the attack was perpetrated by Conrad Kraybill, he committed himself to be more intentional about apprehending the murderer; but, he still wasn't sure how he could expose Kraybill. Then, he thought that he didn't have to do that at all. Kraybill, a desperate man, sometime soon would do another foolish thing on his own. Adriel needed to be cautious and ready, though these measures seemed to him to be inadequate considering the circumstances.

The next day Adriel was re-united with Annie. Jennie visited the day after that. Word tends to get around very quickly in a small community. When Jennie's parents found out, they were beside themselves. Jennie, though, wouldn't concede an inch, saying that she'd find another place to live before forsaking Adriel.

Jake Brenneman came to see Adriel the morning after the incident. Since a crime had been committed, he would initiate an investigation.

After sitting down in a chair while Adriel sat upright in bed, Jake said with serious aspect, "Adriel, I'm glad you're not dead."

"You're a good friend to be so thoughtful," was the tongue-in-cheek reply.

"Somebody is intent on killing you. I could arrest Kraybill on suspicion; however, I couldn't hold him long without more evidence. An intelligent hunch won't get us far. I could take the bullet over to Dunlap's and demand Kraybill produce any guns he owned. The problem is that he could deny he had any guns."

"I realize that. The fact is that I don't have anything more than what I had at the beginning—a tie pin found years after the murder. I noticed that he was wearing a tie pin in the shape of a fly when I went over to the Dunlap's recently; but, this doesn't get me very far."

"You're right that the pin isn't much good for catching him," Jake agreed.

"The only thing I know to do is hang out some bait, but what? I already have. I've probably aroused his suspicions with my last visit to Mr. Dunlap. In any case, I'll be ready for this 'Lord of the flies' one way or another."

"How will you be ready?"

"I'll be expecting anything at any time."

"That'll be exhausting."

"I've no choice."

"I'll help, though, I don't know how much help it could be. I'll check over here every once in a while."

"Thanks, Jake."

Adriel realized that the next weeks were going to be filled with tension. He was more worried about Jennie than about himself. She might again be a target.

The next day, Jennie stopped to see Adriel after school. She brought with her some fruit and baked items, favorites of Adriel that she made the evening before. All the food was neatly packed in a wicker basket and covered with a new, clean towel. Jennie was always showing her consideration in specific ways. Her gesture showed her kindheartedness, especially toward Adriel. She added to the basket a book of poetry by Herman Melville, entitled *Battle-pieces and Aspects of the War*. She knew that Adriel thought much about the war and spent time thinking about its meaning. Jennie also placed in the basket a book of love poetry by Elizabeth Barrett Browning, entitled *Sonnets from the Portuguese*. She marked Sonnet 44 for his special attention. A bouquet of flowers accompanied the basket.

Jennie opened the door and entered the room; and, while placing the basket and flowers on a table, she greeted Adriel. Annie, locked out inadvertently, followed her into the room with canine enthusiasm. Jennie walked over to Adriel, bent down and kissed him. "I thought of you all day while at school. I could think of nothing else. It was the longest day of my life. How are you today, Adriel?"

Adriel looked up into her gentle blue-grey eyes; and though he could have become lost and speechless in his attention to her, he was able to say softly, "Thank you for coming. I love you."

Jennie pulled up a chair next to the bed, took his uninjured arm to stroke his hand, and said, "I love you, Adriel. I don't want to lose you."

"I'll do what I can to stay alive, and I'll find the man who killed Abigail and is trying to kill me."

"I'll pray that you are safe and successful." Jennie turned to the basket behind her on the table. "I brought some things for you." She retrieved the basket and flowers and brought them to the bed.

"It looks like if I die, it won't be for lack of food."

"I made some cookies and your favorite pie."

"Oh good, you baked me a mud pie." Jennie laughed when he said this. Adriel actually liked cherry pie the best, and that's what she baked.

"Yes, a mud pie and sand tarts," Jennie came back quickly, unfazed. She was used to Adriel's frequent attempts at humor, many of which were successful and some not so.

"Good reply."

Jennie took out the pie, and with a knife she brought along cut two pieces. She then went downstairs to ask Adriel's mother for some milk and a vase for the flowers.

After Jennie arranged the flowers and the two of them ate pie, she, setting aside the dishes, pulled out of the basket the two books. "I brought you two books to while away the hours. Herman Melville's Civil War poems and Elizabeth Browning's sonnets."

"I've wanted to read Melville's poems for the longest time. Where did you acquire the books?"

"I've had them for a while. I bought them in Lancaster."

"Wonderful! And you brought me some love poetry?"

"Yes, for you and me."
"Would you read me a few?"
"Here's my favorite."

CHAPTER EIGHTY-TWO

HALCYON DAYS: UNSETTLED NIGHTS

Belovèd, thou hast brought me many flowers
Plucked in the garden, all the summer through
And winter, and it seemed as if they grew
In this close room, nor missed the sun and showers.
So, in the like name of that love of ours,
Take back these thoughts which here unfolded too,
And which on warm and cold days, I withdrew
From my heart's ground. Indeed those beds and bowers
Be overgrown with bitter weeds and rue,
And wait thy weeding; yet here's eglantine,
Here's ivy!—take them, as I used to do
Thy flowers, and keep them where they shall not pine.
Instruct thine eyes to keep colours true,
And tell thy soul their roots are left in mine.
— Elizabeth Barrett Browning, Sonnets from the
Portuguese, XLIV

The days that followed Adriel's harrowing encounter were ones of healing, spiritual as well as physical. He soon got outside and, with a sling on his arm, walked as he used to walk in the woods surrounding the cabin.

Adriel stopped by the cabin to make sure all was in place. He was relieved to discover that everything seemed to be in order. He spent the afternoon enjoying the late summer weather in the vicinity of his home.

For Adriel the days and nights seemed a contradiction. Daylight was bright with hope, as Jennie and he made plans for their wedding by the end of the summer; night time signified a dark, ominous presence that could pounce out from almost anywhere. The prowler had the advantage. He saw; Adriel was seen and didn't see. The watcher had something of the quality of omnipresence, at least in Adriel's mind. Night represented the threat of disaster, literally meaning ill-starred. He had never known such contradiction. During the War the days and nights caused unrelieved dread. On picket duty he could have been killed at any moment; in the rage of battle, the same. The bugle-calling assembly could blow at any time. He remembered those days and nights and wondered how he escaped what seemed a certain death.

Adriel now thought that the sun put to flight what lurked not far from him; its setting brought the night fiend that wished to end his life. The advantage over his time in the military was relief from fear during the day; the disadvantage was the daily setting of hope with the sun despite the fact that most attacks had occurred during the day. Adriel was a victim of his own state of mind, an emotional weariness, that was under the mistaken impression that the killer would no longer strike by day.

His love for Jennie and his hope for a bright future lent to how he felt about the danger that threatened him. He feared great loss. The peril he faced was not yet completely known. During the War he knew with absolute certainty who the enemy was. Adriel was determined that the menace would stop, and soon. He hoped that the one lying in wait would make his move to reveal himself despite the danger to Adriel.

The next day when Adriel arrived at the cabin, things were not in order. The front door was damaged from being forced open. He walked in cautiously in anticipation of an assault. No one was there. His feelings of safety during the day dissolved. He found a note on the long dining table made out in print rather than longhand, sloppy, but carefully wrought, as the note attached to the stone. It read: YOUR LIFE IS AT RISK. GIVE UP THE SEARCH. There was no signature. Adriel knew what "the search" was. He wouldn't give it up. He would find the one who killed Abigail and was the cause of the hanging of Caleb Landis. He would find him and bring him to justice. There was no way that he'd relent.

While the nights were dreadful, Adriel's days, before returning to work, were filled with Jennie. Every day after school she would stop by to see him—he could not yet ride Bunyan so his father met her at school each day-- and often eat dinner with him and his parents. This practice made things harder for her at home; but, her love transcended this difficulty.

Jennie and he talked about Melville's poetry. The poet's elegance brought back memories. Words from Melville's piece on Fort Donelson resonated with Adriel—in fact, all of the eloquent words of Melville did.

>   A crackle of skirmishing goes on.
> Our lads creep round on hand and knee,
>   They fight from behind each trunk and stone;
>   And sometimes, flying for refuge, one
> Finds 'tis an enemy shares the tree.
> Some scores are maimed by boughs shot off
>   In the glades by the Fort's big gun."
> (Herman Melville, "Donelson, February 1862," from Aspects
> of the War and Other Battle-pieces)

Adriel had worked within himself an accommodation to the War. He occasionally had bad dreams and tears for lost comrades, especially his good friend Michael O'Brien now buried in Poplar Grove National Cemetery with many heroes of the Union. The slaughter of the war horrified him; but, Adriel was not bent into a permanent emotional and spiritual disfigurement that happened to many soldiers. He wept on the shoulder of Christ. He participated in the local chapter of the G.A.R., where old buddies together would talk about their war experiences. They would share one another's burdens and scars left there in the heart and mind.

When Adriel shed a tear for a long-dead comrade, Jennie did what Adriel needed—put her head on his and kissed him. When she was distraught, he would do the same for her. They would hold one another until the pain softened. And so, they talked away the late afternoons until Agatha would call them to dinner, and the little fellowship of believers in Christ would break bread together.

Over those late spring days, Adriel's room became a conservatory, the sun shining in through the big windows to nourish the plants Jennie would bring him. Jennie was the gardener, bringing water as a surrogate for the rain of heaven. Both young people exulted in each other, but especially in the kindly Lord who granted them such love. They only had to overcome the serpent lurking in the garden, not the ancient serpent, but a serpent nonetheless.

CHAPTER EIGHTY-THREE

THE FINAL ENCOUNTER

There come times in our lives that are crucial. They are key to what the future brings or whether there is a future at all. So are these days after Pentecost filled with expectancy of something crucial for Jennie and me.   – Diary of Adriel Peregrine, May 28, 1872.

Adriel was to return to work soon. He no longer wore the sling. He lay in bed looking at the ceiling, thinking about the lurking danger and whether Jennie and he had a future. He couldn't sleep, and it was good that he couldn't sleep. As the house clock tolled 2:00 A.M.—Adriel always counted the chimes when he was awake at night—Annie started to growl as she did at the cabin the time someone was watching in the woods. Then, she began to bark furiously. No one could have stopped her, and no one would have.

Adriel leaped up from bed and quickly dressed. He grabbed the revolver he was keeping with him in certainty that his adversary was armed. He closed his bedroom door, leaving Annie behind. His parents didn't seem to be stirring; but, they would soon be awake with Annie's barking. Slowly, he opened the front door with gun in hand. What greeted him was a thick wall of mist. Visibility was non-existent at best. He asked himself how he was going to be able to overcome his antagonist with his antagonist having such a great advantage. This notwithstanding, Adriel entered the density, not know-ing whether from out of the mist he would be assaulted or shot.

Adriel walked toward the church cemetery on a hunch with no foundation that the culprit would be in the vicinity. Between the cemetery and the Peregrine house was a footpath that led to the quarry—one that he had taken many times before. As he moved forward, the fog thinned a bit, making it easier to find his way. The visibility, though, was still poor. As he trod into the danger he felt an intolerable but unavoidable suspense. He crouched behind a tree located next to the trail, not moving for what seemed to him to be the longest time. He looked all around him several times, knowing he could be attacked from any direction.

Adriel was beside himself trying to locate his antagonist, wondering if, at any moment, he would be shot. Then, a shot was fired, missing Adriel by a hairsbreadth as so many bullets did during the War. He fired back in the direction he thought the bullet may have come from. Nothing came of it. For what seemed the longest time, Adriel remained among the trees and off the path. He then ventured back onto the trail that led to the quarry. The trail veered to the right about thirty feet from the edge. As Adriel approached the turn, the foe fired a shot while stumbling and then sprang at him as his gun hit the ground. When the assailant knocked Adriel down, Adriel's gun fell from his hand. The two men were wrestling in a life-and-death contest. Adriel couldn't make out who it was amidst darkness, mist, and struggle. The encounter later reminded Adriel of that between Jacob and the man at the Jabbok; but, the man Adriel fought was not God, but a foe of implacable hostility.

The two antagonists drew closer and closer to the edge of the quarry. One or the other or both were bound to hurtle down into the darkness, hitting the hard surface of the pit. The opponent held Adriel in a stranglehold right at the edge of the craggy height, exhaling a heated, fiendish breath. As Adriel was about to be overpowered, he was able to free himself. His opponent lost his balance and fell over the cliff. In the darkness Adriel heard a cry and then silence. Adriel collapsed on the ground and lost consciousness.

In his swoon Adriel dreamt deeply of heaven. He heard Saint Bernard call to him, "Wake up, Adriel, you have passed from infernal fires to the heavenly empyrean. Behold, the blessedness of this special place of God."

When he awoke, Adriel gazed into the eyes of his father, who was carrying him home.

THE NEXT DAY

Who would true valour see,
Let him come hither;
One here will constant be,
Come wind, come weather
There's no discouragement
Shall make him once relent
His first avowed intent
To be a pilgrim.

Whoso beset him round
With dismal stories,
Do but themselves confound;
His strength the more is.
No lion can give him fright,
He'll with a giant fight,
But he will have a right to be a pilgrim.

Hobgoblin, nor foul fiend
Can daunt his spirit,
He knows he at the end
Shall life inherit.
Then fancies flee away,
He'll fear not what men say,
He'll labour night and day
To be a pilgrim.
— John Bunyan, Pilgrim's Progress

Adriel lay in his bed where his father put him that night. Doctor Schilling was sitting beside him after having examined him for severe injury. Adriel escaped the ordeal with lacerations to the face and discomfort in the stomach from being punched several times.

Adriel's mother was sitting in a chair crocheting, keeping an eye out for her boy. He survived a war. She was convinced and determined that he would survive this. Sylvan was doing several things around the Alden property. Jennie was on her way to the Peregrine's with food she had made. A substitute was taking care of school for her. Jake Brenneman would stop by in the afternoon with a report on the dead foe.

After the doctor left, Adriel insisted to his mother that he was going to take a walk outside. He had had enough convalescing in recent days. As he opened the door, he could see Jennie getting out of her father's buggy. When she saw Adriel coming out of the house, she set down her basket of food and looked intently at him. She was wearing a calico dress. She was radiant and beautiful.

Adriel walked steadily toward her. Despite his lacerated face, slight limp, sore stomach, and the presence of Jennie's father, nothing could deter him from coming to her and hugging and kissing her. He took in a deep breath of her sweet scent. Mr. Hallewell was smiling as he had been in church. Adriel turned to Jennie's father and simply said, "Thank you, Mr. Hallewell."

"Think nothing of it, Son. I was glad to do it." Jennie and Adriel walked toward the house after Adriel assured Mr. Hallewell that she would have a ride home.

Later that afternoon, Jake Brenneman stopped by. Annie was in her glory with all the visitors. Except for scraps from the table, the presence of guests was her greatest joy. In fact, guests usually meant more snacks for the dog.

As Jake walked into the room, Adriel and Jennie were sitting there with great anticipation. He didn't know for sure who the assailant was, and Jake wasn't going to keep him in suspense. As the constable sat down in the remaining seat, he said, "Adriel, your late night foe was Conrad Kraybill." While not a surprise, Adriel felt himself getting a little lightheaded.

Jennie looked at him and again at Jake and exclaimed, "What a vile man!"

"Tell me more about what you've found if there is more."

"We found his body at the bottom of the quarry, where he probably died on contact. We found a gun near the edge where you two struggled. Another gun was not far away. We've compared the caliber of both guns with the bullet taken out of your arm. The bullet was the same caliber as one of the guns. This morning Dunlap told me Kraybill was a model employee and seemed devoted to the family. Dunlap, though, knew little about the man except that he hailed from New York City. We checked with their police department about any record he might have. He once was arrested for assault, but never served time. I can only conclude that he was obsessed with Abigail and got carried away the night of the murder. Perhaps, he killed her accidentally; but, he killed her nonetheless. A judicial review, I'm sure, will show Caleb Landis innocent."

"Is Adriel in any trouble?" Jennie asked.

"Not at all, considering the circumstances. It was a fight to the finish. Adriel was attacked and defended himself. There will be a coroner's inquest, typical in a situation like this. Adriel, you are a fortunate man. You could be the body at the bottom of the quarry."

"If I had, I would not have been able to make this meeting." The three of them laughed like people who had been relieved of a great burden.

Later that day, Adriel confided in Jennie something odd that happened on that dreadful night of amazing things. "I was walking down the path when I thought I saw, distinguished from the fog, an apparition of a sort. It looked like Abigail, as if she were leading me to the final episode of this tragic story. She disappeared along the way. I continued to the edge of the quarry, where Kraybill attacked me. While I was unconscious, she said to me, 'Adriel, I'm grateful to you for what you've done. Now be at peace. And know that I'm at peace.' Till the day I die, I'll never be sure if it was simply a dream or an illusion or a ghost." Adriel never again encountered Abigail.

"No matter, Adriel, you've been given a gift."

"I'll remember, always remember. I love you, Jennie," Adriel said and then hugged and kissed his soon-to-be wife.

CHAPTER EIGHTY-FIVE

HAIL THEE, FESTIVAL DAY!

Rise now, O Lord, from the grave and cast off the shroud that enwrapped thee; Thou art sufficient for us: nothing without thee exists.

– Bishop Venantius Fortunatus 530-609 the English Hymnal, 1906, Hymn 624 Hail thee, Festival Day.

The Sunday after the incident at the quarry, Jennie and Adriel sat together along with her parents and his at Saint Jude Thaddeus Church. They sang, prayed, listened, and received Holy Communion. It was a glorious day—a day full of rejoicing. Many Sundays would be like this one.

Adriel and Jennie spent splendorous days preparing for their wedding and repeating their vows at the nuptials before Father Derek Ledford. Saint Jude Thaddeus Church and the Red Oak community rejoiced in the celebration. The bride and groom received their guests at Mr. Alden's, where the reception was held. Massey Alden, Adriel's mentor, and his wife, Ebba, proud of the couple, stood by them with both sets of parents. Such happiness Adriel and Jennie had never known before that day.

Three children would join Adriel and Jennie as the years went by. Jenny raised them at home; Adriel replaced her at the school. He also farmed a small patch of land on the Hallewell property and helped James Hallewell with the farm work until the day came when he became the proprietor. They moved to the farmhouse; but, would spend much time at the cabin. Jennie pursued many interests, even producing a book of poems. Adriel wrote several pieces over the years. They never reached a national audience; yet, he was well known in the world he inhabited in central Pennsylvania and throughout the Commonwealth and some other parts of the east.

Adriel was true to his name. He was a Peregrine, both wanderer and then pilgrim. He also was true to his given baptismal name. He belonged to God's flock—his friends, his brothers and sisters, and his companions on a journey.

Adriel and Jennie now rest in the church cemetery under the willows. Their hope was that the day would come when they would rise and celebrate an eternal festival day in company with the saints and martyrs of the ages who now rest in the bosom of the Lord. Until then, they sing the heavenly song in the throne room of God.

*

ABOUT ATMOSPHERE PRESS

Founded in 2015, Atmosphere Press was built on the principles of Honesty, Transparency, Professionalism, Kindness, and Making Your Book Awesome. As an ethical and author-friendly hybrid press, we stay true to that founding mission today.

If you're a reader, enter our giveaway for a free book here:

SCAN TO ENTER
BOOK GIVEAWAY

If you're a writer, submit your manuscript for consideration here:

SCAN TO SUBMIT
MANUSCRIPT

And always feel free to visit Atmosphere Press and our authors online at atmospherepress.com. See you there soon!

ABOUT THE AUTHOR

MICHAEL TAVELLA was born and grew up in Lancaster County, Pennsylvania. He spent his career of forty-four years as pastor with his wife, N. Amanda Grimmer, at Saint Andrew Lutheran Church in Hurst, Texas, and Holy Trinity Lutheran Church in Abington, Pennsylvania. He was involved in the establishment of the North America Lutheran Church and served as dean of the Atlantic Mission District of that church body. He had been among the adjunct faculty of the Reformed Episcopal Seminary in Blue Bell, Pennsylvania, teaching New Testament, Pastoral Counsel, and Christian Ethics.

Presently, he is the Executive Director of Sarnelli House, a hospitality center for the people of Kensington, Philadelphia, Pennsylvania. He has written a previous novel entitled *The Light in the Ruins*. He resides with his wife in the greater Philadelphia area. Amanda and Michael have one son.